MISS HONORIA WEST

Ruth Hamilton

CORGI BOOKS

MISS HONORIA WEST
A CORGI BOOK : 0 552 14410 X

Originally published in Great Britain by Bantam Press,
a division of Transworld Publishers

PRINTING HISTORY
Bantam Press edition published 1999
Corgi edition published 2000

1 3 5 7 9 10 8 6 4 2

Set in 11/12pt Baskerville by Falcon Oast Graphic Art.

Corgi Books are published by Transworld Publishers,
61–63 Uxbridge Road, London W5 5SA,
a division of The Random House Group Ltd,
in Australia by Random House Australia (Pty) Ltd,
20 Alfred Street, Milsons Point, Sydney, NSW 2061, Australia,
in New Zealand by Random House New Zealand Ltd,
18 Poland Road, Glenfield, Auckland 10, New Zealand
and in South Africa by Random House (Pty) Ltd,
Endulini, 5a Jubilee Road, Parktown 2193, South Africa.

Reproduced, printed and bound in Great Britain by
Mackays of Chatham PLC, Chatham, Kent.

Ruth Hamilton is the bestselling author of *A Whisper to the Living*, *With Love From Ma Maguire*, *Nest of Sorrows*, *Billy London's Girls*, *Spinning Jenny*, *The September Starlings*, *A Crooked Mile*, *Paradise Lane*, *The Bells of Scotland Road*, *The Dream Sellers* and *The Corner House*. She has become one of the most popular authors who recreate the lives and places of the north-west of England. Ruth Hamilton was born in Bolton and has spent most of her life in Lancashire. She now lives in Liverpool.

Also by Ruth Hamilton

A WHISPER TO THE LIVING
WITH LOVE FROM MA MAGUIRE
NEST OF SORROWS
BILLY LONDON'S GIRLS
SPINNING JENNY
THE SEPTEMBER STARLINGS
A CROOKED MILE
PARADISE LANE
THE BELLS OF SCOTLAND ROAD
THE DREAM SELLERS
THE CORNER HOUSE

and published by Corgi Books

For Avril Cain, who stumbles on regardless

In reply to many kind enquiries about my animals:

Fudge (*huge* chocolate Labrador) ate the landing – a lot of carpet, the step into my office, several spindles up the stairs, the edge of a lovely oriel bay window, some skirting board, an antique spinning wheel and the toilet doorframe. The stomach medicine cost a fortune. Nevertheless, he is gorgeous.

Sam (very slim black Labrador) continues neurotic and adorable. His chewing days are over, thank goodness. A true guard dog, he sniffs everyone's credentials before allowing entry into the house.

Sophie (an extremely beautiful male cat named in error) is slowing down, so most of my blackbirds survived this year. He is forgetting to be feral, and now demands attention.

Bodie (green budgie) died, leaving Ladybird (blue budgie) very lonely. So we stuck her in with Dumb and Dumber (cockatiels, real names Jack and Vera), where she rules the roost. Jack is now twice henpecked – literally.

Oh, a bit of advice to anyone with a baby Labrador: develop insomnia for eighteen months. Your looks may suffer, but the Axminster should survive.

Acknowledgements

Many, many thanks to:

Diane Pearson, generous friend, excellent editor.
  Michael, David and Elizabeth, my family.
  Gillian Currie for support and encouragement.
  Jennie Currie for age charts and character cards.
  Kevin Currie for walking the dogs.
  Louise Currie for being Louise Currie, the best eleven-year-old dirty dancer in Liverpool.
  Martin Cain for motorbikes.
  Robin Cain for llamas and Huddersfield in the rain.
  Diane Jenkinson-as-was, my 'accountant' circa 1953.
  Joanna Frank, my new agent.
  Last but never least, all my good friends at Transworld Publishers for a great time in London . . . even though they failed to kidnap Colin Firth for me.

MISS HONORIA WEST

One

Hyacinth died on the Thursday night. She did it decorously, quietly and with all the dignity available to a seventy-odd-year-old woman with worsening arthritis. In spite of worn and painful joints she had flattened her slender frame on the bed, as if to make work easier for the undertaker. Hyacinth had always been so self-effacing, thought Honoria, as she gazed dispassionately upon the stilled features of her older sister. So eager to please, unselfish, forgiving, such a damned fool.

Saucer and cup, the latter still half full, rested on the bedside table, while a pair of crippled hands were folded on a bosom that had never been generous. Her teeth, Steradented every night, lingered in a glass jar near the handbasin, uppers and lowers frozen in a smile that mocked the newly deceased. She was wearing pink, of course, a colour in which she had placed her trust. According to Hyacinth, pink was stimulating, especially when its wearer indulged in painting and other gentle arts. For all Hyacinth's insistence, pinks had undernourished the muse throughout a long and, apparently, unsuccessful career as poet and painter.

Miss Honoria West, sister of the dear departed, was a woman not given to excesses of emotion. When Friday morning arrived, she relieved the table of Hyacinth's last drop of cocoa before contacting the doctor and Philip Pointer, producer and director of *Monday's Child*, the play in which Hyacinth had been due to star in a month's time.

'Good God!' the great man screamed. 'She was the third Alice, the most important character in the play. It's hard enough finding trios of everybody – why April had to stretch the thing through three generations ... What the dickens am I supposed to do now? Hyacinth looked right in a wheelchair. People who use wheelchairs in their everyday lives are so much more convincing. I was relying on her, utterly and absolutely.'

'I know,' agreed Honoria. It was plain that Pointer required due notice if a member of his cast intended to die. Honoria understood his single-mindedness, accepted him as he was. In fact, in so far as she was capable of feeling approval, Honoria was rather taken with him, as he did not suffer fools. 'I could do it,' she suggested, in a tone meant to be timid. 'She practised her lines with me, so I know most of them, plus all the cues.'

A short silence ensued. 'You?' he boomed. 'You haven't been out of your flat for ten years, at least.' As ever, he dived straight to the point, no emotion, no time for dallying. 'No, no, that will never do, my dear.'

'But this is an emergency,' replied Honoria. 'I couldn't bear to have the play cancelled. Hyacinth would have wanted *Monday's Child* to go ahead, I'm sure.'

12

When the conversation was concluded, Honoria reclaimed her semi-permanent position at the corner window, double-glazed, which had framed her view of the world for the past decade. On the triangular sill, a leather box was hidden discreetly behind some large planters. Inside the concealed container, a pair of expensive binoculars nested, lenses polished and ready, strap adjusted to the absolutely correct length.

From a well-padded rocking chair, Honoria was able to pursue her hobby. People-watching had been her joy for some years and, just now, the pot was beginning to boil. Things were happening out there, intrigues and machinations that had kept the plump, spry woman riveted to her vantage-point for hours on end. In fact, she had probably been sitting here at the time of Hyacinth's demise.

As the window was wrapped around the corner of Cavendish Mansions, Honoria could keep her eyes on two avenues, moving only her head when wanting a change of scene. Currently, she watched Philip Pointer's house, imagining him storming about in his dressing-gown, cordless phone in one hand, cheroot in the other, ash all over himself and any piece of furniture within his immediate sphere. He lived alone, entertaining few visitors, since no one but the most patient of souls could stomach his wildly varying moods. Honoria had always tolerated him. He was, to say the least, honest about his pride and prejudice. He did have a particular weakness, though. Honoria almost licked her lips at the thought of his 'secret'.

Her eyes slid over the rest of the house, taking note of new curtains in Simon Halliwell's dining room, a smart up-to-date car outside the home of a recently arrived couple. How did they afford it? she mused. Perhaps, like many in these parts, the brace of teachers might be up to no good.

April Nugent's vivid blue Micra hove into view, stopped outside Philip Pointer's gate. 'Oh, no,' breathed Honoria. 'There'll be all that to go through now, I suppose.' She watched April as she struggled out of the driving seat and into the arms of Pointer. It was clear that the woman was weeping copiously, while he, still talking into the cordless, made a half-hearted stab at helping her into his garden. April had been close to Hyacinth and was going to feel the loss acutely.

The doorbell sounded. Honoria rubbed her eyes in an effort to make the lids red, nailed a 'brave' smile to her face then opened the door. 'Dr Benson,' she wailed unconvincingly. 'Poor Hyacinth. She must have slipped away during the night.'

David Benson, like most folk in these parts, nursed a strong dislike for Miss Honoria West. He had never been able to place a finger on the source of his antipathy, though a finely tuned medical brain doubted the veracity of Miss West's many complaints. She suffered from dizzy spells, though her ears, blood pressure and all other possible contributors showed no cause for the slightest concern. Agoraphobia had kept her indoors for several years, as had a fear of becoming one of many in enclosed spaces, so she neither shopped nor worshipped. A Sainsbury's Helping Hand fetched home the groceries, while Father Michael Browning, the priest from St Thomas's

Roman Catholic church, brought God to visit Honoria every fourth Monday.

'Do come in,' she gushed now.

The doctor entered, immediately feeling her eyes raking over him. This was supposed to be his day off, so he was dressed in T-shirt and jeans, with an ancient suede waistcoat slung over his upper body as protection against a skittish breeze off the Mersey. 'In her room?' he asked.

'Yes.' In Honoria's day, doctors had worn dark clothes, proper suits and brogues, not these glorified gym-shoes called trainers. He looked like an overgrown child on his way to a football game or a conkers expedition. Still, his life was in a bit of a mess, she supposed. Did he know about his wife? Well, he would soon, she told her inner self. Yvonne. What sort of name was that for the wife of an up-and-coming medical person?

David Benson entered Hyacinth West's bedroom, closing the door firmly in his wake. Hyacinth had been a cracker, a real lady. She looked peaceful, at least, with most of the pain ironed out by the hand of death. There would probably be no need for a post-mortem, as Hyacinth had been in the care of specialists for some years. Arthritis, diabetes and a heart condition had called for frequent monitoring; she had been existing on borrowed time for many months.

The door opened. 'Cup of tea, Doctor?'

'No. No, thank you.' It was just like any other day to Honoria, he guessed. She had her disability allowance, her share dividends and a pension from the Civil Service. She had the *Daily Express* word games to keep her occupied, the binoculars through which she watched her neighbours, and an endless supply of mixed biscuits, an apparently uncontrollable passion for which had led to a great increase in breadth across the beam.

'Would you prefer coffee?'

David's skin crawled. Yes, Honoria was a self-centred bitch, but how on earth could she remain so perfectly calm when the older of her two sisters was as cold as ice in the second bedroom? The main room, the master, was Honoria's, of course. It had better views, a larger radiator and its own *en suite* bathroom. 'No,' he mumbled. He would sooner have taken a sip from the cauldron on Macbeth's heath. Hyacinth was cold, had been dead for some hours.

'Sugar?'

'I said no, thank you.'

She studied him, sensed his hatred, almost basked in it. He was a no-mark, as Mrs Collins would say. Well, the daily cleaner had often talked to Hyacinth while Honoria had listened in. Mrs Collins, who had kept house for the West sisters since 1986, had a wonderful turn of phrase when describing people. 'See him over there?' she might say when cleaning windows. 'That one, walking his greyhound back from the beach. He hits his wife, but he's not the full quid. Bit of a divvi if you ask me . . .' A 'divvi' was a stupid person, Honoria supposed. While this doctor chap was possibly a no-mark, another category known to the Mrs Collinses of this world. Not that Gill Collins had ever passed judgement on the doctor. It was Honoria herself who classed David Benson as a man whose eventual

16

passing would leave the world intact, unaffected.

'Was she ill last night?'

Honoria sniffed. 'No worse than usual, poor soul. She took her arthritis medicine.'

Poor soul? For years, until arthritis had dominated her life, this woman had done everything for Honoria, had shopped, cooked, washed dishes. Even lately, Hyacinth had continued responsible for housekeeping accounts and the ordering of groceries. Until the wheelchair's arrival, the elder Miss West had been little more than a slave. Since Hyacinth's deterioration, Gill Collins had taken on a lot more responsibility with little extra pay to show for her pains. 'And your sister had her insulin yesterday?'

'Of course. The nurse came in, because Hyacinth's hands had become rather troublesome.'

'Quite.' He drew the sheet over the dead woman's face. 'The old heart finally gave out, I'd say. Not exactly unexpected, since she would carry on with her thespian activities. Hadn't she taken on a rather demanding role this time?'

'Yes.' Honoria joined him at the bedside. 'Will there be a post-mortem – an inquest?'

'That will not be necessary.' He walked to the dressing-table and scribbled on paper. As he wrote, he felt a change in the atmosphere, as if the whole room had breathed a sigh of relief. For a split second, his hand hesitated, apparently unwilling to sign the necessary documentation. No, he told himself determinedly. Even a fish as cold as Honoria would not be capable of raising a hand to the sweet, naïve Hyacinth. 'Was your sister insured?'

'Yes.'

He placed a full stop alongside his name. 'You will need the death certificate for the insurance company.' David Benson turned, saw a flash of steel in Honoria's eyes. It was as if she defied him to take away her sibling's body, have it cut up, analysed, pored over, only to return with a red face and an apology. 'You had better contact the undertaker,' he said. 'The sooner the better.'

'I shall.'

'And I am very sorry for your loss.'

Honoria nodded stiffly, a monarch acknowledging the existence of a minion.

'Will you attend the funeral?' he asked. Would agoraphobia keep her in this time?

'Of course,' she replied. 'With the help of God and diazepam, I shall survive the ordeal, no doubt.'

David glanced through the window, saw April Nugent walking crabwise across the road. 'The playwright cometh, God bless her,' he muttered to himself.

'*Monday's Child* is the STADS latest production,' Honoria stated. 'Hyacinth was to play the oldest Alice, which is a sizeable role. I've offered to take her place.'

David swivelled to face her. 'What?' His lower jaw dropped, and he snapped it into the closed position rather quickly, biting his tongue in the process. 'But you never go out. Surely a leading theatre role would be demanding?' In that moment, he realized that Honoria was jealous of her sister, that the envy continued even now, while Hyacinth lay dead in an adjacent room.

18

She lowered herself on to an old and beautifully carved monk's bench. 'Perhaps I seem rather withdrawn, Dr Benson, but I can assure you that I feel things very deeply.' She pressed clasped hands against a rigidly confined bosom. 'Hyacinth was my dear sister. She lived for poetry, for plays and books. No marble monument could ever provide an adequate tribute. She was a wonderful woman, Doctor. If I can take her place, play her part in *Monday's Child*, that will mean a great deal. For her sake, I shall conquer this wretched agoraphobia.'

The challenge was there again. It sparked from her eyes like white-hot splinters in a foundry. What was he meant to say or do? 'If you can overcome your illness, that will be remarkable,' he said finally.

'Absolutely,' she agreed. 'It was Hyacinth's dearest wish. All she wanted was for me to be able to go out with her.' She dabbed at her eyes with a nonsensical scrap of lace-edged lawn. 'I counted my blessings every day, Dr Benson. She was at the top of my list each time. Without Hyacinth, my life would have been completely unbearable.'

He snapped the fastener on his bag. 'What will you do now?' he asked.

Honoria shook her Margaret Thatcher hairdo, the movement displacing not one single glued-down tress. 'I suppose I shall have to bring Hilda to live here.' Hilda was the third of the West sisters. She lived in the Lancashire farmhouse where all three Wests had been born, was still active and hard-working. Hilda was not quite up to scratch in Honoria's book. She was open, common and far too conversational.

David Benson lifted his case and walked to the door. 'If you experience any distress, feel free to take an extra five milligrams.' As he walked down the stairs, he found himself hoping that she would swallow the lot. She hadn't cared a damn for Hyacinth, had often left her to struggle across the landing in her wheelchair, had neglected to help with the stupid, unpredictable lift. Bloody woman. She should be hung out to dry, he thought viciously. But this was no way for a doctor to feel, he said inwardly, as he reached the path outside Cavendish Mansions. Though Miss Honoria West was horrible through and through.

He stood for a few seconds outside the Mansions, which were aptly named as the block managed a fair imitation of similar buildings in Chelsea and Kensington. An apartment here was worth a small fortune, far more than the new, supposedly executive detached dwellings that surrounded it. From this vantage-point, he could see his own house, though his size nines suddenly seemed reluctant to walk towards it.

'Oh, Dr Benson.'

He stopped and smiled at April Nugent. April was the embodiment of mankind's finer points. A victim of multiple sclerosis, she stumbled through life with a smile on her face and a pleasant word for everyone, often missing her footing, seldom missing the mark when it came to clear thinking.

'Hello, Mrs Nugent. How are you today?'

'Sad,' she answered, leaning heavily on the wall. 'It's a left-foot morning, I'm afraid. Not surprising, really, in view of the shocking news. Poor, poor Hyacinth. Of course, everyone will miss her, but I liked to count myself as one of her closest friends.'

David shook his head. April, like the month for which she had been named, was a breath of fresh air. He remembered the day on which her diagnosis had been confirmed. April had sat in her chair, had expressed her pity for him. 'The carrying of such tidings must be so painful,' she had said.

'Have you still got me on computer as being in need of a full body transplant?' she asked him now.

He grinned. She had stood there while he had fed in the ridiculous request. 'Wasn't it Demi Moore?'

'As near as you can get,' she answered. 'Dolly Parton might be worth a try, or Cher. Never mind, I'll let you choose.' The happy face clouded over once more. 'Did Hyacinth have the heart-attack we were all dreading?'

'I'm afraid so.'

'And after you told her to take things easier. It's my fault. I should never have chosen this particular play. It's a bit like Shakespeare's Scottish tragedy – there's always an accident of some sort, or a death.'

'This is not your fault, Mrs Nugent.'

'April,' she told him. 'A man who has seen me naked so many times shouldn't need to use the full title.'

He saluted her comically before walking home to breakfast and unhappiness.

April dropped into one of the benches at the front of Cavendish Mansions. After half an hour of Philip Pointer's ravings, she was considerably the worse for wear. Poor Philip lived for the theatre. A retired chemist, he had been a member of St Thomas's Amateur Dramatic Society since the early fifties, had strutted and perspired his way through comedies, tragedies and histories. Really, any play with Philip in it had been a comedy, as his acting was pure ham-on-the-bone, rigid, dominant, loud.

Now he was self-appointed leader of the pack, a grizzly bear of a man who wore a fedora and, sometimes, a scarf longer than Dr Who's. At every rehearsal, he carried chalk and a tape measure, marking out carefully each actor's position, calculating the number of steps for every entrance, almost pinning his cast in place, precluding any chance of personal interpretation of a script. The poor man was a dodo, born out of his time and with a personality that precluded negotiation.

Forgetting her sadness for a moment, April almost giggled. This would be the second of her plays to be slaughtered by PP. The first, a comedy about sixties youth in Liverpool, had been a resounding success all over the country, yet Philip had managed to render it feeble and mundane. Now he was working on the destruction of *Monday's Child*, April's best-known theatre play.

She glanced upward, caught sight of a movement in Honoria's famous corner window. Her skin crawled for a second or two. She had not based the characters on those three sisters, surely? Like Hyacinth, Honoria and Hilda, the play's three protagonists were sisters, their names all beginning with an A. But Alice, Amelia and Annie bore no resemblance to the Wests. April had chosen A because her own name began with that letter.

And yet . . . and yet Alice, the eldest, was pretty, sweet and kind. Amelia, the middle sister, was jealous and nasty, just like . . . Oh dear. Annie was down-to-earth, plain-spoken, yet just. Annie probably had much in common with Hilda, the youngest of the Wests. Whatever, April Nugent had not consciously used the lives of the West sisters as a basis for *Monday's Child*.

Upstairs, Honoria lost interest in April, who was simply resting in order to achieve sufficient steadiness to tackle the lift. The grieving sister was far more intent on watching David Benson as he made his way homeward, shoulders sagging further with every step he took. Did he know? she wondered. Had he noticed a cooling in his wife's demeanour, a slight absent-mindedness perhaps?

The houses in Oak Avenue and Beech Gardens were executive detached, all with a minimum of four bedrooms, double garages, two bathrooms. Some were blessed with swimming-pools, jacuzzis, saunas. Honoria had fought grimly against the development, believing that the new, possibly tacky homes would undermine the value of the Mansions, but she and a couple of other objectors had been overruled. In fact, the buildings were rather elegant, while their inhabitants had provided Honoria's greatest pleasure.

If she looked through the right-hand side of her corner viewpoint, or straight ahead, she saw the comings and goings in Beech Gardens, while the left-hand pane overlooked Oak Avenue. Newcomers were mostly young, the majority in their mid-thirties, some with children, others concentrating on careers. The latter faction was Honoria's preferred group: children were messy, noisy creatures who should be reared in communes somewhere, returning to the bosom of their families only when civilized. Some remained savages, however. At eighteen and nineteen years of age, they waited until their parents went out before blessing the whole neighbourhood with loud, angry so-called music. About that, Honoria had done nothing so far, though other householders had taken up the cause with moderate success.

Dr Benson disappeared into number 6, Beech Gardens. Honoria counted beats of time by listening to the tick of the grandmother clock. After thirty-nine seconds, Yvonne Benson emerged from the same door, leapt into a large four-wheel-drive affair and set off towards Crosby. Forty seconds later, David Benson appeared in his front garden and began to attack his roses with a sharp pruning knife. The surgery he performed was swift and vicious. Honoria imagined that he might well have preferred to inflict similar wounds on the neck of his pretty wife.

Quickly, Honoria turned to the left and picked up her binoculars. Yes, there she went, Mrs Yvonne Benson, tall, elegant and almost perfectly beautiful. A well-thought-of geriatric nurse, Yvonne Benson was blotting her copybook, was seeing rather a lot of someone who lived down Poplar Grove. Or was she? Had Dr Benson's wife taken a lover? Sometimes, Honoria felt thoroughly thwarted. Poplar Grove was not within her visual sphere, which was a source of great disappointment. Ah, well, it was time to kick agoraphobia into touch. Genuinely afraid of outdoors, Honoria had been indulged, first by her sister, then by others who had sought to comfort her. She would go out soon, must go out.

The doorbell sounded. Honoria could see that April remained in her seat down below, so this must be the undertaker. Wearing a mournful expression, Honoria went to admit the man on to her territory.

When allowed in, Mr Monkhouse stood in the hallway, removed white gloves and nodded sombrely at his hostess.

'She's in the bedroom,' said Honoria. 'Through that door.'

Mr Monkhouse lingered. 'Would you like to keep her at home?'

Honoria's eyebrows shot up. 'Here?'

He coughed, a hand coming up to hide the sound. 'Some people like to keep the loved one at home until the funeral.'

Honoria had not considered the options. 'Take her away,' she ordered. 'Don't you have one of those chapel places?'

'Of course.'

'Then . . . Oh, just do whatever you do, but not in the flat.'

He placed his gloves on the hall stand. 'I'll get a copy of the certificate from the doctor,' he told her. 'Now, will this be a burial or a cremation?'

'Cremation.' God, what a fuss this was becoming.

'And the coffin – linings and so forth?'

A steely glint crackled in Honoria's eyes. 'Just give her the best, bearing in mind that a cremation probably merits a different sort of coffin. Less expensive?' She paused. 'Put her in pink.' She waited again, received no response. 'Will that be all?'

'Er . . . there's the date to be decided. St Thomas's, I take it?'

She nodded curtly.

'Then the notice for the newspapers, which newspapers, flowers and so forth—'

'Pink,' she snapped. 'The flowers must all be in shades of pink, since that was my sister's favourite colour. She liked white, too. As for the notice, put it in the *Crosby Herald* and the *Liverpool Echo*. Plain statements, please.' There had been enough soppy poetry during Hyacinth's life – no need to go waxing lyrical now.

'No nationals?'

'No nationals,' she repeated, the syllables separated by mock patience. 'Will there be anything else, Mr Monkhouse?'

He hesitated, decided against questions regarding the number of cars, a burial plot for the urn, mass cards for Catholics. 'I'll . . . er—'

'Get on with it, please.'

He turned towards the flat's entrance door, stopped in his tracks.

'Whatever now?' She should have been watching the progress of Mrs Yvonne Benson, who was, in Honoria's opinion, doing damage of some sort down Poplar Grove.

'I must return later with a colleague,' he explained nervously. 'It takes two of us, you see, to remove the deceased. I shall probably bring my son.'

Impatiently, Honoria opened the door for him. 'I shall leave it on the latch,' she snapped. 'Let yourselves in, out, or whatever. I have things to do, letters to write and so forth.'

On the landing, Eric Monkhouse shivered. He had been in places far colder than this one, yet the woman inside this mansion flat was chillier than the morgue. Still, there was a job to be done and, according to local opinion, Miss Hyacinth West had been a sweet lady. For her, he would pull out all the stops.

Two

Confusion was becoming a prime number in Yvonne Benson's life, something she was rapidly getting used to. Indeed, having come to expect bewilderment, she staggered through each day with no expectations of anything approaching sense or reason.

She applied the handbrake, then tapped her fingers on the steering-wheel. 'Crackers,' she told the dashboard. 'Absolutely pots for rags. I'll start twitching soon, twitching and forgetting name, rank and number. Did I have breakfast today? And, if I did, was it toast or cereal?' The last question was directed at her companion in the rear seat.

Bertrand Russell, unmoved by his mistress's angst, yawned, scratched an ear and rounded off his performance by staring lugubriously at a large black cat sat on April Nugent's gatepost. He thought about barking, decided against it. That particular cat was known to him; that particular cat was not impressed by the silly yappings of a mere Jack Russell terrier.

'It's not as if anything's happened, Bertie,' continued the captain of the stilled vehicle. 'Nothing

28

ever happens, so how do I manage to be so upset?'
A partial answer to Yvonne's queries peeped over
layers of mental cloud, and she dragged it out and
gave it the once-over before shoving it back into
cerebral Bedlam. She was, she suspected, upset
because she wasn't upset. Daft. No, no, it wasn't
daft at all. A woman who was considering ending
her marriage should be extremely sad, and she
wasn't sad at all. Yes, she was. 'Dafter by the
minute,' she concluded. Perhaps the human brain
turned to mush after a lengthy diet of daytime TV
and soppy novels. What would Richard and Judy's
agony aunt say? 'Stick with it, you're just going
through a bad patch'?

David had persuaded Yvonne to give up her
nursing job. He had his practice, his house, his
cars. He now wanted a child to set against his carefully constructed backdrop of perceived normality.
His wife had been briefed, and was expected to
conceive and deliver an intact child of exceptional
beauty and intelligence. She managed to feel
numb and sick simultaneously. It was always David,
David, David. Yvonne was cook, bottle-washer and
intended incubator. She was also fed up to her
wisdom teeth. Because, in spite of his failings,
David remained a kind man. What a mess. People
would talk, would wonder how and why she had
stopped loving such a considerate, gentle man,
such a good doctor. Let them talk, said an inner,
stubborn voice.

She had felt unable to discuss the problem with
friends, as friends had a habit of being too kind,
too understanding. They also tended to divide
themselves into factions, each group attaching

itself to one or other of the separating parties.

She had not been looking for a confidante, yet she had acquired one quite by accident in Sainsbury's 8 Items or Less queue. And what a bargain, she mused. Karam Laczynska, spinster of this parish, commonsensical, owner of enough degrees and doctorates to paper a small bedroom, had become Yvonne's loyal companion. April Nugent had followed Karam into the arena, had brought with her a sense of humour and a deep, instinctive knowledge of the human animal. Poor April. April was going to miss Hyacinth terribly. The two of them had been so close. Honoria, of course, would never miss anyone. Yvonne's mind was all over the place again.

She closed her eyes and floated back into Sainsbury's. Blessed with an urge to analyse people by judging the contents of trolley or basket, she had looked down into a jumble of tins and packages that advertised their owner's single status. 'You're Karam,' she had declared eventually.

'What's the matter with him?' Karam had asked by way of response.

Both women had fixed their eyes on a middle-aged man in flat cap and tweed jacket. He had been negotiating a deal with the check-out girl, something connected with the closing date in the small print of a *Daily Mirror* offer for Cadbury's Fudge bars.

'Summit conference.' Karam had grinned ruefully. 'Which-ever queue I get in, there's always a NATO meeting.'

Karam's basket had held Cumberland pie for one, a cluster of baking potatoes, small tins of beans, a new toothbrush and a packet of marked-down crumpets. She was extraordinarily beautiful, with eyes of a dark, smoky grey, while her skin was clear and shaded like milky coffee. Brown, almost shoulder-length hair was in enviable condition. Psychotherapy in the cheap lane, Karam had always called it after the event. Of course, the two women had already known one another via the St Thomas's Amateur Dramatic Society, but it had taken a millionaire called Sainsbury to bring them together as soul-sisters, drinking partners and members of a pub quiz team.

On this, the morning after Hyacinth West's death, the doctor's wife's Range Rover was parked at the bottom of the cul-de-sac named Poplar Grove. Yvonne kept thinking about poor Hyacinth. She'd been a grand old bird, always chatty, friendly, very much a part of the community. Even in her wheelchair, she had sat outside the Mansions in good weather, knitting, crocheting, kitting out little dolls for jumble sales.

Yvonne sighed. In spite of pain, the old lady had been a dab hand at steering herself in and out of lifts, at getting from A to B in the motorized wheelchair stored in a cupboard on the ground floor of Cavendish Mansions. Though, after becoming so ill, she should not have continued with the drama group, not on the acting side. Hyacinth West had missed her way – of that there could be little doubt. She had been an actress of note, whose stuff should have been strutted the length of Shaftesbury Avenue. But no. Hyacinth had settled for next to nothing, had written poetry, had painted watercolour flowers, had subjugated herself to the will of a tyrant. Honoria West, queen of all bitches, had made her sister's life a hell on earth.

'And I'm another bitch,' Yvonne said aloud. 'He has never hurt me, has never been cruel.' Some marriages went out with a whimper rather than with an explosion, it seemed. She would have felt better if there had been rows, fights, some peg on which she might hang her hat in defiance, anger or hatred. She admired her husband. Like most mortals, he had some annoying habits, yet David Benson was a superb physician, a just man, one who would champion the cause of the underdog even if such actions might prove injurious to himself. 'Oh God, how I hate you, Yvonne Benson,' she told her reflection in the rearview mirror.

She moved her gaze to fix eyes on an uncertain future, her body held perfectly still in her parked Range Rover. 'Just one run at life,' she informed the dog, who had now installed himself in the front passenger seat. She had never been fond of terriers, had considered them busy and snappy, but little Bertrand Russell had crawled out of April Nugent's animal sanctuary and into her heart. 'That's all we get, Bertie. No dress rehearsal, nobody in the wings with a prompter's copy. This is it, lad. This is our one-night stand.' After all, what was seventy-odd years? Just a microscopic dot in the space–time continuum.

Bertie, who entertained no opinion on the subject of quantum physics or whatever, simply wagged his tail, trod invisible reeds into a circular pattern, then settled for a snooze.

Karam's house was the last on the right-hand

32

side of Poplar Grove. It faced April Nugent's home, and both buildings dated back to just before the battle of Waterloo. Karam's number 10, also named Jasmine Cottage, boasted white stuccoed walls, a lion's-head knocker on the solid front door, and some rather fine poplars at the bottom of a long rear garden. This was a beautiful place, a proper home. The kitchen was probably unhygienic, was certainly stuck in a time warp with its porcelain sink, wooden drainer, pulley clothes-line, aged dressers, coal-fired boiler behind an ancient black grate.

Yvonne glanced across at April's place, noticed new paintwork and some faithful replacement windows. Yes, it looked as if April was solvent again. At the rear of April's house, dogs, cats and even horses were kept on a large plot of land acquired for that purpose. Volunteers laboured day in and day out to feed, clean, walk, train and rehome mankind's rejected animals. April loved all creatures, no matter how unclean and unhousetrainable they might be.

After winding down a window to allow the dog some air, Yvonne jumped out of her status symbol. David drove a large navy-blue hatchback, while his wife used the statutory off-the-road vehicle. She had no children to ferry to school and no intention of driving through rough terrain in search of white rhino. A Golf or a Micra would have been adequate, but no, David had to potter around washing the loves of his life every Sunday, sloshing about with power hose and chamois, waxing wings and swilling mud from beneath the sills. It was all very sad and very stupid. He was a nice man, she reminded herself for the umpteenth time. Perhaps she didn't want a nice man.

She took a key from beneath a terracotta pot and let herself into the back porch of Jasmine Cottage. The smell of oil paint touched her first, followed by the subtler aromas of home-grown herbs and beeswax polish. Karam was out, would be lecturing on art history down at the University of Liverpool. Yvonne grinned. According to Karam, some of her current students were more interested in partying than in Picasso. 'They don't know their Renoir from their Rembrandt,' she was often heard to moan.

In the kitchen, Yvonne boiled the kettle and placed a new filter in the coffee pot. Karam, though absent, seemed very much here. The magic touch showed in the careless yet perfect arrangement of pine-cones, sea shells, pebbles, fruits and home-dried flowers on a gargantuan unglazed earthenware plate, in a busy lizzie exploding from a lidless teapot, in the placement of two Victorian flat-irons press-ganged into supporting Mrs Beeton, Ken Hom and Jane Asher. Irons press-ganged? She must remember to tell Karam that one.

While water dripped through a generous helping of Kenya blend, Yvonne took herself up to the attic studio. On the staircase, she paused to look yet again at black-and-white photographs taken in Peru, where Karam had helped to build a school while working with Voluntary Service Overseas. 'Too good to be true, you are,' she told the willowy figure surrounded by olive-skinned urchins.

Yvonne had never considered herself beautiful,

34

but the painting in the studio made her so. The long-limbed, creamy-skinned blonde lay naked against a background of varying blues, one hand dropping to the floor, the other draped along a shapely hip. 'Utter bias,' she told the sun-scalded room. 'Painted as seen through the eyes of a compassionate friend, no sign of cellulite or freckles. We shall call it *Lies, Damned Lies and Vital Statistics.*'

Downstairs again, she sat with a mug of coffee and the *Financial Times*, eye raking across the pages where her few shares were listed. So far, so good, though there seemed little chance of a real killing in the present climate. She removed her John Lennon reading glasses and bit into an apple.

It was so comfortable here, so undemanding. Her own kitchen was sterile, a germ-free and streamlined environment where appendectomies might have been performed with impunity. There was a dishwasher, a water purifier, a waste-disposal unit, and Dettox filled the under-sink cupboard. She had automatic peelers, corers, sharpeners, an electric carving-knife, a microwave and two fan-assisted ovens. For what purpose? So that she might stand each Sunday arranging medallions of beef on a bacteria-free platter while he washed cars?

The back door crashed inward. 'Buckets of blood and guts,' cried an unseen person. 'Are you there, Yvonne?' It was too late. Files and books spilled on to the flagged floor while Karam swore under her breath.

'I'm here,' announced Yvonne unnecessarily.

'God, that coffee smells good.' The files,

shepherded into some sort of order, were dumped without ceremony on the pine table. 'I went Dutch today,' she grumbled quietly. 'Dutch masters, the greatest of the great. It was like casting pearls before swine. I'm thinking of becoming a road-sweeper.' She gazed hard at Yvonne. 'Are you all right?'

'Yes,' answered Yvonne.

'Fair enough.' Karam whistled until Bertie put in an appearance. 'I released the hound from hell,' she announced cheerily. 'He was trying to gnaw his way through the steering-wheel.'

Yvonne cleared her throat. Did Karam know about Hyacinth? No, she would have said something. 'I have decided to leave David,' Yvonne whispered hesitantly. The words made it real, scary, but undeniable. She would wait awhile before passing on the message about Hyacinth, would save that bad news until Karam was seated and settled. 'And, if your offer of help still stands, I'd be grateful for a bed if things become ... difficult.' He would sulk. Sulking was one of his talents, and Yvonne could not bear it. 'Coffee in a large mug?' she asked.

'Thick, strong and laced with brown sugar.' Karam threw herself into an Ercol armchair that had arrived in the kitchen by accident, had stayed and had been reunited with its matching twin three days ago. In these two chairs, Karam and Yvonne had sat half the night discussing the state of Yvonne's marriage. 'Think carefully, Yvonne,' she said softly now. 'You know April and I will be here for you, but it's one huge step to take. April's divorce was no picnic.'

Yvonne poured coffee. 'I couldn't have managed without you and April. I've become weak and uncertain. It was as if David was there to do all the intelligent stuff, while I was around just to keep the house going. I had no strength, no sense of myself.'

'Forget it, kid.'

Yvonne waited while her companion sipped some coffee. 'Sorry to be the one to break this, Karam, but Hyacinth died last night.'

Karam's eyes were rounded in shock. 'What?'

'Hyacinth. In her sleep. PP was on the phone to me at the crack of dawn, fussing about the bloody play. He thinks life begins and ends with the rise and fall of a curtain, awful man.' She sighed. 'Anyway, Honoria took it well, according to David. He went along to do the necessary.'

Karam closed her eyes and leaned back in the chair. 'Poor Hyacinth,' she whispered. Karam had met Hyacinth while painting flats for STADS, a job she had done many times since arriving in Blundellsands. She had scene-shifted, arranged sets, had even prompted and dressed cast. 'She was a really good woman, one of the best.'

'I know. I can scarcely get her out of my head. I believe April Nugent was very cut up. They were close, she and Hyacinth.'

Karam nodded thoughtfully. 'April's a member of the blessed minority who can walk right past Honoria without feeling the need for garlic flowers and crucifixes. She sees only the best in people.'

'There is no best in Honoria.'

'True.' The dark grey eyes opened. 'Perhaps April imagines it.'

'Perhaps.' Yvonne fiddled with her mug and spoon. 'I shan't leave David until after the funeral – perhaps not until after the play, if the play goes on without Hyacinth. There'll be trouble enough without me creating waves.' Her own problems seemed pathetic now when laid against Hyacinth's sudden and final exit.

Karam closed her eyes again, hands gripping the coffee mug. She wanted to cry for Hyacinth and to rejoice for herself. All she required emotionally was here in this room. She longed to wake with Yvonne, to fall asleep with her, to feed her, drink wine with her, to celebrate life with her. This could be their kitchen, their house, their little dog curled on a hessian mat. Yet she could say nothing, because she knew that Yvonne might be frightened off by avowals of eternal devotion. Tell her, ordered the voice of conscience. Why should I? replied Karam's pragmatic side.

Yvonne bit her lip. 'She made me laugh,' she muttered, almost to herself. 'She and April were two of a kind, forever making fun of their dis- abilities.' The tone was raised. 'Remember the scenes in the village?'

Karam nodded.

'April using Hyacinth's wheelchair as a walking frame, Hyacinth acting as map reader. Always finished up in Ethel Austin's instead of the Halifax.'

'Or the other way round.' Karam opened her eyes. 'I can't take it in,' she whispered. 'I'll still be waiting for her phone calls and the poems on my answer-machine.'

'I know.'

A small sob escaped Karam. 'So frail, yet Hyacinth was everyone's backbone. She straightened things out, made them clearer.' Sniffing back tears, Karam forced a smile. 'She wouldn't want us crying.'

'No, she wouldn't.' Yvonne counted to five, decided to take her friend's mind off Hyacinth by producing yet another difficult topic. 'I think I might be pregnant.' Perhaps Karam would not want a child in her house. There was always April, but April was not well, and her house always seethed with animal life, much of which was not healthy.

'I see,' was the too-careful response from Karam. She didn't want to see, could not bear to imagine, Yvonne with a lover.

'Sometimes I'm too tired to say no. It's almost easier to lie there and accept the inevitable.' Taking the line of least resistance had become Yvonne's way of coping.

'Good job you weren't a passenger on the *Titanic*, then.' Karam paused, reeled in her instinctive, unjustifiable anger. 'I'm sorry,' she said. 'That was nasty.'

'It's OK.'

'What will you do?'

What would she do? For five afternoons, she had glued herself to cable TV, had watched *Coronation Street* episodes from the Bronze Age, *EastEnders* from its shaky beginnings, anything at all to take her mind off the waiting and the worrying. 'I've got a QVC membership number now,' she said absently, her mind wandering into safer territory. She did not want to think about babies, yet she must, sooner or later.

'You've got a what?'

'The shopping channel. A diamonique ring and a non-stick wok. What's the point of a non-stick wok, Karam? How can I season Teflon?'

'Yvonne, I—'

'What's the point of anything?' She pressed her hands against a flat belly. 'I can tell you what I'm not going to do. There'll be no abortion. The bottom line is, I shall be leaving David anyway. Whether you accept me into your home is a separate issue, as is the baby. If there is a baby.'

Karam leapt to her feet, the tears gushing in spite of firm resolve. 'Oh, Hyacinth,' she wept. 'How she would have loved to see your child. Yvonne, this makes no difference whatsoever.' Hyacinth had known about Karam's love for Yvonne, had expressed no opinion, had offered no lectures, no criticisms.

'Are you sure?'

'Yes, yes, yes!'

Yvonne opened her bag and lifted out a box. 'This is the tester kit. You are my anti-hysteria kit. You see, I'm not sure how I'll feel if I am or if I'm not. I think it's called mixed feelings, and I know it's no stranger to insanity. I need not to be alone when I get the result.'

Karam nodded, and the tears stopped.

When the process was over, the women sat side by side on Karam's bed. 'Feeling better?' asked Karam.

Yvonne shrugged, tried to picture a small cluster of dependent cells, a pinhead-sized sliver of life that would, fate willing, develop into a full-blown human with gifts, faults and physical individuality. 'I'm scared,' she whispered. 'I'm a registered nurse with an RMN and—'

'A what?'

'I'm qualified to deal with mental illnesses, particularly the elderly confused.'

'That's why you chose me as a friend. You could see that I needed help to stay out of the asylum.'

Yvonne had never even attempted to choose. She had been invited for coffee, and the bonding process had begun. Men didn't seem to have friendships like this, she mused. Men were too busy competing for the better job, the bigger car, the longer list of sexual conquests. 'I'm qualified and terrified.'

Karam stared at the ceiling. 'What if he makes trouble?'

'He won't.'

'How can you be so sure?'

Yvonne turned to look at Karam. 'His receptionist makes me sure. After all, he needs sexual release. They all do.'

'I hadn't realized.'

'So he takes what's on offer at the surgery. You know Deirdre – that redhead stacked like a page three – lives just round the corner from me, in Oak Avenue, hangs around at rehearsals. She's separated from her husband and usually from her underwear. Deirdre Mellor's skirts are so tight you can see a slight umbilical rupture. She wears black stockings and sling-back shoes so high that the heels come with a government health warning and a cylinder of oxygen.'

A clock chimed twice. 'That's me back at work

in an hour,' sighed Karam. 'And, if you've stopped loving him, why do you hate Deirdre so passionately?'

Yvonne averted her gaze. 'It's purely territorial and nothing to do with love. It's like . . . like a kid stealing your skipping rope. The rope's too short for you, you're finished with it, but why should the other child have it?'

Karam jumped to her feet. 'Then don't let her steal him – give him to her. Tell her she's welcome to your leavings.' She stood tall, yawned and stretched. 'Aren't men silly?'

'Have you had many boyfriends?' asked Yvonne.

Karam swallowed the reply she should have made. 'Not many. Too ambitious, you see. I carry few passengers, and most of them are women.' No, no, she must say no more.

Occasionally – frequently, in fact – Yvonne Benson wondered what on earth Karam Laczynska saw in a friendship with a rather ordinary nurse. Karam had studied in Paris and Milan, had helped to restore priceless paintings in Florence, had travelled in South America. Yet Karam, for all her clever remarks, was sometimes insecure, uncertain. 'You're so kind to me.'

Karam pulled on an ancient, paint-streaked cardigan. 'When he learns about the baby, he'll hang on for all he's worth.'

'The baby could be anyone's. I might have had a rampageous affair with the caretaker at the clinic.'

'And you're the nurse? What about blood tests, DNA?'

42

Yvonne nodded. 'Of course. Never mind, because babies are almost always kept with their mothers.'

With a dyke in the house? Karam wondered silently.

Yvonne rose from the bed. 'Perhaps I shouldn't park myself here after all. Perhaps I should find a room elsewhere.'

Karam considered the options. There was her work, both here in the attic studio and at Liverpool University. There was Yvonne and her baby. 'You could go to the old homestead for a while,' she suggested. 'It would give you some space.'

'What? Where?'

'Yorkshire, just outside Huddersfield. It's no more than an ancient pile of stones with a silly old chap bumbling about inside. The point is, it's usually peaceful unless Seb decides to turn up and as long as Father isn't being inventive. Sebastian is my little brother, the famous one; the aforementioned old bumbler is my father, of course. He came over from Poland just before the last war, neglected to go home, then married my mother. She was a young thing, English and thirty-some years his junior, but he wore her out. The main thing is not to worry about explosions and so forth. Mother was of a nervous disposition, you see.'

'Explosions?' Yvonne sat down again. Could she deal with a whole family of geniuses? Even for a few weeks?

'Papa's a chemist and a life peer. The length of his life thus far is a source of great wonder to

43

me and Seb. It's a big house, or it was before Father started to blow it up. You'd have to stay away from the laboratories. If you lived over in Yorkshire for a while, no one would find you. You'd get a breathing space, at least.'

'So your dad's a lord?'

Karam grinned broadly. 'Lord Laczynski of Horsefield. Horsefield is a village of ten houses and a pub. He's a mischievous old bugger, I must say, though most of the testosterone should have leaked away by now. He's about ninety, you know. Yes, he was sixtyish when I was born, sixty-odd-ish when Sebastian put in a premature appearance.'

Yvonne processed this new information. Until this moment, she had known little about Karam's background, except that the name was Polish. 'Sebastian Laczynski?' she asked firmly. 'ITV, Sundays, a bit arty, unheard-of sculptors and unpronounceable writers?'

'That's my brother, all right. God knows who he had to sleep with to get the series.' She pondered. 'No, Seb wouldn't do that. He's OK, really, the least eccentric of us.' She paused. 'No,' she murmured. 'He's his own kind of weird.' Dragging a hand through wilful hair, she continued. 'So . . . with poor Hyacinth dead, I dare say the play will be cancelled?'

'Probably.'

'And your exit from home?'

'When I hear from Philip Pointer, we'll decide what to do. After all, few decisions can be made until the maestro has been consulted.'

'Fair enough.' Karam dived for the door. It

was Botticelli this afternoon, but at least students were kosher and not a part of some government-invented foundation course designed to keep the unemployed off the streets. Botticelli. To deal with such a master, one needed to be early and prepared.

Three

April Nugent followed her left foot into the flat. It was a law unto itself, forever getting the message too late, then continuing along a course from which nothing would divert it. When she hit the coat-stand, April, forced to stop, took a deep breath, then did a short, involuntary maypole dance around her walking-stick. 'Honoria,' she began, as she turned for a third time, 'I thought I'd just, as I'm on my way to the—'

'Do come into the drawing room, dear.' Now all the wearisome sad stuff would begin, no doubt, people dropping by to express their condolences, some leaving cards, others bringing casseroles and quiches and cakes. Still, April Nugent must be entertained and respected in spite of her childish sentimentality. April was published, had been broadcast on radio and television, had seen her work performed in theatres. April was someone to be cultivated: she had friends in high places. 'Sit down,' said Honoria. 'I'm so glad you came. I caught sight of you earlier, but—'

'Sorry. I decided to go shopping first because I needed to pick up my prescription. And the old legs aren't up to much. Damned nuisance, this wretched disease. Wish I could get my bearings.' She flopped into a chair. 'Poor Hyacinth,' she said softly. 'Dreadful loss.'

'Quite.' Honoria poured two dry sherries.

'Is she still here?'

Honoria glanced at her watch. 'The funeral director should arrive in a few minutes. He went to fetch someone to help him, then I telephoned and asked him to leave . . . her body until after your visit. But because of the warmish weather, he said two thirty was as far as he dared stretch.'

April struggled to her feet, gulped down the sherry and made off towards the hallway. This would be her last chance to see a woman who had been kind, generous and loving.

Honoria listened while the visitor fought to control desensitized extremities, heard a muffled curse, flinched when the walking-stick bounced off skirting board and radiator. April knew something. Poplar Grove was not densely populated, so she must have seen Yvonne Benson's Range Rover going up and down. But the trouble with April Nugent was her dislike of gossip. There must be a way of asking without appearing to be over-curious . . . After the funeral, perhaps.

April placed herself on Hyacinth's dressing-stool and looked at the remains of her dearest friend. Although the curtains were closed, she managed to see quite clearly the sweet, gentle features of Hyacinth West. 'You were good to me,' she said. 'Always there to fill in the missing word, never impatient with me.' When the MS hit her speech, April had been only too happy to keep company with those who prompted and guided her through the stutters and stammers. 'I shall be at a loss without you, my dear friend. As far as I'm concerned, no one could hold a candle to you.' She rubbed her eyes with balled fists, thought about her mother. 'You even taught me to forgive myself when I could no longer care for Mum.' April's mother, a sufferer of senile dementia, was in a Chester nursing home. 'Thank you,' whispered April.

Hyacinth had been beautiful, even in later life. Photographs taken in her youth proved that she had always been a stunner. Rumours about her past and her single status had been abundant. She had been crossed in love, her young man had died tragically, had been married already, had left her at the altar.

Now only April Nugent knew the unhappy truth. Honoria would have an account of it, of course, but tales told by the two sisters had always varied wildly, and April had learnt to accept Hyacinth's versions with unquestioning confidence.

It seemed that the young Honoria West, plump and fresh-faced, had come between Hyacinth and her fiancé, had fallen in love with him, had run screaming rape from a barn with torn clothes and a bloodied face. Naturally, the whole unsavoury business had been hushed up, since Mrs West could not have borne to expose herself and the family to publicity involving charges of attempted rape. 'Why did you come to live with her?' whispered April. Elsewhere, Hyacinth might have enjoyed a degree of tranquillity in her later years.

A bluebottle circled the still form on the bed. As far as April was concerned, the noisy intruder was doing his job, since everything recycled itself if left alone. She believed in nature and in God's plan, was prepared to negotiate peace with every creature on earth, and Hyacinth's stiff-lipped sister was no exception to the rule. Honoria could not possibly be completely bad; she was simply mistaken. Some people made many, many bad choices, and Honoria was one of them. 'You were not happy here,' April advised her silent friend. 'You should have stayed on the farm with Hilda.' Yes, wild, open spaces would have suited the poet in Hyacinth.

In spite of her open-mindedness, April shared Hyacinth's suspicion that Honoria might have planned the scenario in the family barn, but she squashed the thought each time it surfaced. Honoria was an unhappy woman. She suffered so badly from agoraphobia that she had not been out for years. And yet there was so much more to the story of Honoria . . .

The fly buzzed excitedly.

Honoria West suffered so badly from agoraphobia and claustrophobia that she had volunteered to play Alice, Monday's Child grown old and infirm. Perhaps the offer had been made in the heat of the moment, just after

Hyacinth had been found dead. The drama society had lost a valued and gifted member . . . But Honoria could never be Hyacinth, would never match her for talent, for looks, for sheer, dogged staying power. 'You were perfect as my Alice,' she told the deceased. 'Ninety per cent perspiration, wasn't it, my dear? Even talent requires application, dedication and pure, honest sweat. You knew that.'

April closed her eyes and cast her mind back to when Hyacinth had been at her most magnificent. How firmly she had stood by April's side when removal men had arrived to erase the final traces of Mark Nugent, April's ex-husband. Mark, like so many before and after him, had not coped with his partner's illness. Faced with an uncertain future, he had hopped off with an overblown blimp of a woman from the advertising firm for which he, too, had worked.

Recently, April's fortunes had improved immensely. Exhausted after scripting two highly successful television comedy series, she had returned now to her animals and to her real hobby, the love and bane of her life. Once again, she was quarrelling with Philip Pointer, was enjoying seeing friends and neighbours performing her plays on the amateur stage. 'You were the best,' she advised her closest ally. 'If only you had enjoyed some self-esteem, the stage would have been your oyster. And thanks for being there when Mark made his exit. As for Mum – well, I'd never have managed to let go if you hadn't been here for me.'

The said Mark Nugent, now made redundant

by the firm to which he had dedicated thirty-odd years, had taken note of his wife's name sliding up the TV screen once a week, and had returned, armed with flowers, a sickly smile and a bottle of cheap bubbly, intending to renew his acquaintance. Hyacinth had supported April once again through the dilemma. 'He may not allow you to keep your animals,' Hyacinth had insisted. 'And he will spend all you earn, just as he did every other time you enjoyed success.'

April opened her eyes suddenly. It was as if Hyacinth had just spoken, so clear had been the voice in April's head. 'How right you were, Hyacinth. I sent him off with a whole hive in his bonnet, silly, stupid man.'

She missed him, though. She missed sex, felt deprived, neglected, almost valueless. What was the point of eight thousand pounds an episode when there was no one to share in the triumph, no one to roll about the champagne-damped bed with? Her husband had rendered her almost bankrupt, but he had been there. Yet Mark was a hollow shell, a person without guts, without substance. That was how he had been made, and there was no cure for his condition, just as there was none for hers.

And what a damned fool of a disease this was, too. There were days when she felt almost whole, hours so precious that she would write about them. Walking down to the shore, watching the sun going to bed behind the sea's edge, taking photographs of birds on Crosby's beach, meandering, albeit in a crooked line, along the coastal path towards Formby.

Other times were not so wonderful, yet she managed, somehow, to deal with stupidly rigid muscle, with shooting pains that left her sweating and distressed, with a sudden inability to speak, to swallow, to focus. Always, she had to continue for the sake of her animals, some of them pets, others waiting to be rehomed. Volunteers worked marvels, but April visited her rescued friends on all but the very grimmest of days.

The bluebottle stopped bumbling around and rested on Hyacinth's forehead. 'Why did you leave me?' asked April. Stupid question. The good woman was dead, and she had not chosen to depart. 'There's no one I can talk to now.'

'Yes, there is.' Again, Hyacinth's voice came from within April's imagination.

'Who?' she asked.

'Yvonne Benson is going to need you, as is poor Karam. Yvonne is not a lesbian, April. Things will go wrong there, I'm sure. And Honoria watches them, you know.'

'Yes.' Hyacinth and April had talked for endless hours about Honoria's spying, about Karam falling in love with Yvonne, about how that love would probably never be reciprocated. And now those conversations were rattling about in April's head, so clear, so well remembered.

Honoria watched everyone. She sat day in and day out at the wrap-around window in a corner of the lounge, binoculars at the ready, tea or coffee on the windowsill with the biscuit barrel and a copy of *Woman's Own*. What pleasure did that woman derive from meddling in the miseries of others?

With great difficulty, April got up and joined the other mourner at the bedside. He was a very large chap, his body far too fat for his wings. How did he manage to fly? 'How do I manage to walk?' she asked him. 'It's because we must, I suppose.' The bluebottle groomed himself, too lazy to attempt escape from the live one.

The door opened. 'Mr Monkhouse is here, April,' announced Honoria.

April leant over the bed. Hyacinth's face was completely serene, white and bloodless. Age-thinned skin was settling on fine, high cheekbones, but her mouth, unsupported by dentures, was drawn inward, making her almost ugly. 'Honoria?'

'Yes?'

'Ask him to put her teeth in, will you?'

'Of course.' The door closed.

'Heaven is richer today, but we are poorer.' April kissed the forehead, causing the dozy fly to raise himself and hover, buzzing angrily, in the air.

Honoria leapt across the room and swatted the intruder with last week's *Woman's Own*. A black mark appeared on the wallpaper, and Honoria swept it off with the magazine.

April, who had thought that Honoria had left the room after their brief conversation, jumped, lost her footing and fell to the floor. 'You startled me,' she managed when her breath returned. 'When I heard the door close, I thought you had gone out again.' She looked up, saw Honoria weeping. Honoria weeping? The woman was not capable of grief, had been made with a few bits missing in the emotional department.

Miss Honoria West looked down upon the remains of her sister. Hyacinth, the oldest of the Wests, had been so blessed, so loved, so molly-coddled. Hilda, the youngest, had received more than her fair share of spoiling. In the middle, in no man's land, Honoria had existed, had watched Daddy's big fine girl being made much of, had seen her mother crooning over baby Hilda, so precious, so unexpected.

'Don't cry, Honoria,' begged April, as she struggled to raise herself from the floor.

Honoria closed her eyes, allowing the last drops to escape down her cheeks. She was alone now. Unless Hilda could be persuaded to live here, there would be no one in the second bed-room. Loneliness was a grim prospect.

'Honoria?'

There had always been someone.

'Please don't upset yourself. Let them take her now. You can't hang on, Honoria, because this isn't Hyacinth – it's just an empty shell.'

A series of female paying guests had failed to live up to Honoria's standards, but Hyacinth had stepped into the breach, had lived here for a dozen years. 'What shall I do?'

'You'll go on. We all have to go on.' April, depending heavily on her stick, managed to stand at last.

'I can't live alone.'

April fought to keep her composure. Yes,

aloneness was a dire state, yet Honoria was feeling the wrong sort of grief: there was no mention of Hyacinth, just Honoria in the frame. It would be so easy to dislike Honoria. 'She was a good companion to you,' answered April.

Good companion? Hyacinth's diabetes, diagnosed in her youth, had rendered her infirm recently. What with kidney infections, angina and the dreaded arthritis, the woman had been useless after a handful of years. 'She did her best,' admitted Honoria grudgingly. 'And at least she was always here.'

'She was good to you, good to all of us.' Until the arthritis had taken over completely, Hyacinth had done everything for her sister. Even when almost completely crippled, Hyacinth had maintained a measure of independence, had seldom asked for anything from Honoria.

Honoria gazed at the wall, remembered her older sibling messing about with bits of poems, learning scripts, telephoning members of STADS, rallying them to attend rehearsals and meetings. Then there were the paintings, endless sheets of watercolour daubs – flowers, butterflies, birds. Lately, though, Hyacinth's hands had been so crooked that using the phone, painting or cooking had become virtually impossible. And yet she had managed, somehow, to get out and pretend to be normal.

'I'll visit you,' promised April rashly. Although she found Honoria's selfishness hard to understand, she was prepared to persevere. After all, in this last decade of the century, too many women lived alone and unloved. 'I think

Honoria is simply evil,' said Hyacinth's voice in April's head. 'She's dangerous . . .'

Honoria sniffed, dabbed at her nose. 'She was quite a handsome girl, always pursued by callow young men. Hyacinth had that chocolate-box prettiness, the kind that attracts attention from the wrong people.'

Chocolate box? Hyacinth's had been a lasting, raving beauty. April listened to the words, heard the hurt, the envy.

'Of course, men would start off with her, then turn to me. She was not a good conversationalist when she was young. For her sake, I stayed single. We remained a matching pair right to the end.'

A matching pair, indeed. April chased from her head images of a Ming vase alongside a cheap plaster imitation bought at some market stall. Often, being a writer was a sore disadvantage, forcing a person to listen too alertly, to watch too closely.

'I'd better let them get on with it, then.'

Honoria and April sat in the lounge while the undertaker and his son tried to do their job noiselessly. After a few minutes, Honoria stood up and wandered with studied carelessness in the direction of her window. She picked up a book and flicked through the pages, her head moving as she followed the progress of Yvonne Benson's Range Rover.

'Shall I put the kettle on?' asked April.

'I'll do it in a second.' She didn't want April Nugent doing one of her involuntary dances in the kitchen while juggling with decent china.

Yvonne looked flustered. It was a warm day, but not hot enough to merit that degree of personal disorder.

April recognized the sound of Yvonne's car. Karam would probably be giving a lecture, so poor Yvonne had been forced to come home. Home? Yvonne's heart and soul no longer belonged in the Benson house.

'Yvonne has been down Poplar Grove again,' said Honoria. 'Perhaps she was intending to visit you, but you are here. I wonder where she's been this past hour?'

April said nothing.

Hyacinth's door opened. Steps muffled by carpet made progress along the hall. 'Come away from the window, please,' begged April. 'They're taking Hyacinth out now. Really, you should close the curtains.'

Honoria noticed the hearse at last. Impatiently, she dragged green brocade across her view. Now they would all start to arrive. Sighing, she went into the kitchen to do battle with sandwiches, cups and saucers. Yvonne Benson was definitely up to mischief, the sort her husband would be interested in, no doubt.

Carol Halliwell arrived, apologized for her husband's absence. Simon had taken a crowd of disadvantaged children on a camping holiday. 'He'll be back for the funeral, I should imagine. This is the trouble with teaching – there's always something extra to do.'

Deirdre Mellor was the next to appear, tight-curled auburn hair framing a face that looked unhappy in the heat. Nevertheless, she was gorgeous, round and voluptuous, with wide green eyes and a remarkable figure, ridiculously tiny at the waist, full around bust and hips.

Philip Pointer bustled in, the sweat marks on a blue silk shirt advertising his state of agitation. He carried a copy of *Monday's Child* and a bottle of Chivas Regal. In his wake trailed Maureen Dawson, Jenny Marsh and Barbara Trueman, a forgettable trio christened by Honoria the Three Graces. Bringing up the rear, Yvonne Benson, neat in white blouse and navy skirt, closed the door and found a seat.

April watched Yvonne, and Deirdre Mellor. Their body language was eloquent, each sitting at a slight angle from the other, several yards of Axminster between them. Deirdre, separated from an estate agent who had neglected her woefully, was probably having an affair with Dr David Benson. Yvonne, similarly ignored by the same doctor, was enjoying a relatively new friendship with Karam Laczynska. For Karam, it was so much more than a mere friendship . . .

As for the rest of the crew – well, Honoria probably kept files on all of them.

Honoria rattled her way in with trolley and food. Immediately, a line formed in front of the fireplace, each person queuing to offer condolences to the hostess. Philip Pointer, true to form, delivered a lengthy homily on which he had worked all morning. As he wittered monotonously about rising stars and waning moons, April decided to butt in. 'Do shut up, dear,' she begged. 'We're all exhausted after the shock. It was good of you to speak up for the rest of us and you are greatly appreciated. But poor Honoria has made tea and it is cooling fast.'

The great man grumbled under his breath, found a tumbler, then immersed himself in Chivas. What a fine state of affairs this was. Only a month to go, and the actress chosen to play his senior Alice had skipped off to meet her Maker. Jenny Marsh was making a fair stab at the teenage Alice, while Yvonne Benson was playing the heroine in her early thirties. But the late-sixties part was now as dead as poor Hyacinth West.

'A sandwich, Philip?'

He glanced up, saw Honoria's plump face, looked at sausage-like fingers clasped around the edge of a gold-rimmed platter. Could she do it? Would she? But, oh, what a poor replacement she promised to be. Hyacinth, some five years older than her sister, had been slender, elegant. Even in a wheelchair, the senior Miss West had carried herself well. 'No, thank you.'

She studied him for a couple of seconds. 'I meant it,' she whispered almost coyly. 'If you need me, I shall be there to play the part, my dear.'

Philip took another swig of courage. Was there no one else?

'I do know the lines.'

'Yes, but we may call the play off because of Hyacinth.'

'She would not want that.'

He raised a shoulder. 'I must bow to the will of the members. I am but one man, dear heart.'

Honoria relieved herself of the sandwiches

and clapped her hands. 'A moment, please,' she begged.

Everyone froze.

Honoria smiled. 'First, I want to thank you all for coming today.' Her voice travelled well, she thought. It was definitely as strong as Hyacinth's had been. 'We are easily a quorum, though I, myself, am not a member of the drama society. I wondered whether you might take a vote, as I have offered to take on my sister's role in *Monday's Child*. I shall, of course, leave the room while you decide. In fact, I shall take myself outside for a breath of air.' Terrified, Honoria walked out of the room. She had to do it, had to overcome the phobias. Panic rose in her chest, but she carried on. Hyacinth's time was over; this was Honoria's turn.

April absorbed everyone's shock after the front door closed behind Honoria West. Honoria had not even spoken her dead sibling's name, had not expressed any sense of loss, any real sadness or regret. Perhaps Honoria had not changed, had not improved . . .

'But she never goes out,' exclaimed Deirdre Mellor.

'That's a first,' said Jenny Marsh.

Barbara Trueman ran to the second window, an ordinary pane that turned no corners. 'She's sitting on the bench,' she cried.

Philip Pointer rose to his feet. 'We're in a damned awkward spot,' he opened grimly. 'We have to take her on – there can be no other course of action.'

Jenny agreed. 'If it gets her out—'

'And it would be a rather nice tribute to Hyacinth,' chipped in Barbara.

The Third Grace, Maureen Dawson, offered no opinion.

April listened to the ensuing chatter. An icy chill moved up her spine. It might be the MS, she told herself. Sometimes, she experienced the weirdest sensations, usually when standing in queues or walking into church. One of the more interesting feelings imitated a cascade of water flowing down her left leg, but she had not had the shivers before. 'She's dangerous,' repeated the familiar voice. 'She may have changed, or she may be resting, waiting . . .'

'April? Are you with us?' boomed PP.

'I beg your pardon?'

'How do you feel?'

'I'm all right, thank you,' she replied.

Pointer tutted. 'April, how do you feel about Honoria taking the part?'

Still shivering and now ill at ease, April picked up her stick and pushed herself into a standing position. Everyone stared at her, each waiting for her to make her pronouncement. At first, she thought her speech had gone again but, after a few seconds, she realized that anger was blocking her throat. Honoria, cool as ice, was stepping into her dead sister's shoes, intending to replace the irreplaceable.

'April?' insisted Philip Pointer.

'Do as you will,' she answered.

Philip held out large, cigar-stained hands to demonstrate his need, looking for all the world like something out of a French classic or *Fawlty*

61

Towers, an over-expressive actor with no real sense of how to play. 'But, dear April, we need your blessing.'

'No,' she snapped. 'You need my formal permission to put on the play, no more than that.'

The silence that followed was not comfortable. The Three Graces huddled together like frightened rabbits, Deirdre and Yvonne actually glanced at one another, while the rest suddenly found the carpet engrossing. Pointer was the only one outwardly unaffected. 'We need more than that. We want your support,' he gabbled.

April looked him up and down. 'Last night, a sweet soul departed this life. We are here to condole, to support one another, yet what is the topic of conversation? A bloody stupid play. I wrote it, so I am well qualified to call it bloody stupid. Hyacinth is dead. I remind you all of that. Why is everyone worrying about *Monday's Child*? Does Hyacinth not deserve your attention? Does she not merit your time, your thoughts and prayers?'

At last, the leader of the pack returned to his whisky.

April walked to the door, her movements suddenly straight and sure. In the lift, she did not cling to the handrail, scarcely needed the support of the cane.

Honoria, still seated on the bench, raised her face expectantly.

April planted her feet well apart and fixed her eyes on Miss Honoria West, watched the smile fading, noted that Honoria averted her gaze within seconds.

Honoria opened her mouth, but no sound emerged. Anxiety flooded through her, making her hot and causing palpitations. But her opportunity was here and now, her chance to prove to anyone and everyone that she was as good as Hyacinth had been.

April saw the perspiration on the woman's upper lip, watched as it flowed through the thin canals of age towards pursed, ungenerous lips.

'Have I offended you?' Honoria asked eventually.

'I am feeling unwell, so I must go home.' Why couldn't she tell this awful female the truth? Why couldn't she say, 'Hyacinth told me everything about your nasty behaviour, so stay away from my play'?

'I hope you are soon better,' Honoria said.

Without uttering another syllable, April walked to her car, climbed in and drove off smoothly. Hyacinth was dead and April was just beginning to mourn.

Four

Honoria wore a dramatic, tilt-brimmed white hat with a black band and some interesting lacework covering her face. Her rather squat frame was draped in a Dawn French-style suit, long skirt, knee-length jacket and rather full sleeves. Had there been a bit of white at the throat, she might have resembled a Sister of Charity with a weight problem.

The crematorium was packed. Every flower was pink or white, and the still air was weighty with the heady scent of roses. April, who was having a particularly spectacular multiple-sclerosis day, remained at the back on a chair provided by the ever-attentive Mr Monkhouse. She watched the proceedings as if in a dream, her throat refusing to open for the hymns, tears creeping silently down her cheeks when 'Abide With Me' was blasted from half a dozen speakers. This wasn't any old version of the hymn: the jagged, uneven recording had been made at Wembley in 1992, when Hyacinth's beloved team had routed

Sunderland by two goals to nil in the FA Cup Final.

April sniffed back a huge sob and rubbed her eyes on the sleeve of a borrowed blazer. She didn't go in for black, always felt anaemic in it. Still, Karam Laczynska wouldn't mind an April shower on her jacket. Karam was halfway along a middle row breaking her heart, while the woman she loved, Yvonne Benson, stood with her husband in the opposite pew. What a bloody mess.

When the long-dispersed football crowd had finished murdering the hymn, Liverpool supporters raised their voices once more, this time singing 'You'll Never Walk Alone'. Many would think this a strange service, football hymns and chants, but April remembered Hyacinth's fanatical love for Liverpool and was grateful to Honoria for allowing the unconventional funeral to take place.

And suddenly she was back at Wembley with Hyacinth, each sitting for the first time in the shadow of the hallowed twin towers. They had both wept at the end, had clung to each other in sheer joy before heading off to seek out one coach among several hundred. The next day had found them on Queens Drive in Liverpool, watching 'the lads' standing in an open-topped double-decker, Mark Wright holding the trophy, Rob Jones wearing its lid.

What a day that had been. The Blues had come out, too, Everton supporters from divided families, Dad in red, the kids in blue, Mam neutral in the middle doling out pop and crisps. In those days, Hyacinth and April had been whole-bodied, more or less. How they had missed Anfield with its tepid coffee, cold meat pies and sizzling hot players. Now it was cable, sanitized action replays accompanied by silly swishing sounds, adverts at half-time, stuffed-shirt retired footballers dissecting the game at the end, full post-mortem and—

Post-mortem, inquest, suspicious death. Jealousy, insulin, hypodermic. God, what a thought! Had Honoria finished Hyacinth's life? No, no, April ordered herself. She must strangle these ideas, sever them before they took root.

Blue velvet curtains opened to welcome the coffin, the opulent fabric swaying gently like the flowing skirts of the doomed Anne Boleyn's ladies-in-waiting. A clinically correct bit of Bach accompanied the measured, almost stately process. Yvonne Benson, guided by God alone knew what, turned to the man at her side. 'I'm leaving you,' she whispered. It seemed the right thing to do. The occasion marking the end of a life should also indicate change, new beginnings. Shouldn't it? Oh, what had she done now? Hormones, she supposed vaguely . . .

David's head swung round so quickly that he cricked his neck painfully. 'What?'

'You heard me. Deirdre's welcome to you.'

David rubbed his aching nape. This was a funeral, for goodness' sake. What was Yvonne thinking of? He glanced up, saw vibrant red hair two pews further up. It had taken ages for Deirdre to grow the now shoulder-length shock of auburn curls. 'We shall discuss this later, in a more appropriate setting,' he told his wife. So

66

she did know about Deirdre. And couldn't she try to understand that such a dalliance was merely recreational, like a round of golf or a few frames of snooker?

She shrugged. 'Please yourself. I have nothing more to say to you.'

At the front of the church, Philip Pointer stood between Honoria West and Gill Collins. Gill, housekeeper to the West sisters, could not bear to rub shoulders with the leading light of St Thomas's Amateur Dramatic Society so she edged closer to Hilda West, younger sister of the deceased. Hilda kept both feet on the ground. Although Gill had met the youngest Miss West just a few times, she recognized a kindred spirit.

Gill Collins did not look forward joyfully to the future. Hyacinth had been a real love, a pleasure, always grateful, always caring. Honoria was a dragon. Had it not been for a sick husband and three children, Gill would have told Miss Honoria to take a running jump into Liverpool Bay. Oh God, it promised to be all doilies and antimacassars, bring-me-fetch-me-carry-me, don't forget the picture rail, make sure you dust my television screen, the brasses are looking tarnished.

Gili sighed, wiped a tear when Hyacinth's coffin rolled away towards the furnace. The dear lady had taken so little, given so much. And Honoria wasn't even weeping, the old cow. Also, who the hell wore a white hat to a funeral?

Philip Pointer was dying for a cigar. He rattled coins in a pocket, stilled all movement when Honoria sniffed. Hyacinth was sliding away, taking with her any chance of success with *Monday's Child*. The real core of the play was rooted in the third act, when the heroine was nearing her end. Now Honoria was to take the part. Honoria? An orang-utan might well be preferable to that harridan. And what about her phobias? And would Karam Wotsername get round to painting the flats?

Karam glanced across at Yvonne, noticed that she was talking to her husband. Hating herself for the stab of jealousy that ripped through her chest, Karam averted her gaze and watched Hyacinth as she embarked on her last journey. 'I'm a lesbian,' she had told this sweet woman.

'I know. And you love a married woman.'

'Not by choice.'

The silvered hair had blown loose in the breeze. 'Love lands where and when it wants to, Karam. It never touches down in quite the right place. It flitters off into the blue just when we decide where we'd like it to settle, only to hover above the head of a target we never sought to hit. But do not expect Yvonne to return your feelings – she must follow her own star, Karam.'

'Were you ever in love?'

'Oh, yes. Once, a long, long time ago.'

Hyacinth had said no more, yet Karam had felt her pain. Fading eyes had stared out into the estuary, then a dog had arrived, its owner chasing along behind. Hyacinth grabbed at the animal's collar and almost toppled out of her wheelchair.

Karam sobbed. She had lost a soulmate, a true friend, while the world had been deprived of a gentle, self-effacing star.

Hilda West grabbed Gill's hand and hung on tightly. She would need to hang on, because Honoria had already broached the subject of her aloneness. She probably expected Hilda to take Hyacinth's place, but Hilda had her own ideas. Be strong, she told herself. You don't need to do as she says. Stay on the farm. Remember how Honoria used to be, what she did, what she continues to do. Now she has no real power. No one can make anybody do anything. But Hilda swallowed. Honoria had a way of making things happen . . .

Mark Nugent, minus his overweight lover, sat in a rear pew, wondering what the hell he was going to do. He had no job, no home and no prospects. The new love of his life had placed her house in the hands of agents and was about to exit in the direction of Derbyshire, where her parents lived. April had to take him back – she simply had to. Life was too short for quarrels. Here was the evidence, a coffin containing earthly remains sliding away into God knew what, just a sprinkling of ashes and no more to be said.

The Three Graces, Barbara Trueman, Jenny Marsh and Maureen Dawson, wept, dabbed at noses and eyes with Kleenex from little handbag-sized pack. Having shared between them a Max Factor mascara guaranteed not to run, they cried without worrying about the after-effects. With their husbands out at work and dinners in the hands of sophisticated oven-timers, they had not been too badly put out by the afternoon funeral. As the coffin glided away, they opened bags, disposed of sodden tissues and prepared to go on to the funeral buffet.

As the curtains closed behind her friend, April suddenly noticed a man in the left-hand rear corner of the chapel. He was tall, stately and well dressed, very Savile Row, in a suit that must have cost well into four figures. Motionless, with precision-trimmed beard and whiskers, he looked to be in his seventies. A silver-topped ebony cane leant against the wall beside him.

Trying not to be too obvious, April turned in her seat to get a better view of him. Although he remained still, April sensed his distress. She did not recognize him and, since he stood alone, she guessed that he must have arrived un-accompanied. Who was he?

The stranger moved at last, picked up his cane and walked quickly towards a side entrance. April, her antennae in full working order, watched him as he stopped and nodded in the direction of Hilda West. Hilda, who had turned slightly at the sound of footfalls, smiled at him.

Outside, people gathered in small groups, their voices muted to match the occasion. Occasionally, a small burst of laughter was strangled at birth. They should laugh, thought April. If they believed in God, they ought to be rejoicing, because Hyacinth's entry into heaven was a sure-fire certainty.

Hilda took her sister on one side. 'I'm going now,' she said timidly.

'Going? Where?'

'Home.'

Honoria eyed her blood relative. 'We are having a cold buffet at the George,' she said, her tone as chilled as the promised food. 'I've paid for it.'

Hilda took a step backward. 'I'll go halves if you wish,' she muttered.

'That is not what I mean. There are things to discuss – the will, Hyacinth's bits and pieces, arrangements for the future.'

Hilda bit down on her lower lip. 'Arrangements?' she achieved at last.

'Yes.' Honoria all but stamped her food in its black suede court shoe. 'I cannot live alone. You must come to Blundellsands. Hilda, neither of us is getting any younger. We need one another, you and I. How would Mother and Father feel if they knew that we were living so far apart?'

Hilda bit down again.

'You can't just go.'

The elegant stranger stepped forward. 'Miss West?' He was addressing Honoria.

'Yes?'

'I am your sister's neighbour. She is depending on me for a lift, and I must return to Bolton immediately.'

Honoria eyed him coldly. 'And you are?'

Hilda spoke up. 'He's Mr Stoneway. Mr Stoneway, this is my sister, Honoria.'

The man bowed. 'I am so pleased to meet you. However, Miss West and I must leave directly.'

Honoria was not pleased. And anyway, who, in this day and age, used the word 'directly' in such a context? Had he leapt from the pages of some Edwardian novel? 'Hilda may stay the night with me,' she insisted. 'There is Hyacinth's room.'

Hilda shivered. Poor Hyacinth had died in that room, in that very bed. 'I am going home,' she announced firmly. 'I shall telephone you in a day or two.'

Honoria, almost open-mouthed, stood and watched while Hilda and Mr Stoneway walked off far too quickly. This was appalling. Surely Hilda had feelings? How could she hurry away so uncaringly at a time such as this? Her jaw loosened even further when the two figures reached their car. A chauffeur in a peaked cap leapt out of the Rolls-Royce, stamping hard on a cigarette end. Mr Stoneway clapped the man on the shoulder, plainly forgiving him for indulging in tobacco while waiting for his master's return.

The whole party was still, as if breathing had been suspended until further notice. The Rolls-Royce, silent as a snake, crawled out of the crematorium grounds.

'Who was that?' Philip Pointer asked.

Honoria adjusted her ridiculous hat. 'That was a close friend of the family, an old acquaintance of ours.'

Hearing untruth in Honoria's wavering tone, April smiled. Sometimes, Honoria fell off her horse with extreme ill grace.

'There's money about somewhere, then,' grumbled Philip. 'How long have you known him?'

Honoria almost squirmed. 'Oh, the Stoneways have known the Wests for generations,' she lied airily.

'What line is he in?' April could have kicked herself as soon as the question left her lips. Although she did not exactly love Honoria, she was not in the business of making anyone's life more difficult.

'Do you know,' said Honoria slowly, 'I can't remember. The Stoneways have been landed for so long – they've been gentry since my grandparents were alive. It might have been cotton, but I'm really not sure.' She pulled on her gloves. 'Come along,' she ordered. 'Let's go to the George for refreshments.'

The party split up, each smaller group making off towards cars in the marked-out yard next to the chapel. Only April remained, her eyes fixed on a thin plume of smoke rising from the crematorium's small chimney. As the day was still, Hyacinth ascended in a straight, barely visible plume, no deviation towards any point on the compass. 'That's it, girl,' she whispered to herself. 'Straighten up, get out of jail free and collect two hundred pounds.' Monopoly with Hyacinth had been hilarious, as she had insisted on changing all the rules. 'No hotels on Park Lane if there's an R in the month, eh?'

Mr Monkhouse touched April's arm. 'Are you all right, madam?'

'No,' she told him. 'My best friend is dead and I'm a bloody cripple.'

Eric Monkhouse's mouth twitched. 'It's a bugger, isn't it? A bugger of a life, and then you die.'

73

'Yes,' she replied. 'It certainly is a bugger.' It was, too.

As Mr Monkhouse walked away, Mark Nugent hove into view. He looked the picture of misery, but he had always been good at that.

'April,' he began.

'Shut up,' she said mildly. He had obviously been hiding behind the building. 'I am saying goodbye to Hyacinth.' After which, she would say goodbye to him, too.

He hovered like a black cloud in an uncertain sky.

'Right,' she said eventually. 'To what do I owe the pleasure of your company?'

Mark groaned inwardly. April was in one of her we-shall-not-be-moved moods. What could he say? 'I – I lost my job. We all got paid off, but the money wasn't enough to last a couple of years, let alone a lifetime.'

'Then you'll have to find another job.'

He inhaled deeply. 'Nobody wants me.'

April nodded. 'It appears, then, that I am not the only human creature with good taste and high standards.' He was shaken – he looked like a child whose last sweet had been taken away. 'What about your lover?'

'She's selling up and moving back to Derbyshire.'

April leaned on her stick, suddenly in need of support. The divorce case had been interesting, to say the least. With the stalwart backing of Hyacinth, and in view of her condition, April had insisted on keeping the house, most of the contents and the land she had purchased after her first TV success. 'I'm glad we had no children,' she said now.

He used a handkerchief to wipe beads of sweat from his upper lip. 'When we were divorced, I was in full-time employment. That fact was taken into account. Now I have no income, nowhere to live and—'

'And you wish to renegotiate?'

He offered no reply.

April raised her free hand in a gesture usually reserved for moments of road rage. 'You understand the message I wish to convey?' she asked. Without waiting for an answer, she continued, 'Go away. Immediately, if not sooner.'

He opened his mouth to speak, but April had embarked upon a zigzag journey in the general direction of her car. She fumbled with the lock, dragged herself into the driving seat and turned on the ignition. Mark Nugent could find another damned fool to keep him in the manner he felt he deserved.

In an upstairs room of the George, Philip Pointer was delivering a sermon on the art of acting. When April arrived, he stopped.

'His battery's gone,' Yvonne whispered to Karam.

Karam grinned. 'How did he take it?' she asked.

'He stopped lecturing,' Yvonne replied. 'April makes him lose his momentum.'

Karam pulled herself together. 'Not Pointer, you silly woman. I was talking about David.'

Yvonne took a sip of her spritzer. 'Oh, him. I don't know, really. He said something about a discussion, but he hasn't spoken to me since. I expect a rather special evening.'

Karam considered these words. 'He won't get violent, will he?'

Yvonne choked. 'Stop it,' she ordered, when her throat cleared. 'He couldn't knock the skin off a rice pudding, wouldn't hurt a flea on Bertie's back. That's the trouble, you see. He's a nice man.'

Karam dug Yvonne in the ribs. 'Look,' she murmured, 'he's trying to get away from Dreary Deirdre.'

Honoria bore down on April. April had not visited Honoria since last Friday, the day on which Honoria had ventured out to sit on the bench, when April had delivered that particularly dirty look.

'How are you?' gushed Honoria.

'Fine.'

'That's wonderful. Do you think you might be in remission?'

April grabbed a glass of sherry from a passing waiter. 'I have absolutely no idea.' She swallowed the sherry in one go.

'It was a nice service,' Honoria said.

'Very nice. If you like funerals.'

Honoria, trying to feel her way, was running out of inanities.

April, who wanted nothing more than to get the whole thing over with, dived in. 'Look, I'm considering playing Alice myself – playwright's prerogative, I suppose. If I decide against it and if you still want to play Alice, get on with it.' She cast an eye over her companion. 'I wonder, were your phobias about to clear up anyway, or did Hyacinth's death prompt the miracle?'

Honoria's all in-one foundation garment was suddenly tighter than ever. 'I had to overcome my panics just to get to the funeral. There was no question of Hyacinth going to the church and the crematorium without her sisters. I am using will-power and, of course, tranquillizers.'

April, almost hating herself, entertained once more the idea of Honoria's dishonesty and sheer nastiness. 'I have known several people with agoraphobia and so forth. They have never achieved what you have managed, Honoria. Going outside is a gradual thing – first the garden gate, then a lamp-post a few yards away. You know, I think Hyacinth has reached down and performed her first miracle.'

Honoria opened her mouth to speak, closed it again. It was plain that April Nugent had developed a dislike for her, which was a great pity, as Honoria might be in need of April's help soon.

April staggered off to talk with the Three Graces. Honoria, temporarily at a loss, decided to transfer her attentions to Karam and Yvonne, who were having a quiet talk in a corner. 'I'm so glad you could come,' she told the pair. Surely Karam knew what was going on between Yvonne Benson and a neighbour? There were only four houses in Poplar Grove, one belonging to this rather elegant artist, another the property of April Nugent.

Yvonne looked straight into the eyes of the recently bereaved. 'Your sister from Bolton didn't stay, then?'

Slightly deflated, Honoria sought to reply. 'Well, Mr – er – Mr Stoneway had some pressing business. He was kind enough to give Hilda a lift, and she accompanied him on the return journey.'

'Beautiful car,' said Karam.

'Yes.' Honoria glanced from one to the other. Whatever they knew, they were sitting on it, guarding it like the egg of a dodo.

Philip Pointer butted in, already the worse for wear. 'Well?' he asked Honoria.

'I am well enough, thank you.' Occasionally, Honoria could not quite manage to admire Mr Pointer, in spite of his thorough single-mindedness.

'What did April say?'

Honoria glanced across at April and the Three Graces. 'She doesn't seem to care.' Let him find out for himself that April might play Alice. The shock would probably kill him, anyway, as he was terrified of April.

'But she did not offer support?'

'No.'

Pointer took another swig of whisky. The withdrawal of April's backing would be a twin-edged sword. On the one hand, she obviously knew the play better than anyone else. On the other, she would not be there to complain, to ask him to relax his rules. 'We don't need her, I suppose,' he said.

Karam swallowed the dregs of her burgundy. 'What a shame,' she said casually. 'You may have to manage without me, too.'

The man staggered back. 'What?' he roared.

Karam shrugged. 'When term ends, I shall probably be going home to see my father. At ninety, he cannot have many years left.'

Philip Pointer bit back an expletive. *Monday's Child* covered the heroine's whole lifetime. Although all acts were set in the one room, subtle changes to décor and furnishings were required, and this girl with the unpronounceable surname was wonderful with sets. Things were not looking promising – Hyacinth dead, the author refusing her blessing, now the painter backing out. As for Honoria – well, Honoria did not bear thinking about.

Five

Although things were not exactly on a comfortable footing, Honoria accepted the lift offered by April Nugent. They were summoned to the offices of Cain, Cain & Satterthwaite, solicitors representing the recently deceased Miss Hyacinth West.

'What about Hilda?' asked April, as she drove towards Crosby. 'Isn't she mentioned?'

'No,' replied Honoria. 'When our mother died, the farm was left to Hilda.' Hilda, Mother's favourite, had done well out of the estate. While Hyacinth and Honoria had received stocks, shares and a few thousand pounds each, Hilda was now in possession of property valued at well in excess of half a million – land, the house, livestock and so forth.

April was trying to work out her own part in Hyacinth's posthumously acted drama. There was no earthly reason why she should have been mentioned in Hyacinth's will, but at least she had been forced to contact Honoria and to act in a fashion that might be construed as civilized.

She didn't enjoy disliking people and was determined to have another stab at friendship. After all, the other business was all in the past – Honoria must be given a chance, which everyone deserved. Nevertheless, April's skin crawled as she recalled tales of pure horror, told in Hyacinth's soft, gentle tones. 'You cannot imagine what we all went through at Moortop Farm, April. That beautiful place became hell on earth.' Had Honoria changed? Were people like Honoria capable of improvement?

'Here we are,' declared Honoria, as they drove along College Road. 'It's between the fish shop and the haberdashery.'

They stepped out of the Micra, April struggling slightly with stick, keys and handbag. As ever, Honoria appeared not to notice her companion's difficulties, and carried on into the solicitors' premises without a backward glance.

In the waiting room, Honoria flicked through *Lancashire Life*, her face deliberately serene. She was not happy. What was April Nugent doing here? Surely Hyacinth had not left much to her? Perhaps a couple of trinkets or some bits of jewellery had been put on one side for April, a mere tit-bit out of one of Hyacinth's many little boxes and pots. The money would stay in the family – of that there could be little doubt.

April read leaflets about divorce, litigation, conveyancing. Whether Honoria liked it or not, she was in for a shock unconnected with April.

The shock arrived in a Range Rover, two young women climbing down, Karam entering the offices first, Yvonne staying behind for a moment to ensure Bertie's safety in the vehicle, opening windows just an inch, so that the little dog could breathe but not escape on to one of Crosby's busiest roads.

Honoria's head shot upward, while *Lancashire Life* fell to the floor. Why were these two here? Perhaps they were seeing a different man about a legal matter quite unconnected with the will . . . But no. Something in April Nugent's face advertised pre-knowledge. Not to be outdone, Honoria rose from her seat. Pretending that she had expected the newcomers, she reached out to greet them. 'Ah, so you got here.' The expressions on the three faces confirmed Honoria's suspicions. She congratulated herself inwardly on her presence of mind.

Karam and Yvonne sat together with their backs to the window. The room was not air-conditioned, and the sun beat on them mercilessly.

Honoria retrieved her magazine and pretended to take an interest in verdigris garden ornaments. April fiddled with her stick, while the two more recent arrivals simply stared at the floor.

A young man poked his head through an inner doorway. 'Are you all here for the reading of Miss West's will?' he asked.

'Yes,' replied Honoria. 'I am her sister. These other ladies were friends of hers.'

The three women crept behind Honoria into the sanctum. The man was arranging chairs. 'Good, good,' he said repeatedly, as if training puppies to sit and stay in their baskets.

Honoria tried to keep still, but disobedient fingers tapping away on the side of the brown leather handbag said much about her real state of mind.

Karam held her breath, wished that she had stayed at home, but, summoned by Hyacinth from beyond the grave, both she and Yvonne had felt obliged to come. April wished she had brought her little battery-operated fan, as the heat in the room was oppressive.

'I'm Mr Moss,' the man announced, after fiddling with a cardboard file, 'and Miss West's will was signed here in the presence of witnesses some months ago.'

Honoria's heart sank. Until now, she had imagined that the document was several years old, as each sister had made a will in the late eighties. So Hyacinth had changed her mind, had she?

'The bones are as follows,' he intoned after reading out the statutory paragraphs relating to wholeness of mind, the settling of funeral expenses and the paying of bills. ' "To Karam Laczynska, I bequeath five thousand pounds. To Yvonne Benson, I bequeath five thousand pounds. To both, I leave my wish that they will follow their dreams." '

Honoria stiffened. Trinkets? These two women had just relieved Honoria of a large chunk of her liquid expectations.

' "To my sister, Honoria West, I leave ten thousand pounds, which, together with her own assets, should suffice to keep her in comfort for the rest of her life. I also give to her my share in

83

the dwelling known as 8 Cavendish Mansions, Blundellsands, together with any furnishings, contents or personal effects purchased by me." '

The lawyer, perched on the rim of high drama, paused for effect, clearing his throat and sipping water from a glass.

' "To my dear friend, April Nugent, I leave the rest of my estate, including all remaining monies contained in bank accounts, building-society shares and stock-market holdings." ' He shuffled more papers. 'The actual amount has yet to be calculated under probate.'

Silence hung in the air, kept company with dust motes drifting along shards of fierce sunlight. The lawyer rose and adjusted the blinds.

'The actual amount is a not inconsiderable sum,' said Honoria. 'How could she do this to me? Have I no redress?' Her voice was thin, the vowels narrowed by damped-down temper. 'I shall fight,' she added.

April closed her eyes. This was terrible. Of late, she had not been pleasant to Honoria and now the final blow had been delivered. 'I don't know what to say.'

'Don't you?' Honoria's tone was stronger. 'You planned this. My sister was not in good health, and you persuaded her to make a new will favouring you.'

April stood up, her hands gripping the edge of Mr Moss's desk. 'This man is a witness to your slander,' she replied carefully. 'I had no idea about the bequest.'

'Well, a legacy of this size should keep your flea-ridden dogs in Pedigree Chum for a while.'

Honoria turned to Yvonne. 'As for you, madam, I dare say your carryings-on will be made easier now.'

Karam and Yvonne got up without a word and left the room together.

April sighed. 'How do you manage it, Honoria? I have noticed lately that you are becoming even ruder and less tolerant.' She decided to ignore Mr Moss. Like a priest or a doctor, he had probably signed something or other that would gag him. 'Honoria, I know what happened. I know everything about your past, about the goings-on at Moortop, about your father and—'

'Do you?' Plucked and pencilled eyebrows were raised. 'She was raving towards the end.'

'No, she wasn't. If necessary, her general practitioner and her specialists will vouch for Hyacinth's wholeness of mind.'

Mr Moss coughed. 'Ladies, I wonder—'

'That's my money,' spat Honoria. 'Mine. I put up with her stupidity for years.'

'God grant that we all might be as stupid as your sister was,' replied April. 'The woman was a star.'

'Really?'

'Really.' April struggled to her feet. 'By the way, as you probably know already, the meeting held by STADS on the day after Hyacinth's death reached no agreement with regard to casting. After all, the members were in mourning. Anyway, Philip Pointer and I have reached an agreement. I am to play the oldest Alice in *Monday's Child*.' Puerile, chided the inner voice of conscience.

Honoria's face was turning an interesting shade of purple. Mr Moss, fearing that she was about to have a fit, pushed a glass of water into her hand.

With unerring accuracy, she threw the contents into April's face. 'That should cool you down a bit.' The Bolton accent showed, just as it often did when Honoria lost her temper.

April grinned. 'Thanks,' she said. 'I really needed that. Yes, it is very warm in here.' She walked out and joined the other two women on the pavement.

'What happened?' asked Karam.

'Honoria happened. I'm afraid everything got too much for her, especially when I told her I'd be acting in my own play.'

'Whoops,' said Yvonne.

'Indeed.' April wiped her face on a sleeve. 'She's not very happy, poor love. And now, what the hell am I going to do with all that money?'

Karam chuckled. 'Let's away to my house and discuss it. I've a nice salad already prepared, and I bought some fabulous peppered steaks from Frank Smith's. A few Jerseys in their jackets and a bottle or three of Nuits St George – heaven.'

'Indeed,' agreed April. 'What about . . . ?' She jerked a thumb towards the solicitors' offices.

'Let her walk,' said Yvonne. 'Or take a cab.'

The two vehicles set off in convoy, Yvonne's Range Rover leading the way. 'Five grand each,' she said softly. 'She must have loved us both, Karam.'

'And follow your dreams.'

Yvonne turned left towards Blundellsands. 'I think April knows stuff about Honoria.'

'She knows stuff about everyone – that's how she manages to write so realistically. She won't say anything, won't tolerate questioning. Whatever information she has, she'll hang on to it until it's needed.'

Yvonne agreed. 'She's a good egg.'

'Which is more than can be said for Honoria.'

They turned into Karam's driveway, sat for a while. 'I wouldn't put anything past Honoria,' said Karam, after a short silence.

Goosebumps appeared on Yvonne's arm.

'Are you shivering, love?' asked Karam.

'Someone walked over my grave.' Visited by a sudden prescience of doom and gloom, Yvonne clung to her friend. 'What did the old girl mean about my carryings-on? I haven't been carrying on with anyone.'

Karam gulped. 'Take no notice,' she advised. 'If nothing happens at the other end of her binoculars, she probably makes it up.' Tell her, ordered a guilt-ridden inner voice. No, answered Karam silently. Where would she be without me? I cannot frighten her away when she needs me so desperately. 'Don't worry. Please don't worry.'

Yvonne straightened and turned to look at Bertie in the back seat. 'David still hasn't said anything. It's over a week now. He comes home in the evenings, shuts himself in the office, not a syllable out of him. At mealtimes he just eats. Rather noisily.'

'It's up to you, then.'

'Oh, no.' Yvonne shook her head. 'I've done my bit, told him I'm leaving him. He said we should talk about it and I said I'd nothing further to say. I'm in the spare bedroom and he keeps to himself. I mean, he can't have misheard me at the funeral. If nothing's changed, what am I doing sleeping on my own?'

Karam sighed deeply. 'Well, as soon as *Monday's Child*'s over, we go off to Horsefield and stay there until October. Apart from a couple of museum meetings in London, I shall be free all summer. If Papa has allowed Horsefield Manor to remain standing, we shall stay there.'

Yvonne settled down, her skin temperature returning to normal. Karam would always be here for her, she reassured herself. But life at home was becoming difficult. Nausea was the biggest problem, especially in the mornings.

April arrived wearing dry clothes and wielding a bottle of burgundy. She waved the wine, swung sideways into the hedge and started to giggle. When Yvonne arrived at her side, she was weeping. 'She left it all for the animals, you know. Hyacinth understood that all my money goes to the sanctuary. But I still feel so guilty and, oh God, how I miss her.'

Between them, Karam and Yvonne heaved April into the house. They stuffed her into an armchair in the living room, then Karam went off to make tea.

'I don't want a cup of tea,' wept April. 'I want Hyacinth.' She rubbed at her nose with a closed fist. 'Hell, I sound just like a child, don't I? Like Monday's child.'

'No, Monday's child is fair of face. You're all red and blotchy,' replied Yvonne.

April managed a smile. 'With friends like you, who needs Paul McKenna's DIY confidence through hypnosis? Oh, I didn't expect this legacy, Yvonne.'

'We didn't expect five thousand each, either. But she wanted us to have it, obviously.'

April closed her eyes. She heard the story all over again, saw her dear friend's face, the features strangely serene as she recounted a tale of pure horror. It had taken three sessions, five or six hours during which Hyacinth had, for the first time in her life, delivered all the facts in an even, almost disinterested tone. 'Don't hate Honoria,' she had begged. 'I won't,' April had replied. 'It's not in my nature.'

Her eyelids opened. 'I think it is in my nature after all.'

Yvonne waited for a second or two. 'What's in your nature?'

'No matter.'

The aroma of peppered beef drifted through from the kitchen, the rich scent accompanied by Karam's famous rendition of 'Clementine'. 'You have my deepest sympathy if you are thinking of living here,' April told her companion. 'That has to be the worst sound I ever heard.'

Yvonne considered this statement. 'No,' she said eventually. 'Remember that cat? The one who got his head stuck in your fence?'

'Ah, yes,' replied April. 'That was worse, but only just.' This light-hearted banter seemed to calm her, and she wiped the remnants of tears from her face before tottering off to the bathroom. Karam was getting in too deep, she told her reflection, as she washed her hands. Karam was in love, while Yvonne had no idea that her new-found friend wanted to be so much more than that.

They settled down to their meal, deciding to make it a celebration, a festival dedicated to Hyacinth's memory. They toasted her five times, April and Karam getting drunker by the minute, while Yvonne, deliberately sober, stuck to fruit juice after just one glass of wine. They laughed, joked, calling to mind some of their friend's more unusual behaviour. 'That was the first time I'd ever seen someone painting in the snow,' concluded Karam.

'Yes, I remember that,' said Yvonne. 'Christmas Day, and there she was, right in the middle of the road, muffled up in scarves and a silly hat.'

April grinned. 'Hyacinth said she wasn't very good at architecture so the snow hid a multitude of mistakes.' She paused. 'God bless and keep her, she was frozen to her paintbrush. I swear she had icicles dangling from her eyebrows.'

'Honoria said she lived on top of a radiator right through to New Year.' Yvonne bit her lip. 'What the hell are we going to do about Honoria?'

April continued to overdose on wine. There was nothing to be done about Honoria, because Honoria had already done it all, had broken rules of God and man alike, had caused havoc throughout most of her life. Although April tried hard not to believe in the existence of people who were basically bad, her mind was changing. For a start, there were the animals she received into her care, dogs rescued from motorways, litters of kittens thrown into dustbins, rabbits used as footballs, horses with stab wounds. And then there was Honoria. 'Perhaps she's intrinsically bad,' she offered finally.

Karam eyed April. 'What did she do?'

'Who?'

'Honoria, of course.'

April drained her glass, then produced a badly rolled joint. She had been cultivating her own cannabis for some time, insisting that it made her symptoms less severe. On David Benson's computer, she was listed as in need of a new body and in favour of legalization of weed, though she never offered it to anyone for recreational purposes. It was her medicine, and no one else was allowed to use it. 'Don't ask.'

Karam eyed her neighbour. 'I'm curious. We both are.'

April clicked her lighter and set fire to the half-dozen badly glued together Rizlas. 'Continue curious,' she advised. 'Idly curious is best. After all, you know what killed the cat.'

Yvonne persisted, 'It must have been very bad.'

'It was,' replied April infuriatingly.

'Then tell us.' Karam's tone had risen by almost an octave.

'No.'

'April, we—'

91

'No.' She shook her head. 'One day, perhaps. But not yet.'

Karam and Yvonne began to clear the table. Yvonne carried out a pile of plates and placed them next to the sink. 'Karam?' she whispered.

'What?'

'I've had my last glass of wine tonight. Junior must not be born an alcoholic.'

April, who never missed a trick, called out to the pair, 'That's quite right. A pregnant woman should never drink or smoke.'

'How does she do it?' asked Yvonne.

Karam sloshed some water into the ancient porcelain sink. 'She's a witch. A white witch.'

April, full of wine, weed and bonhomie, joined the pair at the sink. 'Yvonne, you're one of those unfortunate women who show early. Not with a bulge, because you're as flat as a pancake and I hate you for that. But your hair and skin have changed.'

Karam concentrated on washing up. It was true – Yvonne was blooming. There was a sheen on her hair, a glow to her skin, a light in the beautiful eyes.

'David will notice,' continued April.

Yvonne laughed. 'Will he, now? Look, I've been stuck in that house for so long that I know the cast of *Home and Away* intimately, plus the plot of *Neighbours* right up to last Wednesday. He comes, he goes, he sees nothing. With a job as consuming as his, he's in and out at all hours. But we haven't spoken properly since the funeral.'

92

'Really?' April inhaled a mouthful of exotic-smelling cannabis.

'As Hyacinth drifted away, so did I. In fact, I severed the marriage contract right there and then, before the curtains closed. Strange. It was as if Hyacinth pushed and encouraged me.'

'You told him at the funeral?'

'She did,' answered Karam. 'He decided that they needed to talk about it, then put the shutters up, not a word out of him.'

April did not like the sound of this. In her experience, a problem undiscussed tended to grow until it exploded. 'What are your long-term plans?' she asked.

'Yorkshire soon,' answered Karam. 'Beyond that, we're not sure. It's just a case of making things as easy as possible for Yvonne.'

April pondered. Was Yvonne planning never to tell David about the baby? She could not hide in Yorkshire for ever. And was Karam using Yvonne's pregnancy as a reason to court her away from Liverpool? Surely not. Karam was as direct and honest as she could possibly be. But she was also in love. 'Well,' declared April at last. There was little she could do to alter the situation, so she must simply go along with it for now. 'Karam will make an excellent auntie. Anyone for coffee?'

Six

David Benson sauntered along Beech Gardens towards Poplar Grove. Honoria had been on the telephone, had ranted and raved at great length because Hyacinth had willed money to April, Yvonne and Karam. 'You want to get yourself along to Poplar Grove,' she had yelled. 'Don't for one moment imagine that your wife is closeted indoors all day with Sky Movies and rented videos. She's always down Poplar Grove. She's found a man.'

'How do you know that?' he had asked. 'Binoculars at dawn, is it? Are you taking notes, photographs, statements?'

'Listen, Dr Benson.' The voice had been high and harsh, much rougher than normal and built around the flat vowels of inner Lancashire, which Honoria had always fought to disguise. 'There are only four houses in that avenue, and two are occupied by April Nugent and Karam whatever-her-name-is. They both know what's going on. You're being made a fool of, a cuckold. April must have noticed, as must that Karam woman.'

'Laczynska.'

'Yes, the foreigner.'

'She's as British as you and the rest of—'

'Don't bandy words.' David remembered holding the receiver away from his ear. 'Your wife has a lover, I'm absolutely sure of it.'

He slowed down and frowned at a crack in the pavement. Someone might fall here, he thought absently. He would contact his councillor tomorrow, try to get the section made good before some old person broke a femur. Honoria West was watching. He could feel her eyes boring into the back of his neck like a Black & Decker drilling through butter.

'I'm leaving you.' As Hyacinth's coffin had begun to move, Yvonne had made that statement. David wondered whether he had imagined it, but he hadn't, of course. She had moved herself into the spare room on the day of the funeral. What the hell was he meant to do now? If he talked to her, he might receive some unacceptable explanations. Yet keeping quiet made him an ostrich. 'It's my own fault,' he mumbled. 'Too busy to notice my own wife, too happy screwing around with bloody Deirdre. Stupid.'

On a whim, he swung round and waved at Honoria. At the same time, he saw Deirdre standing at her front door. The wave died, causing him to look rather foolish, he supposed. Determinedly, he revived the movement, smiling grimly to himself as Honoria walked away from her notorious vantage-point.

'Good evening,' Deirdre called.

'Good evening.' This was another problem, one that needed sorting out forthwith. From the start, his cards had been laid on the table, the very desk across which Deirdre had displayed her undeniable and, at that point, irresistible charms. 'I love my wife,' he had told her.

'And I love my husband,' had been the reply. 'He'll come back to me sooner or later.'

He had explained away his behaviour, had even spoken to himself in the mirror. 'Yvonne will come out of it,' he had advised the handsome-ish, blue-eyed, dark-haired reflection. Yvonne was almost certainly suffering from clinical depression. Depression inevitably resulted in a diminished libido, and she would get over it in time. She had refused chemical assistance, had been unwilling to see a psychiatrist or counsellor. After agreeing to give up her job, she had become passive, had sat for hours in front of *Brookside*, *EastEnders*, *Emmerdale*. David closed his eyes. She always sat so neatly, knees drawn up in a self-protective way that went halfway to imitating the foetal position.

He turned right into Poplar Grove and sat on a tree stump. He had excused his own behaviour. He was a man, and men needed sex. Deirdre Mellor was a gorgeous woman with a voluptuous figure and few inhibitions. She was hungry for physical contact, as was David, so they had been consoling each other for several months now. Because of Honoria's all-seeing gaze, such needs had been indulged in David's hatchback, at the clinic, in motels and, once, in a barn just outside Formby. Nevertheless, whatever the excuses, David Benson was not cut out for dishonesty. It had to stop, all of it, had to—

'David?'

Startled, he looked up. 'Deirdre! What the hell are you doing here? You know about Honoria's little hobby. The bloody woman's like a hyperactive hawk. She'll have seen you, added two and two and she'll—'

'She'll have come up with four. Or three, perhaps.' She pondered for a moment, long white fingers twisting a ringlet just behind her right ear. 'It could be four, I suppose. Twins do run in my family.' She smiled seductively. 'You, me and baby. Or babies.'

He swallowed. She was on the pill. After the first few encounters, he had stopped using other methods, had allowed himself to be convinced that this red-hot lady was not after commitment. 'Deirdre.' His throat was suddenly like sandpaper. Obtusely, he comforted himself with the knowledge that Deirdre was not a patient. Messing about with colleagues was frowned upon, of course, but the sin was not as bad as it might have been. Why, why was he always so damned practical? Had medical science taken away his imagination? Oh, no, not at all. He imagined at this very moment that Deirdre might just become difficult . . .

'Well?' asked Deirdre. 'Where do we go from here?'

She suddenly looked over-emphasized, loud, almost common. 'You are going home,' he said, 'while I shall continue my walk as planned.'

'To the house of sin?'

He stared blankly at her.

Deirdre grinned, displaying flawless teeth made imperfect by a smear of lipstick on an upper incisor. 'Your Yvonne is a raving bloody lesbian.'

David managed not to react.

'She spends a lot of time with Karam Laczynska.'

'I know that.' He had been neither worried nor impressed by Honoria's advice. Yvonne's friends lived in Poplar Grove; there was no reason to suspect her of an affair with either of the men who occupied the other two houses. Yvonne helped April with her animals, posed for Karam, enjoyed the company of two intelligent women.

'I can smell it a mile off,' declared Deirdre, her tongue flicking like a snake's as she used it to smooth lipstick over luscious but overblown lips. 'And I've heard rumours about Karam.'

'Really?'

She nodded, causing curls he had recently considered beautiful to bounce around like a young Bonnie Langford's ringlets. 'I've seen them. They were in the cloakroom at St Tom's during a rehearsal. Arms round one another, your wife's head on Karam's shoulder – very lovey-dovey. They're what you might call an item, I'm sure of it.'

He swallowed again.

'At first, I thought you knew, with her going off normal sex. I really believed that you'd made up the depression to cover the truth. Anyway, the decision's been made for you, Daddy. Let's stop messing around, get rid of Paul and Yvonne, then we can start our life all over again.'

She was acting like a child. David raked his fingers through his hair, wondered what the hell to say. He didn't want Deirdre. She kept the patients happy, was reasonably proficient on a computer, had a brain that was competent, no more. But she was . . . shallow. In spite of that, though, she wielded the sort of power born of confidence in her physical charms. Dangerous females were not created through education: they built their power on men's weaknesses and on their own irresistible sexuality.

'Well?' she asked, one foot tapping the ground, arms folded beneath a bosom that began to bear a strong resemblance to an old-fashioned bolster.

He glanced down, saw strappy sandals and an ankle chain, legs that had wrapped themselves around him like twin boa constrictors. Oh yes, she knew how to play to a man's baser instincts. 'We must talk soon,' he replied carefully. He hadn't even spoken to his wife – how was he going to manage this situation? Like an ostrich again?

'The sooner, the better,' she said, before flouncing off homeward, her exit marred by the stumble caused by a stiletto sticking in a crack.

He watched her as she recovered and sashayed along like an upmarket whore, plenty of swing, lots of bounce. This one wouldn't sit quietly while he thought things through, while he hid in his office playing Freecell or Solitaire on the laptop. Yvonne and Deirdre might both be women, but beyond that they were chalk and cheese.

Yvonne a lesbian? No, she wasn't the type. Deirdre had probably misinterpreted a hug prompted by Yvonne's chronic anxiety and depression. As a doctor, he knew full well that women often turned to female friends in times of trouble. Over fifty per cent of nervous disorders in women were cured at coffee mornings and Tupperware evenings, not on a psychiatrist's couch. Husbands had to accept that their wives were often closer to and more open with members of their own sex than with themselves.

He remained where he was, his mind a tangle of rapid, nervous thoughts. First, Deirdre's pregnancy must be confirmed or otherwise. She was just about daft enough to have miscalculated or to have assumed that one missed period meant a baby. Second, he needed to sort out the mess with Yvonne. She had given no signs of leaving, had made no change in her routine apart from the separate bedrooms. She still stared at the TV, still cooked, washed and ironed, continued to shop, to get her hair done once a week by that mobile hairdresser.

The light was fading when he got up and began to walk again, his breath almost held as he approached the bottom of the grove. Apart from a light in the porch, April's house was in darkness. He let himself in through the gate of

Karam's Jasmine Cottage, flinched when a hinge begged for oil. Before he was halfway down the side of the property, he heard laughter from the large kitchen. Through an open window, his wife's voice floated out to meet him. She was screaming with glee, making the sort of noise he had not heard from her in ages. For a split second, he was chasing her into the Med, watching her as she sank beneath waves just off the Moroccan coast. How she had adored North Africa.

He paused, listened. It was plain that they were playing Scrabble. Scrabble. Yvonne was murderous at that, coming up with words that begged to be challenged, always poker-faced, often cheating. When had he last played a board game with his wife? When had they last enjoyed a proper conversation, one that went beyond the mundane?

'That is definitely not a real word,' shouted April, obviously the worse for drink.

'It is,' replied Yvonne. 'Tell her, Karam.'

'Leave me out of it,' said Karam. 'I can't say I'm familiar with it, but who am I to argue?'

But are you familiar with my wife? asked David Benson silently.

'Listen,' said April. 'I've heard of an endomorph and an ectomorph – I think – but never a morph.'

'A morph is normal,' insisted Yvonne. 'Ectos are thin, endos are fat and morphs are somewhere in the middle.'

There followed a longish diatribe from April, loud enough for David to pick out words like

101

'cheat' and 'liar'. Yes, Yvonne was up to her usual tricks. He pictured her waving a dictionary and bidding her companions to seek the word. If the word was listed, Yvonne would get double points. She was a clever girl. He had married a clever wife.

Someone banged on the table with an item of cutlery – to bring the gathering to order, he supposed. David knew it was his wife. He realized how much he had missed her. Fish, chips and beer in the back of Dad's car, lovemaking in a shallow stream, running naked into the sea at Blackpool for a dare one midsummer night. Honeymooning in Paris, Yvonne closing her eyes at the top of the Eiffel Tower, scared of heights, more scared of missing something, peering through her fingers. 'Look, there's Sacré-Coeur. God, isn't this place beautifully geometric?'

He sniffed back a tear. Who or what had stolen her away?

'It's a word,' she was insisting now, her tone youthful, strident. 'I'm a nurse and a morph is a morph.'

'I'm a wordsmith and you're bluffing,' retorted April.

Karam, often quieter than the others, said nothing. She was, David supposed, a true intellectual, an artist, a sensitive soul. A lesbian? A threat?

Gaining confidence, he ducked under the window and crept to the shed. From here, he could see right through the second kitchen window, which overlooked the rear garden of the house. Bertie barked and David flattened himself against a fence.

'All right,' said Yvonne clearly. 'You win. Can I have "moron" instead?'

'Be our guest,' was April's answer. 'If the cap fits, feel free to wear it.'

He watched his wife slamming her tiles on the board. She sank back into her chair and shook her head in pretended misery. Oh yes, he remembered her. 'It's my fault,' he mouthed. 'I did this. I sent her to have fun elsewhere when I caught the disease called ambition.' He had given so much to his work, so little to her. God, how he needed her.

'What's that?' Karam was asking now. 'Snerch?' She pointed an elegant finger in the direction of the board.

April was ready. 'That kid at the back of the class with two green candles hanging out of his nostrils – well –'

'Yuk,' gagged Yvonne. 'That's dreadful.'

'And no hanky,' continued April undeterred 'So what does he do to improve his situation in life?'

'Uses his sleeve?' suggested Yvonne.

'He snerches.' April imitated the ghastly sound.

It happened then. While her husband hid like a thief in the shadows, Yvonne and Karam laughed hard and fell together. David, looking for symptoms, judged their body language to be almost as clear as their voices had been. They chuckled, wiped away tears of mirth, each looking into the other's eyes.

His chest burned. He wondered briefly about a heart-attack, dismissed the idea quickly. This was heartache, not angina. He loved her, had always loved her. She was inside a house with another woman, Karam Laczynska, a person who was respected within her profession, loved by all who knew her. April Nugent, whom David had regarded as a friend, was plainly *au fait* with the score, which had nothing to do with Scrabble. Deirdre was right. Deirdre being right was horrible, as was the thought of Yvonne giving herself to Karam.

He stared hard at his wife and her significant other, was struck by their beauty. Yvonne, her light brown hair hanging down her back, looked right with Karam. Karam, with those mysterious, almond-shaped dark-grey eyes, the near-black hair, the willowy body, was a perfect match for Yvonne. But how could they be right together? It occurred to him suddenly that Yvonne had been looking for love, love of any kind and from any quarter.

'I win,' shouted David Benson's wife.

He watched her clearing away the game while Karam laughed softly, while April pretended to sulk, while the little dog barked. Yvonne looked so . . . so complete. He felt like an outcast, a Peeping Tom. The world created by Karam, Yvonne and April left no space for David, a mere man.

Exhausted yet elated, Yvonne sat down again. Her smile of triumph died as she spoke. 'Well, I suppose I'd better go home. It's been fun, but most good things must come to an end.'

'You'll be all right,' said April.

'I know,' replied Yvonne. 'I've always been all right. He's a lovely man and a damned good doctor, but I should never have married him.'

April stretched and yawned. 'Rehearsal tomorrow, dear heart,' she advised Yvonne. 'Philip Pointer pointing, telling you when to breathe and when to blink. Now, there's a daft old beggar if ever I saw one. As a director, he makes a fair policeman on traffic duty. What's the matter with him?'

Yvonne shrugged. 'Born out of his time. He'd have done very well in eighteenth-century France, daft wigs and classical theatre.'

April laughed again. 'I've had a thought.'

Karam and Yvonne glanced at each other. April's thoughts were usually quite amusing, especially when she was drunk or stoned. At present, she was both.

'Call me Fletcher Christian. We shall organize a mutiny,' she declared. 'Weekend rehearsals in my garden. There are only a few weekends left, but if we work hard enough we might get a bit of movement into *Monday's Child*.'

'He'll freak out,' said Karam. 'I've already frightened him halfway to death by threatening not to complete the set. I shall do it, of course, as I'm not visiting dear old Papa until after the play. Don't upset him any more – the poor man's had enough.'

'And why can't he be like everyone else?' asked Yvonne. 'Most societies put on productions in spring and autumn. Why do we have this summer lark?'

'It's tradition,' replied the other two in harmony.

'Tradition doesn't work,' declared Yvonne. 'If he wants tradition, he should get air-conditioning in the church hall. In this weather, it'll be like putting on a show in hell's hottest corner.'

Karam got up to make coffee. April leant across the table and took Yvonne's hand. 'Something has to be done,' she said softly. 'You'll start to show soon. When on earth are you going to talk to David?'

'I've done my talking. When the play's over, I leave.'

'And he doesn't know about the baby?'

Yvonne shook her head.

David, still outside near the shed, heard nothing of the *sotto voce* conversation between Yvonne and April, though he guessed that its content touched on plans for Yvonne's future. Panic gripped him, his stomach churned and his abdomen stiffened towards cramp. He was terrified. The women had been discussing April's play while he, a participant in his own drama, was centred in a plot too complicated for any stage production.

He lowered himself on to the grass behind Karam's shed, realizing how ridiculous he would look if the women found him. Perhaps they would let the dog out. Bertie was bound to recognize his master and would surely guide the others to him. Master? he wondered. Who was in charge of this particular farce?

Deirdre, who should not be pregnant,

probably was. Yvonne, who should be pregnant, wasn't. David was a husband in name only, while Karam, a woman, was currently playing his role. Hyacinth should have lived and was dead. Honoria lived on . . . His stomach felt so sore.

'Goodness,' called his wife from off-stage. 'What have you put in this coffee, darling?'

Darling.

'It's as thick as treacle,' agreed April. 'The last time I clapped eyes on anything like this, two Irish fellows were making the road good after laying cables.'

A lot of clattering followed these statements: someone was making a replacement pot of coffee. He vomited as noiselessly as possible into Karam's rhubarb. When had Yvonne last called him darling? Years, months ago?

When his stomach had emptied itself, Dr David Benson sat back, his head leaning against Karam Laczynska's garden shed. He didn't know why the hell he had come here. Life had been difficult of late; now it seemed impossible. Good God, what could he do? And how on earth would the practice react to this situation? Oh, he could well imagine Deirdre announcing her pregnancy, acting coy at first perhaps, then allowing his name to fall from her lips – accidentally, of course.

He struggled to his feet. Here he went again, worrying about his professional life, wondering how his career would be affected. Surely the mending of his marriage should come first? But how did one repair a marriage that had gone out of synch, where one partner had decided to

107

dance to a different rhythm and the other was a faithless dolt? 'I could kill her, I suppose,' he muttered, referring to the lovely Deirdre. 'I could kill them both, then top myself.' But that was idle speculation: it took him all his time to stamp on a woodlouse.

He dipped his hands into the rainwater barrel, rinsed his face, took a deep breath. It was time to let everything out. Perhaps it would be easier this way, in someone else's house. After all, he had tried for over a fortnight to talk to Yvonne.

With his heart in his throat, David walked the short distance to Karam Laczynska's kitchen door. They were still laughing and joking about the lethal coffee.

Ah, well, the fun was over. It was time to face everybody's music, including his own.

Seven

It was as if a radio had died as a result of power
failure. When David Benson entered Karam's
kitchen, the atmosphere changed.

April Nugent, definitely the worse for wear,
was sloshing wine none too steadily into a glass.
When she noticed the intruder she froze, her
lower jaw hanging open. 'Good grief,' she
exclaimed. 'Did someone call a doctor? Are we
ill? It's the medicine man, girls.' She batted her
eyelashes at him. 'Do sit down and join me in a
slug of whatever I'm drinking.' She peered at
him. 'My tastebuds gave out about an hour ago.
Never mind. Even if it's anti-freeze, it does its
job OK. And you can always swill our stomachs
out with a bit of old hosepipe and a funnel.'

No matter what the circumstances, David
could never be cross with April Nugent. A
strange mixture of sophisticate and *ingénue*,
April was thoroughly likeable, even when her
behaviour verged on the determinedly eccentric.
He sat at the table and stared hard at his wife.
'We need to talk,' he said. 'About ...' He

looked pointedly at Karam. 'We need to discuss several topics.'

Yvonne made no reply. If he finally wanted to talk, he'd chosen a stupid time and place for it.

'Things must be straightened out,' he insisted.

April took a gulp of red wine, then smiled benignly upon her audience. 'I agree,' she said. 'Especially the Northern Perimeter Road. It makes me dizzy, turning this way and that. I keep forgetting to go left for Maghull, then I finish up in—'

'Shut up, dear.' Karam glared with mock ferocity at her.

It was like a secret society, thought David. When women got together to share intimate secrets, they became a power that defied control. They didn't need to be Freemasons, were beyond requiring pinnies and little trowels; theirs was a clan already waiting for them, a self-perpetuating, impenetrable sisterhood. Deirdre was not a member of such a clique. She had not the easy, sensible manners that attracted the empathy of other women. Hers was the wrong kind of sexuality, feline, predatory and overstated.

'Coffee?' Karam asked. She hated confrontation, dreaded the idea of quarrels. Still, at least she and April were here to watch over Yvonne while . . . while what? And whatever was about to happen, April would be less use than a sheet of saturated blotting paper. Anyway, the poor man looked confused to the point of illness. 'Would you like some coffee?' she asked again. 'We've just made a fresh pot.'

David refused it: he was here to reclaim his wife, not seek refreshment.

April was having difficulty in focusing, keeping still and thinking straight. But she realized that she shouldn't be here. 'I'm off,' she said, falling from her chair and banging several portions of her anatomy on the flagged floor. 'Damn this confounded disease,' she cursed.

David jumped up.

'Leave her,' ordered Yvonne, patience snapping unexpectedly. 'Stop being in charge, stop knowing everything. April spends half her life on the floor. Let her do for herself while she can.'

He forced himself to sit down again.

April reappeared a bit at a time, the top of her head bobbing up and down over the table's edge while her neck negotiated an agreement with the rest of her. 'I am quite capable,' she began before vanishing again.

'She needs help,' stated David.

'We all need help,' answered his wife quietly.

'Capable of looking after myself.' April finally got to her feet. 'There's no cure, you know.'

He nodded.

'Life's an unholy mess,' she continued. 'And I shall leave you now. Good night, sweet prince.'

Bertie barked and jumped on to April's chair. He pushed his nose into the glass and licked up a few drops of wine. Yvonne and Karam glanced at one another. When April waxed Shakespearian, she needed undressing and pouring into bed. 'We'll take you home,' Karam told her.

'I'm all right—'

'And I'll see you later,' Yvonne advised her husband.

'Is he going?' asked April.

'Yes.' Karam awarded April a second supposedly withering look.

'Oh, right,' declared the inebriated playwright, talk-show guest, public speaker, radio broadcaster. 'Then I'll stay. If he goes, I shall remain *in situ*, so to speak.'

Karam dragged April to the door, then waited until Yvonne joined her. Together, they heaved her across the street, into her house, past half a dozen cats, two dogs, a large rabbit and a parrot with thin plumage.

After stuffing April, fully dressed, into her bed, the two women went downstairs to feed the resident animals. The outside lot had been tended by the 'girls', a clutch of females who dedicated all their spare hours to minding April's unfortunate guests.

When dogs, cats, rabbit and parrot were settled for the night, Karam and Yvonne sat down and stared at each other for several minutes. Both felt exhausted and suddenly ill at ease with each other. 'I can't let you go home,' said Karam at last. 'You can't do this alone. David seems so disturbed and upset. What if—?'

'It's my marriage.'

'I'm fully aware of that. I didn't mean to . . .'

'Sorry.' What was going on? wondered Yvonne. Why was everything so strained all of a sudden? They'd enjoyed a lovely evening with April, a delicious meal, wine, Scrabble, coffee that had turned out OK eventually. Then David had arrived out of the blue, not quite as nice as pie, wanting to talk. A light dawned. 'It's Honoria,' she said flatly, her mind suddenly clicking into gear. 'She's up to her old tricks again.'

'Honoria?'

'Of course. She's been plastered against that corner window for as long as I can remember. The turning into Poplar Grove will be visible, especially through binoculars. She's been watching me. And now, with Hyacinth leaving money to us, the old bitch wants revenge. She probably thinks I'm having an affair. I bet she's sent David to rescue me. Remember what she did to that poor woman three doors down from us? They moved house in the end.' She nodded vigorously. 'Honoria has sent him to follow me.'

'But—'

'There are four houses, Karam. Yours, April's, the widower at number two, who must be a hundred years old, at least. And the other cottage has a middle-aged couple living in it. But were I to walk through April's sanctuary, there's a whole new estate of people living at the other side of the wall.' Yvonne pondered. 'He was angry, upset, not at all his usual self. I wouldn't be at all surprised if Honoria's started meddling. I wonder if he's received one of her famous anonymous letters.'

Karam shrugged. 'Your imagination's running away with you. Honoria hasn't been out. She can't know who lives behind April, can't possibly—'

'Of course she can know. People visit her, she asks questions, knows there are new houses around.'

Karam swallowed. She felt as if her heart was splitting in two because she loved Yvonne, would have done anything to . . . To persuade Yvonne Benson that she should love a woman rather than a man? 'Stop worrying,' she said eventually. 'You come into the grove to help with the animal sanctuary. Don't get paranoid.'

'When I help April, I'm dressed in old jeans and jumpers. Honoria would take that into account because she's so damned clever. When I come to visit you, I'm slightly tidier.' She pondered for a moment. 'Do you think it might be Deirdre? She's streetwise, that one. And she wants him, I suppose. Perhaps she noticed my comings and goings and told him. The daft girl could make up her own stories, I suppose, just to get David away from me.'

Karam ran long fingers through her tousled hair. 'Does it matter?'

'I suppose not.'

Karam stood up. She felt useless and stupid. Mooning after a married woman, carrying on like a lovelorn loon – she ought to have known better. But what if David turned nasty?

'Don't fret,' said Yvonne. 'You're a good friend and I've valued your support these past months.'

A friend. No more than that. There could never be more, yet Karam hoped, wished, dreamt . . . 'I can't help worrying. It's in my nature.'

Yvonne said goodbye, told Karam to hang on to Bertie, then walked out of April's house. She left the Range Rover parked in Karam's drive and set off towards the place that was supposed to be her home.

She passed Deirdre's house, thought she saw a curtain twitch. A street-light bounced off the lenses of Honoria's binoculars, confirming Yvonne's long-held suspicion that the woman seldom slept. Did she watch the behaviour of stray cats and hungry foxes once all human life had bedded itself down for the night?

Yvonne's footsteps slowed as she approached her destination. She didn't want to talk to him, hated the thought of causing him pain. David was David, Yvonne was Yvonne, and the two belonged apart. Why couldn't that be the end of it? Surely he must have recognized her unhappiness, just as she had been aware of his terrible solitude? There was no need for excruciating scenes, investigation, recrimination. Did he want his pound of flesh? No, no. Not David.

She let herself in, hung her creased linen jacket in the hall. David was in the living room. Although there was no sound, television pictures were reflected in the overmantel mirror. 'Now is the hour,' she muttered under her breath.

He got up, grabbed the remote and switched off the TV. 'Well?' he began. 'What the hell's going on?'

She threw herself into a chair. 'I am so sorry, David. I'm sorry that our marriage is over, but

115

must we go through a post-mortem?' she asked. 'We don't love each other any more. It happens. You're a good man and a wonderful doctor, but I—'

'But you love someone else.'

Yvonne made no reply. He was going to be infantile, seemed bent on retrieving a ball that had gone missing for ever. 'David, I know about Deirdre,' she said wearily. 'You needed her because I wasn't here for you. I cooked, sewed, washed and ironed. I cleaned your house and did the shopping.'

'*Our* house,' he shouted. 'And Deirdre means nothing to me.'

'But although I performed all those tasks, they were just a means of keeping myself occupied. You persuaded me to give up my job. To be frank, I didn't care one way or the other.' She paused, wound herself up for what had to be said. 'Then I met Karam. Of course, I already knew her, because she'd popped into STADS meetings and she did the sets. But I didn't know her well. In fact, I doubt we'd exchanged more than a dozen words until we started to talk in Sainsbury's. She listened to me and gave me strength.' It had to be said now. 'I want a divorce. There is no one else, though.'

I'll bet Karam gave you strength, thought David, before lighting a cigarette and waving it under her nose. 'Yes, I've taken up smoking again and, no, I'm not worried about it. I ought to be, but I can't manage to care one jot.'

She flinched, pulled herself back. He was in the oddest mood, hardly recognizable. There really was no necessity for any of this. She should have walked away and to hell with *Monday's Child*. 'David, stop acting like a fourteen-year-old caught smoking his first roll-up. What I told you at Hyacinth's funeral was all I needed to say. It's over. There's no more to be discussed.' She inhaled deeply. 'I can be childish, too, you know. I could go on and on about Deirdre.'

'I hate bloody Deirdre,' he spat angrily.

'Why?' she asked, genuinely interested. Yvonne had always disliked the woman, though jealousy had played only a tiny part in her antipathy.

'Because she acted dishonestly. She wanted sex, no more, no strings attached. Now she demands more.'

'Perhaps she loves you.'

He laughed harshly. 'Love? She's no more than a well-wrapped set of female parts.' He paused, hated himself. 'I know it's my fault, Yvonne. You needed me to spend time with you, but I was too busy, too wrapped up in my work. I'm so sorry. And, yes, I used her mercilessly, thought that she was using me just for the physical stuff.' He dragged on his Silk Cut. 'Look, you'll hear it soon enough, so you may as well get it from me. She says she might be pregnant.'

Yvonne's hands crept over her abdomen. 'That's something you've always wanted, isn't it?'

'With you, damn it! Not with her – never with her.'

117

She closed her eyes, wished with all her heart that she could crawl into bed and fall asleep for at least twelve hours. 'David, just listen to us. We're tired and we're concentrating on stuff that won't rot before morning, though it won't improve, either. Let's make things easier and agree to differ.'

He threw the cigarette into the fireplace. 'I won't let you go.'

She opened her eyes. 'How will you stop me?'

'I don't know.'

'Neither do I, unless you plan on nailing my feet to the parquet. So why can't you accept that there's nothing to be said or done? This isn't a clinical thing with a prognosis to be decided. It's not calculable. We're finished and this is point-less, because it's hurting us.'

He ran across the room, dragged her out of the chair and held her tightly. Unable to keep her completely still, he missed her mouth, kissed her neck, her hair, her cheeks instead. She was his. He had a piece of paper proving his ownership of this woman. No, that was not right. He could not make her love him, could not—

'Stop,' she said quietly.

'No.' He didn't know what else to do. He hated violence, oppression, unfairness, yet some primeval ogre overtook him. Sobbing, he tore at her clothes while she yelled and rained blows on his face and chest. And all along she knew that he would not injure her – not intentionally, at least. He had never lost his rag before, and Yvonne still had his measure and was not afraid of him.

He pinned her to the floor and, panting hard, fell like a dead weight on top of her. He loathed her, loved her, wanted her. She had suddenly become so still. Was she hurt? Terrified, he raised his head and looked at her. The beautiful blue eyes stared straight at him. 'Yvonne?'

'What?'

'I thought you were unconscious.'

'No, I'm still here.' Breathing was easier now that he had lifted himself slightly. 'I'm the fool on the floor, David. I'm the fool and you're the total idiot. What will this behaviour achieve?'

He found no answer.

'Let me go. Let me get my breath back and we'll say no more about this unfortunate episode.'

He rolled away from her, tears trickling from his eyes. He remembered Deirdre's little gasps, her moans, the mouse-like squeaks she employed to imitate fulfilment. Deirdre was a fake, all lipstick and mascara, all shell and no innards. 'You and I used to be good together,' he told his wife. 'We enjoyed one another. Lovemaking with you was like a celebration of life. What went wrong, Yvonne?'

She didn't know.

'Was your depression clinical?'

She shook her head against the pale cream Axminster, the carpet she washed almost weekly because of Bertie's pawmarks. 'No. Had it been clinical, I'd have taken pills.'

'Please tell me about it,' he begged.

She took a deep breath. 'The depression was

119

caused by us. I didn't know where to run. At first, I spent time with April at the sanctuary, then I became so tired. You know, some days even washing a cup was an exhausting chore. There was a long, black tunnel with no light at the end of it, like being under the Mersey for ever, stuck there knowing that an enormous weight of water was pressing down on me. The TV kept me from the edge of insanity, just about. But after a while I scarcely knew what I was watching. Movement lulled me, I suppose, helped me to pretend that I was still a part of something.'

He held back another stream of emotion.

'The truth is, I need to get away. I need my friends to help me cross a bridge I've almost finished building. If only you could know how much I care for you and about you. But it's a different kind of love, David.'

He gazed at the ceiling. 'I would like us to try to work this out, Yvonne. We can't simply throw in the towel after six years. Please give some thought to our marriage.'

'I've done that already.' What on earth did he imagine she'd been thinking about all these months? Right through *Morse* and *News at Ten*, during rehearsals, while visiting friends, she had been plagued by guilt, by the need to justify her feelings, her decisions.

He raised his upper body, crooked an arm and leant on it. 'This is a phase, something that will pass.'

'Really?'

What could he say? Karam's a lesbian so stay

away from her? As an often loud defender of minorities, David did not want to cast any stones. Was Deirdre to be believed, anyway? And even if Karam was a lesbian, did it follow that Yvonne was in a relationship with her? If Yvonne was having an affair, did it matter that her partner was a— Oh, his head was buzzing like a jam-jar full of wasps, no sense, just bewilderment.

'Well?' asked Yvonne.

'I'm thinking.'

When was he not thinking? David Benson was always so damned reasonable. Was this lack of fire at the root of the problem? David was kind, generous, handsome. His patients adored him, his partners respected him. He was even prepared to be honest and up-front about Deirdre, so why couldn't Yvonne come to terms with him? 'If I could forgive you, things might be different. But I've nothing to forgive you for. I don't like Deirdre, never have, but I don't mind what's gone on between you. There is no treaty to negotiate. I'm with the wrong person, and so are you. In time, you'll realize that.'

'Oh, will I?' He wanted to tell her that he could not live without her, that his very existence depended on her presence, but he knew she was past listening.

At this moment, Yvonne identified their problem. She and David were a pair of bookends, a perfect matching pair. Each had a temper, each kept the flames under control. They seldom argued, were not in the habit of close communication, were not as verbally and physically

121

expressive as they might have been. 'David,' she said, 'we're like siblings. That's the core of it, you know. We could be twins.'

He jumped up and slammed a fist on the table. 'No, no!' he shouted. 'That is not the case.'

The door flew inward and Bertie leapt into the arena, swiftly followed by Karam. She stood still and surveyed the scene. 'Sorry,' she mumbled, after a few seconds. 'I was walking the dog and he ran in – the door wasn't closed properly.'

David cleared his throat. The woman was extraordinarily lovely. He had learnt, during years of general practice, that stereotypes seldom existed in the real world. He smiled inwardly when he imagined most men's ideas of dykes – granddad shirts, cropped heads, more body piercing than the average colander. Karam was . . . unusual, probably not a man's woman. Was she Yvonne's woman, though?

Yvonne was dragging her tattered clothing together.

'I'll – I'll be off,' said Karam lamely. Her cheeks blazed, because she knew only too well that she had sent the dog in, had deliberately opened the door because . . . because she feared that David might hurt his wife. His wife.

Yvonne stood up and gave Karam a look that begged her to go.

'Is . . . is everything all right?' Karam asked.

'Perfectly,' answered Yvonne.

David turned on his heel and walked into the kitchen.

'Are you hurt?' whispered Karam.

'No.'

'But—'

'I am perfectly all right,' hissed Yvonne, through clenched teeth. 'He got upset, that's all.' She strode towards the intruder. 'You have no need to be concerned, Karam. I've lived here for years with this man. In all our time together, he has never hurt me.'

Karam lowered her chin. 'I'm sorry I came in.'

'Forget it. Bertie can be a bit of a handful.'

'Shall I leave him here?'

'Yes.'

Karam left the war zone. As she walked home, she felt eyes on her, knew that Honoria was watching. 'Keep looking, girl,' she muttered to herself. 'God help us all, but you're the only predictable item in these parts. What a flaming mess.'

Eight

David Benson sat in his surgery, head in hands, the paper evidence laid out below his nose: RESULT POSITIVE, capital letters, straight off a computer, no room for error. He had impregnated Deirdre, a woman who was not fit to look after a dog. He remembered April refusing Deirdre a rescued puppy. 'That one couldn't look after a boiled egg,' April had said.

Outside, patients were waiting for him, as was Deirdre. He was a man with nowhere to run, who understood, at last, his wife's lengthy bout of depression. What the hell was he going to do? Yvonne remained determined, refusing to listen to the voice of reason. Once the play was over, she would be going away to spend time in Yorkshire with Stefan Laczynski, life peer and inventor of some sophisticated explosives, father of Karam Laczynska. He found himself actually hoping that his wife was involved with Karam; lesbianism could be a passing phase, something saved from adolescence that would burn itself out in time. Yet he could say nothing to Yvonne or to Karam: he was clearly in no position to take the high ground, and anyway his own beliefs precluded him from accusing, judging or criticizing another's way of living and loving. But, oh, what a bloody mess.

He stood up, opened a window and lit a Silk Cut. As he puffed away at it, he wondered what the hell he was trying to do to himself. He had hit the bottle, was getting through the best part of three bottles of Scotch every week. He hated booze, fags and drugs with a passion that fell not far short of evangelical. His only exception to his rigid rules was April Nugent, whose symptoms were sometimes alleviated by cannabis. Even there, he had advised her to weigh it carefully and to ingest it rather than to smoke it.

The door opened. 'Dr Benson?'

It was Deirdre. 'Can't you read?' he asked. 'Doesn't the word "engaged" convey anything?'

She stopped dead just inside the door. 'I thought it didn't mean me. I thought—'

'It means everybody.'

She recovered her composure and sidled to his desk. 'I just wanted to know the result. I mean, I've done two at home, but you never know, do you?' The carefully arranged smile faded as she waited for a reply.

He sighed, threw his dog end outside, wafted away the smoke. 'You are pregnant,' he told her.

She simpered, perched on his desk. 'So what happens now?'

David glared at her. She was wearing green eye-shadow, a pink blouse, many of whose buttons

125

were 'accidentally' unfastened, a maroon skirt and yet another stupid grin. 'I can arrange for a termination, if you wish. If you go through certain channels, nothing will be recorded in your file.'

Her mouth fell open.

'Deirdre, we have no future together. When we started our . . . our affair, I made it plain that I did not want a permanent relationship. For your part, you said you were continuing to take the pill and that your husband was going to come back.'

Deirdre's smile was a distant memory. She drew back her lips in what amounted to a snarl, leant forward and gave him the dubious benefit of a deep, rather slack cleavage. 'You've had your fun. Now you can pay for it.'

He nodded his agreement. 'You'll get the best treatment available.'

'I want my baby! You're not killing my baby!'

David picked up a pen and doodled on a pad. 'Right. If you wish to keep the child, that is your prerogative. I shall speak to my solicitor when the time comes, and arrangements will be made for financial support.'

She staggered back as if he had hit her with a heavy object. 'You don't want me any more.'

He threw down the pen. 'Got it in one, Deirdre. I happen to love my wife.'

'She's a bloody dyke.'

'Really? Whatever gave you that idea?'

Nonplussed, Deirdre peered at him, scrutinizing his face through myopic, beautiful eyes.

She could not understand why he was rejecting her. The baby was her passport, her security. David Benson was an honourable man, a man who would not leave his child's mother out in the cold. 'I love you.' She pouted miserably.

'No. We had good sex together, but—'

'And she's got no interest in you.'

He sighed heavily. 'She has been ill. We are sorting things out. And this is none of your business. You'd better leave, because I have patients waiting.'

Deirdre, who had expected better treatment than this, threw back her head and screamed. She howled for several seconds, during which time David stayed in his chair. He could not mend the situation, so he simply allowed it to develop.

Walter Roberts, a decent, ageing Welshman who had set up the practice ten years earlier, burst into the room and applied the laws of a fundamental and long-ignored type of psychology. He lifted a hand and swept the palm across Deirdre's cheek with a resounding slap. 'Shut up at once,' he ordered. 'There are sick people out there, some of them not quite as young as they'd like to be.'

A young Indian doctor pushed her face around the door. 'It's all right, Asha,' said Walter. 'Just hysterics.'

'All right?' Asha Mathur awarded Deirdre a cursory glance. Asha, like many intelligent females, could scarcely bring herself to be pleasant to the gaudy receptionist. 'I am trying to calculate the blood pressure of a very sick

127

man. He has shot right off the top of the scale, while I'm quite weak from shock.' She looked at David, felt pity for him. It didn't take much to guess what was happening here. 'Come with me, please.' The small woman grabbed Deirdre's arm and dragged her from the room.

Walter sat down. 'So she's pregnant, then?'

'Yes.'

'Yours?'

'Of course.'

The older man tapped a pipe on David's desk, sucked noisily on the stem for a while. This was his pacifier, no more than a baby's dummy really. He had not lit the thing for years, though he always carried tobacco and matches, just in case. 'Go home,' he said eventually. 'She's determined to make a stink, no matter what, so leave your patients to me.'

David looked at his senior colleague, assessed his mood. Sometimes, argument with Walter Roberts was futile. 'I'm sorry,' he said. 'This should never have happened.'

Walter nodded. 'I agree. You have been careless and stupid, but you aren't the first man to fall for a sexy figure. Go home and let things cool off for a while.'

David picked up his belongings and made for the door.

'Not that way,' advised Walter. 'Go through the back. If I know anything about human nature, Deirdre will have your name as black as coal by lunchtime.'

David changed direction and went through

an adjoining room where afternoon clinics were held. This was the well woman, well man, well baby, diabetic, sensible eating and maternity room. Would he see his surgery again? he wondered. Would the partners blackball him for his behaviour with Deirdre?

Outside, he opened the door of his car, removed his jacket and threw it on to the passenger seat. Go home? Home was just over a mile away. Half the patients in this place lived within walking distance of his house. He stood in the small car-park and wondered which direction to take, both immediately and in the longer term. He had no wife, no work for the moment and little hope.

For want of ideas, he drove homeward. There was little for him in Beech Gardens: the house would probably be empty, because Yvonne was likely to be with Karam, April, or both. Nevertheless, he pulled into his driveway, got out of the car and pondered for a few seconds before swivelling on the spot to face the face at the window. She was gazing straight at him.

He marched across the road and into the mansion building. Too impatient to wait for the lift, he took the stairs several at a time and bounded up to Honoria's door. With a determined finger, he pressed the bell-push until she answered. Let her have it from the horse's mouth this time, he thought.

Honoria opened the door. 'Doctor,' she cried, 'how good of you to come. I've tried and tried, but to no avail. Outside is just too big for me, too terrifying. We must be telepathic, you and I, because I was about to send for you.'

Without bothering to reply, David followed her into the sitting room. The place was lifeless now that Hyacinth had gone. There were no fresh flowers, no half-read books strewn around, no folders of notes and poems.

'I thought you were about to play your sister's part in the production. You said you would manage it.'

'No,' she replied. 'Sadly, it proved too much for my nerves.'

Her nerves were as strong as reinforced concrete. Nobody wanted her – that was the truth of the matter.

'So April is doing it instead,' she concluded.

'Ah.'

After an awkward silence, she offered him tea or coffee.

'No, thank you.'

Gill Collins came in from the kitchen. 'Hello, Dr Benson,' she said. 'Warm enough for you?' She fanned herself with a tea-towel.

Honoria glowered at the poor woman. 'The doctor is here to see me,' she said icily.

Gill Collins opened her mouth, closed it tightly against a retort that might just have lost her her job, which she despised but needed.

David sat down. 'This is not a professional visit,' he said, making sure that his voice was powerful enough to carry its own weight through to the kitchen. 'I'm here to save you some trouble and, perhaps, to help your eyesight.'

Honoria placed herself in another armchair. 'Oh. Do continue,' she invited.

'It's about your spying,' he began.

'Spying?' she asked, the word almost sticking in her throat.

'The constant standing at the window, the binoculars. We've all noticed you.'

Honoria sat up straight, her spine as stiff as a ramrod. 'What are you implying?'

'I'm here about your Peeping Thomasina act, Honoria.' Cutlery clattered in the sink. Gill Collins emitted a strangled cry and promptly disguised it as a cough.

'Dr Benson,' began Honoria, 'this is a high-class residential district with valuable properties and affluent residents. As many of you work, I keep a watchful eye on your homes just in case burglars should happen along.'

'Really?'

Her hand strayed to her wrinkled throat. 'As I must stay indoors owing to my condition, I thought I might as well occupy myself for the good of the community.'

David nodded slowly, as if taking time to consider her answer. 'Yes, we do realize how highly you value your neighbours, Honoria. The Wilson-Carpenters, for example. Do you remember them?'

Her hand stilled, rested itself on a single row of cultured pearls.

'They sold up. In fact, they fled and left an empty property on the market, causing a severe reduction in its asking price. You made their lives unbearable just by being here. Each time a member of that family stood near a window or walked through their

131

doorway, your binoculars went on red alert.'

'Nonsense,' she cried. 'There was no question of—'

'Oh, excuse me,' he continued. 'Mary Wilson-Carpenter was a sick lady. She needed rest and, above all, a stress-free environment.'

'She had fits,' replied Honoria, her own face almost purple enough to merit a seizure.

'She was epileptic,' answered the doctor.

After a pause, Honoria spoke up again. 'People of that sort should not be allowed to live in areas such as this, falling on the ground and flailing about – she wasn't safe.'

He jumped up, towered over her. 'People of that sort? Of what sort? She was a doctor of microbiology, for goodness' sake. Even if she hadn't had a decent education, Mary would still have been brighter, cleverer and a damned sight more likeable than you could ever be.'

Honoria blanched, the blood draining away from her face so quickly that she felt faint.

'Well, Miss Honoria bloody West,' he went on, still leaning over her chair, 'put this in your diary. My wife and I may be separating. If any of my words are too difficult for you, don't hesitate to ask, as I shall spell them out letter by letter.'

'There's no need for this sort of—'

'And Deirdre Mellor is pregnant. Her husband has left her and, as far as I am aware, Deirdre's condition has not been achieved via the post office.' He looked at the confusion in Honoria's eyes. 'She has not got into her present condition by receiving letters from

132

her estranged partner. The child is probably mine.'

Gill Collins closed the kitchen door quietly, then turned on the coffee grinder.

He walked away from his victim, stood where she usually stood. 'I see the Halliwells have planted some more roses. They were on offer at Safeway, three for the price of two. A bit late in the year for introducing new stock, I should have thought. The Dawsons could do with a better lawnmower, I suppose. Oh, and Jenny Marsh has leaf mould. Pity I can't prescribe for that.'

Honoria stood up. 'I am asking you to leave,' she said.

'Don't worry, I couldn't stay here for much longer if you paid me a king's ransom. The atmosphere doesn't suit me.'

'And I shall not be needing your services as a doctor.'

'Good. Because I shan't be offering to service you. In fact, I am currently suspended for misbehaving, so our choices and decisions will be limited. We are both sacked, it seems.'

David marched to the door, opened it, turned. 'By the way, I have informed the authorities that you are now capable of leaving your house. After all, you managed to get as far as St Thomas's and the crematorium. And you sat outside for about half an hour the day after Hyacinth died. Your disability allowance will probably be reviewed. Goodbye.'

Outside on the landing, David Benson felt truly foolish. 'That has to be the most childish

133

thing I've done in thirty years,' he told the wall. 'And now I'm talking to a wall.' He went home to get drunk.

After two whiskies and a couple of lagers, David became restless. He was unused to idleness, seldom having more than one day a week to himself. The alcohol, unaccompanied by food, relaxed his mind, giving him a veneer of confidence, an outer garment that masked his innermost fears. He would go out again, not in the car, but for a wander down Memory Lane, otherwise known as Poplar Grove.

In Beech Gardens, he stood for at least two minutes, his eyes fixed on the figure of Honoria West. She gave up in the end, withered under his steady stare, withdrawing into the room until the coast became clearer.

Gill Collins slammed her way out of Cavendish Mansions, an expression of hurt and anger on her face.

'Been sacked?' David asked her loudly.

'No,' she yelled back. 'I've told her to take a running jump into the river. I offered to knit her a pair of cement socks, too. She said I was eavesdropping, stupid mare. Eavesdropping?' She walked across the avenue and stood by his side. 'Eavesdropping? Do you know, Dr Benson? She's got books in there, exercise books like my kids use at school. She writes stuff down, like. Every time somebody comes and goes, she makes notes of the time and what they're wearing and where she thinks they might be going or coming back from.'

David sighed. 'Well, I can't say I'm astonished.'

'And she's yak-yak-yak all the while, have I seen so-and-so, do I know who lives down this street, that road, the other avenue.'

'A hard life, then?'

'Oh, yes.' Gill shook her head. 'See, we can't manage without me working. My kids go through shoes like nobody's business. The thing is, I don't mind making do with their clothes, but shoes have to be leather and they've got to fit proper. I know what I'm talking about with my bunions.'

David considered the matter for a second or two. 'You can start working at my place tomorrow,' he told her. 'Three hours every morning, no Honoria on your back all the time.'

Relief flooded her eyes. 'Hey, do you mean it?'

'Of course I do.'

She smiled, her eyes still wet. 'You've just saved my life. And my family, too,' she managed. 'Are you sure? What about . . .?'

'It might be a bit awkward at first, but it'll get sorted out. If Yvonne goes, I'll need a housekeeper. If she stays, she'll probably go back to work.'

Gill dabbed at her eyes with a handkerchief. 'I know who's come off best today, Doctor. And it's not fancy bloody Nancy with her binoculars and her notebooks. We've got her beat good and proper, you and me.'

David wasn't so sure. There was a deep seam of near-evil in Miss Honoria, an element he had never encountered before. It was beyond coldness. She allowed no one to reach her, she needed nobody except a servant to tend to her practical requirements. Poor Gill had slaved for years, only to be driven to resign after all her loyalty. 'She's something else,' he muttered.

'You can say that again.' Gill paused. 'She hated Hyacinth.'

He nodded.

'I wondered . . . You know what I mean.'

He did, but decided to wait.

'With her being on the insulin and all that. Nobody'll ever know now, what with her being cremated. But it would be so easy to jab an extra dose into her. It doesn't go in a vein, does it?'

'No, it's intramuscular.'

'Like I said, it makes you wonder. There's other stuff as well, things I heard Hyacinth saying to April. Nothing you could put a finger on, only it was as if Hyacinth was looking after Honoria. It was her duty, something of that sort.'

David closed his eyes, remembered signing the death certificate. He also recalled being uncomfortable about the look of near-triumph on Honoria's face. 'Don't say I'm responsible for that as well, Gill.'

She placed a hand on his shoulder. 'Listen, lad, there was that much wrong with the poor woman it could have been anything. I might be wrong.'

'You could be right, though.'

She bowed her head. 'Yes, but that's life.'

'And death.'

'Right.' She peered closely at him, caught a whiff of whisky on his breath. 'I'm going now. And, by the way, you'd better stop drinking. It's bad for your health, you know.'

Nine

April Nugent knocked on Honoria's door. Life was too short, and it was time to bury the hatchet. After shopping in Crosby's Dog House for provisions for her waifs and strays, she had decided that Honoria, bad as she might be, was probably another of the world's unfortunate creatures. Also, April was experiencing a degree of guilt: however unwittingly, she had stripped Honoria of her expectations.

She waited, rang the bell. Hyacinth would have wanted April to come. Someone had to look after Honoria, and that someone needed to be in possession of certain facts. However distasteful the history was, Honoria remained in need of care and vigilance. The woman had sacked her excellent housekeeper and could well be in need of help.

The door opened as far as twin safety chains would allow.

'Honoria?'

'Go away. I am not receiving visitors today.'

'Look, Honoria, I just—'

'Look at what? At you in your Oxfam frock and orthopaedic sandals? I'd rather watch paint dry.' She closed the door.

April leant against the wall on the landing outside Honoria's flat. Everyone was in some sort of trouble today. She had heard on Crosby's grapevine about the scene at the health centre, was aware that poor David Benson had hit the booze, the fags and rock bottom. Deirdre was pregnant, as was Yvonne, though the latter's condition was a secret, especially from her husband. David was drinking himself into a semi-stupor because he didn't want the baby he knew about and was not allowed the news that would have delighted him.

April blew a lock of hair off her sweaty forehead. Deirdre had been driven home by Dr Asha Mathur, a sensible young woman who took no nonsense from anyone. Like Honoria, Deirdre Mellor had shut herself away in isolation. Two females in decline promised to add an extra layer of drama, if nothing else.

Karam was upset. Sorely tempted to declare her love for Yvonne, she was too terrified of what might happen if she did. She wanted Yvonne to walk out on David immediately, refusing to accept her insistence that she was safe with her husband. 'Why did you have to choose a married woman?' muttered April. 'Why Yvonne?' After finding Yvonne on the floor in a state of considerable dishevelment, Karam was now worried about rape, murder, Yvonne's unborn baby, Yvonne's morning sickness, the unfinished sets of *Monday's Child*, plus anything

139

else she could manage to fit into her currently hyperactive brain.

'I'm worn out,' April said softly. Yvonne was worried about Karam worrying, about David going into a nose-dive, about being well enough to perform in the play, about worrying during her pregnancy.

Philip Pointer was another one in a quandary. With the author in the cast, mutiny was in the offing. April, considered by Philip a latterday Judas Iscariot, would go her own way and take the rest of the players with her. His experience, his chalk and his tape measure would doubtless count for naught once April got her teeth into the production. He was always on the phone, sometimes trying to be nice, often in belligerent mood. 'You must give me my head,' he kept booming into April's ear.

April was concerned about them all, and about one Mark Nugent, her ex-husband, who was currently living in an old caravan behind hedges at the bottom of April's garden. He was probably unaware that his wife had spotted him, and April was at a complete loss as to what to do about him. She sheltered animals, succoured friends, was supposed to be a caring person, but was Mark making his way back into her life an inch at a time? Today the caravan, tomorrow the stables, then dog kennels, cattery, rear porch, kitchen, onward and upward? He was penniless, jobless and homeless. She, weakened by the death of one dear friend and by the dilemmas of others, was living in a state where sensible decisions were not reached easily.

She stared at Honoria's door, tried to imagine what was going on inside the flat. Honoria had scarcely wielded as much as a duster in recent years. Before disability had overtaken her, Hyacinth had performed the chores not covered by Gill Collins. Both women had become increasingly dependent on Gill, but now Gill was gone.

April walked away and waited for the lift, with a degree of impatience. In her experience, those who accepted help graciously were the same people who offered it when required. Honoria did neither. Right from her childhood, it had been a case of I, me, myself, where Honoria was concerned. She wanted no one and resented everyone.

All the way home, April pondered, but reached no conclusions about Yvonne, David, Honoria, Philip Pointer, Karam, Mark Nugent, Deirdre, Gill Collins, the play. But what she had long realized was that multiple sclerosis was a disease that played to the gallery in times of stress. Her left foot was even more left-footed than usual, while her sight was literally on the blink due to twitching nerves in both eyelids. She had pains in her stomach, her back and her arms. Speech was difficult, and she was concerned that she might lose it before or during the three-night run of *Monday's Child*. 'I've no control,' she said, as she edged homeward in the car at fifteen miles an hour, eyeballs red-raw, hands so numb they seemed to be a mere extension of the steering-wheel.

Shaking uncontrollably, she climbed out of

her Micra, wondering anew how much longer she would be able to drive. This was the final frontier for her: the whole of April's freedom lay within the small interior of her Nissan. For as long as she could take herself out, a limited degree of personal choice remained within her grasp. She patted the car's bonnet. 'My little house on wheels,' she said fondly. Perhaps she would go to Crosby Park and ask the garage to order an automatic for her. Her left foot could rest in peace or in pieces if there was no clutch to depress.

A movement from across the way caused her to turn. There followed a crash, some choice expletives, then a man's head poked itself out of Karam Laczynska's attic window. April screwed up her eyes. 'Is that you, David?'

David Benson caught his breath, coughed. 'No, I'm a burglar.'

April leant against her car. He was drunk – stupidly drunk, and Dr David Benson was no boozer. There would be little sense emerging from his mouth, April decided. What the hell was he doing inside Karam's house, anyway? Had he found out about the girl being lesbian? Did he know that Karam loved Yvonne? And, if he had discovered the truth about Karam's sexuality, was he assuming that his wife was Karam's other half?

April groaned. In the last two or three weeks, life around her had gone pear-shaped, to say the least of it. It had all happened after Hyacinth's death. There had been the Hyacinth era and this was the dawn of the post-Hyacinth age.

Ice-caps were melting, sure enough. One of the liquid results was currently in a very precarious position on top of Karam's house. Even from this distance and with her eyelids jumping up and down like a couple of fleas in a fit, April could see that Yvonne's husband was the worse for fluid, probably Scotch.

She watched David light a cigarette.

'What are you doing up there?' she called.

'I'm being up here and not down at your level,' came the blurred reply. 'And you have fairies at the bottom of your garden.'

April sighed. David had spotted Mark, so she could no longer pretend ignorance of his presence. 'He's not a fairy, David. He's just a rather ugly gnome.'

David climbed fully out of the room, sat on the dormer's edge and dangled his legs down the roof's slope. He held the cigarette in one hand and a bottle in the other. After taking a drag from the former and a swig from the latter, he started to sing 'Heartbreak Hotel'. Behind April's house, dogs awaiting rehoming howled as if begging potential owners to arrive sooner rather than later.

April crossed the road and entered Karam's garden. In the middle of the lawn lay a large canvas, a portrait of Yvonne in the nude. Crudely executed fig leaves had been placed at salient points, the green paint still wet, and Yvonne now sported a moustache, a beard and some spectacles. Poor David had finally flipped.

'Any savage can paint,' he yelled before embarking on 'Peggy Sue'.

143

April was in a quandary. She felt as if she had been waiting for weeks at an unmarked cross-roads. Had Hyacinth held them all together? Was her departure causing the breakdown of society hereabouts? 'Do I get the fire brigade?' she asked herself softly. 'Or the police, the ambulance, the coastguard? Yvonne, Karam, please, hurry up.'

The good doctor was enjoying himself. His situation in the world had improved no end since this morning. From this lofty position, he could see quite a distance. Even without the benefit of binoculars, he was enjoying a whole new perspective. 'April?'

'Yes?'

'Will you let Mark stay?'

She decided to keep him talking. 'Oh, I don't know. When a person is down and out, it's so difficult to refuse shelter and a crust. But Mark isn't a man to be trusted, you know.'

'Did you ever meet a man with no faults?' he asked.

'No.'

'But a woman without fault is not so rare, eh? How you cling together, you females. Unhappily, my wife and Miss Laczynska may have clung rather too closely. Have you seen that painting? Have you scrutinized it?'

'Yes, I—'

He drove straight through her reply. 'The expression on Yvonne's face. That's a woman in love. She used to wear that look for me.'

'David?'

'What?'

'Listen to me. Just shut up and listen for once. Yvonne is not – I repeat – is not Karam's lover. Do you understand?'

In spite of the whisky, David absorbed and accepted her words. April never told lies. But Deirdre had been right after all. Karam was a lesbian. 'Thank you,' he replied, almost sensibly.

Mr Hoskins, the widower from the house next door to April's, had come out to watch the cabaret. He was setting up a deck-chair and had brought out his newspaper, a flask of tea and a rather battered Panama hat. After grappling with frame and canvas, he settled down to a rare form of entertainment.

'Are you well, Mr Hoskins?' enquired David. The old man looked up at his general practitioner. 'Just the piles and the bit of angina. Oh, the knee plays up and I still get the headaches. But I'm not too bad, thanks.'

'Capital,' replied David. 'Splendid, splendid.'

This was a Brian Rix farce, decided April. Any moment now, a trouserless man would enter stage right bearing headless flowers and a half-eaten cheese roll. 'David?' she called.

'Ici, ma chérie.'

A French farce, then. 'David?' She attempted a sterner tone.

'What?'

'Are you listening to me?'

'Yes, dear heart.'

She took a deep breath. 'I can't see properly and I'm in a lot of pain. Will you please come down right away and stop all the nonsense? It's not fair on me, on Mr Hoskins or on yourself.'

David looked at Mr Hoskins. 'The old boy's having the time of his life,' he pronounced. 'As for you, I prescribe a large whisky followed by an afternoon nap.'

April glared at him. This really was too much. Suddenly, exhaustion overcame her and she decided not to care any more. If David Benson wanted to go breaking into people's houses and throwing paintings about, that was his business. If he fell off the roof, what could she do anyway? She had to stop worrying about others and start looking after herself.

As April turned to quit the bizarre scene, Yvonne's Range Rover came round the corner. 'April, stay where you are,' cried the man on the roof. 'I may need a witness.'

April remained where she was, but not because she was being obedient. Her dependable right foot appeared to have gone slightly adrift, which event was new and totally unwelcome.

Yvonne's car stopped and, as soon as the passenger door opened, Bertrand Russell leapt off Karam's lap, bounded out of the vehicle and into the garden.

David watched the little terrier and smiled. 'Good boy,' he said, when the dog had finished relieving himself on the already ruined portrait. 'A dog of excellent taste, indeed.' No, no, cried the voice of conscience. You should not have spoilt Karam's work; Karam did not take your wife away. Your wife took herself away . . .

Yvonne applied the handbrake, looked at

poor April, then at the man on the roof. 'David's cracked up,' she told her companion.

'He wants you to think that,' answered Karam, her hand still on the open passenger door. 'What do you have to say to convince him that you're leaving?'

Yvonne leant forward and laid her forehead on her hands, her fingers still gripping the steering-wheel as if her life depended on remaining motionless. 'I can't go on like this,' she whispered. 'It's hopeless. He's drinking, he was sent home because Deirdre made a dreadful scene. David has a breaking-point and he's getting dangerously near to it.'

'And what are you supposed to do about that?' Karam felt like biting her tongue. The man was suffering: she ought to feel pity, not just fear on her own behalf.

Yvonne kept her head down. 'I don't know. I've never known. We're like book-ends, David and I, so alike that we scarcely recognize one another. Like me, he even gets bloody depressed by life – peas in a pod and we didn't see it. After all, very few of us truly know ourselves. He's my double – should have been my brother.'

Karam shook her head. 'You'd better talk to him. I'll go in and make coffee.'

April, having suddenly attained partial control of both feet, shot forward and knocked on the windscreen. 'He's ruined the painting,' she said, 'and he wants me to stay, but I'm going to bed.'

Suddenly Karam stared into the wing mirror.

147

'Oh God – he's supposed to be wandering about London or Coventry or somewhere looking for a sculptor. She was doing a bust of him for his Sunday-night prog. Shit, he's seen us.'

Yvonne was worried about her companion's sanity. Coventry? Busts? Then she saw the man. He was exactly like his sister, yet he wasn't any more feminine than Karam was masculine. 'Is that Sebastian, then?' On TV, Sebastian Laczynski looked so different.

Karam nodded. Yvonne's husband was balanced on the roof. April's nerves had kicked themselves to life, were causing her to perform a rain dance around her walking stick. The painting, centrepiece of Karam's next exhibition, was ruined. And here came Sebastian. He was about as welcome as a swarm of blue-bottles in a heatwave.

'Very handsome,' said Yvonne. Yes, he was far better-looking in real life. 'Quite an oil painting.'

'And weird,' added Karam.

'You said he was the least eccentric of all your family.'

'Exactly. Weird.'

April decided to wait until later for further explanations. She deserved a break, perhaps a breakdown even, and she was going home to rest.

Yvonne stepped on to the pavement and watched her husband on the roof. Karam walked into the road and into the arms of Sebastian, Sunday-night beloved of pseudo-arty types and old ladies with nowhere to go at weekends. 'Hello, Seb,' she said.

Sebastian grunted. 'I was passing, so I thought I'd call.'

'Nobody passes Liverpool,' replied Karam, 'unless they're on their way to Ireland or the Isle of Man. Liverpool's a place you visit deliberately or avoid deliberately.'

He shrugged. 'Who's the pretty one?'

'That's Yvonne.'

'Ah.'

Karam pushed him away, dragged a hand through her tousled hair. 'You've arrived at a bad time,' she informed him, realizing immediately that the understatement was almost laughable. 'You see, Yvonne's husband is having a bit of trouble getting used to the idea of divorce.'

'I have come at the right time, Karam. I need you to be the subject of a programme.'

'And April's not getting any better—'

'Because Beryl Micklewhite let me down, you see.'

'And there's— Beryl who?'

'Micklewhite. She's the sculptor I was meant to be recording this week, but she became difficult and I had to think of some alternatives.'

'Listen, Seb. Just for a minute, try to live in the here and now. There's a fine man balanced on my roof. He's drunk and unhappy, and we're scared he might jump or fall. Deal with him.'

Sebastian glanced upward. 'Ah, I see what you mean.'

'Come inside and I'll start some coffee.' She thought about David and his hopelessness, knew how he felt. 'Poor man,' she mumbled, as she strode into her house.

Time for a head-count, she thought, while directing boiling water through a filter. April had gone home, Yvonne was upstairs and David was just about to return to *terra firma* via the usual means of descent rather than by jumping, she hoped. 'I had better stay inside,' she whispered to herself. Her heart pounded. Why had David Benson entered Jasmine Cottage? Karam had never taken particular care to conceal her lesbianism, though she had not advertised it. Did he know? Was he going to tell Yvonne? Would Yvonne disappear altogether, afraid of Karam, determined to escape from David?

Sebastian returned. 'He won't budge – his wife's talking to him. Sis, I really do need your help.'

'Seb, I'm in this mess with the doctor on the roof, and I really need some space for the play.' She rambled on, trying to forget Yvonne and David. 'It's in three acts, same setting, but different trimmings, stuff to remember. Like in Act One, there are baby photographs, toys strewn about and so forth. Act Two's all wedding dresses, cakes, hairdos and flowers, then the last's faded wallpaper and a wheel-chair, so it's—'

'Karam?'

'What?' She slammed down the coffee jug. 'Listen, you, you drift into my life at twenty minutes past three on a stinking hot day while other trouble is in motion. You switch on your

150

ego and drive full steam ahead across everybody's plans, sensitivities and requirements.' She waved a spoon at him. 'Sit, zip and wait.'

He did as he was told.

Karam slumped against the table. 'Don't say a word,' she reminded him. She raised her head. 'I am halfway out of my mind at the moment. We have all lost a very good friend. Her name was Hyacinth and she was simply brilliant. "Sad" is too shallow an adjective to touch on our feelings just now. April, who was closest to Hyacinth, is quite ill. Yvonne's husband, a GP, is in danger of losing his job as well as his wife. This is not the time to worry about your programme.'

'I'll go and drag him off the roof.'

'Thank you.'

Sebastian left the kitchen, stormed up two flights of stairs, lifted Yvonne away from the attic window, reached out and hauled David inside. David allowed himself to be manhandled downstairs. There was no point in arguing with this recent arrival: he was fit, impatient and on television twice a month.

The kitchen table was suddenly fully populated. David sat opposite his wife, Sebastian opposite his sister. Yvonne sipped her coffee, clattered the cup into its saucer. Two pairs of grey eyes were fixed on her.

'Are you all right?' asked Karam.

Yvonne jumped. 'Me? Of course I'm all right. Everything is just wonderful. He' – she waved a hand at David – 'is as drunk as a lord. Your painting is spoilt, Karam. Poor April seems to

151

be having some sort of an attack, but no one cares about her. Yes, all's well with the world.'

'Of course we care about April,' answered Karam. 'But the plight of your . . . of David was of paramount importance. A man preparing to jump cannot be ignored.'

Yvonne raised her face and looked at her friend, then at Sebastian. He stared back before returning his attention to his sister. He doesn't approve of me, Yvonne thought, doesn't like the idea of my problems sitting on his sister's roof. He looked like a statue of some self-engrossed Greek god, too concerned with his own perfection to consider the problems and flaws of others. Oh, he was beautiful, right enough, with his dark brown hair, classic features, square jaw with a slight cleft at its centre. Like Karam, he had a generous mouth. Unlike Karam, he appeared to have an ungenerous soul.

David had fallen asleep, folded arms acting as a cushion for his head. Dehydrated and thoroughly drunk, he snored gently, a cup of black coffee neglected at his elbow.

'What shall I do with him?' asked Yvonne.

Sebastian gazed at David, stood up and left the room.

'We'll put him on the sofa,' replied Karam.

Yvonne sipped coffee. 'Your brother doesn't approve of me.'

'Really?' Karam dipped a custard cream into her cup.

'He almost sneers when he looks at me.'

'Take no notice,' advised Karam. 'Sneering runs in the family.'

Yvonne blew out her cheeks. 'He's so hail-fellow-well-met on TV.'

'He gets paid.'

'So he performs to order like a seal? Throw him a bucket of fivers and he claps his flippers?'

Karam put down her biscuit, pushed back her chair and propped crossed ankles on the table. Explaining Sebastian was never easy. Like his older sister, he had deliberately steered himself away from science and into the grip of the arts. Chemical lunacy had been their father's speciality, as had the pursuit of the fair sex. 'He's not like other blokes,' she managed at last.

'Is he gay?'

Karam shook her head thoughtfully. 'He's weird.'

'Stop saying that.'

'All right, all right. I think he's a virgin. Or almost a virgin.'

'There are no degrees of virginity, Karam.'

Karam shrugged. 'See? Weird.'

Yvonne got up and began to clear the cups. Once David was settled, she would look to April's needs.

Ten

'I am rewriting the end,' April said on the telephone. 'Under these circumstances, I'm sure the production can be postponed until October.' She could almost hear Philip Pointer's heart galloping into overdrive. 'Yes, yes, I know poor Karam worked hard to complete the set. Philip – listen, please. Our little society will be the first to deliver the new version of *Monday's Child*. We could even get critics.'

'But we always have the summer play in summer. It's tradition,' came the trite answer.

'Then change the name. Alter it to autumn play. Most civilized amdram groups put on plays twice a year and in cooler weather. Who wants to be stuck in a theatre or a church hall when the most wonderful sunsets in the world happen here? No one can match a Crosby sunset for drama. Even Shakespeare would have had his work cut out. Apart from which, I am the writer and the star and I am ill in bed, Philip. So, dear boy, do shut up.' She slammed down the receiver.

Veetol, a striped cat named after the qualities of certain aircraft whose specifications he shared, leapt off April's bed and spreadeagled himself on the floor. April tutted at him. 'One of these days you'll do the vertical take-off and land on something sharp.'

Yvonne had heard April's telephone tantrum and rejoiced as she entered with a tray of tea and scones. She placed it by the bed, avoided treading on the stretched-out form of Veetol, then walked to the window. The famous playwright was on the mend again, but the momentum must be prolonged and emphasized. Her spirits needed to be maintained to give her a reason to get better. She had been cosseted for long enough and had stopped spilling soup and tea everywhere. Now was the time to strike. 'Funny colour, that old caravan,' Yvonne said to herself. 'It's neither cream nor yellow.'

April was still staring at the phone. 'The bloody man will drive me crackers,' she mused crossly.

Yvonne nodded. One way or another, she would get April out of bed today. 'Yes, I know how you feel. Husbands? Who needs them? David's quite the injured infant, these days. I'm seriously considering putting him back into Pampers. At least Mark's hanging out his washing.'

'I meant PP,' stated April. 'He's on the phone day and night, whingeing, carrying on and . . . What did you say about washing?'

Yvonne gazed across kennels and stables until

her sight rested on April's old caravan. 'He's done his smalls. They're rather grey and hanging on one of those stupid *Magic Roundabout* washing lines next to the caravan. He's also fed the dogs, exercised them and swilled out the play areas and runs. The girls are quite impressed with him. He seems to be developing a fondness for animals.'

April bridled, fastened up the old cardigan that served as bed-jacket and folded her arms. 'Four weeks he's been out there. Well, three and a half.' With a level of alacrity that would have stunned her doctors, April Nugent leapt out of bed. A few seconds later, the disease reminded her of its existence, yet she persevered to the window, steadying herself on furniture and walls.

She looked at him. She had never stopped loving him. She had never quite managed without the weak, stupid, spineless dolt. 'He's got to go,' she told Yvonne.

Yvonne poured tea and spread strawberry jam on split scones.

'He knows I know he's here now. And he knows I know he knows.'

Yvonne placed April's scone and tea on a table by the window.

April lowered herself into a blue wicker chair. Mark was losing his hair. In working gear – washed-out jeans and a Homer Simpson T-shirt – he looked so much older, so vulnerable. 'Yvonne?'

'Yes?'

'Is he a bad person?'

156

Yvonne laughed. Weren't writers supposed to know the answers to such questions? After all, they set themselves up as commentators on the human condition, made sure everyone knew their opinions, listened to their voices, read their words. But when she looked at April's face Yvonne's laughter died. Yes, it was hard to know thoroughly someone who lived too closely for proper focus to be possible. 'He's not a bad man,' she replied.

'But he spent all my blinking money then ran off with Zeppelin Woman. He gave me no respect and he couldn't have loved me because he didn't stay with me. He left me for Bessie Braddock's double, Yvonne.'

Yvonne settled herself at April's feet, leant back against the nicely shaped but sometimes useless legs. 'He was scared of the MS, April. It's such an unforeseeable quantity, isn't it? I mean, look at you now. You've been in bed for over a fortnight, but I bet you'll be shopping at Sainsbury's tomorrow, waving your stick at that poor manager and screaming about price increases, making a scene about tins of tuna from waters where dolphins get killed. The disease is so unpredictable. Perhaps he couldn't get his head round it.'

'And he thinks I can? Do people really believe that this is a piece of cake? I went to the surgery with pins and needles, a bit of an ache in a leg – and what did I collect? And where was he when the diagnosis finally came? In the pub with his friends. Seven months later he's in a nasty little dormer bungalow in Ainsdale, of all places. He

157

hated Ainsdale. He couldn't bear the idea of living in a new shed with shallow skirtings and power points hanging out of plasterboard. But he went.'

'Eat your scone and shut up.'

April stroked Yvonne's hair. This poor kid was going through her own kind of hell. Karam was the one in whom Yvonne confided fully. But Karam, whose year at the university was not over, had gone off with her brother to comb the streets of Doncaster for some missing sculptress who was supposed to be the subject of one of Sebastian's autumn shows. Sebastian, it seemed, did not trust researchers. 'And what are you going to do?' April asked.

'Try to stay slim until October, so that I can still play Alice, I suppose.'

'Beyond that?'

Yvonne shrugged. 'Go towards my kismet.' She tutted. 'Oh, April, I really don't know. There's no easy answer, is there? David will just have to settle down. Deirdre's husband's on the scene again. He's got himself involved in foreign markets, time-share and so forth, so Deirdre's planning to hop off to Majorca for a few weeks soon. That means David won't have her hanging round his neck. He seems to have gone off her.'

April drank some tea, arranged her words as best she could. 'Karam is very fond of you.'

'I'm fond of her, too.'

April just could not do it. Try as she might, she could not tell Yvonne that her friend was a lesbian, that Karam was in love, was bleeding . . .

'She's planning to look after you, then?'

'Yes.'

April said no more on the subject. Who was she, anyway, to question someone else's decisions? She had married a glorified clerk who had been replaced by a photocopier or an answerphone – she could never quite remember which item had been called upon to fill Mark's role at work. His lack of ambition had annoyed April, while David's devotion to his work had irritated Yvonne. It took all sorts.

Before April had fallen ill, Mark had taken advantage of her successes: he had spent her money, had bragged about his clever wife, had become so impossible that April had cried herself to sleep many times. So, having made her own mistakes, April felt she was in no position to pass judgement on anyone. 'What do I do about him out there?' she wailed now.

Yvonne turned round and leant back against the wall, stretching long legs in front of her. 'You give him a kennel. That room off the half-landing will do, the one with a single bed in it. Come on, you do it for dogs. The room's on a different level from your office and your bedroom so he'll soon learn his place. Let him feed himself from your fridge, and he can earn his keep by doing odd jobs and looking after animals. Easy.'

'What? Allow him back into the house?'

'He's potty-trained, isn't he?'

April nodded absently. 'He doesn't want me. He wants my money – Hyacinth's money, too.'

'Then leave him in the caravan.'

159

'I can't.'

'Stalemate,' pronounced Yvonne. Just like me, an inner voice said. David occupied the same house as Yvonne, but they were not together. It was a silly waiting game, an attempt to put up a show for the neighbours, for themselves, for the clinic to which David had returned under a small cloud, where he worked now in a middle-class let's-not-talk-about-it atmosphere. But the community knew, surely. Dr Benson had had his wicked way with Deirdre Mellor, who was pregnant and preparing to go abroad with her husband.

'Are you going to move in with Karam?' asked April.

'Sideways.' Yvonne grinned ruefully. 'We're possibly going to Yorkshire first. She may commute to Liverpool on a weekly basis until . . . until I decide to come back.'

'With David's baby.' This was not a question. 'So, as soon as *Monday's Child* has finished its run, you exit for Yorkshire, where Karam will visit you at weekends. I suppose that's manageable. As long as you don't bloom and blow up, you might get away with all of it.'

'That's the plot.' Yvonne jumped to her feet. 'Speaking of plots, what possessed you to alter *Monday's Child*?'

April chewed absently on a bit of scone. *Monday's Child* was Hyacinth's story. It hadn't started out as that, yet Hyacinth's death had altered things here, there and everywhere. In the play, Alice now had to survive, while the middle sister, a dreadful woman, was . . . 'Has

160

anyone seen Honoria?' The fact was that April still hadn't worked out what to do about either of the horrible middle sisters: the real one was incommunicado, and the paper one was waiting for something or other.

Yvonne raised her shoulders. 'Not as far as I know. Up until a couple of days ago, it was still bandits and binoculars at two o'clock, but—'

'What about food?' Honoria and Hyacinth had always stocked up well, almost well enough to survive war, plague and famine, but surely everything had to run out at some stage? 'I'll perhaps phone Sainsbury's,' she added. 'Hyacinth had an arrangement with one of their Helping Hands.'

Yvonne sighed, decided to give up. No matter what she or anyone else said, April would always worry about other people. She had never become grand, was not typical of that small group of writers labelled successful. She saw to her own family of animals, gave interviews to press, radio and TV, and cleaned up after creatures whose lives had been blighted by contact with humanity. Yvonne had watched April cry after coaxing a terrified dog to take a biscuit, a pat or a drink. 'Why?' April always asked on those occasions, when injured horses and ponies were brought in, when scorched kittens needed expensive veterinary care.

'I've decided,' said April. 'He has to go.'

Yvonne tried to work her way back through her thoughts until she remembered their recent conversation.

'Mark,' continued April. 'I can't lay myself open to that kind of hurt any more.'

'You love him.'

'Exactly. He doesn't deserve me and I deserve something rather better than him.'

Yvonne had to be satisfied with that. Really, April needed someone to live in, just to be on hand if she took one of her funny turns, but if she didn't want Mark then no law stated that she had to let him back into the house.

Velcro strolled in. He was a ginger tom of statuesque proportions, very elegant except for his hangers-on. He had a fondness for sticky plants and was often covered in burrs and leaves of various denominations. Velcro was followed by Vienna, also known as Fast-running Car, then Miss Jones, Rigsby and Veetol. Last in line was Mark Nugent. He knocked lightly on the door before letting himself into his ex-wife's bedroom.

Yvonne, who had suggested that Mark should come in and talk to April, sat down and awaited developments.

April inhaled deeply. 'I thought I told you to carry on waiting in line at the crematorium,' she snapped. 'They're sure to be able to fit you in soon.'

'I'm not dead yet, not quite. I wanted to have a quiet word with you.'

April addressed Yvonne. 'If and when he does drop dead, he'll be doing as he's told for the first time ever.' She returned her attention to her ex-husband. 'That caravan is condemned,' she told him. 'Unfit for animal, vegetable or mineral habitation. And I want you off my property by noon on Friday.'

Mark glanced at Yvonne, clearly expecting a degree of support, but Yvonne picked up Velcro and began to relieve him of his various adhesions.

April folded her arms over a thin cardigan that had seen far better days. 'You're still here.'

Mark turned on his heel and stamped down the stairs

'There'll be an injunction, so mind you get out in good time,' April yelled after him.

'You'll finish up a lonely old woman,' he called back. 'And who's going to look after you?'

'That's for me to know.' April turned to Yvonne. 'Close the door, please.'

Yvonne complied, then reclaimed her seat.

'Don't say a word,' April told her. Her legs ached and she had shooting pains all over the place. MS had taken up the starring role again but, after so many days in bed, she knew she had to get up and about to prevent the wasting of muscle. Sometimes, when she was at her lowest, April had to steel herself to fight back. She could not permit the illness to reign, though: even if, or when, mobility became impossible, she intended to stay on top in the head department, at least.

Yvonne closed her eyes. There were occasions when she couldn't look at this woman. Newspapers crowed every day about exceptional deeds that truly deserved praise. But the unseen and unsung, the Aprils of this world, carried on climbing Everest and K2 behind closed doors, with few witnesses, little encouragement.

'Well, I've had enough of this lark,' said April. 'I'm getting out of jail today if it takes a crowbar and a rasp. Serving wench, bring me my suit of armour.'

The two women struggled until April was wrapped and ready, whereupon she declared that she intended to get down to the business of Honoria. The woman had been locked away in Cavendish Mansions for some considerable time. Binoculars had been spotted, though not within the last couple of days.

The stairs were not easy. Yvonne led, while April descended in a sitting position. By the time they reached the hallway, April was sweaty and pink. Dogs and cats homed in on her, each animal vying for attendance and love. 'Not half as much trouble as humans,' she told them, as she tried to detach herself from a motley collection of limbs, tongues and tails.

After a quick drink of ice-cold lemonade, the women got into Yvonne's car and set off for Beech Gardens, a drive of just a few hundred yards. Outside the Bensons' house, they parked, turned in their seats and looked up at Honoria's flat. All windows were closed and there was no sign of movement. 'Oh, my God,' mumbled April. 'If she's dead . . .' She could think of no sensible end to the sentence.

Yvonne pondered. 'I'm going to get Gill.' She waved in the direction of her own front door. 'She still has a key to Honoria's place.' There was very little for Yvonne to do in her own house, these days. Gill Collins had arrived, had seen, had conquered. Gill and dirt were not on speaking terms: the house sparkled and she was happy. Like David, she believed in sterilizing everything, right down to the last tuft of carpet. 'We've even got a steam-cleaner now. David and Gill have waxed lyrical for days. It defrosts freezers, cleans windows, tiles, ovens. It even gets wallpaper off.'

'Does it mend marriages?'

'No, but it has a powerful iron attached, so it might flatten a few of the creases.' She went to fetch Gill.

April closed her eyes and prayed for patience. The attack had left her more drained than previous episodes, some of which had kept her in bed for longer. Will-power, she insisted. Will-power, patience and love for her fellow creatures would win. Wouldn't they? For how long, though? 'Stop it,' she hissed. 'Stop thinking about the flaming MS. That's what it wants – attention.'

'Greetings, April.'

She didn't bother to raise her eyelids. 'Just go away, PP.'

Like many who consider themselves great, Phillp Pointer did not hear April's command. 'I just wondered about this new ending of yours. How will it affect the present script? Shall we all be ready by October?'

April opened one eye. 'Does it matter? It's a soliloquy delivered by the oldest Alice – me, in other words. It affects no one else.' Waiting until October might well affect Yvonne, though, who would be over four months pregnant. Still, clever clothes might do the trick. And, anyway, what did it matter? As far as April was concerned, *Monday's Child* could keep for a year or more if necessary.

He spluttered, pushed his head further into the Range Rover. 'Of course it matters. We have our audience to consider, our cast. Many have holiday arrangements later in the year. The whole thing could be called off.'

She considered him, ran an eye over his upper body. This was the biggest fool since Oliver Hardy, a large-faced buffoon of a man whose features advertised self-indulgence and a petulant, resentful nature. 'Philip?'

'Yes?'

'Did you know there's a big hole in the atmosphere? Ice caps are melting. Children near Chernobyl are dying of leukaemia and thyroid cancer, others are locked in orphanages. But none of that matters as long as you get to walk about with your chalk and your measuring tape. Take yourself off, dear heart.'

He processed the information, deciding in the end that rumours about authors being mad were not without foundation. After all, he had asked a civil question, made a comment, no more than that. 'I'll – I'll bid you good afternoon, then.' He stalked off towards his house, head shaking slowly as he considered the vagaries of human nature.

Gill and Yvonne arrived. 'Was that the maestro?' Yvonne asked. 'Twitching, too?'

'Don't ask,' pleaded April. 'Just go and find

that dreadful woman. She could be in a coma, dead, whatever.'

Yvonne and Gill crossed to the corner. Gill had an outer key, which overrode the voice-activated door locks. She and Yvonne entered the smart foyer and let themselves into the lift. As they ascended, Gill grew fidgety. 'I've never seen a dead body,' she volunteered.

'I have.'

Gill fiddled with her key ring. 'Yes, but you're a nurse.'

Yvonne touched the woman's arm, felt the tension. 'I'll go in by myself.'

'The chains might be on. She could be dead in there with the chains on.'

'Police and fire brigade,' offered Yvonne. 'Stop worrying, please.' Oh God. Was she going to be stuck with a horrible dead old woman, a hysterical housekeeper, a childish husband and a playwright who was just coming out of a rather nasty MS attack? And where was Karam when she was needed?

Honoria's door swung freely. For a split second, Yvonne hesitated, then she called Honoria's name. It echoed, came back to her, was clearly her sole companion in the apartment. She searched, went into both bedrooms, both bathrooms, kitchen, living room. Nothing. 'You can come in, Gill,' she called.

Gill entered an inch at a time. 'But she's got to be in. She never goes out, does she?'

A clock chimed, causing both women to jump, after which small shock they giggled nervously. 'Cupboards,' said Gill.

'What would she be doing in a cupboard?'

Gill laughed again. 'No, I mean drawers, wardrobes. See if she's took anything.'

Honoria had taken practically everything. Some heavy wintry garments remained, but most of her summer clothes had disappeared. 'A cruise?' suggested Yvonne.

'Not likely. She said cruises were all plumbers with ten-pound notes hanging out of their back pockets. Too common for her, even if she hadn't had that agora-wotsit. And, like I said, she never goes out. I know I keep on about that, but it's true. All the time I worked here, she stopped in and drove me daft.'

They sat down, Gill twiddling the keys, Yvonne twiddling her hair. 'She's been nothing but trouble ever since I've known her,' said Gill. 'Gave us all a rough ride. She knew everything, how jobs should be done, all that kind of stuff.' She paused. 'And she never liked Hyacinth, told her her poetry was rubbish, stopped her from trying to get it published.'

'Jealousy.'

Gill Collins pondered. 'More than that,' she said softly. 'It was as if she really hated her, as if she wanted . . . I don't know what I mean.'

It was a warm day, but Yvonne shivered. 'Come on,' she said. 'Let's get out of here. I feel as if something with a hundred legs has just walked over my grave.'

Eleven

It was truly terrifying. Often, Honoria had doubted herself, had wondered whether she had actually chosen to stay inside the flat for all those years. But now, standing in Bolton's Nelson Square, her heart was all over the place, while both knees seemed to have turned to jelly. She remembered days when she had tried to get out, when excuses had poured from her like flurries of confetti, each component small and separate, the whole a blinding mass that clouded judgement and took the sharp edge from the firmest resolve. The agoraphobia was real, as was the almost overwhelming panic that now filled her head, chest and throat. But she would overcome it, just as she had overcome many of life's obstacles.

A Delta cab driver had brought her all the way from Blundellsands and was now carrying her luggage into the Pack Horse Hotel. The world was so big, the sky too heavy, the lower atmosphere clogged with traffic fumes. This was supposed to be home, though Honoria found within herself no sense of belonging. In this town Mother, Father, Hyacinth, Honoria and Hilda had shopped, visited theatres, walked in parks. Yet now it was just a town, just another place that didn't matter.

She stepped into the hotel's foyer, saw not much more than a notice board announcing meetings, conferences and other forthcoming events. Terror rendered her almost blind, almost deaf. When the key was in her possession, Honoria ascended a wide, sweeping staircase to her room. The porter accepted her tip and left her to unpack.

It was still terrifying. For the first time in years, she had made a decision and had ventured out alone. There were other people in the hotel, but this lonely beige room with its kettle, sachets of coffee and cream, its *en suite* bathroom and serviceable, comfortable furniture was as anonymous and featureless as she felt within her frightened soul.

She retained no love for Bolton. Her reasons for coming here were still unclear, though she did mean to visit Hilda. Hilda lived in the family home, a large farmhouse that was imposing enough to be a manor. On that score, Honoria's anger had never abated. She and Hyacinth had been ignored apart from a few investments; Hilda, Mother's babe right to the end, had come into the house, its land and all livestock.

'Who will she leave it to?' Honoria asked the blank screen of a large television set. 'She has no children to think of.' So why couldn't

170

Honoria enjoy some of the benefits? Were Hilda to sell up, the sisters might afford a home abroad, somewhere to go in the winter. Many of north Liverpool's genteel poor spent three months of each year in Spain, living quite cheaply in the Med's kinder climate, enduring British weather only at its most acceptable.

She sighed, sat down in a rather firm chair. The bit of Bolton she could see had been hacked about. A perfectly serviceable building that had once housed education offices had been eradicated, a faceless red-brick pile standing in its place. A bespoke tailor's had disappeared, though the underground toilets remained in evidence and the Lido cinema seemed to have survived the nationwide cull. She heard the town-hall clock, mellow as ever, sending its gentle tones across the town it had supervised for so many years. Until today, her only recent sightings of Bolton's famous timepiece had happened before or during *Coronation Street*, when titles appeared or when half-time advertisements threatened to interrupt the show.

Honoria rose, picked up a document case and placed herself at a small desk where crested notepaper sat next to top-quality envelopes. Yes, she would be writing a letter or two, but first she had a more important task to undertake. She opened the case and removed several bundles of paper. Taking up a large cardboard file, she wrote on its pristine exterior THE WORKS OF MISS HONORIA WEST. She liked the Miss. It afforded her an air of difference, of quality, since it supported the notion that the author had given up every opportunity and every waking moment to the perfecting of her art. She would show them. Oh, yes, she would show them all.

Two hours later, with the task of sorting papers and notebooks barely started, Honoria let herself out of her room and walked downstairs. The tranquillizers had made her listless, but lack of energy was preferable to panic. Some inner voice urged her on, forced her to walk through her own history, as if she sought some particular time or location. Perhaps she had programmed herself to do the work here, where her roots were supposedly deepest.

Preston's Jewellers was still there, as was the Yates' Wine Lodge, Marks & Spencer, the ancient pasty shop. An Arndale Centre had sprung up like a hitherto dormant volcano, with concrete car-park and closed-in shops that depended too much on strip-lighting and air-conditioning: little bakeries, news-stands, boutiques, cute places full of candles, pot-pourri and baubles, disposable monuments to the quick-fix, throw-away final decade of the century.

She sat on a bench near some high empty birdcages, brainchild of whoever had designed this noisy place. What had happened to the birds? Why was that old man staring at the floor? Ah, he was looking for cigarette ends. Clearly, the living conditions of tramps had improved.

Why the disappointment? Surely she didn't care? A woman who had turned her back so firmly against the world should not concern herself with the follies of others. But she remembered, almost wistfully, an ice-cream place, bacon shops, coffee-houses where Brazil and Kenya had hung in the air, aromatic promises of joys to come once beans had been mixed and ground. Progress equalled subtraction, even destruction.

She walked on, covering more ground than she had trod in years. The Market Hall had retained its roof, but E Quality Sweets had long gone, as had the man who guessed weight for threepence and repaid in full if his estimate was too far out. Glass lifts floated up and down. Honoria felt unsafe on the slick floor.

Outside again, she breathed gratefully, cast a scathing eye over McDonald's, looked at the fountains on the town-hall square. This was a truly beautiful spot, marred only by chunks of stone set around tiled areas where water did not flow. But the lions remained, still proud, still couchant, one at each side of huge double doors. 'Daddy, take me up the steps,' Hilda had begged. Baby and Hyacinth had gone up with Father, while Honoria, scarcely acknowledged by her male parent, had sat at the bottom, waiting, waiting.

Nobody noticed her, ever. She rested now on a bench, watched the world go by, listened to an accent she had not heard for some considerable time. No one looked at her; nothing had changed. Why had she never asked to be taken up the steps, or to the park, or to the fair?

She wandered into W. H. Smith's, bought

pens, highlighters, paperclips. The editing of the work promised to involve a great deal of paraphernalia. Members of staff found what she needed, took her to the front of the queue, offered her every conceivable assistance when she admitted that this was her first shopping expedition in years. In British Home Stores, she found a nice cardigan and a blouse, was beginning to enjoy herself. What a bore agoraphobia had been, choosing clothes and shoes from catalogues or, occasionally, having a selection sent round from local stores.

Ambling along Deansgate, Honoria discovered a smaller bookshop. Sweetens carried a selection of slender volumes produced by local writers, histories of mills, of the workhouse, biographies written by a carpenter, a miner, a cotton worker. As she reached for Norman Kenyon's *I Belong to Bolton*, something caught her eye. With one hand frozen mid-air, she staggered back, catching her hip on a corner of the counter.

'Are you all right?' asked the shop's owner.

Honoria could not speak.

'Would you like a chair?'

It was there as plain as day, prominently placed above all other works by Lancastrian writers.

Sandra Heilberg fetched a chair and pulled Honoria on to it and thrust a glass of water into her hand.

Honoria took a sip. 'When was that published?' Her voice was squeaky, not at all its usual strident self.

Sandra followed the direction in which

174

Honoria's shaky index finger pointed. 'Last year,' she replied. 'We've sold several hundred copies. It's a good read, full of humour. The author died quite recently.'

Honoria stared at *Home From Home*, subtitled *Reflections on a Bolton Childhood*, by Hyacinth West. 'Is it poetry?' she asked eventually.

'It's a mix,' Sandra replied. 'Poetry, prose – and there's a section called "Conversations". I understand that a large publishing firm had expressed an interest in Hyacinth West.'

How? When? Honoria wondered. There had been no extra post, no suspicious parcels, no ... There had been April Nugent. For hours on end, April and Hyacinth had shut themselves inside Hyacinth's room, chatting, laughing, making light of their impaired mobility. Like sisters they had been, inseparable, each interested in the written word, the younger woman wildly successful, the elder unremarkable. April had probably been involved in Hyacinth's project.

'Would you like a copy?' the young shopkeeper asked.

Honoria nodded. 'And a taxi to take me back to the Pack Horse.' Even in death, Hyacinth continued to win. Even in death, Honoria's sister shone.

'Are you sure you'll be all right on your own?'

'Yes, thank you.'

She arrived back at the hotel, sent for tea and sandwiches, then opened her sister's book. It was dedicated to April Nugent, a very dear friend. Honoria squared her shoulders, read some poems, a piece about growing up on the farm.

The 'Conversations' section was interesting enough to make Honoria gasp. How clever, she thought. The truth, not the whole truth – oh, no – nothing like the full truth. And yet how little Hyacinth had really known. Right to the end, languishing in her pink gowns and fluffy slippers, Honoria's older sibling had remained blissfully unaware of a reality that was so radical, so mind-boggling . . . 'Silly old beggar.' Honoria threw the book across her room. 'I can do better than that.'

She spent the early evening doing better, then watched *Coronation Street* and a Bruce Willis film on cable. The hero ran about in a bloodied vest, a Lone Ranger in a terrorized tower block. He was always going to win, because he was Bruce Willis and the baddies sported good clothes and foreign accents.

She picked up the phone, dialled.

'Hello?'

'It's Honoria.' She heard Hilda's sharp intake of air. 'I'm in Bolton doing a bit of research.'

'Research?'

'For a book I intend to write.' Hollow seconds boomed past Honoria's ear. 'I'd like to visit you.'

Hilda pulled herself together. 'Right. Just call me when you're coming so that I'll make sure I stay in.'

Honoria sniffed. 'I'll be sure to warn you, Hilda.' She replaced the receiver, retrieved Hyacinth's writings from the corner.

Where is my father? asked the child
I've searched over moor and brushland wild
I've called out his name til my voice ran dry
And I've screamed my heart up into the sky.
Where is my father? she cried again
Did he leave me alone to suffer in pain?
Your father is gone, the mother replied
Like Grandma and Grandpa, your daddy has
*   died.*
But no, sobbed the child, that cannot be right
He promised to be here to chase away night
To save me from goblins and devils so wild
He never would leave me, his own special child.
The mother looked out across acres of land
Remembered the day when he'd asked for her
*   hand.*
The laughter, the loving, the children who came
To sit at his table, to borrow his name.
Who smote him so cruelly? The answer was clear
But unspoken. The killer was standing too
*   near . . .*

Honoria grinned. Sentimental slop, meaningless rubbish. So Hyacinth had found the
courage to seek publication in spite of her
advice. No doubt April Nugent had used
her influence, because poetry as pathetic as this
needed a little help. The prose was better. The
author betrayed an eye for detail, a marked
ability to describe people and places. 'But I shall
leave you at the bus stop,' Honoria promised
the dead woman. 'The world has seen nothing
yet.'

She took a pack of bond picked up in Smith's,

a common enough type of paper and envelopes. These letters would be posted in Manchester, Bury, Blackburn, hand slightly disguised, surgical gloves precluding fingerprints. Recipients would guess the identity of the writer, no doubt, but who cared? She had been treated badly and would strike back.

First, she acquainted Sefton Police with her near-certainty that one April Nugent was cultivating and harvesting cannabis, nominally for her own use, probably for the benefit of anyone with the price of an eighth. The RSPCA was invited to call, just to make sure that the drug addict's dogs, cats and myriad other creatures were enjoying an adequate level of comfort.

After this enjoyable exercise, Honoria opened her mini-bar and treated herself to a tiny bottle of champagne and a small carton of orange juice. Armed with the Buck's Fizz, she selected her next victim. She could look up the address later, but she carried on doing her duty, informing the University of Liverpool that one of its younger stars, a lecturer in art history, had broken up a perfectly good marriage by persuading the female half to indulge in unnatural practices, commonly known as lesbianism. Deirdre had her uses after all, Honoria admitted silently. Invited in for coffee, the little slut had opened up to her hostess, had spoken of her own troubles and of David Benson's deviant wife. So that was another little job well done.

She then complained to the Hall Road Clinic,

suggesting that not too many patients would be happy to receive treatment from an adulterer whose wife was a practising lesbian and a registered nurse. In the same letter, she advised the institution that Deirdre Mellor, their receptionist, had indulged her fleshy needs with the above-mentioned medical person. Everyone knew the details already, but the written word carried weight.

Paul Mellor, Deirdre's husband, had worked for a Crosby estate agent, so Honoria wrote to him at his office. He was rumoured to be going to work abroad soon with his loud, over-painted wife, the adulterous subject of Honoria's earlier letter, but he would get this message eventually.

Honoria paused, tapped her teeth with the pen. She could not post all the letters at once, but she intended to stay away for some weeks, so she would space them. Let the fools prosecute anyway, she thought defiantly. This wasn't blackmail, as she was not demanding money. And, of course, unlike Hyacinth, she was willing nothing but the truth.

Philip Pointer was an easy victim. For almost a decade, Honoria had kept both eyes on him, especially after the hours of darkness, his preferred time for sinning. Pointer liked young men, the younger the better. The pattern was so tried and tested that countless pairs of boots, shoes and trainers must have worn down the driveway to his ill-kept house. Sometimes a young man would arrive alone; often, Pointer fetched home from the pub whatever he had managed to gather. After five minutes, during which span an amount of alcohol was probably consumed downstairs, the bedroom light would come on. This event was followed by what Honoria termed 'the ceremony of the drapes', the closing of which was always performed by Pointer himself. Lights out followed, then Pointer's partner for the evening left the premises within half an hour. So droll, so infantile. Pointer would shrivel when he learnt that his cover had been blown.

She dropped a line to Dr Benson, who had been quite nasty to her of late. What sort of man lost his wife to another woman? Was he impotent, boring, inadequate? She enjoyed this one. Let him accuse her of writing anonymously – she would deny her involvement to the last ditch.

Yvonne came next. Honoria chewed her pen, indulged her jealous hatred for this young woman with her waist-length light-brown hair, clear blue eyes, flawless skin and near-perfect figure. What the hell was she doing with Karam Laczynska? Karam was striking, of course, creamy complexion, huge dark-grey eyes. But why would the wife of a well-set-up doctor choose to associate with a woman of any description?

She wrote to both, signing herself Concerned Christian. The rest, the supporting cast, she would deal with tomorrow.

That night, Honoria slept the sleep of the just. She had done her duty, had raised her neighbours' awareness of their faults. All that remained now was the task of taking Hyacinth's unpublished work, remoulding it, making it her own.

TWELVE

Hilda West had never needed much in life. The fact that she was a wealthy woman scarcely occurred to her. She lived quietly and simply at Moortop, dedicating her time to running the farm, caring for her workforce and baking, the last occupation being the area in which she had made her personal fortune.

Quite by accident, Hilda had discovered that an ability she took for granted was a saleable service. Few knew of her success, as she conducted her second business discreetly and with the assistance of dedicated managers. She had never told Honoria about Parkside Bakeries, though Hyacinth had been informed. Honoria differed from other people. She had a mean streak, a side to her character that rendered her resentful of others' successes.

Hilda stood now by the huge kitchen fireplace, her face smudged with flour, hands busy poking skewers into her latest experiment. She was the inventor, the one who slaved happily for two days a week in the privacy of her own home, ingredients spread to the four corners of the table, copious notes scattered all over the dresser, a permanent frown creasing her forehead. If something worked it went into production, while failures often formed the basis of her own diet, or the swill for her pigs, depending on the seriousness of the disaster.

Hilda, now in her later sixties, carefully maintained the blonde hair with which she had originally been blessed. These days, a hairdresser coloured her abundant locks, low-lighting, high-lighting and, as Hilda put it, painting by numbers the basically silver mop. Sparkling blue eyes had begun to need spectacles part-time, and her face, though lined by life's joys and sorrows, was still lovely.

The cakes were cooked. She tipped them on to cooling racks and placed herself on a chair while she studied them. Would individual pineapple upside-downers feature on next year's stock list? Time would tell.

She glanced at the clock, thought about Honoria. What was she up to this time? Researching? Hyacinth had been the writer, God rest her. Like Hilda, Hyacinth had kept much of her business out of Honoria's reach. Poor Hyacinth. As the eldest, she had felt bound to live with Honoria, to keep her company, to make sure that she steered clear of trouble. Maintaining personal space in which to write and negotiate with publishers must have been a mammoth task for Hyacinth.

Hilda sighed, pushed a tress of hair off her face. Honoria and trouble were like salt and pepper, inseparable, natural partners. But no, Hilda would not brood. She jumped up, started to tidy away the mess. Leo would be here soon. Hilda's heart leapt in her breast. Single into her seventh decade, she was in love, and as silly as any young girl on her way to the altar.

'Don't think about Honoria,' she muttered to herself as she cleared away the debris. 'It's at least three weeks since she phoned, and there's no sign of her.' But she could not help wondering, with a degree of trepidation, what Honoria had been doing for the best part of a month. She never travelled, seldom left her flat. What had brought her so far east? Agoraphobics did not recover overnight as a rule.

When the telephone's ring cut through the balmy morning, Hilda almost collapsed from shock. Her whole body had been tense ever since Honoria's one and only call. Expecting Honoria had become a full-time job, an occupation that sapped energy and made nerves tighten. She dried her hands and picked up the receiver. 'Hello?' Her voice was tremulous.

'Hilda?'

It wasn't Honoria. 'Yes. Hilda West speaking.' She sank into a grateful heap on a kitchen chair. 'Who's that?'

'It's April Nugent – Hyacinth's friend.'

Hilda found herself smiling. 'April. I wanted

to call you, mainly to thank you for your kindness to Hyacinth, but I seem to have mislaid
your number. How are you?' She waited. 'April?'

'I'm still here, just about. Er . . . have you any
idea of Honoria's whereabouts?'

Honoria. Of course, everything came down to
Honoria in the end. 'She was staying at the Pack
Horse in Bolton. But she rang me only once,
just over three weeks ago.' She paused, ex
perienced a degree of dread before asking,
'Why?'

'Letters.'

Oh, no, not again. 'I'm sorry.'

'It's not your fault,' came April's quick reply.
'Most of us took no notice. I had a wrist-slapping
from the boys in blue about growing my own
medication, but it was no problem.'

Hilda swallowed. 'Who else got them?'

'Just about everybody who knew her.
Fortunately, a few of us got together and had a
good laugh.'

April wasn't laughing now, though In spite
of the distance between them, Hilda could
sense the woman's sorrow. 'Are you still managing to get out and about?' she asked.

'Oh, yes. Usually walking round in circles, but
I get there in the end. Visited Mother yesterday.
She's still not making a lot of sense, poor soul.
But they look after her in the home. She
scarcely knows me.'

After this babbled speech, there followed a
measurable pause. Hilda, made acutely sensitive
by April's discomfort and by her own fear of
Honoria, spoke up. 'April?' she ventured.

'I'm still here, which is more than can be said for poor Philip Pointer. He hanged himself.'

Hilda gasped, searched for words. An icy hand seemed to have clutched her heart. 'Did he – did he get a letter?'

'None was found.' April cleared her throat. 'Knowing PP, he probably destroyed it. There's no doubt in my mind that he received one, though. He was a particularly vulnerable man, tough as old boots on the outside, frightened to pieces underneath. He was a homosexual born in an age when he would not have been acceptable. The man was too scared to take a live-in lover, so he indulged in one-night stands. She must have noticed.'

Beads of chilled sweat poured down Hilda's face. 'So she killed him.' This was not a question.

'Her behaviour did.'

Hilda could not separate essence from behaviour. A person's deeds spoke up for him or her, said more than words, in fact. 'How did Hyacinth manage all those years?' she asked.

'I think her presence kept Honoria from stepping over the edge. The agoraphobia helped, too, because at least Honoria was contained. This going out worries me. If she can drive a man to suicide by remote control, what will she manage if she's out and about?'

Hilda didn't want to think about that. The telephone receiver felt liquid, as if the dreadful news had begun to melt it. 'Have you had the funeral?'

'Yes, he was buried last week.'

'This is terrible.' Hilda was trembling. 'There are other things, you see, things Hyacinth would not talk about to me. Honoria was naughty as a child, too. Do you know any details?'

'No,' lied April. 'Look, I just wanted to see if Honoria was staying with you.' There followed another pause. 'We haven't shown the police our letters. Really, I can't see the point of trying to prosecute her as none of the letters demanded money or threatened violence. Also, although we tried to see the funny side, some of the accusations were nasty. The fewer who saw the letters the better – or so we decided.'

'I see.' Hilda saw, all right. She saw that she had a despicable sister who enjoyed causing pain, a nasty creature with a marked tendency to home in on people's weaknesses. 'Do you want me to find her?'

April laughed, though there was no mirth in the sound she made. 'Losing her would be infinitely preferable,' she replied 'I just don't like not knowing where she is. It's a bit like having a ground-to-air missile on the loose – we know what it is and what it's capable of, but we've no idea where the hell it's hiding.'

Hilda agreed, though she offered no comment.

'What did she say when she phoned you?'

'That she was researching, writing something or other.'

'Poison-pen letters,' said April drily. 'But if she is writing something other than these letters, she's trying to steal Hyacinth's thunder even now.'

187

'Shall I phone the Pack Horse?'

'Leave it, Hilda.' April suddenly sounded weary. 'Just let me know if and when she turns up. And . . . oh, tell her that Philip's dead. Other than that, save your sanity and ignore her.'

Hilda sat with the phone in her hand, trying to remember, her mind flitting about like a butterfly, then landing in places that afforded no comfort. Mother crying. Father in a coffin in the second drawing room, curtains closed. Hyacinth weeping, Honoria dry-eyed, almost triumphant.

The door opened. 'Hilda?'

She dropped the phone and ran to him. 'Leo,' she cried.

'Whatever's the matter?' She looked so pale, so afraid.

'It's Honoria,' she said quietly. 'She's behaving badly again.'

Leo Stoneway folded his arms around the woman he loved. 'There, there,' he said. 'She was always the same. Don't upset yourself. Has she been here?'

Hilda shook her head against his shoulder. 'She made a man hang himself, Leo. She drove him to the point where his life was not worth living.'

'Good God.' He patted her hair, felt his heart lurch in his chest. 'She's beyond all human understanding, I'm sure.' He thought for a moment. 'Look, if and when she does come, I shall be ready for her.' Oh, yes, Honoria was well capable of pushing a human into the abyss. God forbid that she should lift a hand to Hilda, her sole remaining relative.

They separated and sat in ancient rocking chairs, one at each side of the kitchen range. Hilda rocked herself slowly, like a mother trying to soothe an ailing child. The child lived and grew within Hilda's heart, herself as an infant, a girl, a young adult. Dark silences, Father with his mouth set in a permanent line, his brow furrowed, thunderclouds gathering in this very house. Mother fluttering, then growing stronger, always, always watching Honoria. 'Why can't I remember?' she asked, for the hundredth time.

'Sometimes memory is mercifully selective,' he answered. Yet he needed her to remember, willed her to search her past for an answer to a question he could not even put into words.

Hilda stopped rocking. 'It was almost as if Father kept Honoria under his thumb, though he said little. She feared him, I think. After his death, Honoria seemed happier.'

Leo glanced at his watch. If the woman arrived at the farm, he wanted to be here. 'I've some business to attend to,' he said. 'Then I shall go home and fetch clothes and so forth. We are too old, I think, to worry about what the neighbours or the farm workers might think. And, of course, we're not blessed with an Honoria, binoculars and notebooks.'

'But—'

'You must not be alone.'

Oh, how she loved him. He was a tall, imposing man with well-trimmed whiskers and beautiful, understated clothes. She could not imagine what he saw in her, as she was no more than an ordinary woman who could cook and keep a farm ticking over. 'What would I do without you?'

He twinkled at her. 'Hopefully, you won't find the answer to that for many years.'

Hilda found herself blushing, felt ridiculous, blushed all the more. He had sought her out after years of pen-friendship, had travelled all the way from South Africa just to be with her. 'Did you ever read *Little Women*?' she asked him now.

'No.'

'The boy next door married the sister of the girl he really wanted. I always felt very sad about that, because second best is seldom good enough.'

'You're not second best, Hilda. This is a different time and we have changed, both of us.'

'But, Leo—'

'I love you now. Now is all that matters.'

Hilda fell silent.

Long ago, when he had been Lawrence Beresford, a member of the West family had changed his life suddenly, radically and cruelly. 'Yes, I loved your sister,' he said. He thanked God that Hyacinth had given her blessing to him and to Hilda just weeks before her death. Hyacinth had always been a giver, never a taker. In the end, he had attended her funeral. Beyond that, he had been able to do nothing for the love of his young life. 'And now, as I keep repeating, you are the one I love. You and Hyacinth were blessed with the same sweet nature.'

'And Honoria was one on her own,' added Hilda.

'Oh, yes,' he said pensively. 'She most certainly was.'

Honoria had almost ruined him, had driven him to change his name and his job, had caused him to flee the country. 'Perhaps I should have stood up to her.'

'She was too clever, even for you.'

He agreed. Honoria was a viper, an unpredictable creature who pounced, devoured, crept away. Age had not wearied her, then, had not made her mellow.

Never mind, he told himself. Here, with this third daughter of the Wests, he would be happy. He loved the farm, cherished Hilda with a passion he had not thought possible at this stage in his life. She was twenty-four-carat gold right through to the core, just as Hyacinth had been.

He laughed drily. 'Leo Stoneway, once Lawrence Beresford, fiancé of Hyacinth, victim of Honoria, is now engaged to marry the third sister. I suppose this could appear droll to an outsider.'

'Leo?'

His eyes were closed. So lithe, Hyacinth had been, strong as a young sapling, bending but never snapping in the wind. She had danced across fields and into his heart, had screamed at the sky, so carefree, so fresh. In the end, he had abandoned her, had fled from her sister, had run like a coward. Honoria's cuts had gone deep and he had not recovered his equilibrium for years.

Hyacinth was in another dimension now, had gone on into an existence where time and space did not feature. Yet she was telling him something, was calling him in the night, pleading, begging . . . He opened his eyes. 'Tell me the little you do remember,' he asked again.

Hilda shook her head. Leo had asked these questions so many times. 'We were happy till Father died. Mother was ill, but she got better quite quickly. She was always watching Honoria. They scarcely spoke two civil words to one another.'

He waited patiently, hoped that she would say something new. Pieces were missing from his life, as if his picture had never been completed. Jigsaws were easy – one either found the piece or lost it, but the master was usually printed on the lid of the box. He had no whole to which he might refer.

'After Honoria accused you and some time after you left, Hyacinth had her breakdown. Mother put her in a sanatorium for several months. When her health improved, Hyacinth sent me what she called her decorated poems. They are so pretty, with those watercolour flowers painted around the edges.' With eyes blurred by tears, she looked at the framed poems on her kitchen wall.

'And when she came home?'

'She was quiet, rather sad.'

Again, he closed his eyes. In the darkness

behind the lids, he was chipping away at his memory, rooting about like a miner seeking gems in the blackest, smallest recess of a pit. There was something out there, something now, not just a beautiful being who had recently passed on into eternity.

'What are you thinking?' she asked.

'I was thinking about my diamond mine in South Africa,' he replied truthfully. Honoria had the answer. With a blinding certainty, Leo suddenly saw that. She was a sly, secretive sort, who kept things well hidden under her hat until such time as she could capitalize on her knowledge. The woman had all the answers, while he could not even guess the questions. 'She'll come here soon,' he predicted.

'And she may recognize you when she arrives. At the funeral we gave her too little time.'

'It doesn't matter,' he answered. 'Let her know who I am, because it's all water under a million bridges.'

Hilda was tired. She had been baking on a day that was too hot for kitchen work, had sawed away at pineapples, fiddled with cherries, spilt sugar, had learnt that April's friend had taken his life.

Leo stood up. He walked to her side, dropped a kiss on her head. 'I'm off to the bank, but I shall see you soon.'

She went to the window and watched as he drove away. Something was bothering him, but he could not place a finger on it. Leo was searching for something he had not even managed to identify.

193

Hilda West pulled herself together. There were dishes to be washed and cakes to be tasted. And Leo would be back soon.

Thirteen

The death of Philip Pointer delivered a blow to the community. He was missed by shopkeepers, clergymen, road-sweepers, mothers and children. There had been something about this grizzly bear of a man, a quality rarely found in an age when people measured themselves by the size of their car's engine, the value of their house, their job title. He had been an exception, an oddity in an age of conformity, predictability and blind, ruthless ambition.

In his will, Philip had left five thousand pounds to the St Thomas's Amateur Dramatic Society, the rest of his bank balance to AIDS charities, and his house, a substantial if rather neglected modern detached, to a young man called Kevin. The older residents of Blundellsands were somewhat bemused by the contents of PP's will – many had never encountered homosexuality before. If it did exist, its place of abode could not possibly be in this elegant if rather crumbly part of north Liverpool. It was bad enough to know that the borough of Sefton now included areas that were not quite up to scratch; the realization that the so-called decadence of modern society had encroached on their enclosed and double-glazed porches was shocking indeed.

But, as was ever the way with Blundellsanders, they got used to the knowledge, many even admitting that they missed the blundering old fool with his Dr Who scarves, his fedora and his silly capes. Schoolchildren had taunted him, but he had never minded. Whatever else Philip Pointer had been, his faith had remained unquestionable. He was laid to rest among other good Catholics within the bounds of St Thomas's churchyard, sins forgiven, weaknesses accepted.

April sat on a cold concrete step and gazed out at the river. She was troubled, unnerved by Philip's death, realizing how fond she had been of him. Things would never be the same. She closed her eyes and pictured him strutting about the stage in the hall, metal tape measure retracting noisily into its housing, chalked crosses appearing on the boards, purple for one character, green for another. Hero and heroine had always been white and yellow. When colours had got scuffed together, no one would stand in the resulting turquoises and oranges, the cast members taking their opportunity to mock their director's foolishness. But April would miss the arguments, the battles of two opposing wills, the sheer dedication he had brought to his task.

Karam, who was walking with Yvonne on the

sand, paused to look at April, read her thoughts. 'She's remembering him.'

'We all are,' answered Yvonne, who was having trouble with a long leash. At the end of many yards of red webbing, a dog called Stinker dug about among decayed jellyfish and streaks of oil. No one would walk Stinker on a normal lead; his name had been chosen for reasons that became only too obvious in confined spaces or within sniffing distance in the open air.

'Wind him in a bit,' advised Karam. 'He's getting into an even filthier state than usual.'

April looked at the two young women. Philip had been different; Karam was different, too. Karam Laczynska was special. Now, with all Honoria's vicious letters laid out for their recipients to share, Karam's lesbianism was common knowledge. Oh, well. The tide would turn shortly, would erase foot- and pawprints, sending its waters to lap at the very steps upon which April lingered. Out there, near the river's edge, two people struggled with thoughts, consciences and with a dog whose behaviour would not invite many offers of adoption. 'Three displaced persons,' April muttered softly. 'Let's just hope for the best on all fronts.'

The weather over Wales looked a bit grim. Karam and Yvonne were staring at Stinker, scarcely talking to one another. The dog had found yet another dead creature to roll in. April simply allowed life to pass by while she prayed for Philip and blocked out all thoughts of Honoria West.

'You could have told me.' Yvonne dragged

197

Stinker away from a piece of glass.

'I saw no need.' Karam found herself concentrating on the outlines of North Wales's hills. 'Does it make a difference?'

Yvonne shrugged.

'Well? Does it make a difference? Say something.'

'Perhaps I feel that you didn't trust me enough to tell me the truth.'

'I told you no lies.'

'Not the point, though, is it? I mean, there I was, pouring out all my pathetic little troubles, and you said not a word about your own predicament.'

Karam raised her eyebrows. 'Predicament? I'm in no difficulty, Yvonne. I accept myself – my family, too, loves me. Being gay does not imply trouble.'

Yvonne almost flinched. 'I'm sorry. I didn't mean to sound patronizing. But I—'

'But you're worried about being classified through association?'

'What?'

'Everyone will assume that you, too, are a lesbian.' Karam shaded her eyes against a ray of sun and wished that she could shield her heart as easily. 'Don't worry,' she added, almost snappily. 'We'll tell everyone that you still bat for the main team.'

Yvonne turned and stumbled through uneven sand, grabbing a plastic bottle from Stinker's mouth before he could begin to chew at it. She paused, looked at April on the steps, felt Karam's eyes on her own back. 'I care about

both these women,' she told a bemused Stinker.
'I even love them. But surely . . . ?'

Stinker, deprived of his bottle, scratched an
ear. Too old and ugly to be lovable, he had been
thrown from a car on the M62 and had landed
on his feet in more ways than one: he was fed,
warm and grateful. He woofed at Yvonne and
picked up a gull feather.

'She doesn't care for me in that way. Does
she?'

He spat out the feather, sat still and waited to
be walked home.

Yvonne pondered. Why should she assume
that Karam wanted any more than friendship?
Heterosexual women and men could go miles
and years without happening upon a potential
partner. Why presume that the case should be
any different for gays? Anger stirred. Beneath
the small bubble of fury, Yvonne's famous
stubborn streak drew a fine line. Karam
was her friend, would remain her friend. The
world could think and say exactly what it
liked.

'Yvonne?'

She spun round. 'I'm thinking.'

Karam noticed the set jaw, the fingers
clenched on the lead's reel. 'I'm still myself,'
she said.

Yvonne shortened Stinker's tether before
speaking. 'I know that. And I'm still myself, too.
Look, I don't want to be . . . to be explained.
Even to family.' Especially to a certain member
of Karam's clan, that dark, brooding brother
with his paperbacks and his dirty looks. 'If any-

one wants questions answered, let him or her come to me.'

'What about your husband?'

'One size fits all,' answered Yvonne smartly. 'I'm too angry to care. I know Honoria should be the real target for my bad temper, but I feel too . . . adult to be asked about my sexuality. Anyway, stuff like that's personal, isn't it?'

'Integral, I'd say.'

'Exactly. Look, if I'd turned to a man for comfort, there might have been a nine-day wonder, everybody going on about me and who-ever. But it would have been accepted pretty damned sharpish. Let them gossip, Karam. We know who we are and what we're about.'

Karam knew, all right. The woman she loved was out of reach, could not be dragged home with Stinker. Over the years, Karam had become sufficiently pragmatic to accept that most women were not heading in her direction. She tried not to let it matter but, sometimes, her heart and head took widely differing routes. 'Are you sure? Isn't life hard enough already? Pregnant, separated – oh, come on, Yvonne. Perhaps we should tell just a few people, the nearest and—'

'No.' There was vehemence in the word. 'I insist.' She wasn't certain why she was so sure, but it was probably something to do with loyalty. No, it wasn't quite that: this was a matter of principle. Yvonne didn't want to go into a labelled box. No, she wanted to remain in the 'assorted' pile, the clump of humanity whose secrets were often deliberately impenetrable.

Yet if society wanted to exclude her, she would cope. 'We go to Horsefield together, Karam. I'll be glad of the break and I'm sure you need a change, too.'

'But—'

'Exactly. But. Not one word to anyone, Karam. Not even Sebastian.' Especially not Sebastian. Let him sit in silent judgement till doomsday, Yvonne said inwardly. 'Agreed?'

Karam lowered her chin. 'OK. And take no notice of him. I adore my brother, but he's always been a bit pensive.'

'A change from weird, at least.'

'It's a weird kind of pensive.'

'Shut up, Karam. Let's go home.'

The gathering in the kitchen of Jasmine Cottage was a sober one. Occasionally, in an effort to lighten the mood, someone offered a feeble quip, but such attempts died quickly, for lack of nourishment.

Sebastian Laczynski was ensconced near the fireplace, elbows balanced on the arms of an Ercol, eyes fixed on a dog-eared paperback. He had not known Philip Pointer so he had nothing to add to the sporadic bursts of conversation, yet he stayed where he was as if he had been planted, watered and nurtured like a pot of geraniums.

Yvonne, who sat opposite the man she now termed Dark Master, tried hard to ignore his presence. Like Karam, he was easy on the eye; unlike Karam, he seemed a miserable sort. It dawned on her that she had never seen him smile. Would his face crack if he made a small effort? Was he a true intellectual, or was he merely filling a role, pretending to be other-worldly and, therefore, fascinating? And did she care either way?

April, entering a merciful remission, drank coffee without spilling too much of it. She, too, was very much aware of Sebastian as she was to be interviewed by him with a view to appearing on his Sunday-night show in a few months. No one talked or thought about the play any more: it had been cancelled *sine die* in deference to Philip Pointer.

When someone knocked, the resulting sigh of relief was almost audible. Karam rushed to the door, admitted the visitor, performed the introductions, then stood back to view the scene. This was Kevin Brooks, the young man to whom Philip had left his house and its contents.

Kevin presented as unique, to say the least. He was dressed in flares fashioned from purple crushed velvet, high wedged shoes and an orange T-shirt, which had been deliberately butchered and tacked together again with nappy pins. He wore in his left ear a dangling silver cross and four round-headed studs. His hair, shoulder-length and streaked, was plaited, with little bead stoppers at the end of each braid.

'Blimey,' breathed April softly, when the vision appeared.

Sebastian, who watched life for a living, raised his head for a moment before continuing to read his tattered book. Yvonne swallowed and tried to imagine Philip, all precision and opinions, in the company of this odd-looking young man.

Karam, triumphant because she had managed to coax Kevin along to her house, continued to stand back and watch the expressions of her friends. With the possible exception of Sebastian, this was one gob-smacked kitchen.

'Would you like anything?' Yvonne asked, keen to fracture the silence.

'Coffee, please,' replied Kevin. He hitched up the insane trousers from just above the knee, perched himself on a stool, crossed his legs and smiled nervously upon the company.

April, as ever, was the bravest creature present. Even Bertrand Russell, that noble and worthy terrier, had secreted himself beneath the table. The hungry-for-material playwright stood up, tottered about and circled the new arrival. 'Who got you ready, love?' she asked. 'And what have you come as?'

The room held its breath. Even Sebastian ignored his book for a few ticks of the clock. Kevin smiled, displaying a full canteen of polished and even teeth. His eyes crinkled, then he started to laugh. It was a Father Christmas type of chortle, a noise that failed to match the fine frame and raw-boned features. He wiped bright-blue long-lashed eyes. 'Sorry,' he mumbled. 'That's the first time I've laughed since . . . for ages.' He placed a hand on April's arm. 'You're April Nugent,' he informed her. 'PP was terrified to diarrhoea of you.' Sensing that he was among friends, Kevin allowed himself to relax slightly.

April prodded his legs with her walking stick. 'I had curtains that colour in the seventies,' she said.

'These *were* curtains,' he answered. 'I released them from drudgery and gave them a life.'

April decided immediately that she liked Kevin Brooks. He was a colourful event in a life that had, of late, been grey and depressing. 'PP and I gave each other a hard time,' she told the young man. 'It was part and parcel of our relationship.' She paused. 'How long had you known him?'

Kevin sobered. 'Three years, at least.'

'You were a well-kept secret, then.'

Kevin watched Yvonne making coffee. The sadness was visible in her shoulders, in Karam's face; it was audible beneath April Nugent's banter. 'We were not lovers,' he said easily. Yes, he could tell them. In fact, these folk might even care. 'Philip was my buddy,' he said. 'I am HIV positive, though I don't have the full-blown drama, thank God. Buddies visit and help people like me.'

Karam gasped. She couldn't imagine Philip Pointer actually worrying about anyone other than himself. Such a pompous, bombastic man would surely not volunteer for such a task?

'He was so good to me,' continued Kevin. 'Like a father and a brother rolled into one. All those stories he told me – I feel I know the drama society already.'

April patted his hand, almost falling into his lap when she lost her footing. 'Listen, son, don't take any notice of that old liar.' She shouted up at the ceiling. 'That's all slander, Pointer. I was never on the floor naked with the caretaker.'

Kevin hooted again. Then, when his laughter died, he asked the question. 'Where's Honoria?'

Everyone fell silent.

'Well?' Kevin studied the faces of Karam, April and Yvonne. Once again Sebastian was buried in literature.

'She's away,' replied Karam eventually.

'She killed him,' declared Kevin. 'There was a letter. He wouldn't discuss the contents, but it doesn't take a genius to guess.' He dropped his head for a second, then raised it defiantly. 'That woman is dangerous.'

Karam's gaze travelled around the room. Everyone here had been targeted recently by Honoria. The woman was a strange mixture of evil and naïveté: she had failed to conceal her identity, had scarcely disguised her hand and had posted the letters in Lancashire, all within the space of a fortnight. Sebastian hadn't had one, she reminded herself, but Honoria did not know him. And, with a sheet as dull and clean as his, he would never be a likely candidate.

The unshaven TV personality looked up. 'Did someone mention coffee?'

'God, he's alive,' exclaimed Karam, glad of a chance to break the tension. 'Even if our dear Sebastian ever received poison messages, he wouldn't notice them.'

Kevin jumped down from his stool and helped Yvonne with cups and coffee pot. 'I'm going to live in that house,' he announced. 'Probate can be ignored because Philip gave me a rent book. According to records, I have been a sitting tenant for twelve months.'

'Good,' said Karam. 'That's excellent news.'

Kevin grinned once more. 'And I may decide to bring one or two needy friends to share it with me. Honoria will love that, I'm sure. She'll have disease on her doorstep. That should make her binoculars mist over. And I shall search for that letter until my dying day.' His movements were exaggeratedly camp, small steps, a wiggle of the hips, his hands, once free of crockery, mobile and fluttery.

'So PP told you about her,' said Yvonne.

He nodded, causing plaits to fly and beads to collide. 'Oh, yes, he said the odd word. The rest of you he loved, praised you to glory at every opportunity.'

The three women stared at one another. PP had seldom praised anyone, let alone the poor devils who had volunteered to work with him. Nothing had ever been good enough. He had been a rigid and stylized taskmaster and had seldom varied his routines. For Philip, the theatre had been a reason to live. Until Honoria had snuffed him out, of course.

Yvonne passed a cup of coffee to Sebastian, who growled what might have been a thank-you. She glanced at Karam. 'Why does he snarl at me?' she asked. The two women had fallen into the habit of talking to one another about Sebastian, usually in his presence, as he had become particularly withdrawn of late.

Karam smiled. 'Take no notice. One of our ancestors was a high-ranking Labrador retriever.'

Kevin spluttered, coughed, spilt coffee all over his T-shirt. 'Is there anybody normal here?'

April looked hard at the young man. 'Well,' she began, 'you're not exactly soup of the day, are you, dear?' She cast an eye over the rest of the company. 'Seb you will recognize, though he looks different in real life. He does *Arts Forum* on a Sunday night. You may have noticed him sandwiched between Heinz ketchup and Birds Eye fish fingers. He chases round looking for sculptors and the like. Anyone who works in TV is a weirdo – and I should know, because I've been there.' She considered Yvonne. 'That one's married to a doctor, good prospects and so forth. So she's moving in with Karam, who's an art historian and a painter, therefore completely insane.'

Kevin mopped at his front. 'And you?'

'Oh, I'm all right,' insisted April 'They let me out on Thursdays as long as I don't howl at the new moon. I live across the road with a lot of animals and a husband who is parked at the bottom of the garden in spite of threats and solicitor's letters. Mind you, he was never very good at reading big words. I keep telling him to wander off, but he's very attached to a caravan and a rotating washing-line.'

Sebastian looked up. 'It was an Afghan hound,' he informed his sister. 'On the distaff side.'

Karam stared at him. Sebastian could read,

listen and write a script simultaneously. Once upon a time, he might have been referred to as a genius. In actuality, he had sat unnoticed in various classrooms for thirteen years, emerging with enough bits of paper to enter Cambridge, where he had gained a first in English and a reputation as a debater. 'There is no Afghan in me,' she advised him loftily. 'I am half English, half Polish and my name is Egyptian, I think. Mummy spent time in the Pyramids.'

Sebastian's mouth twitched.

'I would not say woof to a goose,' Karam concluded.

He turned a page, continued reading.

'Are you gay?' Kevin asked Karam.

'Yes,' she answered immediately. 'How could you tell?'

The visitor smiled. 'Takes one queer soul to know another.'

Sebastian flicked over another page. No way could anyone read so quickly, thought Yvonne. She was the one he wanted to flick over, dismiss, brush off like a fly. The man was assuming that she and Karam were partners, and he did not approve. He didn't hate her, not quite, not yet. Perhaps he wasn't enamoured of the idea of anyone taking his sister away from him. Did he dislike all lesbians except his own sister? Or was Yvonne herself so detestable?

'Shall we go and look at your house, then, Kevin?' asked April.

The general consensus was supportive of the suggestion, but Yvonne, after muttering something about following on later, started to accumulate mugs and cups in the sink. While the others left, Sebastian and his reading matter remained where they had sat for over an hour, the former rigidly upright, the latter still droopy round much-thumbed edges.

Yvonne continued to clatter until well after the others had left. No one expected Sebastian to move or to take an interest in Kevin's house. No one ever expected Sebastian to do anything, or so it seemed. Was this because he was on TV for an hour or so on some Sunday nights? Did being on TV mean that a person need not be civilized, pleasant, or even human?

He was occupying Yvonne's chair. Had he sat there deliberately to stake his unspoken claim? Of course, Yvonne had the ability to put his mind at rest, to explain that she and Karam were not lovers, that Karam had become a good friend, no more than that. But she would not do it, refused to make an issue where there was none. Assumptions? Let him manufacture them, let him wonder and worry.

She rinsed off the Fairy and stacked the pots in the drainer. He was staring at her again. Like something off one of Captain Kirk's strange planets, Sebastian was drilling holes into an innocent human. Yvonne didn't need to look over her shoulder: the heat was between her shoulder-blades, dead centre and dead on target. 'Beam me up,' she mouthed silently.

'Did you say something?'

She spun round. 'Did you actually ask me a question?'

Sebastian Laczynski closed Terry Pratchett

and placed him and his Discworld creatures between the coal bucket and a brass companion set. He prepared to stand, but Yvonne was upon him.

Standing so close to him, she caught the scent of Imperial Leather and the sight of Karam's amazing skin and eyes. He wasn't merely handsome in the Brad Pitt or Pierce Brosnan sense: brother and sister were absolutely beautiful, almost flawless, so dark-eyed and creamskinned, so perfectly etched. 'What the hell have I done to you?' she said quietly. 'I come into the house and I hear you and Karam talking, laughing. As soon as you see me, you rush off or start Pratchetting about, all turning pages and mean looks.'

'I beg your pardon?'

She pushed him back into his chair. 'You heard me. Don't make me repeat myself.'

He made a church steeple of his fingers and pressed the index pair against his mouth.

'You are annoying me, Sebastian. Don't you like my coffee? Are you suffering from chronic indigestion? Did someone thwart a childhood ambition to become an engine driver? Or do you just hate me, myself, *moi-même*, personally?'

'I don't hate you,' he replied eventually. 'My sister and I are very close—'

'Your sister and *I* are very close,' she told him.

Sebastian dropped his hands. 'Karam and I fall back into our old ways whenever we meet. Sometimes, we carry on a conversation started months ago – few would understand us. As for Pratchett, I'm studying him because I'd like to do a feature about him if I can catch him. Unfortunately, he's yet another elusive genius.'

Yvonne did not flinch. She held his gaze steadily, stepping back only when the back door crashed inward.

Three suitcases entered the arena, followed quickly by two Sefton Council bin liners and a series of cardboard boxes. 'Your luggage, madam,' yelled David.

Sebastian stood up and placed a protective arm across Yvonne's shoulders. He had witnessed some of David's recent ongoings and was not impressed. 'Can we help you?' he asked.

Yvonne sighed heavily when her husband's tousled head poked into the room. Sebastian remained by her side, his arm tightening across her back.

'Good-oh!' yelled David Benson. He staggered and grinned, clearly the worse for alcohol again. He addressed his estranged wife. 'Are you doing job lots now, Yvonne? Brother and sister, two for the price of one?'

Sebastian moved across the room like greased lightning. He was not an unusually big man, just about encroaching on the six-foot mark, and his muscles did not exactly bulge beneath the short sleeves of his *Arts Forum* logo T-shirt, but he lifted David off his feet in one smooth movement and dumped him into a chair. 'Can we help you?' he repeated, no breathlessness in his voice. 'And please show some respect for this woman.'

David looked up into a very famous face. 'I've seen you on TV,' he babbled. 'You're so much smaller in real life.' He narrowed his eyes. 'Is this real life, Mr Laczynski? Or are we in the middle of some shared nightmare?'

Yvonne glowered. Had the situation been different, these two might have been fighting for her favours, all clenched teeth and fists, meet me at playtime behind the bike sheds, the winner takes her home on his handlebars.

'You're making your own nightmare, Doctor,' answered Sebastian. 'I've seen too many decent men ruined by booze.'

So he does notice stuff, thought Yvonne irrelevantly.

'Are you leaving, or shall I throw you out?'

David grinned inanely.

'Leave him alone, please.' Yvonne could see only too plainly that David was no match for Sebastian. 'He'll go. He always goes quietly in the end.'

'You don't like him?' David hiccuped loudly in Yvonne's direction.

No one offered a reply.

David nodded rapidly. He knew where he had gone wrong. Had he immersed himself in paint and thinners, or in airy-fairy nonsense spouted through a tube at the weekend, Yvonne would have loved him. He was too medical, too bloody normal and ordinary by far. 'You think you're so clever, don't you? Just because you've survived three rounds with Robbie Coltrane and Dame Barbara Cartland—'

'Both very nice people, by the way.'

'—and your name floats up a screen after you've delivered a load of crap, you imagine

212

you can grab anybody's wife with impunity.'

'And that wasn't easy to say, was it, David?' Yvonne chipped in. 'Not after – how many large whiskies?'

David managed to focus on her. He wanted her. He didn't want her. He didn't know what he wanted apart from a painless existence. She looked beautiful, all soft focus and composed – a bit like a model at a shoot, filtered lighting, not an eyelash out of place. The waist-length brown hair was sun-streaked and thick all the way down, not tapering off into rats' tails, while her eyes were so clear, so lovely. 'What happened to us?'

Sebastian turned to Yvonne as if waiting to courier an answer back to the man heaped into Karam's chair.

'I told you, David. We're too alike.'

The TV personality of 1994, darling of every ageing female who had wanted a son to be proud of, went down on one knee and started to scrape together some of Bertrand Russell's biscuits, most of which had jumped for the hills after a close encounter with April Nugent's walking stick. He could not leave Yvonne with her visitor, yet he did not wish to eavesdrop.

'You are no dyke,' shouted David.

'Change the record,' Yvonne suggested. 'It's the same tune over and over. Please, please, shut up, go home and have some sleep.'

'So I have to leave you here with your lady-friend and her nancy-boy brother.'

The nancy-boy banged his head on the table

in the act of retrieving a Bonio. No one said a word to him so, having spotted a clutch of Spiller's Shapes, he threw himself back into his work. Used to being called nancy, powder-puff and other such daft names, he had become inured to the gibes.

'Seb is not gay,' Yvonne informed the drunk to whom she remained married.

'How do you know?'

'I just know.'

'The wisdom of womankind.' David heaved himself up and staggered to the door. With a piece of pure ham that might have delighted Philip Pointer, Dr Benson delivered his exit line from the doorway. 'I'm selling up and moving to Manchester in six months,' he declared. 'You'll get half of everything.' He stumbled off.

Yvonne and Sebastian heard him tripping over the dustbin, caught the expletives, tried not to smile.

'How do you know I'm not gay?' asked Sebastian.

'I just know,' Yvonne repeated, before stalking off to change her shoes. Men were a breed apart, they really, really were.

Sebastian Laczynski had another go at Terry Pratchett, but failed to get into it. He was uncomfortable with himself, moody, too sensitive by far. He didn't know who or what to blame, so he ditched Discworld and had another stab at the crossword. Karam had been at it. Karam laboured under the delusion that any word would do as long as it fitted.

'Four across is carnation.'

She was leaning over his shoulder. 'And three down should be assimilate,' she suggested. 'I think we should buy Karam one of those electronic gadgets with the built-in crossword buster.' She prodded the page. 'Try blackboard.'

He made the necessary adjustments.

'Aren't you coming to see Kevin's house?' she asked.

Sebastian threw down his pen. Her hair smelled like a spring morning, fresh and newly washed. He didn't like her one bit, didn't want her hanging over him like an extra sister. 'I'm going to pack,' he muttered. 'Time I went to see the old man.'

'Karam and I thought we might all travel to Huddersfield together,' said Yvonne.

Sebastian shrugged. 'I'll speak to Karam.' Relief flooded his veins when the bloody woman finally moved away. He had to come to terms with this, had to find a way of tolerating Karam's lover. 'I'll walk up to the house with you,' he said.

'Don't do me any favours,' she answered.

Sebastian put on his expressionless face, the non-judgemental veneer that had made him a national darling. 'Lead on,' he said.

Yvonne stared at him. Like his sister, he was extraordinarily attractive. But inside, this young man was not easy at all. Yet she wasn't going to put his mind at rest. Oh, no. What right had he to choose his sister's friends, companions, lovers? 'Come on,' she snapped. 'I can't wait to see what Kevin makes of PP's house. It's all scripts and cigar butts.'

Sebastian followed, closed the door behind him. Often, particularly where women were involved, the line of least resistance brought the happiest results.

Fourteen

Miss Honoria West had taken on a cottage just half a mile away from Moortop Farm. Dressed in sensible tweeds and sturdy brogues, she marched about the moors with a walking stick and binoculars, wondering how on earth she had managed to suffer so long from agoraphobia. She found foxes and badgers, rabbits and birds, wild flowers and fruits. She also discovered a nice spot from which she could watch the comings and goings of Hilda West and her fancy man.

The fancy man was extraordinarily handsome and he was living quite blatantly with Honoria's younger sister. Hilda had a youthful spring in her step, a phenomenon that was easily visible through Honoria's powerful lenses. Hilda was not the type to express *joie de vivre*. Hilda was stodgy, commonplace, more at ease in her farmhouse kitchen than in the presence of monied folk.

Honoria parked her hired Escort on the gravel pathway that led to Brookside Cottage.

After three driving lessons, she considered herself sufficiently refreshed to tackle anything but motorways. When visiting other towns like Blackburn, Preston and Chorley, she took the longer, scenic routes and was coming to depend less and less on that little magic bottle labelled diazepam.

The house was quaint, roses round the door and on most wallpapers, an inglenook fireplace, a good bathroom, television, decent plumbing and exposed beams. Strangely, she was not afraid on her own in the middle of the countryside. She had now convinced herself that Hyacinth had held her back, that the death of the oldest West had released her from imprisonment.

In the living room, she removed her hat, poured a generous sherry, sat down and switched on the TV news. There was trouble all over the world, but Honoria scarcely noticed the grim pictures. Her mind was engrossed in other matters, things closer to her rented cottage and far more pressing than explosions in Belfast. Hilda had a man. Hilda, that boring, unprepossessing woman, was clearly in love.

She drained her glass. The feeling was reciprocated. Mr Leo Stoneway, the stranger at Hyacinth's funeral, was as besotted with Hilda as Hilda was with him. Astonishing. He always helped Hilda into the car, always held her arm as they walked to the house. Even from the little copse, Honoria had seen smiles, gestures, a kiss. 'Ridiculous,' she told the opposite chair. 'She's a mess and she never did have sex appeal.'

Stoneway seemed as rich as Croesus, sometimes arriving home with masses of flowers, sometimes in the company of a liveried chauffeur who would then drive away the Rolls to wash it, service it, or whatever else uniformed retainers did with cars between journeys.

'I've seen Mr Stoneway before,' she told her empty schooner. 'Before the funeral, before Blundellsands, before . . .' Before what? She rose and refilled her glass from the Harvey's bottle. There was something familiar about Mr Leo Stoneway, but he was from another time, a different age. 'I shall follow him,' she advised the room. 'He must go somewhere on a regular basis. As for Mother's little pet lamb, she's worth watching, too.'

Honoria sat at a small desk and picked up a letter. It was a reply from the publisher who had handled Hyacinth's work. He expressed his sorrow about Hyacinth's death, then his interest in Honoria's submissions. 'You obviously have the same talent,' he opined. 'I would certainly be interested in seeing more of your pieces.' Honoria grinned. She would have her day with both her sisters, would outrun and outlive the pair of them.

She worked on a poem, then a short story, carefully editing and altering Hyacinth's notes. She was no longer the middle sister: with the eldest dead, Honoria wore the leader's shoes. Perhaps she should not have phoned Hilda during her stay at the Pack Horse. Yes, that had been a mistake, because Hilda would be expecting her, waiting for her. No matter. Everything would fall into place. As long as she was careful, Honoria's triumph was practically guaranteed.

After a light supper of Marks & Spencer's smoked salmon with salad, Honoria set forth into the night, binoculars and a small torch her sole companions. She liked the darkness. It provided a natural cloak, a protection against discovery. Her night vision was remarkable for a woman of her age, as was her ability to walk without pain on the most uneven surfaces. When she neared the edge of the small wood, she slowed, wondering if she dared go nearer to the farm this time.

The house was magnificent. Even in darkness, its solid perfection was outlined against a star-sprinkled sky of deepest navy. A shy new moon flirted with gossamer clouds, the resulting filtered light offering a soft, romantic glow to the buildings. Although Moortop was very much a working farm, it had been designed as a work of art, a miniaturized stately home with balustrade, pediments and balconies. Formal gardens fronted the house, large sweeps of lawn punctuated by flower-beds, fountains, ornate bridges spanning a small stream. 'And it's all hers,' grumbled Honoria.

The moon danced behind a haze of moisture, reappeared, skipped off again. Honoria fixed her eyes on the columned open porch, watched Mr Stoneway as he emerged with Hilda. They got into a car and swept off along the wide drive-way. Did anyone live in? Honoria wondered. Probably not. Hilda would have help in the house, but servants, these days, usually travelled in on a daily basis. There would be no house-keeper: Hilda was too domesticated to hand over the reins completely.

Honoria sat on a tree stump. The porch was lit by carriage lamps, but there was likely to be no lighting at the rear. She remembered the back of the house, its squared-off yard bordered by barns and stables. That was where the precious Hilda had played with her dolls and her tiny tea-sets, where she had made a shop and a little house for Marigold, Poppy and Violet, three porcelain-faced 'babies' whose clothes Mother made. Of course, when Hilda's pot children had needed to go into the dolls' hospital, blame had always been apportioned to Honoria.

'She had her own way every time,' said the middle child who was now the eldest, 'while Hyacinth was perfection on legs. Damn them both, damn them all.'

Honoria got up and smoothed the dog-tooth check skirt. 'I wonder if she ever got the locks changed?' Honoria had taken a souvenir with her all those years ago, a spare key to the back door. Had it been a mere memento, or an insurance against a night such as this? 'I wonder if there's a burglar alarm or a dog?' Still, who would hear a dog? Set in acres of its own land, Moortop had no really close neighbours. What if the dog was fierce? Never mind – she might not even get inside the house.

It was just as she remembered it. The horse trough remained, though it now overflowed with the dying plants of summer. All outbuildings were secured, and no horse whinnied inside the stable block. Father's horse had been a black brute called Ebony. Honoria remembered the shot, that single report that had ended the creature's life. Even now, she smiled as she imagined how the light would have died in those white-edged terrified eyes. She had got the blame for that accident, too.

The back of Moortop was plain, just bricks, windows and doors. After waiting for several minutes, Honoria drew from her shoulder-bag a key of at least four inches in length and inserted it carefully into the solid back door. It grumbled for a second before the mechanism turned, allowing the visitor to step into a house of which, she felt, she should have been part-owner, at least.

To the left of a short hallway, a room that used to be a laundry now posed as an office of some sort, word-processor sitting on a bench, recipes pinned to a large cork wallboard. Honoria ran her torch over a sign above the pinboard. Parkside Bakeries? Hadn't she and Hyacinth used that brand? Yes, it was offered by Sainsbury's, some items in tins, some chilled, others available frozen. Cursing her lack of computer skills, Honoria sat in a leather chair and swivelled round. Everywhere there were recipe books, mock-ups of package illustrations, price lists, reminders scribbled on Stick-It pages. Hilda was Parkside Bakeries. Hilda was on sale nationwide in high-class supermarkets.

She flinched when the aged key cut into her

palm. She had not recognized her own tension until metal had dug into flesh. Always, always, she was to be the middle one, the unremarkable child. Hyacinth, though dead, continued the subject of admiration. Dumpy, stupid Hilda was the brains behind a culinary empire. Quietly, Honoria closed the office door.

Opposite, a smaller room contained a washer-dryer, plastic baskets, a pulley line and some peg-bags. Next to that, a cloakroom housed lavatory, washbasin, shower stall, wellington boots and outdoor clothing. Everything was so neat, so carefully arranged.

The kitchen had been transformed into a wonderful mix of ancient and modern, black grate and oven rubbing shoulders with a gleaming Aga, microwave seated on a Victorian washstand, Kenwood mixer flanked by pestles, mortars and stockpots. It was dominated by a massive scrubbed-pine table at which sixteen might have dined with ample room for elbows. By means of her tiny torch, Honoria picked out Hyacinth's early daubs and poems, the work she had done while recovering from the break-down. She smiled grimly. Yes, that had been a breakdown and a half, all hushed tones, dramatic exits and entrances, secrets stored so carelessly that Honoria had fathomed each one. How stupid her mother and her sisters had been, how clever she had become.

The main drawing room retained the magnificence created by Honoria's forebears. Four sofas, nine easy chairs and a plethora of fine wood cabinets, bureaux and tables failed to fill it. There was a fireplace and mantelpiece at each end, twin marble affairs covered in gilded clocks, Royal Doulton figurines and massive candlesticks. She might have been standing in the pay-to-view ancestral residence of some duke driven to show off his home in order to keep it.

The second drawing room, slightly smaller, was just as well furnished. On one side of the chimney breast, a floor-to-ceiling cabinet provided a safe haven for priceless china, while the other recess nursed leatherbound books and items of silver. These were riches indeed, many items acquired after the death of Mother. Hilda plainly took an active interest in antiques as well as in the culinary arts.

Honoria stood in the centre of a silk rug, planting her feet where the coffin had rested. Father had been too battered for an open casket. Mother had sat just there, to the right of the little davenport, her eyes fixed on Father's coffin, those slim hands murdering a scrap of lace-edged linen saturated with tears. Honoria, dutiful in black velvet, had stood with her sisters, had watched them weep, had listened to sobs strangled by the need not to upset poor Mother.

Poor Mother. When had she ever shown love to her second child?

'Woof!'

Startled almost to the point of cardiac arrest, Honoria froze for several seconds before turning to face the door. It was Mason. No, it couldn't be Mason. 'Mason?' she ventured.

Mason the Fifth, a long-haired German shepherd, relaxed. He wagged a dramatic, thick-curtained tail and walked slowly towards the visitor. At nine years of age, he was not as vigilant as he had been, but he had the experience now to recognize the difference between a thief and a guest. This woman, whom he had never met before, was a clan member. He could see it in her stance, could smell it on her skin. He licked her hand, returned to his basket on the landing and fell asleep.

Honoria breathed again. She didn't like dogs and, on the whole, they tended not to be overfond of her. But, had she been forced to keep an animal, it would have been a German shepherd. They were intelligent and discriminatory, at least. She sat down, recovered her composure and looked at the paintings on Hilda's walls. A genuine Stubbs nudged a couple of impressionist prints, and Hilda had obviously invested in the works of a few unknown, possibly up-and-coming artists, the subjects of whose paintings were recognizable objects rather than stupid daubs.

Honoria got up and played her torch on a still life: dried flowers, fruits, crockery and a dull, possibly pewter coffee pot. It was signed KARAM L. Oh, didn't those people get everywhere? Even in the middle of Lancashire, Karam Laczynska pursued Honoria, insinuating herself on to the very walls inside which the Wests had all been born and bred.

Life was so sickening. No matter what she did, no matter what she tried, someone else always got there before Honoria. Anger bubbled, simmered, almost got the better of her. But control was the key. In order to be in charge of everything and everyone around her, Honoria must first overcome her own weaknesses. She was managing the phobias, was driving again, was living alone, had achieved sufficient confidence to enter this house.

Upstairs was interesting. She missed out the ground-floor study, dining room and morning room, passed Mason on the landing. There were five bedrooms and three bathrooms, one of the latter having been added since Honoria's time. The two residents were sleeping separately, it seemed, though one could never be completely sure of that. Mr Stoneway's room was clinical – stripped-pine furniture, double bed, built-in shower cubicle.

He was reading a Mary Wesley and a book about the Amsterdam diamond market. Inside the drawers, socks and underwear were folded perfectly, while a large wardrobe contained half a dozen suits, some jackets and flannels, three bathrobes and a rack of silk ties.

Hilda, still the baby, had a fluffy boudoir, all peach and cream. Incredibly, she harboured a shelf of soft toys – rabbits, bears, a grey elephant with a red bow. The wallpaper boasted clumps of roses and tiny sprigs of forget-me-nots, and the cream-coloured dressing-table bore many pots of cream and bottles of lotion. It was a child's room, a playroom, a special nest for a special little girl.

Honoria cracked a capsule of vitamin E,

allowed the viscous substance to caress her fingers. Johnson's baby powder and baby oil nestled together behind a basket filled with pastel-coloured balls of cotton wool. The woman was emotionally retarded, locked into a time that was long past, long finished. Honoria's hatred for her younger sister received a fresh charge when she noticed Hyacinth's book on a bedside cabinet. The owner of Parkside Bakeries no doubt showed off about her sister, the writer. She probably never bothered to mention Honoria, who had more brains than the other two put together.

Obeying an instinct for which she would never be able to account, Honoria picked up a bottle of perfume and pushed it into her hand-bag. Knowing that this was stupid, she could not quite manage to replace it on the dressing-table. She wanted something, anything, needed to take a token prize just to prove to herself that she had been here.

Back downstairs, she looked at the face of the grand-father clock, remembered Father winding it, pocket-watch in his hand, frown creasing his brow as he synchronized the two pieces. Such an exact man, he had been, so correct, so masterful. She opened the case, grabbed the pendulum and held it still. When the mechanism stalled, she took a handkerchief from her pocket and wiped the pendulum clean. Her fingerprints were all over the place, she supposed, as she held the torch in her mouth and directed light on to the brass disc. Oh, let them worry. She had not finished with these two people, not by a long chalk.

'Keep an eye on her,' Father had said to Mother. 'Make sure she doesn't slip into bad ways again.' Bad ways? She had been an infant, a child trying to gain attention and affection. 'She will always need watching,' he had insisted.

Watching? All her life, Honoria had merely sought to make her presence felt. If people ignored her, she punished them – it was as simple as that. First Father, then Mother had become watchdogs. Honoria, having escaped to Liverpool, had taken a job in the tax offices, had led a blameless life until . . . until an unfortunate incident about which she preferred not to think. Then Hyacinth had arrived, had installed herself in the Mansions, had insinuated her persona into Honoria's life until Honoria had been reduced to helpless agoraphobia. But now they were all dead. Mother, Father and Hyacinth had returned to the earth; only Hilda and her stranger remained.

'I'll wipe your eyes for you,' she whispered into a hallway lit only by spillage from carriage lamps in the porch. 'Wipe your eye' was another of Gill Collins's Liverpool sayings, mused Honoria, as she let herself out by the rear door. The moon had disappeared, so the only light available was from her torch. She allowed her vision to adjust, then set forth towards the side of the house. Crunching gravel advertised the arrival of Leo Stoneway's quiet car. Honoria flattened herself against an end wall, listened as the two of them stepped out of the vehicle.

'Stop worrying,' the man said.

'I can't help it,' replied Hilda. 'I just know she's round here somewhere.'

'Well, she's left the Pack Horse.'

After a short silence, Hilda piped up again. 'She made that man hang himself, Leo. Just by writing her evil letters, she caused Philip Pointer to commit suicide.'

Their voices tailed away as they entered the house.

Honoria steadied herself. She had done nothing wrong; she had told only the truth. With her wonderfully selective memory kicking into gear, Miss Honoria West made her way back towards Brookside Cottage. Everyone was misjudging her again. It was nothing new, but it was still terribly tiresome.

Fifteen

When the Great War ended, Thomas James West, having served his time as an officer in the Lancashire Fusiliers, came home from hell and, the following year, married the supposed love of his life. Isobel Craven, daughter of a local mill-owner, brought into the marriage ten thousand pounds, two servants from her parents' home and an adoration for her husband that went beyond the usual bounds of human affection. She worshipped him, indulged his every whim and waited on him hand and foot.

She had always wanted to marry him. Ever since childhood, Isobel had felt as if she hovered on the breathless brink of a life that could never be complete without the owner of Moortop Farm. When he went away to fight the Hun, she knitted for him, wrote to him and prayed for him constantly. He returned a decorated hero, and she adored him all the more for that.

Thomas, only child of Mr and Mrs Archibald West, had been an orphan since his late teens. A sober young man, he had simply stepped into his father's shoes, supervising the running of the family estate, then marching off to war at the first sign of hostility. He believed in God and in England, could scarcely separate the two within the narrow, blinkered bounds of his basic and uninformed philosophy.

Isobel was married in white, a long dress worn by her mother and by her maternal grandmother. Her wedding day was fine and her future happiness seemed guaranteed. The perfunctory nature of Thomas's lovemaking did not worry her, as she had no experience and no way of assessing his performance. He said little when in bed with his beautiful wife, simply labouring over her for a couple of minutes and impregnating her within a few months of the wedding night.

Hyacinth was born in the spring of 1920. Thomas, though anxious for a son to follow in the footsteps of the Wests, was immediately enamoured of his baby daughter. She was a quick, pretty child whose precocity made her the centre of her father's existence. An early walker, she talked sensibly before the age of two and became her father's shadow as he marched across his extensive estate supervising those who worked for him. The next child would be a son, he felt sure.

Honoria came along after a gap that drifted into 1925. Isobel, having endured terrible pain during the delivery, was too ill to care for the newborn girl. Thomas, who did his best to hide his disappointment, employed a wet-nurse and a nurserymaid, then continued as before, the five-year-old Hyacinth his closest companion on a day-to-day basis.

Isobel lingered in bed for weeks. Minnie Kershaw, a fat woman abundant in both milk and common sense, nurtured the tiny Honoria, but Isobel could not take to the child.

'She's bonny,' Minnie would enthuse in the presence of the listless mother.

'Get Bertha,' was Isobel's inevitable reply. 'I can't bear the crying, Minnie.'

Minnie, whose instincts were acute in spite of poor education, would shake her head sadly as she carried 'madam's poor little mite' through to the nanny in the nursery. 'Here, Bertha,' she would say. 'You be mother while I go and suckle my own little chap. No good'll come of this, you know. Mrs West's hardly touched yon baby since she were born. It's not right.'

Bertha Mills knew it wasn't right. The Wests had wanted a son, and Honoria, a sufferer from infant colic, was not the easiest baby in the world. Also, Honoria seemed to understand from a very early age that she was little more than a wrapped item in a game of pass the parcel, something to be shuffled about and handed along the line until she decided to lie still and shut up.

Hyacinth loved her baby sister. At every opportunity, she stuffed the child into dolls' cots and prams, walking her round the grounds until the crying made way for sleep. She propped her up on pillows, read to her, sang to her, played little games of house in which

232

Honoria took the part of a living doll among many plaster faces.

Thomas West developed no particular fondness for his second child, the one who ought to have been male. He allowed Hyacinth to bring the baby on several walks and visits to tied cottages, but the infant was so noisy and red in the face that he eventually banned her from accompanying him on such expeditions.

The crying stopped eventually, but Honoria remained sullen and withdrawn. When Hyacinth tried to play with her, the younger girl refused to co-operate, often smashing toys and throwing missiles at windows, at walls and at Hyacinth.

Hilda dropped into the world in 1927, literally parting company from her mother after just one scaring pain. So profuse was Isobel's bleeding that she had to be rushed off to the infirmary, where she and Hilda remained for several weeks. Exhausted and isolated from the rest of her family, Isobel West developed a close relationship with her youngest child, a bond so tight that no one would ever find a doorway into that special world created during the hospital days

When, at last, Isobel and Hilda returned to Moortop, Thomas seemed to have distanced himself completely from his wife.

'Why?' she asked repeatedly, over breakfast, lunch or supper. 'What is wrong?'

He would shrug and offer no reply.

When Isobel could endure the silences no longer, she knocked on the door that separated their bedrooms, walked in, found him sitting as still as stone near the window. 'Thomas?' she ventured.

Slowly, he turned to face her. 'There can be no more children,' he advised her, somewhat brusquely.

Isobel sank on to her husband's rather firm mattress. She stared at him for at least half a minute before speaking again. 'Why?'

'Because you might bleed to death.'

Isobel closed her eyes and inhaled deeply. 'You need a son,' she told him, 'and I am prepared to risk anything and everything for you.' Was she? Could she really leave her girls, especially the beautiful Hilda? Oh, yes, she would do anything for Thomas, even now. 'We must have a son,' she repeated.

Thomas was not a demonstrative man. Mistaking terms of affection for weakness, he maintained a stiff upper lip at all times, yet he was touched by the sheer devotion of his suddenly paler, thinner wife. Try as he might, the words would not come. Annoyed with himself and with life in general, he often looked sullen when faced with situations such as this.

Had Thomas West been endowed with the ability to look at his own make-up, he might have noticed, in time, some marked similarities between himself and his cold, taciturn middle daughter. 'I absolutely refuse to be the cause of your death, my dear,' he managed finally, in this particularly difficult moment.

'But the land, the future—'

'There is nothing to be done,' he replied.

Isobel squirmed. Delicate matters were difficult to discuss with Thomas – with anyone, in fact. Having married into the heady realms of landed gentry, she was now a lady, and ladies were not meant to express opinions on certain subjects. He never visited her bed unless intending to fulfil his husbandly duties. Isobel could not recall one single occasion when they had simply kissed, cuddled and talked. 'I shall miss you,' she murmured, biting back a comment about how she had already missed him for years.

'It cannot be helped.'

She felt the heat in her cheeks. 'There are times when ... when a woman is unlikely to conceive,' she muttered, her voice thinned by embarrassment. 'We could still be together without ...' Her words died suddenly.

'To what end?' he asked. 'Marriage was created primarily for the creation of children.'

Tears welled up, spilled from her eyes. 'What about mutual comfort, Thomas? What about companionship and closeness? We aren't animals designed just to produce. I love you. I have loved you since I was ten years of age.'

The aspect of Isobel's character most admired by Thomas West was her self-containment. She never wept, seldom complained, was biddable, sensible and calm. Was he, like so many of his acquaintances, about to be saddled with a petulant, dissatisfied wife? 'We are adults now,' he answered, 'with responsibilities. We have three children to rear, while I must carry on supervising the running of Moortop.'

She stared hard at him. 'You don't love me,' she accused resignedly. 'You never have.'

Thomas gazed through the window, though he saw nothing of the scenery available to him. He watched boys going over the top, bayonets at the ready, guns loaded. He heard their screams, received bloodied bodies into his hands before going into the fray with the rest of the officers. Corpses everywhere, a boot containing a severed foot, broken faces howling, railing, refusing to go softly into that final good night. How could he tell his wife about haunted sleep, about midnight wakefulness filled only with the sight of gore and the stench of contaminated mud?

'Thomas?'

'Don't weep, because I cannot bear it.'

She dried her eyes.

'I have always loved you,' he said, the syllables almost sticking in his throat. 'Though I scarcely know what love is.' He faced her. 'Before the war, I was different. Something happened to me, to all of us over there, I expect.'

She awaited further explanation.

'I lived on top of death for over three years. For every yard of territory gained, I lost a dozen or more soldiers. And that was just me, just my little piece of foreign soil. All along the lines, the same thing was happening.' He bit hard on his lower lip. 'Sometimes, those who survive feel guilt for ever. I . . . I didn't survive inside. I sent children out to die, fresh-faced lads who had scarcely finished rudimentary education. Isobel, our daughters will not perish in the trenches, but a son might. The war to end all wars? It will happen again.' He clung to the thought, used it to compensate for the knowledge that the Wests were about to die out.

This was the longest speech she had ever heard from him. His eyes were empty as he spoke, almost as lifeless as those in the faces of several million dead soldiers. 'You could talk to me more often,' she told him. 'I could comfort you. There's no need for you to lie alone at night.'

He nodded curtly. 'We'll see.' He already felt less than a man, had already failed her by dragging her into his murky past. 'I must go now and speak to the new steward.' He walked past her and on to the landing.

Isobel sat for at least ten minutes in her husband's bedroom. She would no longer be a wife to him, would no longer be able to enjoy those brief moments when he had visited her bed. Life stretched before the young woman like an uncharted road, territory that she stood little chance of comprehending. 'Why?' she whispered to the mirror. 'Why can't he want me as I want him?'

She stood up and walked to the window, looked out on a garden that had been regimented into a shape as rigid as a military battalion. Even pain would be better than this dreadful nothingness. He had hurt her several times, but that had not mattered, because his body had been on top of hers and she had touched him, had held him tightly to her needful flesh.

Hilda wailed. Immediately Isobel ran to comfort her child. As she rocked the baby towards sleep, she did not notice the two-year-old in the doorway, failed to see those sad, hardening eyes in the face of a neglected infant.

Honoria crept away, found Hyacinth's favourite doll and smashed it apart with a shovel.

Hyacinth was at school most of the time. Honoria, just three and a half years old, was bored beyond measure. No one seemed to care whether she came, went or stayed, so she took to wandering a little further each day, often imposing herself on the families of farm labourers and sitting, silent as a graveyard, watching life as it ought to be. Nobody told her to go away, as each and every man, woman and child depended for roof and bread on Honoria's father.

Honoria had what many called 'queer' eyes, of a colour so unusual that it managed to be neither blue nor green. As she grew older, the hue would settle somewhere towards greyness, but twin turquoise orbs in the head of the infant Honoria caused more than one adult to squirm in his seat.

The little girl learnt about head lice, fleas and ringworm, sometimes standing next to a mother and helping to crack the bodies of 'bollies' newly ripped from tousled heads. She ate jam and bread, cow heel, tripe, sugar butties. She drank thick, treacly tea, dandelion and burdock and, occasionally, a mouthful of beer from a cracked pint pot.

People got used to having the child around. They found jobs for her, taught her how to peel potatoes, how to spread butter very thinly on shives of bread. After a while, she became part of the environment, something that got missed when it wasn't there. Folk who had not seen her for a day or two began to enquire after her, while mothers in particular missed that extra little pair of hands when vegetables wanted preparing.

Honoria got truly close to no one. As she neared her fourth birthday, she fell into the habit of categorizing people. There were those who noticed her, those who took her for granted and, lastly, a group who disliked and feared her. One such was Frankie Kershaw, the thin, sickly child with whom Honoria had shared mother's milk. She had never been suckled by Isobel, had not even been granted sole ownership of a wet-nurse. No, she had taken milk out of a blowsy woman whose son now sported a permanently snotty nose, red-rimmed eyes and clothes that were usually filthy.

They played together one day on one of the bridges that spanned a small stream running through the gardens of Moortop. The activity was not strictly play, as the rules were that Honoria did the telling and Frankie did as he was told. Honoria was the boy's superior in more ways than one. Not only did she come from the Big House, she was also tall and strong, was already beginning to show the promise of becoming weightier and mightier than her older sister. Next to Frankie, she looked truly powerful.

'Hang upside down over the rail,' she ordered.

Frankie rubbed a string of mucus on to the sleeve of a tattered jacket. 'I might fall in.'

'Yes,' Honoria agreed. 'Then I shall rescue you.' A strange excitement rose in her breast. If Frankie fell in, he would be completely at her mercy. 'And I'll get you some scones and a cake,' she promised. She looked over the bridge and into skittish water clear enough for a bed of stones to be visible.

'Me mam'd kill me if I got wet,' he grumbled. 'Cos I've allers gorra cold any road.'

'It would be an accident,' she reassured him. 'Anyone can have an accident, because I heard Father say so.'

Frankie considered his immediate future. Scones and cakes sounded promising, especially if such delicacies had been created within the kitchen at Moortop. But Mam had a temper on her, a red-hot temper, and very large hands.

'You won't fall in, anyway,' pronounced Honoria loftily. 'I shall hang on to you.'

'Will you?' Honoria was from the boss's house. Folk from the boss's family always told the truth.

'Yes, I'll look after you.'

Frankie swung himself over the edge, grimy fingers whitening as he hung upside down above the stream.

For a few moments, Honoria watched him, saw the terror in his eyes, heard him struggling to breathe against the vile slime that invariably occupied his nose. Because of his position,

Frankie could not rely on gravity to relieve the congestion, and it flooded his sinuses, causing him to feel dizzy and sick.

Honoria glanced around, made sure that no one was in sight. Then she picked up a large pebble and smashed it into the boy's knuckles. He yelped, the sound imitating a hurt puppy, removed the injured hand from its moorings and hung, like a rather dirty sheet in the wind, just one peg pinning it to the line. She attacked the second hand, then stood back calmly as he fell into the water.

He continued to scream until Honoria left the ornamental bridge, struggled down the shallow bank, picked up a stone and smashed the back of his skull. There, it was done. The water ran red, parting to make its way round the boy, stroking his body as it continued on the course from which no mere murder would ever divert it.

Calmly, the almost four-year-old washed her hands and dried them on a clump of grass. The thief was dead. He had got his comeuppance, had deserved it, since Honoria should never have been forced to share nourishment with a creature as low as Frankie Kershaw had been.

'Honoria?'

She swung round, almost losing her footing, saving herself by throwing herself flat and grabbing two handfuls of reed.

Hyacinth put down her bag of books. 'Frankie?'

He did not move.

'He fell in,' explained Honoria. 'He was

241

hanging upside down on the bridge, and he just . . . fell.'

Hyacinth shivered. Here she stood with a child five years her junior, a child with the eyes of a . . . of a person who did not give a handful of straws for anyone. 'Did you do this?' Had Honoria progressed from dolls to humans?

'No.'

Why wasn't she crying, screaming, expressing horror? Hyacinth was hanging on by a thread, because Frankie Kershaw was bleeding, motionless, probably dead or dying. 'I'm going to get Father.'

'Accidents happen,' chirruped Honoria. 'Father says so.'

Thomas West lifted the body of young Francis Kershaw from the stream. He felt for a pulse, found none, and sent Hyacinth to fetch the doctor from Edgeworth Village.

'He fell. It was an accident.'

Until now, Thomas had not noticed that his second daughter was a part of this dreadful scene. 'Did you see this happen?'

She nodded mutely.

'How did he fall?'

She lifted narrow shoulders. 'He was hanging upside down. I told him not to.'

Thomas West was faced now with the grim prospect of informing Mr and Mrs Kershaw that their son was dead. He laid the body flat on the ground, removed his own jacket and placed it over the young, white face. All the time, Honoria stared impassively at her father and the dead boy. Frankie Kershaw was just another accident, she told herself.

Her father pulled back the jacket and studied Frankie's injuries. They seemed unduly severe, not at all commensurate with an accidental drop of two or three feet, the height at which the pretty bridge stood above the water. He looked up. She was smiling. She was standing there with her strong, plump arms folded and an angelic grin on her face.

'Honoria?'

'Yes, Father?'

He could not employ the necessary words, was unable to question and accuse a child so young. 'Go to the meadow and find Bill Watkins. Can you do that?'

Her eyes danced with pleasure. Father needed her, wanted her to help. 'Yes, I can find him, Father.' She skipped away, gladness advertised with every step she took.

Thomas West sank to his knees. Another death, another child wiped out. For poor Frankie there was no hope, no future. The noises came then, blasts from heavy cannon, the screams of dying horses, those awful thuds as men fell back into the filthy trench from which they had emerged only seconds earlier. 'No,' he ordered himself. 'Don't listen, don't look.'

When the doctor and Mr Watkins finally arrived, they found the master of Moortop curled around the body of little Frankie Kershaw.

'I'll deal with this,' said the doctor. 'Take Miss Honoria to her mother, then inform Mr and Mrs Kershaw of the accident.'

Riveted to the spot, Bill Watkins twisted a flat cap between hands gnarled by many years of contact with the earth and its fruits. 'The master,' he managed finally. 'Will he be all right?'

Dr Randall shook his head. 'Shell-shock's a bugger to treat, Bill. I can offer little beyond mild sedation. Please, go and fetch the lad's parents.'

Inside the house, Honoria found her mother seated with the two-year-old Hilda on her lap, Hyacinth wailing into Isobel's shoulder.

'What have you done?' asked Isobel.

Honoria put her head on one side. 'Nothing,' she replied. 'I tried to pull him out, but he got heavy.'

Isobel sighed, her breath shuddering on its way out. Even when saturated, Frankie Kershaw's tiny frame would have presented no problem to this strong girl. 'Frankie was terrified of water,' said Isobel. 'Whatever possessed him to jump into the stream?'

Honoria offered no reply. Mother was looking at her strangely, as if she blamed her. But no one had seen, so no one could be sure.

Hyacinth lifted her head. 'You did it,' she said clearly. 'At first I thought I must have been mistaken, but I saw you. You killed Frankie Kershaw.'

This development was unexpected, to say the least.

'I shall talk to your father,' said Isobel. 'This must be kept quiet, of course.' She turned to her oldest daughter, placed a hand on her head.

'Never speak of this outside,' she said softly. 'The disgrace of it would kill your father.'

Honoria stood her ground, did not flinch or weep. There they sat, Mother with her baby, Hyacinth waiting for her other parent to come in. Daddy's girl and Mummy's pet. Honoria hated them with a deep, quiet, almost emotionless passion.

'Go to your room,' snapped the mistress of Moortop. 'Your father will deal with you later.'

Thomas did not deal with Honoria. He withdrew even further into his shell after the death of Frankie Kershaw. Nothing was ever said. The West family attended the funeral, although Hilda was judged young enough to stay at home with Bertha Mills. The Kershaws' cottage was renovated and decorated, and Isobel West made it her business to ensure that the remaining children were well fed and clothed.

Honoria found herself in a strange position, because although she was ignored by members of her family she sensed their unease, and realized that her power, should she ever care to implement it, was probably without bounds. She took to listening at doors, even secreting herself in cupboards and under beds to spy on her parents and sisters.

School became a necessity once she reached the age of five. Her older sister began to attend a private academy for young ladies, a school to which Thomas moved her before Honoria began to attend the village junior mixed and infants where Hyacinth had received her early education. Honoria did not dislike lessons, though she found little use for what she learnt within the walls of infant academia. She could already read and calculate, so she passed the time of day digesting information contained in books meant for much older children.

Miss Woods found Honoria a strange, clever pupil whose silences managed to be insolent though the girl was not particularly confrontational during her early years. She finished every task set for her, even completing an extremely neat cross-stitched sampler within a very few hours and coming top of the class in most subjects.

When Honoria moved up into Miss Bowker's class, Miss Woods breathed a sigh of relief and got on with her job, pleased that she no longer laboured beneath the damning gaze of Honoria West's strange turquoise eyes.

Honoria hated Miss Evelyn Bowker. A remnant of the Victorian age, Miss Bowker believed in hard work, regular exercise and the frequent application of a ruler across the back of small, naughty hands. She did not discriminate when doling out punishments, so girls as well as boys often smarted after spelling and mental arithmetic tests.

She used her ruler on Honoria West just once, when the child deliberately insisted that seven times seven made forty-eight. Evelyn Bowker knew full well that the bold girl was capable of offering the right answer, as Honoria, at the age of six, was at least as well informed as any child four years her senior. The teacher whacked Honoria's knuckles, staggered back when she saw the huge smile on Honoria's face.

'Forty-nine,' said Honoria sweetly. 'The correct answer is forty-nine.' She jumped up and wrested the ruler from Miss Bowker's hands. 'You will not hit me again,' she stated, before stalking out of the classroom. All heard Miss Bowker's ruler scraping along corridor walls as Honoria left the school.

The giggling started at the back of the classroom, spreading infectiously along rows of children until the whole scene was one of madness and uproar. Miss Bowker burst into tears and ran from her post to the comparative safety of the headmaster's office.

Honoria, in the playground, listened to the delightful sound of chaos. She had made something happen. All it had taken was courage, a sweet smile and a swift exit from the scene.

From that day, Honoria was hailed by her fellows as a hero. In the eyes of Standard Two, she could do no wrong. Miss Bowker left at the end of term to take up a post in nearby Bolton. Never quite the same as she had been, the woman passed the weeks of her notice simply supervising her pupils while they read or amused themselves quietly. Books on her desk were often torn or defaced, while a large spot of ink appeared one day on a scarf draped over the high chair in which she usually sat, but the teacher made no comment about such occurrences.

The perpetrator of these small crimes did not become bolder, as there was no need for self-reinforcement. Honoria simply basked in the praise of her peers, secure in the knowledge that she could deal with any or every one of them if she so chose.

Mr Cullen, headmaster of the school, trod warily around the daughter of Thomas West. An experienced teacher and manager of children, Brian Cullen could not fathom Honoria at all. Often, at the end of a day, he would stand in the doorway of his empty school, pipe clenched between his teeth, hands clasped behind his back, eyes fixed on a horizon beyond which lay the estate of the West family. Uneasy in his bones and unable to account for his tremors, the headmaster could not lay his tongue across one word to describe young Honoria. But he was sure of one thing. All through her life, Miss Honoria West would bring trouble and unhappiness to those around her.

The West girls led sheltered lives. As time passed and they neared womanhood, Hyacinth and Hilda were certainly aware of their parents' protective attitude, though Honoria, guarded more closely than the other two, continued to feel like a prisoner rather than a precious daughter. They were taken out, of course, sometimes accompanying their parents to shows at the Grand or the Theatre Royal in Bolton, sometimes to visit neighbours, occasionally to attend social functions in houses easily as handsome as their own.

Honoria's behaviour, seldom acceptable, had become a source of great anguish, most particularly to her father. Thomas and Isobel had numerous discussions on the subject, many of which were overheard by the topic under scrutiny, who listened behind doors, from within cupboards, even while hiding behind the very chair or sofa occupied by one of the senior Wests.

'She jumped on Hyacinth's pet rabbit, I'm sure of it,' sobbed Isobel one summer evening in 1942, 'and broke all those lovely dolls. Now I don't know where she gets to.'

The seventeen-year-old Honoria lay behind a large, overstuffed sofa in the second drawing room, her mother and father just inches away. 'She doesn't know where I get to,' mouthed the unrepentant sinner.

'Well, we cannot be in two places at once. Short of employing a full-time chaperone or a prison warder, there isn't a great deal we can do,' said Thomas. He had little time, these days. As a farmer, he was expected to produce as much food as possible, as cheaply as possible. While war raged in Europe, Thomas West's struggles consisted of paperwork, trying to run a business without fuel and with a depleted workforce, then more and more paperwork. 'This war doesn't help,' he said unnecessarily.

Isobel nodded. In 1940 she had been saddled with three evacuees from Liverpool, but the parents had reclaimed the children after months without bombardment. 'At least I don't have to worry any more about Honoria hurting our little strangers. Liverpool is very much under fire. But I do hope they don't send us any more, Thomas.'

'Quite.'

Isobel was not comfortable with herself. She felt a large degree of guilt in matters concerning her middle daughter. The girl had been overlooked to the point of neglect, as Isobel's health had been so poor after Honoria's birth. Then, when Hilda had arrived, Isobel's meagre store of energy had been invested in the newborn. 'Hyacinth has always had you,' she told her husband now, 'while I have paid far too much attention to Hilda. But it's too late now, because the damage has been done and we are paying for it.'

Thomas nodded. 'She certainly hates me and makes no attempt to conceal her feelings.' He glanced at his watch. As an ex-officer from the previous war, Thomas also enjoyed the dubious privilege of supervising the local Home Guard. In half an hour, he would have to go along to the church hall for drill.

'She dislikes her sisters, too. Thomas, Hyacinth is twenty-two years of age. How could she bring a young man here?' Hyacinth, in a reserved occupation as farmhand, had been spared call-up. Sometimes, Isobel wished that Hyacinth had gone away, as the oldest West girl, pretty as a picture, was becoming as weathered as the men with whom she worked. The young men had gone abroad, of course. Hyacinth toiled among old people with polished walnut skin and gnarled hands. 'Thomas, even if Hyacinth were to bring a friend home, there is no way of predicting how Honoria would behave. Yet the tenants adore her. She is all sweetness and light to them, helping with chores, nursing the sick.'

'And she killed young Frankie Kershaw.'

There followed a short silence. 'Perhaps Hyacinth was mistaken.' There was no hope, no conviction behind the words.

'Hyacinth was not mistaken, my dear. She was some distance from the bridge, but her eyes are good and she is not given to exaggeration. I suppose we must face the fact that we have bred a monster.'

The monster smiled in its lair.

'Then how does she manage to be so good with your tenants?'

Thomas made no immediate reply. Honoria had burnt down the school. He had discovered paraffin and matches in a barn, had sought out the dress she had worn that day, had recognized the scent of singed wood and accelerant. Brian Cullen, asleep in the schoolhouse at the time of the fire, had perished while trying to save his little world. 'I think we must have her put away, Isobel.'

She gasped, clung to the arm of her chair. 'No,' she cried. 'The disgrace, the humiliation! How would Hyacinth find a husband while her sister is in an asylum?'

'I'm sorry,' answered Thomas. 'But the world needs to be protected from Honoria.' His wife knew nothing of Honoria's involvement with the fire; Thomas, true to form, had kept his counsel.

'No,' repeated Isobel. 'She is not as bad as she used to be. You must admit that she has behaved slightly better of late.'

Again, Thomas made no effort to enlighten his wife. Just weeks earlier, Honoria had been refused permission to attend a function with her older sibling. Hyacinth, five years her sister's senior, was officially out in the world. She needed to meet people of her own age, needed to find a partner, a husband who would guard her well, provide and care for her.

Isobel wriggled in her chair, flinched slightly because of bruising.

Thomas had found the length of fine string that had caused his wife to tumble down the stairway, was in no doubt about who had caused the 'accident'. Yet he had failed, thus far, to find within himself the ability to inform Isobel of the truth. As for Honoria, Thomas was afraid of confronting her, of sending her spinning into a whirl of insane behaviour that might reverberate for ever inside the walls of Moortop.

Behind the sofa, Honoria stiffened. An asylum? She was the cleverest of the Wests, the one who made things happen, the one who would leave her mark on the world. Hatred for her father flooded through her body, almost causing her to faint or to cry out against cramps that suddenly visited her abdomen. She would not allow this man to continue as a threat, would find a way of punishing him, of removing him, if necessary.

'I believe that Hyacinth will become a target for Honoria,' said Thomas. 'Even Hilda could be within her sights. We must be prepared to ask for medical help, Isobel. If we allow her to remain a free agent, God alone knows what she might do to us or to her sisters.'

Isobel pondered, almost destroying the hand-kerchief clasped in her fingers. 'I cannot do it,' she said eventually. 'I cannot stand by while a daughter of mine is dragged off to live with screaming lunatics. Please, please, do not have her taken away.'

'Then you must watch her,' replied Thomas. 'And make her sisters aware of the potential dangers.' To be doubly sure, Thomas intended to tell Hyacinth the full story. That sweet, gentle young woman had a strength of character which, he felt sure, would enable her to cope. 'Also, watch yourself on the stairs,' he added, largely against his better judgement. Poor Isobel had not Hyacinth's strength of mind, and Thomas could not bear to think of his wife living on the edge of her nerves. Now that her child-bearing years were over, the couple had become slightly closer, often sharing a bed and talking things over well into the night. Isobel was frail; he intended to protect her.

Isobel swallowed. 'My fall was an accident.'

'Was it?'

Honoria placed a hand over her mouth. She had not found the opportunity to remove the string that had sent her mother crashing down the stairs. He knew so much, this man who was her father. Honoria was not safe in a world that contained him.

'Please don't do anything just yet,' Isobel begged. 'Poor Hyacinth and Hilda – what will they think of us if we lock up their sister? And our tenants would consider us heartless.'

253

'Oh, yes,' sighed Thomas. 'Honoria has taken care to win their affections. She is so calculating, so cold. How is a child like her to be dealt with, Isobel? She has no human feelings, no pity or sympathy.'

'She must have, Thomas. Surely everyone has feelings.'

He looked hard at his wife. 'Do you remember the day when I took my gun to Ebony?'

She nodded mutely.

'I shall not trouble you with the details, but the horse's injuries were inflicted by . . . well . . . they were deliberate.'

Isobel pushed a clenched fist against her mouth. Thomas had never bought another horse. He still kept shires: they ploughed the land, these days, because fuel for tractors was in short supply owing to the war. But he no longer rode, and riding had been one of the greatest pleasures for him.

'She killed Ebony?'

Thomas nodded. 'I fired the bullet, but I had to put the poor chap out of his misery. She is, without doubt, as evil as any criminal accounted for in newspapers.' He jumped up, paced about. 'First a rabbit, then a child.' No, he still could not bring himself to discuss with Isobel the murder of a man who had devoted his life to educating children. 'More recently, poor Ebony, followed by your fall on the stairs. We are not secure.'

Honoria shook her head. They were talking as if she were a lunatic, a person with no control over herself. Everything Honoria did was carefully planned and perfectly executed. She was no Jack or Jill the Ripper. All she sought was fairness, a commodity that was sorely lacking in these parts.

Isobel was wringing her hands again. 'Could she be treated, I wonder? Without going away into one of those dreadful places, that is. Perhaps if one of those psychiatry doctors spoke to her . . .'

Thomas had already considered that possibility. 'Of all our children, Honoria is, I believe, the cleverest.'

In that moment, the eavesdropper almost forgave her father, almost loved him. Yes, she was the cleverest and the best.

'But she will achieve nothing, I fear,' he continued, 'as she is not capable of steering her gifts in a proper direction. Can you imagine the sort of brain that could work out how to commit crimes such as hers? I think she could easily fool a doctor. Our only course is to try to convince someone of her insanity, have her locked away and allow her to be studied over a period of time. Weekly visits to a specialist would not suffice. She would have him eating out of her hand inside five minutes. In fact, she would probably convince him of *our* insanity and wickedness.'

He was learning, Honoria concluded.

'Consider this carefully,' Thomas was saying now. 'She would kill us all in our beds if the fancy took her.' He regretted these words immediately, had not meant to terrify his wife. 'She won't, Isobel. However, just in case she should lose her temper again, we must consider seriously the idea of putting her into a private clinic.'

But Isobel's mind was made up. She was in charge of the house and the girls, while his function was to ensure that his estate ran efficiently. 'No, Thomas.' She sighed wearily. 'Let us see how she goes on. Perhaps she will grow out of her wicked ways. She must be allowed time to improve.'

Thomas walked to the door. 'I hope, my dear, that we shall not live to regret this day.'

Behind the sofa, Honoria lay still, waited until both her parents had left the room. They didn't deserve her. They had never loved her, had seldom found time for her. Mother was a weak fool, but Father was an actual threat. Honoria straightened her dress, patted her hair and went up to bed. It was time to think, to form a plan. Because she had no intention of entering a madhouse.

Most of the tenants had really taken a shine to Miss Honoria. The other two girls were pleasant enough, but Honoria was one for rolling her sleeves up and getting on with things. If a mother was ill, the middle daughter of Thomas and Isobel West thought nothing of cooking, cleaning, washing and ironing, sometimes spending a week at a time with a particular family, wiping fevered brows, taking the whole-bodied out for walks, amusing babies for hours on end.

'That's a grand lass,' Bill Watkins told his

wife, when she finally showed signs of recovering from a bout of influenza. 'See, she's left you some nice broth, full of nourishment, it is.'

Polly Watkins, brighter than most, had her doubts about their high-ranking nursemaid, though she had, thus far, kept her opinions to herself, since expressing them would have brought the wrath of the whole estate on her head. There was something about Miss Honoria, a way she had of looking at people. She reminded Polly of a reptile, cold-blooded, hard and watchful. Yes, she helped people; yes, she went out of her way to become indispensable. But, even as she washed and cooed over a baby, while she fed the sick and scrubbed floors, she was elsewhere, dreaming, thinking, calculating.

'Will you try a bowl of this?' asked Bill.

'All right.'

He spooned the viscous liquid between the parched lips of his wife. They were surviving the war so far, but in spite of living well beyond the reach of bombardment a little germ had almost taken her. 'What's up now, lass?' he asked.

'Oh, it'll take me a while to get right, love.'

He scooped a few drops of broth from Polly's chin. 'Nay, you're bothered over summat.'

Polly swallowed, hesitated. 'I don't feel comfortable when she's here.'

'Well, that'll be with her being gentrified.'

The sick woman raised weary shoulders. 'She's got a bit of a Lanky accent, gentry or not.' Mixing with ordinary folk since childhood had flattened Honoria's vowels somewhat.

'Aye, but she uses the right words.'

Polly accepted another spoonful. 'I can't put a finger on it,' she mumbled. 'She's . . . she's not like other folk.'

' 'Course she's not. She's a West.'

It was no use. Polly took the broth obediently, tried to get her mind off Honoria. Was she the only person in the world who instinctively mistrusted the girl? 'Where's the kiddies?'

'Gone to the big house with Miss Honoria. She's feeding them in the kitchen – scones and jam.'

'Very nice.' Since the death of little Frankie Kershaw, Polly had been uneasy about her own children going near that stream. Poor Minnie Kershaw had never been the same since her son's death. 'She were with him when he died,' Polly said now.

'Eh?'

'Miss Honoria. She saw Frankie die. Happen it turned her mind, made her a bit thoughtful, like.'

'Aye,' agreed Bill. 'That'll be it. Miss Honoria's looked after that family ever since, so has Mrs West. Did you see the size of the goose she got them last Christmas? That were black market, no mistake.'

Polly remained uneasy. 'Will she bring our children back soon, Bill?'

'You know she will.'

Polly slipped into a fitful sleep. In her dreams, she saw a mad witch wielding an axe and chasing children across bridges. The

258

harridan's face was not visible, but she moved like an older version of Miss Honoria. The scene changed to one of domestic harmony, four children sitting around a kitchen table, cakes and sandwiches spread out before them. As each child bit and swallowed, it shrank until it was the size of a small doll. 'Poison,' said a female voice.

'Miss Honoria!' screamed Polly.

Bill rushed in. As Mr West's steward, he had to go out on his rounds soon, then he was due at the church hall for drill later on. But he didn't like the idea of leaving Polly.

'Don't kill them,' yelled the woman in the bed.

Bill shook his head. This bloody influenza was a pest, and no mistake.

Hyacinth watched Honoria with the Watkins brood. She was so kind, so gentle with them. It was almost impossible to believe that this same young woman had killed Frankie Kershaw, had committed arson and manslaughter, had tortured animals. Father had told Hyacinth everything, and Hyacinth was helping to watch a sister whom she feared more than any missile dropped from stray German aircraft.

Honoria smiled to herself. If any member of her family ever accused her of a crime, the whole community would attest to her innocence. Even the priest was in tow, pleased to have a young lady from a good family who was not afraid to dirty her hands by polishing pews and scrubbing aisles.

'Honoria?'

'Yes?'

'Have you seen Father?'

'No. I've been with Mrs Watkins all day. She is still recovering, so I've minded the children and made broth.'

Hyacinth was worried about Father, though she couldn't pinpoint her reasons, not quite. She placed herself in a chair at the table with Honoria and Polly Watkins's brood, three boys and one girl. They giggled in the presence of their betters, and Honoria laughed with them, plying them with jellies, cakes and jam tarts.

'It's like a birthday,' crowed the little girl.

Honoria was working her way up to something, thought Hyacinth. She had been extra kind and happy just before causing Mother's fall.

'Every day is someone's birthday.' Honoria laughed.

She killed my rabbit, Hyacinth said inwardly. She killed Frankie. *Who saw him die? I, said the fly. With my little eye, I saw him die.* Hyacinth had been the fly, a small speck on the horizon, growing and growing, nearer and nearer until . . .

'More cake?' asked Honoria.

The children continued to stuff themselves in the direction of nausea.

Watching the scene, Hyacinth was suddenly visited by another terrible thought. Mother and Father would not last for ever. Honoria might even . . . No! When Isobel and Thomas were dead, who would watch over this wayward young woman? All Hyacinth wanted was to meet a nice young man, marry and have children of her own. But would anybody be safe?

'He would have been my age almost exactly,' Honoria told the four round-eyed chewing children, 'and he drowned. So that's why I'm telling you to stay away from water.'

Hyacinth met her sister's steady gaze. The eyes had quietened, were now a greyish blue, all hint of green having faded during recent years. The challenge was there, as plain as any thrown-down gauntlet. Hyacinth knew in that moment that she would never marry, that the evil person with whom she shared parents and home would always spoil everything.

Honoria's smile spread, illuminating a fresh, plump face so angelic that it might well have fooled a jury of twelve good men and true. But it didn't fool her older sister. The near-knowledge that something disastrous was about to happen tingled in Hyacinth's veins, causing pores to open and flesh to crawl.

'Are you well, dear?' Honoria asked.

'Yes.' But for how long?

'I shall take the children home now.' Honoria shepherded her borrowed brood through the doorway and into the farmyard.

Thomas came in. 'What is she up to now?' he asked his oldest daughter.

Hyacinth burst into floods of tears.

'My sweet child, don't weep.' Thomas could not bear tears. Whenever Isobel wept, he felt as if a cold hand had reached into his chest to squeeze every last drop of blood from his heart. If only he could say that. If only he had the ability to touch his wife and children, to give them the physical comfort they craved. The thought of touching Honoria made him shiver, though.

'I'm afraid.' Hyacinth composed herself. 'She terrifies me.' Hilda knew nothing. At the age of fifteen, she continued happy, carefree, concerned only with new dresses and hairstyles. 'And Hilda just isn't prepared.'

'To warn her would be to terrify her,' said Thomas. Hilda was a lovely, generous girl, silly at times, sensible on the whole. Hilda's mind was simpler than Hyacinth's, was probably incapable of absorbing with equanimity the knowledge shared by Thomas and Hyacinth. 'I've begged your mother to send Honoria for some kind of treatment, but she won't hear of it.'

Hyacinth dried her face. 'Well, I can understand that. If Honoria were to be put away, our whole family would be forced to share in the disgrace. But, occasionally, such measures cannot be avoided.'

'Isobel will not be moved.'

Hyacinth looked hard at her father. She understood him, was completely in tune with the man who had given her life, who had nourished her, cared for her, made a fuss of her. He was not demonstrative. Many of her friends' fathers were similar, stiff upper lip, wisdom etched into handsome faces, not a word of love out of any of their mouths. 'I love you so much,' she told him.

He pulled at a suddenly tight collar stud. 'I love you,' he answered gruffly.

'And Hilda?'

He nodded mutely, colour high on his cheekbones.

Hyacinth paused for a moment. 'Honoria?'

Thomas put a hand to his forehead. 'That's a difficult question. If I am to be honest, I must say that I have all the instinctive feelings that seem to accompany parenthood. If anyone hurt her, I should probably fight to the death on her behalf. But I cannot love who she is, what she has become. Worse than that, I cannot like her. Living with someone one dislikes is a terrible thing.'

Again, Hyacinth understood. Honoria was family, and blood ties were strong no matter what the circumstances. Yet living with her was like existing on the brink of a precipice whose edges were eroding by the day. 'Father?'

'Yes?'

She took a deep breath. 'I've been thinking about the long-term future, wondering what will happen when . . . well—'

'When I'm dead?'

She blinked away new tears.

'I, too, have given consideration to that. It's very difficult to know what to say to you, Hyacinth. But I have talked to Honoria.'

'Really?'

He nodded. 'I know that it has not been usual for girls in your position to work. But things have changed. With all the young men away at war and, knowing that some of them will not return, it is becoming increasingly common for young women to work, to have a career. She wants to do a secretarial course. I have agreed. With any luck, she'll find a job away from here.'

'And plague other people?'

'What else would you wish to happen?'

Hyacinth didn't know, would never know how to answer.

'Is it our fault?' Thomas asked. 'Did we get what we deserved?'

How often Hyacinth had wondered about that. The conclusion she had reached was not born out of the need to serve her parents well and to save their feelings; Hyacinth had worked out the answer months earlier. 'No,' she said now. 'It is not your fault. Perhaps she needed more attention when she was small, but other people have suffered owing to parental illness or absence. Take as example Maria Compton. Her mother died in childbirth and Maria's neglect was severe. But she survived. She never hurt anyone.'

'Honoria's disposition is determined by her parents.'

'Her constitution is a freak of nature, Father. You cannot be accountable for a character which may have been formed in the womb.'

Thomas still felt guilty. He remembered falling in love with Hyacinth, recalled Isobel's fascination with the youngest of the three. 'Honoria was simply left in the middle to care for herself.'

'Stop this,' ordered Hyacinth. 'I know you are my father and that I should treat you with respect. But what is done is done and there is no undoing it, so I must reprimand you. Life isn't a piece of knitwear that can be unravelled and reshaped. Torturing yourself will get us nowhere. She is seventeen. She is old enough now to know the difference between right and wrong.'

'And she still tried to kill your mother.'

Hyacinth squirmed uneasily in her seat. She and Father had hoped, had prayed that Honoria had grown out of her childhood delinquency. For years, the girl had done nothing untoward. 'It was because Mother refused permission for Honoria to attend a birthday party with me. Honoria would have been the youngest person there, and Mother considered the occasion unsuitable. So, if Honoria does not get her own way, we shall all be in danger.'

'Exactly.'

'I suppose the secretarial course is a good idea.' Honoria would need to work. She wanted occupying. 'If she should ever marry, Father, how would she treat a husband if he tried to be severe? If she had children and they were naughty, what—?'

'I know. These thoughts have plagued me for some time.'

'And yet, if she does not marry, the burden will eventually fall on me and on Hilda. Our husbands and children could be in danger.'

Thomas sighed heavily. 'Most fathers bequeath security to their children – or they try to. To you and to poor Hilda, I shall be leaving a responsibility so heavy . . . Try to find a life, Hyacinth. Something for yourself alone, or for yourself and some nice young man. Get away from here.'

'And Hilda?'

'The same.'

It sounded so simple, but it wasn't. Young men were thin on the ground, most away fighting for king and country, while those remaining at home were unfit or married to work that was essential, many doing twelve-hour shifts. Once the war ended, unless Honoria found a relationship first, she would surely go out of her way to spoil her sisters' chances. Just as she had broken dolls and killed the rabbit, she would ruin any opportunities for Hyacinth and Hilda.

'I'm sorry,' whispered Thomas.

'Don't be. Look, I'll make us both a nice cup of tea and take some up for Mother and Hilda.' She grinned in an effort to lighten the atmosphere. 'Hilda found some material in the loft. She's making herself a suit with a bolero. Just at present, she has a fixation about boleros.'

Thomas thanked God for Hilda's fixation. One person in this beleaguered home was happy and relatively carefree. He watched his beloved eldest daughter making tea, tried to enjoy the ordinariness of this domestic scene. But Honoria would return soon, and the thunderclouds would not be far behind her.

Bill Watkins went down with influenza just as his wife neared recovery. After two weeks in bed, he was rushed off to Bolton Royal Infirmary with double pneumonia. Honoria, expressing her customary concern, moved into Bill's house.

Polly, who was well past caring about folk with strange eyes, left her four children in the care of Miss Honoria and moved to her sister's house in Bolton. Polly's sister lived no more than a cough and a spit from the infirmary, making visiting easier for Polly, who was also glad of her sister's company at this stressful time.

Life on the estate was difficult, as many workers had been called up to serve in the forces. Now, with Bill Watkins on the danger list, Thomas had to knuckle down with the rest and get his hands dirty. In his more honest moments, Thomas admitted to himself that there was nothing he liked better than honest-to-goodness sweated labour. He enjoyed being practical and getting filthy, took pleasure in a good long soak at the end of each day, enjoyed a feeling of pride when he looked upon land he had tended himself.

The old well at the back of the farmhouse had always been a source of worry to Thomas. As it was no longer in use, he had decided that it would be filled in properly once the war was over, but, until then, he repeatedly checked the bolted and padlocked cover to make sure that it presented no problems to youngsters on the estate. Honoria had taken to bringing home the Watkins children and, especially after the business with Frankie Kershaw, Thomas was keen to keep the area as safe as possible.

Isobel and Hilda had gone into Bolton to search for trimmings to adorn Hilda's latest bolero outfit. Hyacinth, too, was out, having promised to meet a friend in Edgeworth Village.

Thomas looked at the well's lid and saw that it had begun to show signs of wear and tear. Two planks had splintered and drifted apart, leaving almost enough space for a small child to fall into a drop of more than fifty feet.

He opened the padlocks and removed the cover. It would have to be mended today, of course, so he went off into a barn to find tools and timber. A feeling of deep unease followed him into the building, and he did his best to shrug it off. Honoria was nowhere to be seen: she was at the home of Polly and Bill Watkins, was caring for the family while the parents were away.

After three hours, the lid was mended and reinforced. All he had to do now was to replace it and fasten it down securely. He stood by the well and set the heavy, repaired cover on the ground while he drew breath after such a long stint of labour.

When the first blow struck him, he crumpled, falling to his knees like a Christian at prayer. He saw her, watched from the corner of a shock-dulled eye while she brought the plank down for a second time.

'They're at school, Father,' she told him, 'so I thought I'd pop home and see how you are.'

He was still conscious. How strong she was, how powerful, how evil. He was lifted, heaved about and draped like wet washing over the edge of the well. Thomas West was strangely unsurprised to find himself falling into a deep, black hole from which he would not emerge alive. Isobel and Hyacinth were foremost in his mind as he bounced against cruel, sharp stones. What would become of them? The murderer above was laughing; the eerie sound pursued him for what seemed like hours.

At last, he reached the bottom. The water was icy and not very deep. Mud closed over much of his body, entering his mouth, causing him to gag against the vile, dank taste. She was replacing the lid. No, no, she was balancing it across half of the aperture. So clever. It would appear now that he had tumbled while trying to cope single-handedly with a job that required two men. Oh, she was stronger than two men; her fury made her brawnier than a dozen farm labourers.

Well, it was over. He went through it all, his childhood, the deaths of his parents, his marriage. Hyacinth, Hilda and Isobel were beyond his reach now. He could not warn, save or protect them from the dangerous Honoria. Unconsciousness threatened and, his body racked with pain, Thomas entered a place where there was no hurt, simply closing his eyes and welcoming the warm, safe blanket that sometimes covers those whose deaths come as a result of sudden assault or shock.

Honoria, far enough from the house to be invisible to daily domestics, finished her task by disposing of the weapon, allowing it to fall among several other discarded lengths of wood beside the well. She then ran like the wind through fields and meadows. Entering the back yard of Bill's cottage, she turned right immediately and went into the lavatory shed. Here, she picked up a large paintbrush and dipped it into a bucket of whitewash, making sure that much of the paint marked her clothes as she sloshed it about.

'Still at it, Miss Honoria?' yelled Minnie Kershaw from next door.

Honoria poked her face into the yard.

'You look like a ghost,' said Minnie. 'I reckon there's more on you than what there is on t'wall. Eeh, but you're a grand girl, miss. There's not many as would move in and look after them four. Aye, you're a good lass.'

'Perhaps I was reared on good milk,' replied Honoria.

Minnie, who had never managed to be fully content since the death of Frankie, beamed with pleasure. She had lost a son, but she had nurtured a daughter-by-proxy who now belonged to a whole community, a young woman whose charitable works made her an asset to all who lived hereabouts.

Honoria returned to her work, humming merrily in spite of the stench in the outbuilding. She had been whitewashing all morning, had not left the premises. There was stew cooking on the kitchen range, the children's clothes were clean and waiting to be ironed. Tomorrow, she would fill the copper and wash all the bedding. After all, this was a diseased house and Polly's children must be saved from influenza.

They found him, realizing right away that an accident had taken place, as Thomas West would never have left the well cover half on and half off. Landowners from surrounding areas sent labourers and equipment, the most useful item being a long rope ladder with hooks that clamped over the rim of the well. John Patterson, one of the Wests' men, went down and struggled through slime to secure a heavy rope around his master.

When the broken body lay beside the well, Isobel and Hyacinth ran towards it, but workers held them back. Thomas's descent into the well had left its marks, while the corpse had made violent contact with uneven walls on its way back to the surface.

Hyacinth understood why the labourers wanted the women to stay away from Father. 'Mother, you must not look.'

'I must see him!' screamed the dead man's hysterical wife.

'Let them clean him first,' begged Hyacinth. 'The doctor must be sent for.' She turned, saw Hilda sobbing against the shoulder of a rough clad man who made no attempt to stem his own tears. Everyone was weeping. As they stood around, unsure of what to do next, the sun was obliterated by a sudden scud of clouds. The light had gone out, thought Hyacinth. Thomas West, a taciturn man with a heart of gold, had given so much to so many, had certainly been completely unaware of his own value, his own goodness. 'Come along, Mother,' she whispered. 'There is nothing to be done. Let's go inside.'

Isobel took to her bed and was sedated by the doctor. Hyacinth lay next to her mother, while

271

Hilda sobbed quietly on a *chaise-longue* beneath the window. Someone would have to go and tell Honoria. A dart of pure horror stabbed its way into Hyacinth's breast, but she chased it away. No. Surely not? 'Hilda?'

'Yes?'

'Lie here with Mother in case she wakes. I must go down to the cottage and tell Honoria.'

Hilda sat up. 'Don't go,' she pleaded. 'Send someone. I'm sure Honoria will know anyway – the news will have spread.' She looked nervously at Isobel, who still moaned in her sleep in spite of the drugs. 'I shouldn't know what to do if Mother woke, Hyacinth.'

The door opened. Honoria's face insinuated itself into the resulting gap. 'Mother?'

'She's been sedated,' replied Hyacinth.

Honoria entered the room and closed the door quietly. 'Poor Mother,' she said. 'She will miss him so.'

As soon as the newcomer turned towards the bed, Hyacinth knew beyond a shadow of a doubt that she was looking into the eyes of a murderer. The plump, open face did not fool the oldest West sister, not for a single second.

Honoria held Hyacinth's gaze. 'Is Mother ill?'

'Our father has just died,' replied Hyacinth, almost snappily. 'She is bound to be out of sorts. We all are.'

Honoria walked across the room and placed herself in a chair. Again, she stared into Hyacinth's all-knowing eyes. It was no matter. Let Hyacinth think what she would – there was no proof.

Hyacinth closed her eyes and saw her father's face. In her mind's eye, he sat astride Ebony, as straight as any soldier, as comfortable as only a practised horseman could be. He clicked his tongue, told his beloved steed to walk on. 'Oh, my dear God,' she wept. 'Please, please, look after him.'

Hilda sobbed anew, curled herself into the *chaise-longue* with her face buried in her hands.

Honoria studied them both, saw Hyacinth lying close to Mother, Hilda breaking her heart. Well, let them. The man was dead and Honoria was no longer threatened with incarceration.

'Where have you been all day?' asked Hyacinth eventually.

'Whitewashing, cooking, looking after the cottage.'

Hyacinth's weeping slowed. 'We knew that Father intended to make the well cover good today. He told us all. You were here when he said it.'

Honoria stood up. 'Is this leading somewhere, Hyacinth?'

'I wish I had guarded him better, that's all.'

'Accidents cannot be predicted,' announced Honoria.

Hyacinth nodded just once.

'And it was an accident.' There was an edge to Honoria's words. 'It's plain that he fell in while trying to mend the cover. He should have waited for help.'

Hyacinth sat on the end of her mother's bed. 'You have not cried, Honoria.'

'If and when I do, it will be when I am alone.

Shows of emotion mean nothing. And weeping will not bring our father back.'

Hilda howled again.

'I don't know why she's in such a state,' declared Honoria. 'She still has her mother. You, Hyacinth, have suffered the greatest loss. I have meant little to either of my parents. You were his favourite, while Hilda is Mother's.'

Hyacinth felt a cold shiver making its way from the base of her spine to the top of her head. This seventeen-year-old girl had committed patricide today. There was nothing in her face, no grief, no guilt, no discomfort. 'You are quite the coldest person I have ever met,' whispered Hyacinth. 'There is no love in you.'

'Affection breeds affection.' Honoria's reply was swift and clear. 'To give, one must receive.' Having made this statement, she left the bedroom.

Hyacinth went to the *chaise-longue*, knelt on the carpet and tried to comfort her fifteen-year-old sister.

'Just because I wanted a bolero,' sobbed Hilda.

'No, no. Hilda my dear, the well is invisible from the house. Even if you had stayed at home, the same thing could have happened. I went out, too, you know. I walked to the village to meet Maria and we went to Joan Dobson's for little more than a trivial chat. While we talked about parachute silk for Joan's wedding dress, our father was being . . . was having his accident. No one is to blame.' Honoria was to blame.

Hilda sighed, sobs causing her breath to

shudder on its way out. 'How shall we manage without him?'

'I'll take over.' When she heard those words emerging from her own mouth, Hyacinth was as shocked as Hilda. But Hyacinth knew more than anyone about Father's estate. She felt as if a dark, heavy curtain of responsibility had suddenly descended upon her. Father was hardly cold, and here she sat, considering the future. 'I must,' she explained. 'Someone has to look after Mother. That job will fall to you, Hilda. I shall have to be the man of the house.'

'I'll help you,' said the ever-practical youngest child. 'We must all help one another now.'

'Yes.' Honoria would help only herself, of course. God forbid that she might find the need to dispose of the rest of her family.

'Mother is awake,' said Hilda.

They walked to the bed, found Isobel staring up at the ceiling, no expression on her face. Eventually, she noticed the two girls. 'Oh, my poor daughters,' she mumbled, her speech slurred. 'What will become of us now?'

'We'll manage,' said Hyacinth. 'We have one another.'

'Where is she?' the mother said.

'You were asleep when Honoria came,' replied Hyacinth.

'Good. I have no desire to see her . . .' Isobel drifted back to sleep.

Hilda touched her sister's arm. 'What does she mean?'

'Nothing,' said Hyacinth. 'The drugs are affecting her, that's all.'

275

* * *

The funeral was almost as well attended as it might have been without the war. People from miles around came to bid farewell to a man who had been a kind neighbour, a dependable ally, an excellent employer. Men in good suits cried openly, all thoughts of propriety deserting them. Landed gentry stood shoulder to shoulder with common working folk, each reaching out to the other while the Catholic requiem droned on and on in ancient church Latin.

Polly Watkins, whose husband was on the mend, made it her job to look after the master's girls. Their mother was elsewhere, present in body alone, her mind obviously drifting as she gazed round the church smiling and hailing familiar faces.

'She's as drugged as a nobbled horse,' whispered Dr Randall to Hyacinth, 'but as long as she can put one foot before the other that's as much as we can expect for now.'

The coffin was beautiful, all shiny and new, with heavy brass handles and heaps of flowers decorating its lid. 'Pretty,' mumbled Isobel.

Polly Watkins put one arm round Hyacinth, the other round Hilda. Honoria needed no one. Slightly separated from the rest of her family, she occupied the end place in the pew, the area furthest from the coffin, nearest to the wall. All this rubbish and pomp meant nothing to her. She went to confession rarely, never told her worst sins, as she was above and beyond the reach of all this praying and moaning. She was busy studying Pitman, had every intention of passing her examinations and making her mark in the world of industry. In fact, she had a typing examination in a few days and could have done without all this time-wasting.

Isobel looked at Polly Watkins. 'What are you doing here?' she asked, in a voice loud enough to drown the priest's mutterings.

'Helping you,' answered Polly.

'That's very good of you.' Isobel turned round. 'Where's Thomas?' she asked.

Several women went outside to cry in the graveyard. Hyacinth turned and looked at Honoria. As she scrutinized the killer's face, a thought scuttered across Hyacinth's mind. Honoria had probably wiped the murder from her mind. She had the ability to commit a crime, then to banish it from her memory. There was no doubt that Honoria was evil, that she chose to do the wicked deeds, yet she was so wonderfully, unbelievably calm.

They buried Thomas West while his wife prattled on about knitting patterns and cross-stitch. Hyacinth threw soil on the coffin, as did Hilda. But Isobel continued to describe a table-cloth she had recently embroidered, while Honoria simply disappeared.

'She must be too upset,' said Minnie Kershaw, referring, of course, to the middle daughter of the recently deceased. 'She saw my Frankie die, now she's lost her dad and her mam's gone funny. She'll likely be crying on her own somewhere.'

She wasn't, of course. Honoria was at home

brushing up her shorthand. Determined to do well, she employed every spare moment in the pursuit of her goal. With a plateful of sandwiches culled from the post-funeral buffet, she scribbled and checked, chewed and swallowed.

After half an hour of peace, Hyacinth put in an appearance. 'What on earth are you doing?'

'Studying. Secretaries are needed during the war – as well as in peacetime. I shall have to do something, or I shall get called up, so I'm making sure I don't have to become an unofficial Land Army girl. Farming is not my idea of fun. So I have to get on with my studies.'

'Today?'

'Why not?'

'If you don't know why not, there is no point in telling you.'

Honoria stood up. 'You hate me, don't you?'

'No.'

'Well, you should, because I have no time for you or Hilda.'

Hyacinth stood absolutely still. There was too much danger here, far too much wickedness. In order to keep everybody safe, nothing contentious must be said. Honoria had literally got away with murder. Again.

Sixteen

Isobel West hovered for many months in an area where sanity and madness held an uneasy truce. She divided her time between her bedroom and long walks, for many of which she was not always suitably dressed. On more than one occasion, she was brought home in nightwear and slippers by one of the workers or by Hilda, whose unenviable task was to look after Mother.

Honoria, at eighteen, had been allocated a wartime post as secretary in the offices of a Bolton local-government official, whose filing system she reorganized and whose love life she affected within a short space of time. The infatuated man followed his wayward assistant around for a few weeks, then gave up and returned to a wife who would never forgive him. Honoria moved onward and upward at lightning speed, eventually coming to rest in Bolton town hall, where she settled down to run the life of the chief librarian, a bookish gentleman who never noticed her advances.

Hyacinth administered the estate with an efficiency that was much admired. 'She's her father's daughter, all right,' the fully recovered Bill Watkins was often heard to opine. Everyone agreed. It was plain that Miss Hyacinth West had a good business head on her, because she bought land, sold it, studied husbandry, gave each tied cottage a piece of soil on which families could grow their own produce, keep chickens or geese. Any idea that saved money or made money was implemented immediately.

Hilda, youngest and loneliest of the three girls, seemed to shrink further into her shell as time went on. She lost interest in her appearance, stopped meeting friends, spent most of her time chasing Isobel or helping in the kitchen. At sixteen, she was already middle-aged, resigned to a life without colour or promise.

She was in the kitchen when it happened, when Isobel finally returned to the land of the consciously bereaved.

'Hilda?'

The servants had gone home, and Hilda was experimenting with flaky pastry, an item that had defeated her for some time. Apart from anything else, even within a farming community, ingredients were still thin on the ground.

'Rest it,' said Isobel.

'I beg your pardon?'

'Put it on the marble slab in the pantry for half an hour. Don't refrigerate it.'

Hilda complied, one eye on her mother as she closed the pantry door.

Isobel sat at the table. 'Before I married your father, I was not terribly grand,' she began. 'We were comfortable – trade, not landed. We had four servants, two of whom were a wedding present to Thomas and me – my father paid their wages for years. Mother liked to do her own cooking. I think she was glad to lose a couple of servants.'

'I love cooking,' said Hilda.

Isobel nodded. 'You will have inherited that from your grandmother. Well, she did the most amazing things in the kitchen. There was always game, and she produced the most wonderful game pies, very rich and juicy. The housekeeper was quite demoralized, because Mother outdid her every time. Such marvellous cakes – they melted in the mouth.'

This all added up to at least thirty seconds of sensible speech. Hilda lowered herself gingerly into a chair and waited for Isobel to ask for Father.

'After a while, people actually begged for dinner invitations. We had a strict rota so as not to appear to show favouritism. Your father always enjoyed dining at our house.' She twisted the wedding ring round a finger that was much too thin for it. 'I shall get this made smaller,' she added.

Hilda knew that her mouth was hanging open, so she closed it determinedly.

'How long has he been dead now?'

'Almost a year.'

'I've been unwell, haven't I?'

Hilda inclined her head. 'Yes.'

'It must have been extremely tiresome for you, dear.' Isobel smiled ruefully. 'You were the most beautiful baby, all yellow curls and gurgles. Of course, we couldn't have any more children, or I might have died.' She sat for a while, remembering. 'I loved him so much. He was the finest man I ever knew. Some found him quiet, even sullen, but he was just a thinker. I miss him, Hilda.'

'So do I.'

Isobel rubbed her nose with the heel of a hand. 'It was too much for me to take in, I expect. Was I dreadful?'

Hilda hesitated. 'You were unpredictable, very sad. You didn't always make sense.' Sense? Running around, calling Father's name, throwing food at the walls, screaming to be put out of her misery – 'Let me die. If I die, I might find him!'

'Bring the pastry,' ordered Isobel, after a few more minutes of chat. 'I shall show you how best to fold it. The secret is trapped air, you see. Oh, and put the kettle on. Is there any Earl Grey? Is food still on ration? What on earth have you done to your hair? Where's Hyacinth?'

In the pantry, Hilda leant her head against the wall and allowed the pent-up tears to flow. The doctor had said that Mother might come back eventually, but he had said nothing about how sudden it might be. For ten months, Hilda had cared for a woman who had been incontinent from time to time, who had refused to eat, who had made life excruciatingly painful.

'Hilda?'

She turned, could not stem the flow of emotion. 'Mother?'

Isobel entered the pantry. 'I have stolen your happy years, my darling.'

'No, no, you haven't.'

'You must begin again, go out and about, meet people.'

Hilda sniffed, drew a handkerchief from her sleeve.

Isobel took the square of cotton and dried her baby's eyes. 'Does Hyacinth have a young man?'

'No. People hereabouts call her Farmer Hyacinth now. She's all trousers and wellington boots.'

'And Honoria?'

Honoria had had several, though they never lasted long. 'I'm not sure. She meets people at work, I expect.'

Isobel drifted back to the table. What would Thomas say if he were here? Girls wanted watching, needed guidance from their mother. Hyacinth must be ... oh, twenty-three by now, while Honoria would be eighteen. Honoria. A rabbit, a child ... No. Isobel must look forward, not back. 'We shall be a family again.' She rolled and folded the pastry, showed Hilda how to keep it pliable. 'Don't punish it,' she said. 'Go gently, tease it into doing your bidding.'

Hilda set the kettle to boil, returned to her mother's side. It was hard to believe the change, the miracle. But, as she looked back over recent days and weeks, she realized that Isobel had shouted less, had asked more questions. Perhaps the recovery had not been so sudden after all.

Honoria came in from the hallway, stopped at the open door and studied the scene. 'You managed to get her out of bed, then?'

Isobel rose to her feet. 'I got myself out of bed. I even clothed myself.' She crossed the room and stopped just inches away from her second-born. 'I'm back,' she whispered. 'And I'm here to stay.'

Honoria did not flinch beneath her mother's icy stare. 'We're very pleased – aren't we, Hilda?'

Hilda, who felt the undercurrent and failed to understand it completely, nodded. 'Yes, we are.'

Honoria turned to leave the kitchen.

'Was my darling husband heavy?' Isobel asked, very softly so that her words would not reach Hilda's ears. 'Wasn't that well cover a terrible weight? How did you do it? How could you?'

Honoria swung round. 'Perhaps you are improving, but your recovery is plainly incomplete.' She left the room, slamming the door in her wake.

'What was that about?' Hilda asked.

'Nothing,' answered Isobel. 'Nothing at all.'

The years drifted by, Christmas making way for spring, summer turning to autumn in the blinking of an eye. Without the Germans to worry about, life was easier, though shortages prevailed long after the signing of treaties.

Hyacinth, weathered and fit, realized with a sudden jolt that she was twenty-eight years old. She and Hilda seldom left the estate. Honoria, on the other hand, led a life whose details were largely unknown to the rest of her family. She came and went as she pleased, seldom informing the servants or her mother of her intentions. No one had any idea of where she stayed when she wasn't at home, and no one cared or dared to ask. At twenty-three, she was a handsome if rather weighty young woman with a passion for clothes and shoes. She did not contribute to the domestic coffers, as there was no need for her money, so she spent every halfpenny on herself and still took her allowance from Mother each month.

Hyacinth refused to be properly recompensed for her labour. She received a very small wage on top of her allowance, as did Hilda, who showed no inclination towards socializing among her peers. Still a mother's girl, she stayed at home, cooked, sewed and kept Isobel company.

It was June 1948 when Honoria decided to have her garden party. Plainly out to impress someone or other by bringing him to see the estate, she announced her intention over supper one evening. 'I shall pay the caterers,' she said airily. 'There is no need for any of you to be put out.'

Isobel, who was no longer afraid of Honoria, placed her knife and fork on the plate and wondered what was going on now. Honoria had never brought friends home, had seldom mentioned the names of those with whom she spent time. 'There is no need for caterers,' she said. 'Lottie and Sarah will be pleased to work overtime. And Hilda will have an excuse to show off her skills as a cook.' Hilda, at twenty-one, needed something to do. Perhaps there would be a young man for Hilda or for Hyacinth, though Isobel wondered whether Honoria's friends would be suitable partners for the other two girls.

'As you wish,' said Honoria. 'I think compromise would be the best solution. I shall have some food prepared and brought in, and Hilda and the servants can do the rest.'

'How many?' asked Hilda, her heart in her mouth. It was so long since she had been among company – the very idea terrified her.

'Forty or fifty.' Honoria got up. 'I need an

285

early night,' she said, before leaving the room.

The three remaining women looked at one another. Isobel and Hyacinth seldom said much about Honoria in Hilda's presence, as they sought to protect her from the unsavoury past of her other sister.

'I've never cooked or baked for so many,' moaned Hilda.

'I'll help,' offered Isobel.

Hyacinth placed tanned, supple hands on the table, the fingers clasping each other as if in need of support. 'So we are to meet her friends at last.'

Isobel wished that her older daughter would use hand and face creams. Hyacinth was beautiful, but her skin needed care. 'Hyacinth,' began Isobel, 'I really think you should get Bill Watkins to run the estate. You could continue to supervise finances and to make the larger decisions, but there is no need for you to be running around like a member of the Land Army.'

'I must work.' Work meant movement and movement meant tiredness. Since the death of her father, Hyacinth had seldom enjoyed a full night's sleep, but sleep came more easily at the end of a busy day. Occasionally, during a particularly bad night, Hyacinth would lie in her bed and wonder about craziness. Honoria was as cracked as an old cup, Mother had endured a bad breakdown, Hilda lived on the edge of fear, hiding in Moortop in case anyone should see her or talk to her. Hyacinth herself had often glanced across the thin line that divided reason and chaos, especially when sleep had eluded her for several nights in a row.

'We shall have to buy new clothes,' ventured Isobel.

Hilda sighed. She hated shopping for clothes. Had she not gone for trimmings that day, stupid trimmings for a bolero, Father might not have—

'Hilda?' Isobel knew her youngest girl's thoughts.

'Oh, just get me some material, Mother. A nice blue cotton, I think, perhaps with a bit of white. I shall make my own outfit.'

Hyacinth and Isobel glanced at each other. 'You will come with Mother and me,' insisted Hyacinth. 'We shall be wonderfully reckless, new shoes, perhaps a bit of jewellery, blow all our clothing allowance in one fell swoop. Let's make a day of it. Now that I have the car, we could go to Southport, perhaps. There are some lovely shops in Lord Street.'

Isobel studied Hilda's dejected face. 'A week's holiday,' she suggested. 'Just the three of us. We could take in some sea air, have a rest, then do our shopping.'

'What about Honoria?' asked Hilda.

Hyacinth all but ground her teeth before replying. 'Honoria has her job. She wouldn't want to come, I'm sure.'

Hilda closed her eyes and thought of Southport. They had always stayed at the Prince of Wales, a very grand hotel with rich carpets and sumptuous décor. Father would sit on the beach in all weathers, even if he had to huddle alone on sands abandoned by every sensible person in the town. 'Remember Father and his deck-chairs?' She opened her eyes.

'Don't remind me.' Isobel actually laughed aloud. 'In the pouring rain, too, sitting there like King Canute, master of the elements and a saturated *Manchester Guardian* in his hands.'

'There's no need for King Canute in Southport,' said Hyacinth. 'You have to walk miles, sometimes, to get your shoes moist.'

Hilda was smiling. 'He always had a stick of rock. Do you remember, Mother? Even though he was so elegant, his pink rock had to be eaten on the beach.'

'Oh, yes,' replied Isobel. 'That was a religious ceremony, very nearly as important as confession and communion. Then there was the fair, of course. He was such a good marksman that the shooting gallery banned him. Thomas won so many teddy bears he was thinking of opening a shop.'

'I remember him walking along the beach to find children. He would ask them if they could recommend a good home for his winnings.' Hyacinth's eyes filled. 'Giving away those toys brought him so much pleasure. There'll never be anyone like him.' The daddy's girl shook herself out of her reverie. Father was a hard act to follow. She had taken on his workload, had learnt what people had thought of him. More importantly, Hyacinth had realized some time ago that no man could be her husband unless he matched Thomas West for goodness and strength of character.

'Right, we are decided,' said Isobel. 'Southport, here we come.'

'I haven't decided.' Hilda's nervousness made her words shiver as they left her lips.

288

'Ah, but this is a democracy and you are out-voted.' Isobel patted Hilda's hand. 'Just a few days. You'll enjoy it.'

It rained, of course. The three women plodded up and down the covered side of Lord Street, bought numerous items of clothing and lunched in a different restaurant each day. In their suite on the top floor of the hotel, they tried on their purchases and paraded up and down like models in a fashion parade.

After forty-eight hours of freedom, Hilda began to relax. Isobel bit back tears as she watched the girl growing younger and sillier with every hour that passed. Hilda bought makeup, experimenting with it, sometimes decorating her face properly, sometimes making a clown of herself with garish rouge and lipstick. When she eventually ventured outside on her own, Isobel breathed a sigh of relief that was almost gale force.

'We forget how young she is,' said Hyacinth.

'My fault.'

'No, Mother. Never your fault.'

Isobel, deep in thought, stared at the floor. 'You are so alike, you and Hilda. Both practical, hard-working.' Even their features were similar – lovely blue eyes, high cheekbones, soft hair. Hyacinth's was light brown, Hilda's blonde.

'I am not really practical,' said Hyacinth. 'There are many things I can do, but I would much rather . . . oh, write, I think. Poems, short stories – even a novel.' She laughed. 'You see, Mother, when I am outside pretending to study the crops and the animals, I'm really waxing lyrical over shades of green and how pretty the clouds are.'

'I'm not surprised. You were always a great reader, and that is how writers are made.'

Hyacinth laughed again. 'Yes, I think that must be true. Perhaps each writer absorbs the already written words, jumbles them up and regurgitates them in a different order. Blatant plagiarism.'

A tea trolley was wheeled in by a maid. As they ate cucumber and salmon sandwiches, Isobel looked at Hyacinth and asked, 'What does she do? Where does she get to?' There was no need to identify the 'she'.

Hyacinth swallowed the last of her sandwich, drained her cup and poured more tea. 'Brace yourself, Mother. She is having an affair with an alderman. He is sixty and married – a grandfather, in fact. She seems to be working her way through the council.'

'Oh dear.'

'Power attracts her. I live in the vain hope that no one upsets her. If she commits a crime out in the world, she could lose her freedom, even her life.' She paused, took another sip of tea. 'I try not to know what she's doing, Mother. And I'm glad to be outside when she's at home.'

'You don't love her.' This was not a question.

'Strangely, I do. I don't like her, not at all. But there's something about her, as if she's a poor, sick thing with no idea of how to live, how to get through the years. And, having just made that statement, I don't understand a word of it.'

Isobel nodded. 'Complicated, isn't it? Did she kill my husband, her own father? I'm half sure that she did, because Thomas wanted her put away and Honoria was a great one for eavesdropping. Yet hope springs eternal and I try to believe that she didn't do it.'

Hyacinth said not a word. But her mind leapt back through the years and landed on a day when she had picked up a bloodstained plank, when she had thrown it into the very hole from which her father's body had been dragged.

Why? she asked herself once again. Mother had gone strange, Hilda had been heartbroken, while Hyacinth herself had lost a father and a best friend all contained within the one package. She had disposed of the plank, she supposed, to save the family any more trauma. And now, with the well concreted and impenetrable, the evidence lay beyond the reach of human hand.

'What's troubling you?' asked Isobel.

'My tea is cold,' lied Hyacinth. 'I think I shall send down for more.'

The weather was perfect for Honoria West's garden party. On a hot Saturday in July, a marquee was erected on the front lawn and a small band practised on a portable rostrum. Honoria, elegant in grey silk from some black-market source, sashayed about giving orders, the slightly over-plump hips wobbling as she went about her business.

Isobel watched her. Honoria's was the sort of prettiness that would not last. She had not been born with the excellent bone structure of her sisters, was not blessed with true beauty. But, as Isobel was forced to admit, Honoria exuded sex appeal. Isobel had no doubt that Honoria's virginity had been thrown away some time ago.

She had the appearance of an experienced woman, versed in the arts of physical entrapment.

By the time people began to arrive, Hilda had whipped herself into an advanced state of nervousness. Surrounded by fresh fruit salads, home-made ice-creams and cakes, she rushed around the kitchen, flustered to the point of speechlessness. Rationing made things so difficult. Would people notice that she had mixed dried eggs with real ones for the cakes? Oh, if only the hens would increase their rate of production, then there might be—

'Out,' ordered Hyacinth. 'Go and get a cool bath, then put on your new suit. Your face is so pink, you'll be clashing with that gorgeous material.'

'But what about—?'

'Out!' yelled Hyacinth.

Hilda ran, then turned in the doorway. 'I'd forgotten how beautiful you are,' she told her sister. Hyacinth was dressed in mint green with dark navy accessories. 'You could have been a film star,' said Hilda.

'Get in the bath now, this minute.'

Left to herself, Hyacinth placed the ice-cream in the freezer, the fruit salad in the fridge. Honoria had provided the savouries, while Hilda, meticulous as ever, had made a superb job of all the sweet dishes. Hyacinth picked up a small cake, bit into it.

'Caught red-handed,' called a male voice.

Hyacinth swivelled, dropped cream on the floor. 'Do you always give people heart-attacks?'

'Sorry.'

Hyacinth pretended not to study him. He was

tall, dark, elegant and very well spoken. He had straight eyebrows, a square chin and a slight wave in his hair. 'I'm Hyacinth West,' she said, after gulping down the cake.

'Lawrence Beresford.' He shook her hand, picked up a napkin and wiped a blob of cream from her nose. 'Honoria's sister?'

She nodded mutely. 'And you?'

'I'm in shoes.'

She looked down at his feet. 'Isn't everyone?'

The newcomer laughed. 'I own the Beresford chain. My father left it to me, though I think I've managed to forgive him at last.' He bent and wiped up the mess on the floor.

Hyacinth suddenly felt silly and girlish. Here she stood, twenty-eight years of age, yet she bubbled inside like a sixteen-year-old with a passion for a boy from the school next door. 'I – I run the estate here.'

'That would account for your lovely tan.'

She felt the heat in her face. 'Mother wants me to stay in more. She says that the weather will age me, and she's spent a fortune on moisturizing creams. But I love the outdoors.' She was gabbling like a teenager, too.

'So do I. In fact, I live not too far from here in a pair of cottages made into one. Country walks are my hobby.'

Had she died and gone to heaven? No. There would be a wife outside, a china doll with yellow curls and a yellow dress, all sunshine and smiles. 'Were you looking for someone?'

'No. I tend to wander. If there's an open door, I take it as an invitation to explore.'

293

'You might be arrested one day as a burglar.'

'Yes. Then there would be no open doors, I suppose. Just a locked cell and a mattress. Still, I appear to have got away with it for well over twenty years. I shan't start worrying now.' She was lovely. He, too, felt that his luck had taken a turn for the better in recent moments. 'So you are all three single and available?'

'Old maids,' she replied.

'Just like me.'

He was humorous without trying, kind without making a fuss. More importantly, he was a bachelor and he lived nearby. 'Shall we go outside, then, Lawrence?'

He crooked his arm and guided her out to the yard.

As they rounded the side of the house, Hyacinth noticed Honoria watching them. Honoria took a step towards the pair, thought better of it and walked in the direction of the marquee.

Lawrence turned to the woman by his side, suddenly feeling that she had always been there, perhaps round a corner, perhaps in the next room, waiting for him just as he had waited for her. 'Are you in garden-party mood?' he asked.

Hyacinth had never in her life been in garden-party mood. 'Honoria would not be pleased if I wandered off,' she replied carefully. 'And Hilda needs support – she's the youngest of us. I think we should stay and mingle.'

He squeezed her arm gently. 'Perhaps we could share a country walk soon?'

'Of course,' she replied. 'I must go now and find Hilda. She's rather tired after all that baking.'

He released her arm. 'You all begin with H,' he said.

'Yes, though Honoria's H is silent.'

Lawrence grinned, brightening eyes so dark that they appeared to be almost black. 'Trust her to be different,' he said. 'I shall see you later.'

Honoria was different, all right, thought Hyacinth. She was making a bee-line for the newly released Lawrence, all smiles as she gave him a peck on the cheek. For a brief moment of time, the two sisters' eyes met, and Hyacinth felt threatened. But no, there were plenty of young men here, more than enough to go round. It was plain that working in the town had spread Honoria's net very wide indeed.

Hilda was still all of a fluster, but very pretty in her new rose-coloured outfit. 'Hyacinth?'

'Yes?'

'You look different.'

'Do I?'

'Has something happened?' Excitement seemed to ooze from Hyacinth, forming an almost visible aura that emanated from her, making her vibrant and even more lovely than before.

'I'm just hot. Come along, let's see how the savouries are going. I've put ice in those buckets to keep the ice-cream cold when we take it to the marquee. Well? What are you waiting for? They're only people, Hilda.'

Hilda swallowed her misgivings. Reassured by her sister that her underskirt did not show, that her lipstick was not smudged, that her stocking seams were straight, Hilda went forth to cope with the guests.

All afternoon, Hyacinth felt his eyes on her, wondered whether he was aware of Honoria staring at him. Although there were at least four dozen guests, Honoria was plainly interested in just one, who, in his turn, was intrigued by Honoria's sister. This promised to be difficult, Hyacinth told herself more than once. While she studiously side-stepped all contact with Lawrence Beresford, she knew that Honoria was on red alert.

Lawrence was doing his best to keep away from Honoria. Having met her through some mutual friends, he had not liked her, had been in two minds about whether to come to her party. But, had he stayed away, he would not have met Hyacinth. It was an ill wind, he told himself.

The ill wind, eating a bowl of strawberries and cream, saw how self-consciously Lawrence and Hyacinth avoided each other. Hating her sister was becoming so, so easy.

The rest of the summer was idyllic for Hyacinth and Lawrence. She handed over most of the estate work to Bill Watkins, while Lawrence, no more than a figurehead in the shoe-retailing business, was largely free to come and go as he pleased.

Isobel was cock-a-hoop. She looked forward to seeing the young couple almost daily, as did Hilda, who took to Lawrence right away. He didn't make her feel awkward or stupid, was so complimentary about her cooking and her appearance that she all but died of happiness. She was a person, a real person, and a grown man liked her, appreciated her.

'He has such lovely, completely natural

manners,' said Isobel, one afternoon when Hyacinth and Lawrence had left. 'That is a born gentleman, you see. And he's wealthy, of course, which always helps. It's no use fastening yourself to a fortune-hunter, Hilda. Remember that when your turn comes. We are not exactly millionaires, but we are much better off than most.'

Hilda piled teacups and saucers on to a tray. 'We mustn't tell Honoria, then? Does she like Lawrence? Does she want him for herself?'

Honoria wanted the whole world and all its surrounding planets for herself. According to Hyacinth, there were telephone messages for Lawrence all over the country, little reminders left by Honoria so that the man she had in her sights would not be allowed to forget her existence. 'He loves Hyacinth, I'm sure,' answered Isobel carefully. 'Honoria becomes very cross if she doesn't get her own way. It's far easier if we say nothing. Let Hyacinth handle the matter.'

Hilda carried the tray into the kitchen. Although she was happy for Hyacinth, she felt a terrible dread, an inexplicable apprehension that made her shake to the point where she actually dropped a piece of Crown Derby, which shattered.

Lottie came in from the yard, washing basket balanced on a hip. 'Let me clean that up, miss. Come on, don't cry.' She led Hilda to a chair. 'It's only a saucer. We'll pick another one up in Whittaker's when we go to town.'

Hilda leant against the loyal and loving servant. 'Lottie, you know that feeling you get just before a thunderstorm?'

Lottie looked through the window. 'But the

sky's clear, Miss Hilda. Look, there's not a cloud in sight.'

Hilda sobbed quietly. 'There's a storm coming. Believe me, Lottie, we are in for some bad weather.'

They ran together across the moor, Hyacinth opening her arms as if trying to embrace the whole world. Lawrence stopped from time to time, just to watch her and listen as she answered birds and sang silly songs, words and music made up as she went along.

For the first time since the death of her father, Hyacinth West was truly happy. Occasionally, when apart from her lover, she became frightened, remembering how her father had been taken so suddenly. Would fate or Honoria strike again? Surely not. At twenty-three, Honoria was quieter, not quite as angry as she had been five years earlier. And Lawrence was just another bachelor, one among many. If he chose to marry Hyacinth, surely Honoria would find someone else?

Behind a clump of trees, Honoria West watched the couple cavorting, running, catching one another and kissing, their body language betraying that they knew one another in the biblical as well as in the merely social sense. It was just as it had always been, Hyacinth and Hilda first, Honoria piggy in the middle, the least important, a spectator allowed to view life only from a distance.

She had set her sights on Lawrence Beresford months earlier while indulging her passion for shoes. He had been visiting his outlet in Newport

Street, Bolton, in which shop an acquaintance of Honoria's worked. It had not been difficult to wangle an invitation to a Beresford function at the Aspen dance hall, had been easy to arrange an introduction to the man himself. He had been polite, civilized and very attractive, so Honoria had moved him to the top of her short-list. On the look-out for a husband, she had mended her ways and was trying to erase her reputation as a flighty woman.

And now Hyacinth had pushed herself forward. Hyacinth was slim, elegant and extremely beautiful. Of late, a new radiance had made her all the more attractive. The cause of Hyacinth's glow was currently locked in her arms, was moving his hands up and down his loved one's back in a way that was familiar, to say the least.

A red glow began to form beyond Honoria's eyes, a layer of anger that felt ready to ooze down her cheeks and scar them for ever. There could be no more ... terminations. With a selective memory, Honoria found it easy to ignore certain portions of the past, almost deleting them from her consciousness. But there had been reprisals, yes. To stand alone and unaided in the shadow of destiny was a terrible thing. Alone, she had fought; alone, she would continue so to do. This time, a degree of intricate planning was required.

Lawrence and Hyacinth reached his cottage. Panting for breath after running and laughing, they collapsed on the sofa. 'Oh, my goodness,' gasped Hyacinth, 'I have a stitch in my side and I think my feet are going to drop off.'

'That'll do my business no good,' he grumbled.

'If feet start dropping off, I shan't have a leg to stand on.'

'Or a sole to bless.'

'Poor,' he judged. 'That was below the belt.'

Hyacinth closed her eyes and leant back into the deep, feather-filled cushions. 'Is Honoria still leaving messages? She must have gathered by now that you are not on your travels.'

'Well, she left a few *bons mots* here and there. I imagine that she knows by now that I am here, not out and about my business.'

'She knows we're together, you and I.' Her tone was resigned and sad. With humour all forgotten, Hyacinth continued. 'Lawrence, I can't betray her or my mother, but Honoria has very little self-control in times of stress. Things have gone badly awry in the past when she's been slighted or threatened.' The understatement almost stuck in her throat.

He pulled her into his arms. 'Then we get on our horses and get out of town,' he drawled, in the manner of a Texan cowboy. He planted a kiss on his beloved's head, pulled a few blades of grass out of the soft brown hair. Sensing her seriousness, he quietened for a few moments. 'You're really afraid of her, aren't you, my darling?'

She nodded.

Needing to see her face more clearly, he separated himself from her, moving away to watch her expression. 'Is she actually dangerous?'

'Yes, she can be.'

'And you won't give me any details?'

'I have promised my mother.'

He appreciated that. A woman who refused to

gossip, who kept her promises, was as rare as a flawless diamond. She looked absolutely terrified. 'You can't carry on living like this,' he told her. He rooted in the canals of recent memory, a slight discomfort crawling into his veins. Honoria's behaviour had always been odd. She hung around like a bad smell, insinuating herself into any and every situation in which there was a chance of meeting him. There was no let-up; she seldom paused for breath, did not pause for anything. She was simply there, always there. 'Honoria the Ubiquitous,' he muttered, almost to himself.

'She's very determined. Whatever she wants, she goes for it and doesn't care how many faces she has to tread on along the way.'

Lawrence thought about Honoria for a full five minutes. He did not speak; neither did Hyacinth. 'We could live elsewhere,' he suggested at last. 'Put a few miles between us and her.'

'No, no. You don't understand and you never will, not completely, but I have to stay near Mother and Hilda. You see, when Father died, I did my best to take his place. Mother was so terribly ill, Hilda was only fifteen. Honoria – well, she was Honoria. I'm sorry, Lawrence, but I'm afraid I bring luggage with me. Whoever marries me takes on the responsibility of caring for me, for Mother and for Hilda.'

'I will gladly do that.'

'I know.' He was the only man for her. As steady as Father, Lawrence was a kind, gentle lover who wrote poetry with her, read aloud to her, made her feminine and lively. After a matter of weeks, she had felt that she could not live without him.

'So when shall we marry?' he asked.

Hyacinth sighed. This was not the first proposal and she had already agreed to become his wife. 'It would be better if we grabbed a couple of witnesses off the street and went to the register office. Mother would understand, while Honoria would be presented with a *fait accompli*.' A proper wedding with all the inevitable preparations was not an option. What havoc might be wrought by Honoria during those weeks? It did not bear consideration.

'And we would live at Moortop?' he asked.

'It's a big enough house, but I would rather we kept the cottage. If Mother needs us, we can stay with her for a few days, then return here.'

He was the happiest man on earth. Even a cloud labelled Honoria could not mar his sky. Hyacinth was everything he had wanted in a partner.

The cloud labelled Honoria moved away from the open window of Lawrence Beresford's cottage. Light on her feet and adept at moving quietly, she was so furious on this occasion that she could scarcely walk. It seemed that she had been plotted against all her life, betrayed repeatedly by her own family, by Father, Mother, Hyacinth, by Mother's little Hilda. Now the very man she wanted to marry was on the verge of abandoning her for Hyacinth.

Had Honoria been capable of rational self-analysis, she would have realized that Lawrence was not the only man in her world, that it was Hyacinth's affection for Lawrence Beresford that made him more desirable. Honoria simply wanted everything, wanted the unreachable most of all.

She entered Moortop and marched up to her room. Having taken a day off work, she intended to use it well. She lay motionless on her bed, eyes staring blankly at the ceiling. This could not be allowed to happen, she told herself. Whatever it took, she would formulate an idea that would wipe out Lawrence Beresford and Hyacinth West. No, perhaps she would not . . . would not wipe them out literally, but she intended to end their relationship, no matter what that implied. Murder was not always an option; as an adult, she understood that subtler methods were required.

Isobel, knowing that her second daughter was in the house, felt far from easy. She paced up and down the drawing room, a terrible feeling of foreboding preventing her keeping still. The air was electric, as if about to give birth to a tempest of enormous proportions. She could do nothing. Her powerlessness made her worse, causing perspiration to flow down her forehead and into her eyes, yet she shivered. On a whim, she grabbed a cardigan, pulled it on and fled from the house.

Isobel stood on the very bridge beneath which little Frankie Kershaw had perished all those years ago. 'I'm so sorry, Frankie,' she whispered. 'I am so sorry, Thomas.'

It was a beautiful day. From nearby trees, a wood pigeon mocked the world, while swallows and swifts formed up in the air, the famous V shape advertising the nearness of autumn. Who decided? she wondered. When the front bird, the leader, was chosen, was there a vote? Did they sit in a parliament? No – only crows had parliaments. Did they perch in a tree and say, 'Who's the front flier this year? Not you again, George, you did it last time.' When had Honoria first decided to make herself leader, creator of decisions, chief juror, judge, executioner? 'Hang on,' Isobel told herself. 'Keep your sanity, because Hyacinth will need you.'

She sat on a bench, folded her hands in her lap and waited. Hilda had gone into town with Lottie and Sarah. The servants were doing their own shopping, while Hilda was looking for bits of china to replace a few broken items.

Except for the movement of birds, Moortop was still, seemed not to breathe. Everything was waiting. These very trees had witnessed actions so foul, so nasty; had they been capable of speech, the birches and elms would have screamed Honoria's guilt.

'Thomas, what am I to do? She's upstairs and she's thinking. I'm sure she knows about Hyacinth and Lawrence. I'm sure—' Yes, she was sure. There was only one solution to the problem, and she would implement it this very day.

As she walked towards Lawrence's cottage, Isobel considered the other option. She could gird her loins and bring in the law. But Honoria was clever, wise enough to rely on Isobel's breakdown. 'Mother was never well. She made up these stories and even got my sisters to listen. I have never hurt a soul . . .' Then, the disgrace of it all would damage Hyacinth and Hilda. Whether Honoria should be found guilty or innocent, the name of West would be punished for ever.

So this much was plain. Isobel had to warn Hyacinth and Lawrence, must get them to go away immediately. They must be safe, had to snatch their chance of happiness, too.

The cottage was empty. Tired and hot, Isobel let herself in and sat for a while to regain sufficient strength for the return journey, which measured over two miles. On Lawrence's mantelpiece, a silver-framed photograph showed Hyacinth at her best, relaxed, happy, head thrown back as she laughed.

A side table bore Hyacinth's mark, too, in the form of a hairbrush, a powder compact and a small bottle of perfume. They were lovers in the complete sense. Isobel found herself smiling, imagining Hyacinth doing her hair at the mirror while he, laughing and joking, spoiled her work by running his fingers through those brown tresses.

Older and wiser, Isobel now knew that the intimate side of her marriage had lacked something, that Thomas's natural shyness and quietness had held him back. 'But I have no regrets, my dear,' she told her dead husband. 'Except, of course, there is Honoria.' Isobel leant back, eyelids drooping, memories flooding her mind and turning quickly into dreams. Exhausted, she fell into a fitful sleep, yet she found no rest, as demons plagued her for several hours.

It was Hilda who ran outside when the screaming began. Lawrence, with deep scratches raining blood down his face, entered the kitchen of Moortop just as Hilda scurried into the yard. He stood as still as stone beside the table, stared blankly at Hyacinth when she came into the room.

'Lawrence!' she cried. 'What happened?'

He suddenly began to shake from head to foot, and no words would form.

'Lawrence?' She went to the sink, poured cold water on to a tea-towel and brought it to him. 'Here.'

He made no move.

Hilda returned, Honoria dragging along behind her. 'She's . . .' Hilda, too, seemed to have been struck dumb.

Honoria shrank away from the man, tattered blouse held tight against her upper body. A blue skirt was torn from hem to waist; stockings lay in jagged pools around her ankles. Her face was filthy, almost as bloody as his. 'Where's Mother?' she asked, her voice a mere whisper.

No one replied.

Honoria raised an unsteady finger, the movement causing one of her breasts to break free of ruined underwear. 'He tried to rape me,' she gasped.

Hyacinth blinked as if to clear her head. So this was to be Honoria's *pièce de résistance*. She was too cautious now to try murder, so she was trying to assassinate the character of an excellent man who had rejected her. 'Lawrence would not do that,' she answered confidently.

'Let's see what the police have to say about this,' snapped Honoria. 'He dragged me into the stables and – and look what he did to me.'

Lawrence sank into a chair. 'Good God,' he managed. 'What an evil piece of work you are.' Untroubled by Honoria's partial nudity, he stared at her until she averted her gaze and attempted to cover herself.

Hyacinth stepped forward. 'Go to your room, Honoria,' she ordered. 'And put on some clothes.'

Hilda, shocked beyond measure, escaped into the hallway. Where was Mother? Lottie and Sarah were long gone and Hilda was beginning to worry about Isobel.

Lawrence looked at the woman he loved. 'I didn't touch her,' he said. 'I was on my way home after leaving you here, and she leapt on me. Her clothing was already as it is now. She scratched my face and started to scream.'

'I know,' said Hyacinth. 'We all know.'

They sat together at the table, hands joined across its breadth, fingers intertwined as they waited – for what? 'I didn't do it,' he said repeatedly. 'I would not, could not—'

'We know she's a liar,' answered Hyacinth. 'And she seems to have calmed down, at least.'

But Honoria had not calmed down. Locked in a bathroom, she tore out a few handfuls of hair and allowed them to fall among the remains of her ruined clothing. She scratched her face, banged her head twice against the tiled wall, rubbed a bit of soap into the corner of an eye to cause inflammation. In Isobel's bedroom, she used the extension telephone to summon police and an ambulance.

She sauntered down to the kitchen, her dishevelled blouse and skirt covered by a dressing gown. 'The police are coming,' she announced casually. 'You have two choices, Mr Beresford. You may stay and face the music, or you may clear off and never come near my sister again.' She glanced at her watch. 'It'll take them about fifteen minutes to get here. If you promise to leave the area forth-with, I'll say that I did not see my assailant's face. If you remain here, I shall have you charged with attempted rape. If you return, I shall suddenly remember the identity of my attacker.'

Hyacinth gasped. 'Why? Why are you doing this? Why did you do any of it?'

'Any of what?'

Hilda rushed in and, to everyone's amazement, hit Honoria across the face with a resounding crack. 'You ruin everything. I hate you and I hope you burn in hell.'

Honoria grinned. 'Thank you, dear. The more bruises, the better. Shall I turn the other cheek?'

Lawrence jumped to his feet. 'I have nothing to fear,' he said.

'We'll see.' Honoria left the room.

Hyacinth turned to Hilda. 'Say nothing,' she babbled. 'We need time to think. When the police come, don't mention Lawrence.'

Hilda, still trembling after hitting Honoria, nodded her agreement.

Hyacinth dragged Lawrence into the yard. 'Go home,' she said. 'Pack a bag and make for London. If she decides to accuse you, the marks on your face will back up her lies, so you have to get away. Remember, too, that Honoria has many influential friends. She is not beyond persuading them to bend the law in her favour. Write to me, telephone me.' She kissed him. 'Go. Please go. You have no idea what she is and what she's capable of.'

'But—'

Hyacinth took a deep breath. She had no choice

308

– caution must now be thrown into the four winds. 'My sister is a killer. She murdered her first victim just before her fourth birthday. There is no proof, because we have protected her. Please, please, go while you can.'

He could find nothing to say for at least ten seconds. 'Will you be safe?' he asked eventually.

'Oh, yes,' she answered with false confidence. 'She won't hurt us. Go on.'

He left. Hyacinth stood and watched him as he ran homeward, her mind filled by just one thought. With a certainty that was rooted deep in the marrow of her bones, she knew that she would never see Lawrence Beresford again.

October arrived, became November. Hyacinth learnt from the newspaper that the Beresford shoe chain was the subject of a takeover bid by a firm called Hunt's. The 'attempted rape' was hushed up, as the influential widow of Thomas West, together with other members of the dead man's family, was not keen to have the incident broadcast. No attacker was found, so no charges were brought and, after a visit to the hospital and a fortnight in her bedroom, Honoria went back to work and carried on as if the episode had never taken place.

'Why doesn't he write?' Hyacinth asked her mother repeatedly.

Isobel, who blamed herself for falling asleep in Lawrence's cottage on the day in question, could never find a feasible reply to her daughter's inquiry. After waking, she had walked home along the lanes, while Lawrence, probably in an attempt

309

to avoid police, had gone through the fields. The result of that particular quirk of fate was that they had failed to meet, and Isobel had arrived home to scenes of chaos. That Honoria had invented the whole story was certain.

Honoria was walking on air. Unbeknown to her family, she was rising earlier than normal and sorting through mail before anyone else could get to it. In her bedroom, inside a locked box, Lawrence's letters were stacked in chronological order. He had not telephoned, he explained, as he could not bear the thought of what he might do if Honoria answered. 'I almost wish she were dead,' he had written, 'and I feel horrible for having such nasty feelings. But I could not be answerable for my actions were I to come into contact with her again . . .' He informed his beloved about the quick sale of his business, about his intention to go abroad. 'Please get yourself ready to come with me.'

Christmas passed almost unnoticed. Isobel was concentrating on Hyacinth, whose health seemed to be deteriorating fast. The girl had virtually stopped eating, was not reading or listening to the radio, did not work or go out for walks. She seldom had a conversation with anyone, and she took no care of her appearance, sometimes neglecting to wash herself or change her clothes.

Hilda and Isobel decided to send for the doctor at the end of December. He prescribed a tonic and advised Hyacinth to pull herself together. Hyacinth looked straight through him and, as soon as he had left the house, curled herself into a ball on the sofa and went to sleep.

'Mother?'

Isobel sighed, put down her sewing and answered her youngest daughter. 'Yes, Hilda?'

Hilda searched for kind words with which to frame her statement. 'When Father died, you went strange. Well . . . Hyacinth is a bit like that now. She reminds me of you.'

Isobel rubbed a hand across tired eyes. She could scarcely bear to entertain for a second the concept of her daughter inheriting some weakness from the Craven family. 'My parents were never mentally ill,' she ventured.

Hilda was quick to intervene. 'No, Mother, this isn't that sort of illness. I got a book from the library. Some people are depressed on and off all their lives, but others get affected by what happens around them. They become very sad, uncontrollably miserable, when life goes wrong.' She paused. 'I suppose that losing Lawrence was a bit like you losing Father. And Hyacinth has . . . Well, two people have gone away. She still misses Father, and now there's no Lawrence, either. We have to get some help.'

From Hilda, this speech was a marathon. Isobel felt touched when she thought of Hilda going out of her way to study her sister's illness. 'I shall send for Dr Randall again,' she decided, 'and Hyacinth can go into some sort of rest home for a while.'

Hyacinth West, totally compliant and biddable, was removed from the bosom of her family in January 1949. She was placed in the care of a select nursing home just outside Preston, a luxurious environment into which the upper crust deposited embarrassing members of a society in which they

311

could no longer function without bringing discomfort upon their families.

Isobel never brought Hilda or Honoria to visit their sister. The former was a sensitive girl, while the latter would probably have derived great pleasure from seeing Hyacinth so diminished. Bill Watkins drove Isobel to Park House every Saturday without fail, remaining in the car until Isobel, usually in tears, reappeared to face the long journey home.

Bill and most other tenants had revised their attitude towards Miss Honoria. She had outgrown them, had begun to ignore them in her late teens. Their hearts now belonged to Miss Hyacinth, that sweet, gentle soul who had nursed them all through the death of their beloved master, Thomas West. The Wests were Catholics, as were many of their tenants, so not a week passed without a mass being dedicated to the recovery of poor Miss Hyacinth.

Hyacinth lay in a trance for much of the time. He had left her, abandoned her, and she had made a subconscious decision not to thrive. Doctors spoke to her, nurses fed her and gave her medicines. Lying there was so easy. She wanted silence, inaction, nothingness. Mother appeared occasionally, but she was probably just another dream, another memory from which there seemed no escape.

It was the end of April when Hyacinth, in considerable pain, was taken to a general hospital. As far as she was concerned, it might have been just days after her removal from home, as time had ceased to have significance for her. She was trundled off to theatre, anaesthetized, operated on and housed in a room in the private sector of the hospital. The pain lasted for a few days, at the end of which she was packaged up and posted back to Park House. Strangely, it was the reality of physical pain and the trauma of surgery that brought Hyacinth back into the present tense.

After the appendix operation, she began the process of recovery, often sitting at a chair near her window, beginning to notice birds, squirrels and even people, waving at familiar faces, calling out to other patients and the nurses who accompanied them on walks.

When Hyacinth asked for books, pens, paper and a typewriter, Isobel went to church and thanked God for all His kindness. She had a mass said for Thomas and for little Frankie Kershaw, placed flowers on both graves and went to bring home her daughter from Preston.

Honoria packed her bags, making sure that she collected all Lawrence Beresford's letters to take with her. The last message, stolen by Honoria just after Christmas, announced that he was leaving for South Africa and a completely fresh start. 'As you have answered none of my letters, I can only conclude that you have lost all interest in me or that you now believe me guilty of molesting your sister. Please accept my warmest wishes for your health and future happiness . . .'

With a taxi waiting outside, Honoria clattered down the stairs, intending to ask the driver to collect her things from the bedroom.

'Where are you going?' asked Hilda.

Honoria opened the door and instructed the

man. When he had climbed the stairs, Honoria gave her answer. 'Liverpool. I have a post in the tax offices.'

'But Hyacinth is coming home today.'

'Exactly.'

'And Mother has gone to collect her. Can't you wait just to say goodbye to Mother?'

Honoria pulled on a pair of thin gloves. 'Look, Hilda, let's put the cards on the table, shall we? Hyacinth was the light of Father's life; you were the same, but for Mother. I was just an optional extra, something that didn't count. I've been accused of crimes and I was almost raped by Hyacinth's fancy man. Nobody gives a damn about me. By the way, I've left a note so that Mother can pay my allowance into my bank account. I shall forward an address when I am settled.' She followed the driver outside.

'Honoria?' Hilda stood next to the taxi. 'I hope you'll be happy.'

'Thank you.' Honoria did not even turn to look at her sister. 'Drive on,' she snapped.

Hilda, her cheeks wet with tears for which she would never account, stood alone outside a large empty house. The sun had dipped low in the sky and the world was preparing for sleep. With a dull ache in her heart, Hilda West leant against the door jamb, watching the taxi as it drove slowly towards the road. It stopped, waited for a second, then turned right and made off in the direction of Honoria West's future.

Seventeen

'It's like leaving a child,' Yvonne told April. 'I can't stop worrying about him. You must know how I feel, because Mark is still here. Responsibility doesn't go away just because a marriage is over.'

April looked through the window at Mark Nugent, who was playing with a dog in a lampshade, a plastic collar designed to prevent the animal from worrying its own damaged flesh. The little mongrel, survivor of a recent road accident, was clearly pleased to have some company all to himself. 'You're so right,' said April thoughtfully. 'They are children, you know. Most of them leave their real mother for someone else who will do the cooking, then they don't move on again until they find another bed, breakfast and evening meal, plus sex, of course.' She paused. 'I'm giving Mark room and board without the sex,' she said. 'He can look after the place while I come with you and Karam to Yorkshire. After that – well, we'll just wait and see.'

Yorkshire. Yvonne dropped into a chair. 'I can't go to Horsefield,' she said. 'What if David does

315

something silly? And this is his baby. If only he were a bad man, I wouldn't hesitate. But he's a good man, an excellent man. It's not his fault that I've stopped loving him. I mean, it was getting to the stage where everything he did infuriated me – his walk, the way he eats, toothpaste dropped in the washbasin.'

'Well, that can only get worse,' replied April. 'Most marriages end with a whimper rather than with an explosion. It's the tiny details of life that erode the surface and leave us raw and aware. His eating will become noisier and the blobs of toothpaste will grow larger. And you'll end up hating him. Better to employ damage-limitation tactics and get out now, without acrimony.'

Yvonne picked up Veetol, who had just landed at her feet after rearranging some grapes on the sideboard. The cat purred musically, his nose pushed against Yvonne's right ear. 'Sebastian wasn't very nice to David when he brought my clothes to Karam's house. It's strange, because I can be as nasty as I like to David, but if anyone else gives him a dirty look I'm all up in arms. Stupid. Of course, Seb is a past master when it comes to dirty looks.'

'Sebastian is seldom nice to anyone.'

'I wonder why?' Yvonne asked.

April shrugged. 'Perhaps he's a genius. Karam certainly is. Geniuses can go about offending people with impunity. I like him,' she proclaimed, after a short pause for consideration. 'He says little, but he can be acutely droll. He had quite a long conversation with me when we were planning the TV show. My work was just an afterthought – he was coming out with all kinds of jokes. I had to tell him to shut up before I burst my corsets.'

'He hates me.'

'Don't be silly.'

'But he does,' insisted Yvonne. 'Which is another reason why I don't want to go to Horsefield. He makes me feel so uncomfortable, as if I'm an intruder.'

April rounded on Yvonne. 'Look, I didn't want to say this, but you are in danger of becoming an indecisive and petulant moaner, which is precisely what Karam does not want at this juncture. Just make your mind up and stick with it, because she needs consideration, too. If you opt to stay with David and be miserable, then do it. If you want to go off on your own to avoid Sebastian, fair enough. Damage limitation, Yvonne. Put everyone, including yourself, out of this misery.' It was not April's place to tell Yvonne that Karam was in love, so she picked up her stick and walked with unusual steadiness out into the garden. If Yvonne could not sense Karam's dilemma, then Yvonne was rather less than alert.

Yvonne, slightly shaken, remained in the chair. Veetol took off, projecting himself into the atmosphere and landing on a coffee table. After sliding across its surface, he tumbled to the floor, licked his chest, twitched his tail three times and followed his mistress outside.

'I'm just like that flaming cat,' mumbled Yvonne. 'Take off, land, bugger the consequences.' Much of her problem lay in a lassitude that had begun to visit her body soon after the pregnancy had been confirmed. She wasn't herself, didn't know who she was. Being an incubator had swollen her belly very slightly, had diminished considerably her ability to think in a rational, straight line. 'I'm becoming paranoid. Nobody likes me, everybody hates me, I think I'll go and eat worms.' April was right, as ever. April could be quite annoyingly right.

She picked up her bag and left the house. No longer the driver of a Range Rover, she climbed into her recently acquired Fiesta and drove round the corner, pausing outside the house she had shared with David Benson. Now a lodger at Jasmine Cottage, Yvonne rarely visited her ex-home. Gill Collins was hoovering the ceiling in the living room, the vacuum attachment skating over Dulux Brilliant White in search of cobwebs.

Honoria's flat displayed empty, sightless eyes. Where the hell had she gone and what was she up to? Kevin, resplendent in blue overalls and beaded plaits, waved from the garden of Philip Pointer's house. He was hoeing indiscriminately, probably digging up the plants and saving weeds.

Yvonne glanced at her watch. Here she sat, outside her own property and on the edge of indecision: should she, shouldn't she, how many beans made five, how long was a piece of string. Grinding gears and teeth, she shot off in the direction of the clinic.

Again, she remained in the car at the end of the journey. The surgery was almost over, so now was the time to collar him. Perhaps not. Perhaps she should just go back to Karam's house and make the spaghetti sauce. No. She couldn't do that, because Sebastian had stayed and was in the kitchen with a pile of books and a dish of nectarines. Karam had gone to Chester to examine a painting in which the Walker Gallery had expressed interest. Karam was an expert in art history, her brother was a much-loved TV star, while Yvonne was just a pregnant pause. And she felt sick into the bargain.

'To what do I owe the pleasure?'

'Ah. David.'

He walked round the car, opened the door and sat in the passenger seat. 'I thought you were bound for Huddersfield?'

'Horsefield,' she replied. 'According to old Lord Laczynski, Horsefield was where they kept the horses, and Huddersfield was where they kept the cows. Some posh person put an H in front of udders, hence we have Huddersfield. Of course, he very probably makes all of this up as he goes along.'

'Strange family.'

'Yes,' she agreed, without hesitation.

'So when do you go?'

'Tomorrow.'

'Ah.' He waited. 'Did you come to see me?'

'I think so.'

He looked around the interior of the car. 'I suppose this is OK, as far as used cars go.'

'It goes far enough. That's all I need. It starts, travels and stops.'

'But you can keep the Range Rover, if you wish.'

Oh, how she dreaded his generosity. 'David, I just wanted to tell you again that this is all my fault. You did nothing wrong. Turning to Deirdre was natural, because I wasn't there for you.' She

319

inhaled deeply. She had to be fair, had to tell the truth. No way could she take off with Karam without first—

'What is it?'

Yvonne gripped the steering-wheel with both hands, wished that she could gain similar purchase on life and all its vagaries. 'David, please don't go mad. Promise me you won't drink, deface paintings or hang out of bedroom windows.'

'I promise.' He was over all that, working hard, slowly getting used to living without an unhappy wife. 'Go on.'

'I'm pregnant.' There, it was said. She suddenly felt as if a lead-lined cloak had been lifted from her shoulders. 'And I want you to be a father to him or her.'

He sat very still, wondered how to feel. Love was a two-way ticket, and Yvonne did not love him, so he was training himself in the art of detachment. There would be someone else for him, surely? But now this. 'Will you come back to me?' Did he want her back? He had wanted her back a few days earlier . . .

'No. After Horsefield, I shall come and live at Karam's. She's longing for the child to be born – we've discussed it and she's glad to be an auntie. I really believe that it would be unfair to separate you from your own child.'

He coughed. 'You know that Karam is a lesbian?'

Yvonne gritted her teeth. 'Of course.'

'And you?'

She forced herself to relax. This was the one man with the right to an answer. 'No, I'm not. But don't broadcast that, David. I don't quite know why, but I feel that I should not be questioned and that Karam is a fine person who doesn't deserve to be put on trial. Let everyone think what they like – I'm on her side.'

'I understand.' This was the truth. 'Yvonne?'

'What?'

'Is she in love with you?'

Seconds ticked by. 'No. No, she isn't.'

He waited for more, but nothing was forthcoming. 'You know I've been offered a post in Manchester?' When the words were out, he realized how silly they were. What did a bloody job matter when he was about to become a father?

She nodded, launched into speech. 'Even with the motorways, the journey is a nightmare. The problem is Crosby. It can take three-quarters of an hour to get to the M57. This place is just a bottleneck.' She forced herself to stop the nervous babbling. 'What will you do?'

'I don't know.'

'At least you know the facts now.'

'Yes.' He placed a hand on her shoulder. 'Don't worry about money, Yvonne. You'll both be well taken care of. And you know where I am if and when you need me.'

She bit her lip to hold back the flood. 'I'm sorry,' she managed.

'Stop saying that. It's happened. Perhaps you'll change your mind in time and decide I'm not so bad after all.'

Yvonne sniffed back unwanted moisture. 'But will you change yours?'

'I beg your pardon?'

He was not the same. He was no longer desperate, no longer afraid. She was glad that she had come to see him, partly because she could now stop worrying, mostly because he knew about the child. 'You've come to terms, haven't you?' she asked. 'On your own, you've had the chance to arrive home without dreading the company of a miserable wife.'

He smiled. 'Oh, I don't know about that. Gill's taken me under her wing – it's all pans of scouse and liver casseroles. I feel quite threatened because I'm sure she searches the bins to make sure I haven't thrown any away. I tell you, Yvonne, if I see one more shepherd's pie, I shall run for the hills with my crook and my sheepdog.'

'Simple,' replied Yvonne. 'Take the meals to April's refugees. Bertie will be one of them, because I'm not hauling that poor mutt into Lord Stefan's lair. So you can feed him, take him for walks and offload Gill's cooking all in one go.'

He grinned broadly. 'Nice one, Yvonne.'

'You're welcome.'

He opened the car door. 'I have to do the rounds now. And I'm so glad about our baby. We'll sort something out.'

She sat and watched him walk out of her life. Yes, he was going forward now, even though he did stop, wink and wave at her. Everything was all right. She could settle down with the baby, live with Karam until the divorce was over, then she could buy or rent her own place. She would have no need to hide her pregnancy – and what relief that thought gave to her. She could even deal with Sebastian and his endless silences. Well, probably.

David pulled out of the car-park and turned left. Yvonne followed, but turned right. At last, they had agreed to differ.

He looked up, allowed his eyes to travel the length of her body as if criticizing her dress sense, her imperfections, her very existence. 'Hello,' he said eventually.

Yvonne nodded at him, grabbed an apron, a knife, a cutting board and an onion. Karam loved Yvonne's spaghetti sauce. 'Have you packed?' she asked, in an attempt to make polite, meaningless conversation. It didn't do to get into anything deep with Sebastian, as his knowledge on most subjects was practically boundless. 'I don't know how long we'll be away, so I don't know what to take. It'll probably be just a few weeks, because Karam will be back at the university soon.' And there would be no need for Yvonne to stay behind in Yorkshire, as she had come clean with David about the baby. 'What do you think?'

Sebastian carried on reading.

'I asked you a bloody question,' she said, the knife waving in the air. She slammed it down, wondered anew whether she and this – this person could possibly co-exist for much longer. It wasn't so bad here, on territory she knew and understood, but Yorkshire was another bag of washing altogether. This man was probably responsible, at least in part, for Yvonne's current state of indecision and her tendency to moan. No, no, it was her own fault. Everything was her own fault . . . She was so tired, lethargic, stupid.

He turned a page. 'I've packed. What the hell has that onion done to you?'

'Nothing.' She chopped mercilessly, sending slivers of perfectly innocent vegetable matter flying all over the table. Her eyes pricked, and she hoped with all her heart that this arrogant bastard didn't think he had upset her to the point of tears. 'Except it's making my eyes sting.'

'What did he say?'

She paused. 'Who?'

'Your husband, of course.'

The knife was laid to rest again. 'How did you know I'd been to see him?'

He shrugged. 'I can read you like a book.'

'Well, you've had plenty of practice with books these past few weeks. If you really need to know, David and I parted on good terms. I told him about the baby and he seems quite happy to let me go. So that should upset you for the rest of today, Seb. After all, you do want me as far away from your sister as possible, don't you? Well?' Did this – this dolt really believe that Karam and Yvonne were some kind of item, a pair, a set?

He turned another page. 'You really should curb your imagination, Yvonne. Or, perhaps, put it to constructive use. Karam is an adult, as are you, as am I.'

But he talked to her as if she were a child. She stabbed a fork into a tomato, held it in a gas flame to crack the skin for peeling. It was like being in a home-economics class at school: teacher sitting in judgement, pupil trying to look nonchalant and competent.

'Shall I make some coffee?' he asked.

324

Yvonne sagged against the stove. 'What? You mean you actually know how to make coffee?'

'First-class honours,' he answered. 'And I do tea, cocoa, Bovril, Alka Seltzer, Beecham's, lemonade spritzers—'

'Get on with it.' He was just like Karam, yet he was . . . he was male. She didn't know how to cope with him. He was her greatest friend's brother and she could not work him out. Perhaps his fame overwhelmed her; but April was famous and easy to know. Yvonne battered peeled tomatoes to a red pulp. Damn bloody Sebastian bloody Laczynski. She felt tempted to scream, 'I am not a lesbian,' but she stuck to her guns. Her movements slowed for a few seconds. Karam? Karam in love with her? Ridiculous.

'Would you like me to finish that sauce?' he asked. 'Shouldn't women in your condition rest or something?'

'Oh, make the coffee and shut up,' she snapped.

He lifted his hands in a manner that was decidedly Eastern European. 'I can't win with you. If I don't talk, I'm being silently critical. When I open my mouth, you jump into it with spiked boots. I give up.' He rattled a few cups, ground some beans, found a filter and set the pot on the stove.

'I'm sorry,' she said.

'That's all right. You're probably hormonal.'

She glared at him. 'Why is it that men blame the world's ills on women's hormones?'

He opened the fridge and searched for milk. 'It's not just women, I can assure you. My father was disgustingly hormonal for years. In fact, his hormones were responsible for quite a few bits of bother over in Yorkshire. Such was his reputation that Karam and I left home at the first opportunity.'

Yvonne sat down. Without warning, she began to laugh uncontrollably, almost hysterically. Stefan Laczynski, whose knowledge of explosives had won him a peerage and acres of space in newspapers and periodicals, was a dirty old man.

'Have you no brown sugar?' asked Sebastian, apparently unmoved by her sudden silliness.

She shook her head, unable to speak.

'Well, I must say, this is a terrible attitude. I make the coffee, but you show no gratitude.' There was laughter in his tone.

'There is sugar somewhere,' she said at last. 'I don't take it, though.'

He walked to the window. 'Yvonne, don't mind me, I beg you. I am of a taciturn nature and can seem standoffish, to say the least. It's just how I am made. My sister is very similar, but you are too close to see that, and you've probably got through her barrier. Pretend I'm not here.'

She couldn't.

A roaring noise from outside made them both jump. They looked at one another, listened more intently. 'She's finally done it,' said Sebastian.

'Who? What?'

'My sister. A motorbike.'

'Good God.'

'Exactly. She passed the test years ago, then seemed to lose interest. The trouble with Karam is that she often picks up where she left off, and without warning.'

'Unlike you, of course.'

Karam burst through the door. She wore leathers and a hideous helmet with blue wings painted on a silver background. When the tinted visor was lifted, she grinned, then pulled off the helmet, shook the mane of hair and smiled benignly upon her world. 'He threw in all the clothing and the crash hats, too. It's a Harley-Davidson, practically mint condition.'

Yvonne could not associate the sweet, romantic, artistic Karam with motorbikes. 'But we have my car.'

Karam laughed. 'It's not the same, dear heart. The smell of fields, the wind beating against you, the sense that you're rushing through life and—'

'And waiting for an ambulance,' said Sebastian crossly. 'Take it back, or sell it.'

Karam stared hard at him. 'Don't go all Victorian on me, please, Sebby.' She turned to Yvonne.

'Don't look at me for support.' Yvonne returned to her sauce. 'I don't like them much, either. My ... David wrote out enough death certificates when he was doing his hospital service. Too many young men die on motorbikes.'

Karam dropped into one of the Ercols.

'There was no painting to look at, was there?' asked Sebastian.

'The painting is here,' replied his annoyed sister. 'It's you standing and pointing into the snow, *Never Darken My Door*. You are such a prim and proper, unadventurous soul. How on earth did I manage to get you for a brother?'

Yvonne was searching for Parmesan. Sebastian

picked up an arts magazine and grabbed a nectarine.

'Is no one going to have a look at my new toy?' cried Karam. She noticed a look passing between Yvonne and Sebastian. 'Are you two intending to conspire against me? Seb, you know I've always wanted a Harley.'

'Stupid,' he pronounced. 'And probably far too heavy and powerful for you.'

Yvonne walked to the door. 'Come on, then,' she said to Karam. 'Let's see what you've brought home.'

It was enormous, a great, ugly monster with a huge petrol tank and a saddle big enough to seat a family of three. 'Good grief,' exclaimed Yvonne. 'How on earth do you control it? It's bigger than the Aga.'

'Mind over matter.'

'And no small matter.' Yvonne walked round it, making sure that she gave it a wide berth in case it fell over. 'Well, you won't get me on that.'

'Yes, yes, yes!' April, appearing from nowhere, startled them both. 'Oh, joy,' she declared. 'Have you got two lids?'

'Er, yes,' answered Karam.

'I've got my thick jeans on,' said April. 'So what are we waiting for?'

Ten minutes later, Sebastian and Yvonne stood together in Poplar Grove while Karam rode away with April clinging to her waist. Yvonne leant on April's walking-stick. 'Don't you think that life gets stranger every day?' she asked.

Sebastian grimaced. 'You haven't met my father yet.'

'I can't wait.'

They went back inside, Yvonne returning to her sauce, her companion to his research.

'Sebastian?'

'Yes?'

'Is your father an impulsive sort? Does he get an idea into his head, then does he just do it?'

His mouth twitched. 'Something like that, yes.'

'A bit like your sister, then.'

He grinned. 'At last, you're getting the plot.'

Eighteen

Honoria managed to find the address of Mr Leo Stoneway. She did this quite easily, following his driver one morning after Leo had returned to Moortop. Although he was living quite openly with Hilda at the farm, Leo still retained a house in Blackburn Road in Bolton. His home had started life as a chapel-cum-school, and it had been converted beautifully into a sizeable residence with its decorative brickwork and much of the original stained glass. This was the residence of an extremely wealthy man.

On a side wall, a for-sale sign was displayed. After returning to her car, Honoria made a note of the estate agent's details before turning round and heading back to town.

First, she visited her publisher, a one-man band wedged inside a smoke-filled cupboard above a draper's shop in Bradshawgate. This was the one who had been responsible for Hyacinth's local success, so, although he seemed rather less impressive than Honoria would have liked, he had been good enough for Hyacinth and must suffice for Honoria's purposes, also.

She drank a cup of coffee in a small café, then walked in the direction of Newport Street and the estate agent's. Standing on the pavement, she ran hungry eyes over the window display, finally discovering the information she sought. Leo Stoneway's house, described as a one-off opportunity, was photographed, detailed and listed as a great bargain at a price just pennies short of three-quarters of a million pounds.

Honoria entered the agency and was greeted by a woman dressed for business, clothes understated and powerful, a few strands of gold at the throat, two eye-catching rings and blatantly false nails. 'Can I help you, madam?'

Miss Honoria West did not attempt to explain her true status. In fact, an invisible husband might be useful in a case such as this. She sat down in a comfortable chair and smiled benignly at Mrs Jennifer Evans-Jones, whose name was printed on a small brooch pinned to a crisp lapel. 'Estella Hamilton,' she replied.

'Were you interested in a particular property?'

The Chapel House in Blackburn Road. It seems very reasonably priced. We have viewed it from the outside, of course, but my husband has been called away quite suddenly to Europe. It is difficult to assess how long he will be away. Tell me, have there been any offers?'

Acrylic nails tapped furiously at a keyboard. 'Not as yet,' replied Mrs Evans-Jones. She leant forward, her demeanour suddenly conspiratorial. 'I shouldn't be telling you this,' she looked over her shoulder, as if expecting to find a large audience, 'that place is easily worth the three-quarters, but the vendor may well be disposed to consider a price slightly lower even than the one displayed, as he is in a hurry.'

'Really?'

The bleached head inclined to one side. 'It's so sweet, because he must be seventy, but he's getting married soon.'

A small beat of time passed. 'I see.'

'And, of course, he needs to be rid of the house, since his fiancée owns a large property, too. There's no shortage of money, and I think he wants to shed his own place just to tie up loose ends.'

Honoria forced a smile. 'May I confide in you, Mrs Evans-Jones?'

'Of course.'

It was Honoria's turn to lean forward. 'My husband and I have just sold our house in Hale Barns. He is retired, you see, though it would appear that the European Community cannot do without him. We want to settle here, as James used to live in Bolton.' She paused. 'Well, it was a nightmare, my dear. People tramping through our home, many time-wasting. I'm sure that when an expensive property comes on the market some take appointments just to pry and to get ideas for décor.'

The woman nodded sympathetically.

'I decided there and then that I would not put anyone else through that. So I should prefer to see the Chapel House while the owner is out. I must be accompanied by an agent, of course. You see, one does not like to inspect possible faults too closely when the owner is present.'

'I understand. You can't really look in cupboards if the vendor is standing by your side.'

'Quite.'

The nails rattled again. 'I'll just find a window for you.'

'Would you accompany me, dear? It's so seldom, these days, that one manages to find a person as professional and charming as your good self.'

Rose-tinted lips parted to display some excellent dental caps. 'I am sure that can be arranged, Mrs Hamilton. Shall we say six o'clock this evening? And do you have transport?'

'Oh, yes. I have hired a little runabout so that I might look at a few houses. However, I'm sure that this one will be eminently suitable for us.'

'It's a very large house, Mrs Hamilton.'

'We are a very large family. Four children, all married, seven grandchildren. There are quite a few visitors, especially at Christmas time. And we want to invest in a property that will increase in value. Money is safest in bricks, even these days. After we die, the house can be sold and—'

'Quite. But I think you have a few years left yet, Mrs Hamilton.'

Mrs Hamilton hoped so. There was so much to do.

Honoria had rediscovered shopping after many years of deprivation. Although the panic attacks came and went, sometimes lasting for several minutes, she had managed to move up into a higher gear, was travelling at a speed she had not experienced in ages. She felt young again, determined and free, just as she had when dealing with ... with other matters, happenings she had almost forgotten.

The town-hall clock chimed three times as she stopped outside a jeweller's. Her eyes wandered greedily over diamonds and emeralds, finally coming to rest on a high choker of pearls which would be eminently suitable for hiding the crêped base of her neck. Walking had helped the weight to melt away somewhat, but her skin, no longer elastic, was showing signs of wear.

She had followed Hilda, who was already inside the shop with her fancy man.

Honoria almost giggled. As well as enjoying shopping, she had got into the habit of following Hilda and Leo whenever possible. Perhaps she ought to have been a private detective? Heavily disguised in large hat and sunglasses, she entered the establishment, ducked behind a screen where a table and two chairs had been installed to allow privacy and, perhaps, safety to staff and public who wanted to look at expensive items. The happy duo stood at a counter across the room. Honoria, having hidden herself, could not see them, but she could hear some of the conversation.

His voice was familiar, an echo from long ago. Hilda's had remained high and girlish, singularly unsuitable for a woman of substance, mastermind behind a food empire, owner of a small mansion and several hundred acres.

'Not too wide,' Hilda said.

'Try this one,' the assistant replied.

A man bustled behind the screen and hovered

over Honoria. 'Would madam like to see something?'

She put a hand to her mouth. 'Laryngitis,' she whispered. 'I'd like to look at the three-strand pearl choker, please.'

He went off to rattle about in the window.

'Next Thursday afternoon, three o'clock,' Hilda was saying. 'At the register office. No fuss, not at our age.'

'So, if you downsize this to a P, and stretch mine to a U, we should be well suited,' Leo was suggesting.

No Catholic blessing? Mother and Father would be turning in their grave. Hilda and Leo were buying wedding rings, then. Love's young dream, thought Honoria. Hyacinth had been a great success in amateur theatre, had been published; Hilda had triumphed in business and was about to be married. 'We'll see,' Honoria muttered, beneath her breath.

She tried on the choker, paid for it, waited while the man boxed and wrapped it.

'That's far too much to pay, Leo,' Hilda uttered.

'It's a beautiful piece,' interspersed the salesman, obviously interested in commission.

'But I have a lovely engagement ring.'

'Then you shall have an even lovelier eternity ring,' boomed Leo. 'It fits perfectly, so we shall take it now.'

Honoria listened while the assistant waxed lyrical. 'Your fiancé knows his diamonds, Miss West. And so he should, I expect, since he mined enough of them in South Africa.'

The eavesdropper remembered the book at

Leo's bedside, a huge tome about the Amsterdam market. Well, that certainly explained his expensive clothes, the car and the house. He was probably a multi-millionaire. Why should the dowdy Hilda do so well for herself? How had she managed it? South Africa? Someone had mentioned that years ago. Who, though?

The happy pair left the shop, Honoria warmish on their heels, maintaining a discreet distance between herself and them. Hand in hand, the lovebirds strolled through the town centre, not a care in the world, not a cloud on their horizon.

It was as she passed the police station that a panic attack of enormous proportions overcame Honoria. She sagged against the wall, heart beating like a pneumatic drill, arms tingling as the adrenaline flowed unchecked through her system. She was going too fast altogether, she told herself. From a casual walk through a town centre, Honoria had gathered all the symptoms of a climber who had just tackled Everest.

A young constable found her and led her inside. Luckily, the police surgeon was in the station. For privacy's sake, he and a female sergeant took her into a vacant holding cell. Her heart was judged to be in excellent condition, while her blood-pressure reading was as good as any forty-year-old's.

The doctor smiled encouragingly. 'Are you under stress?'

Was she under stress? 'I'm recovering from a long spell of agoraphobia. These panics just seem to hit me from nowhere.'

'Have you had counselling?' the young man asked.

'No.' Breathing was difficult, each draught of oxygen a bonus for which she was ridiculously grateful.

The doctor rooted about within the depths of a huge leather case, clattering his way past bottles and tubes until he emerged triumphant with an audiotape. 'I've been working with the pain-control unit at the Liverpool Royal,' he told her. 'This recording was made for those patients whose illnesses are not curable. It's part of an effort to teach them to relax, thereby limiting their discomfort. It also works on people like you.'

'How?'

He pushed the tape into Honoria's handbag. 'Twice a day, listen to this man's voice and follow his instructions to the best of your ability. I guarantee that it will put you into a sort of trance – it will even make you sleep.'

He seemed to care. This was how it felt when another human gave more than a damn. Tears welled, but she held them in check. 'Thank you,' she said.

The policewoman led her outside and walked with her all the way to the car-park. 'Take it easy,' she advised. 'Don't do anything unusual, try to stick to a routine.'

Alone in her hired car, Honoria almost screamed. She had to do the unusual, had to fight back and leave her mark. The poems and stories would be published, Hilda and her fiancé were going to get a few surprises. If the price was to be anxiety attacks, then so be it.

The Chapel House was truly amazing. Polished wood floors punctuated by Chinese silk rugs, furniture that must have cost a whole world war of bombs. The upper choir stalls had been converted into a minstrel's-cum-art-gallery, while the area below was a large living room filled with a strange yet tasteful mix of ancient and modern pieces. On the ground floor, there were four reception rooms, a massive kitchen, laundry and bathroom, plus a library, a games room complete with snooker table, then an indoor pool surrounded by exotic plants and wicker chairs.

'Impressive, isn't it?' asked Jennifer Evans-Jones.

They were now upstairs in one of the five bedrooms. Each had its own bath or shower room, walk-in wardrobes, television set, music system. 'Amazing,' agreed Honoria. What was he going to do with all this money? Leo Stoneway was far too old to make proper use of it. Did he have children from a previous marriage? 'It's certainly very large for one person. Does he have relatives who stay here sometimes?'

'I don't know,' answered the agent. 'Right. I'll pop back downstairs and leave you to browse.'

Alone, Honoria walked from room to room, this time looking more closely at photographs and ornaments, anything that might give a clue to the identity of this man who was familiar, yet whom she could not place.

She found what she was looking for on a dressing-table in the biggest bedroom. It was in a silver frame about four inches by six, a black-and-white snapshot of Hyacinth West. Hyacinth was in a field, her arms held up as if to hug the sky, head tilted back, the long, elegant throat decorated by a locket, a Christmas present from Father. Which Christmas? Honoria wondered as she sank on to the dressing-stool. 'Thirty-eight, probably.

When the photograph was back in its proper place, Honoria opened her mind and allowed memories to trickle back, carefully sifting out the bits that were too unpleasant. The owner – or, in Mrs Evans-Jones's parlance, the vendor – of the Chapel House was none other than Mr Lawrence Beresford. He had abandoned poor Hyacinth, of course. After attacking Honoria, he had fled like a coward, a yellow-bellied slug, back under the pile of stones from which he had crawled. Except that this time he had chosen valuable stones. Diamonds, no less. Yes, there had been a mention of South Africa in one of the . . . confiscated letters.

She breathed slowly, hoped that the adrenaline rush would disperse quickly. So he was back. With a pseudonym and money to burn, he had returned to pick up where he had left off. He clearly intended to carry on meddling in the affairs of the West family. Did Hilda know who he really was? Well, of course she must.

'Mrs Hamilton?'

'I'm just looking at the bathrooms,' Honoria called.

She bent and scrutinized the picture of Hyacinth, realized how beautiful she had been when young. Her fingers itched until she had picked up the item once more, then, after a split second of hesitation, she placed the photograph in her handbag. It was hers, after all.

She sauntered down the stairs and met Mrs Evans-Jones, whose carefully applied mask of patience was slipping. 'It's rather late,' said the estate agent.

Honoria agreed. 'You were right,' she said. 'The place is far too big. It has a feeling about it, a coldness. No, we could not live here.' She walked to the door.

Jennifer Evans-Jones chased her prey. 'We have other properties on our books, if you would like to—'

'Thank you. I'll let you know.' Honoria climbed into her car, slammed the door and drove away.

It seemed that every fireman and engine in Lancashire had rolled up to play a part. They fought for over two hours, training water on timber that was long seasoned, battling to save an irreplaceable piece of history. The Chapel House had always been there in one capacity or another. Groups of old people, some of whom could just about remember attending school in the building, leant on one another for support, while residents and shopkeepers stood shoulder to shoulder, silently saying goodbye to a part of their lives which they had taken for granted.

The blaze, visible for miles, attracted a sizeable crowd, and police were brought in to clear the resulting congestion. Cars and buses passed by slowly, as if each driver paid tribute to an item of beauty whose death throes were a reminder of the frailty of humankind and his trappings.

Hilda and Leo sat in a side-street, the nose of

their car pointing towards the burning building.

A policeman tapped on the window and waited for Leo to open it. 'They've found Coca-Cola cans near the back door,' he said. 'And crisp packets, empty fag packets, that sort of thing. It looks like kids, Mr Stoneway.'

Leo nodded.

'Just out of interest, sir, are you insured?'

'Yes.'

'I'd bring the strap back if it was down to me,' said the sergeant. 'They want a good hiding, nothing better to do than hang around taking drugs and setting fire to places.'

Hilda, uneasy in her bones, waited for the policeman to walk away. 'Leo?'

'Yes, my dear?'

She swallowed, searched for words. 'If Honoria did this, she could well be setting fire to the farm while we sit here.'

He sighed. 'Hilda, you heard what the policeman said – cigarette packets and so forth.'

'With Honoria's prints all over them, I'm sure.'

'No,' he answered quickly. 'If she did this – and I have serious doubts – she would have wiped off any evidence. We are in danger of becoming paranoid. She may well have gone back to Liverpool—'

'She hasn't. I phoned April Nugent yesterday. There's been no sight of Honoria. Had she turned up today, April would have let me know.' Hilda was not satisfied. She had to fold her hands tightly in order not to bite her nails, a habit in which she had indulged as a small child.

Someone else tapped at the window. Leo

341

pressed a button to lower the tinted glass once more. It was Peter Thompson, the estate agent who had been handling the sale. He clung to the mobile phone via which Leo had contacted him. 'Just an old lady from Manchester,' he said breathlessly. 'A Mrs Estella Hamilton. She has a husband, children and grandchildren. Mrs Evans-Jones foolishly neglected to get an address from her. She wore tweeds, walking shoes and had a purple rinse, apparently.'

Leo turned to Hilda. 'A purple rinse? Tweeds?'

Hilda shrugged. 'Disguise,' she suggested.

'Aren't we in danger of becoming imaginative?'

'You don't know her,' Hilda insisted.

Leo knew her well enough. She had changed his whole life, had destroyed every chance of happiness for him and for Hyacinth. He smiled at the estate agent, thanked him, then closed the window. 'Do you really want her caught and arrested? Can you imagine what life would be like if that happened? We would have to leave the farm because the press would be hungry for details.'

'And we'd be safe.'

'Would we? They'd bail her, Hilda. She'd be like a black widow spider looking for someone to eat. And I'm sure that she was not responsible for this.'

Hilda all but squirmed in her seat.

Twenty miles away, Miss Honoria West held court in a small country inn. After driving so quickly, she was quite animated, was telling tales about her fascinating life. In setting the fire, she had been extremely careful, had not poured too much lighter fuel through the letterbox. It would have been slow to start, would not have blossomed fully until she had put space between herself and it.

Laughing at one of her own clever jokes, Honoria West ordered another round of drinks for her captive alibi. She had bitten back once more, and no one would ever suspect her.

Nineteen

As they came over the top, reaching the pinnacle of England's spine, Karam stopped. She swung the bike sideways and grinned at Yvonne and Sebastian, who were behind her in the Fiesta. Yvonne, exhausted after a journey of long silences punctuated by stilted, abortive bursts of conversation, slowed gratefully to a halt. She left the car, stretched her legs and gazed into what must surely be one of the most amazing sights on the mainland. Bringing up the rear, April parked and clambered out of the Micra.

'Yorkshire,' breathed Yvonne. 'We think it's all wool, cutlery and football, but . . .' There were no words for what she saw. What she saw was a soul-stirring mix of God and man, wildness and artifice side by side. The unfinished works of creation teetered impossibly, great boulders that seemed to have paused mid-tumble, rough patches dotted among lush pasture, bald areas where nothing would ever grow. Into this rough landscape the Yorkshire folk had planted themselves so neatly, so quietly, little rows of houses built of stones hewn from the very land on which they stood. 'The scenery defies belief,' she whispered. 'I could live here.'

'You will be living here,' replied Sebastian, who had left the car and was standing beside her. 'For a while, at least. It is beautiful, isn't it?' He swept a hand across the view. 'Sometimes, I come and sit here, just to think. It's as if time stops. Until the sheep get curious, that is. They always seem to find me.'

Yvonne, shocked because the Master had spoken more than half a dozen words, said nothing.

Sebastian turned. 'April?' he called.

'I'm all right.'

'She isn't,' said Karam softly. 'She went to Chester again yesterday to see her mum. No improvement. The end isn't far off.'

April blinked back a tear, looked upon the beauty of East Lancashire and West Yorkshire, remembered coming over Snake Pass years ago with her parents. Dad, a taciturn man, had sucked on his pipe, had said little. But Mum, that busy woman with apple cheeks and soft eyes, had spoken for everyone. 'Perhaps heaven's a bit like this,' she had declared. Then, 'April – have you got your vest on? It gets a bit chilly high up, you know. Fasten that cardigan, love.' Mum. So practical, so sweet, now just a bundle of bones in a nursing-home.

'April?'

She turned. 'What?'

Sebastian offered his arm for support. 'If you want to go back to Chester tomorrow, I'll come with you.'

She glanced sideways at him. He never said much, but he took it all in. 'Thank you,' she replied. Then she remembered why this man's manners were so familiar. 'You remind me of my dad,' she told him. 'We used to wait hours for him to speak, then, when he did say something, it was either momentous or hilarious – sometimes both.'

'Sounds a bit like our old man, too. Though he's more shocking than hilarious.' He pondered. 'When I come to think, Papa's nothing like that at all – he seldom shuts up.'

April laughed. 'When I was about five, Dad bought our first washing-machine. Till then, it had been the launderette twice a week, Mum pushing my old pram there and back. But, when she got her toy, she wouldn't use it for the dog's blanket, said the hairs would stick in the works and break the motor. The dog's blanket went in a dolly-tub in the back yard.'

He waited, allowed her to travel back forty years or more.

'I was sitting on the back step, watching her while she washed our very hairy mongrel's bedding. My dad pushed past me and grabbed Mum by the front of her frock – like they did in old gangster movies. She didn't flinch. Even at my young age, I could see how relaxed she was. "Listen, Enid," he said. "I've told you before about washing our dirty linen in public." Then he kissed her. It's one of those abiding memories, like a snapshot in my head. He died of a stroke just after my twenty-first. A truly unforgettable man, ordinary and so precious.'

Sebastian nodded just once.

'Magic moments,' she continued, almost to herself. She raised her voice. 'There's a widely held opinion that good marriages breed good marriages. And I really did expect Mark and me to go on for ever. Sometimes, parents are a hard act to follow.'

'Yes.'

She brightened visibly. 'Glad you're talking to us at last.'

He shuffled about, kicked at a small stone. 'It takes me a while to get comfortable with people.'

'Except on TV.'

Sebastian laughed. 'I'm paid for that.' He looked at Karam and Yvonne, two beautiful women in a wonderful setting. They were giggling, probably sharing lovers' secrets.

April, antennae on full alert as always, touched his arm. 'Things are not always what they seem, son.'

'I beg your pardon?'

She bit her tongue, ordered it to be still. Yvonne continued to insist that she wanted no explanations, that she refused to justify herself. If people wanted to view her as Karam's partner, then that was their prerogative. 'Nothing,' said April finally. 'I'm just a wandering old playwright who thinks aloud.'

Sebastian scratched an ear. 'You'll be in good company soon,' he promised. 'Papa talks to himself all the time. Nobody else will listen, so he has to be his own audience.'

April looked again at the view. 'This must mean a lot to you.'

Sebastian closed his eyes for a second. 'It means

everything to me. This is the gateway to my home, my place in the world. Here we sit in our cars, or, as in Karam's case, on an expensive motorbike, while families in Bradford get no chance to look at such views. No job, no transport, no bus fares, just enough to eat and a TV with no licence. Sights such as these no longer come free.'

She had never heard him so passionate, or so talkative. During *Arts Forum*, he interviewed guests, yet the Sebastian who lived in the real world was not one for chatter. 'You're a socialist, I take it?'

'I'm not an anything-ist. No party in this country will mend the schools system, create a health scheme that will actually prove adequate, work on an economy that will give jobs and dignity to ordinary people. It's too late for all that.' He was quiet for a moment. 'Perhaps not. Perhaps some of the fractures can be mended. Which is why, I suppose, I intend to go into politics.'

'Really? As a what?'

'As a politician.'

April extracted her arm from Sebastian's and leant on the Micra's bonnet. She had decided to bring her own car so that she could travel home whenever she chose. She grinned impishly. 'See that sheep over there?'

They both turned, eyed a tatty-looking animal that sheltered beneath a rock of uncertain stability.

'I wonder if he feels safe under that thing?'

'That stone's been there for millions of years,' replied Sebastian.

'My opinion exactly,' said April. 'It could roll at

any minute. Anyway, he doesn't seem to have thought it through. Not very sensible.' She noticed how the young man's eyes continued to seek out his sister and Yvonne. He was different, more open, yet still closed. How she wished that she could tell him that these two women were not lovers. But why did he care so much? Did he seek to protect Karam, or was he falling in love with Yvonne? 'People are very complicated,' she said. 'And so are sheep.'

'Wait till you meet my father,' warned Sebastian yet again. 'He's a Yorkshire Pole, a fatal combination. Compared to him, sheep are easy to manage.'

Karam arrived. She pointed up into a sky that promised fair weather in the morning. The sun hung low; the moon, begging for a place within the kingdom of Earth's warming star, glowed politely and hopefully in full sight of its brighter master. 'Isn't this glorious?' she asked.

Falling in love with Yorkshire for the umpteenth time was so easy. As they drove through villages and past distant rows of houses perched halfway up hillsides, Yvonne let her heart roam free amidst God's raw creations and among aged dwellings with dry stone boundaries and poky little windows. 'Wonderful,' she breathed several times.

'Prepare yourself,' warned Sebastian from the passenger seat, 'for we are about to enter the twilight zone.'

Yvonne didn't know whether to laugh or worry.

'Don't smile at him – he'll think you're propositioning him. Don't laugh at his pathetic jokes, or he might imagine that you like him. I suspect that he may still have half a teaspoonful of testosterone secreted somewhere about his person.'

'But he's ninety.'

'He's ninety going on seventeen.'

The convoy drove through large wrought-iron gates. On one of the flanking posts, HOR FIE D H LL was announced, the missing letters nowhere to be seen. 'They fell off when I was a mere sapling,' explained Sebastian. A long-neglected garden boasted thistle, dock, dandelion and buttercup. The house itself was an interesting wreck, all drooping shutters, rotted paintwork and cracked masonry.

Yvonne got out of her car. HORSEFIELD HALL was advertised completely in stone above the arched front doorway. 'Bit of a mess,' she told Karam.

'The inside's even better,' laughed the daughter of the house.

Sebastian joined them. 'Does he know we're coming?'

His sister shrugged. 'He's been told, but that doesn't mean he knows. Mrs Isherwood is expecting us.' She turned to Yvonne. 'Mrs Isherwood is our father's live-in housekeeper. We think she performs light duties in the bedroom, too, for which we are greatly indebted to her. It keeps him calm.' She considered her statement. 'Well, calmer,' she amended.

Yvonne was expecting a monster. What she got was a sight that would stay with her for the rest of her life. From a small jungle to the right of the house, a figure emerged. It turned out to be a tall, thin and very ancient man in knee-length khaki shorts, an old-fashioned cricket cap and brand-new Adidas trainers. On his upper body, he wore a string vest over which a stopwatch dangled. 'Twenty-three minutes,' he announced, to no one in particular. He peered closely at Karam. 'Is that you?'

'I think so,' she answered. 'It was me in the mirror this morning.'

'April's legs are playing up again,' said Sebastian. 'She's gone into the shrubbery, so I'll dash off to see if she's all right.' He left to deal with her.

Lord Laczynski was helping himself to a tour around Yvonne. 'Who are you?' he asked.

'I'm Yvonne. Karam's friend.'

He clicked his tongue, loosening the upper denture and flicking it back into place with a resounding crack. 'Another bloody lesbian,' he assumed aloud. 'What a waste.'

Karam slapped her father's hand. Even if Yvonne had allowed the truth to come out, Karam would have preferred her father to remain in the dark. Lesbians were not his forte. 'Keep away,' she ordered. 'No fussing and fumbling – all right?'

He glared at her. 'I neither fuss nor fumble, child. I have never needed to fuss and fumble.' He decided to explain himself to Yvonne. 'Women have fallen at my feet for decades.'

Yvonne glanced at the feet in question, which loomed very large in front of him. The pristine trainers probably made them bigger than they really were.

April arrived, Sebastian in hot pursuit. She travelled sideways and rather more quickly than intended, almost knocking over Lord Laczynski of Horsefield as she neared the house. 'Sorry,' she said. 'Multiple sclerosis.'

'May I call you Multi for short?' asked Stefan. 'And you may call me Stef.'

Karam looked up to heaven for help. 'He knows you're not called Multiple Sclerosis,' she explained patiently.

'I know he knows,' replied April. 'And he knows I know he knows.' April enjoyed a certain notoriety for the 'he knows that she knows et cetera' stunt. 'Are you warm enough?' she asked the old man. 'And where are your other two fingers?'

Stefan held up his left hand, which boasted a thumb, a forefinger and a little finger. 'Gone with the wind,' he answered smartly. 'I had an accident in 1942, an argument with a detonator. Fortunately, I was working in miniature, or the rest of me might have followed. I am an expert in explosives.'

'An expert would own a full set of fingers,' replied April.

'And a dining room with plaster on the walls,' added Karam softly.

It was Sebastian's turn to look to the skies. He prayed silently that Stefan would not begin to set his cap at April. April had not the agility to steer herself clear of predators. His father liked feisty women, and April was certainly a lively soul.

An overweight female had positioned herself in the doorway of Horsefield Hall. She wore a white peasant-style blouse, from the elasticated top of which bulged huge breasts. Her lower half was covered by a garish cotton skirt, all purples, greens and reds. Long grey hair hung limply on beefy shoulders and, between heavily painted lips, a cigarette managed to look like a permanent fixture. 'What's he been up to?' The cigarette bounced about, though it did not impede the words.

Karam laughed. 'Mrs Isherwood. Nice to see you again.'

'Dolly,' said the woman. 'I've told you to call me Dolly.'

'Right.' Karam drew herself to full height. 'Dolly, this is April Nugent, the playwright.'

The cigarette quivered in response.

'And Yvonne Benson, my friend.'

Dolly achieved a slight nod. She glared at Stefan. 'I told you to stop in,' she grumbled. 'It'll be dark in an hour. Every time I turn round, you've gone off somewhere. Get in here now.'

The newcomers stood back and watched Stefan obeying the orders of his housekeeper.

'Good God,' exclaimed April when the two had disappeared inside. 'Is she a jailer or a servant?'

'Both,' replied Karam and Sebastian simultaneously.

'And what a lovely Yorkshire accent she has,' continued April. 'Your father retains his Polish accent, too. I'm going to enjoy myself here.'

They went inside, Sebastian supporting April, Yvonne staying close to Karam.

The hallway was a huge flagged area, in the centre of which a big bulbous-legged table struggled to support several hundred books. 'He's been sorting out his library since 1989,' Karam explained. The books were very dusty. 'Dolly refuses to do the hall,' continued Karam. She pointed to a jangle of metal in a corner. 'That's what's left of an aeroplane engine. It fell out of the sky during the war and Papa rescued it, intending, I'm sure, to turn it into something useful. The piano was my mother's and the suit of armour was here when Papa bought the house from a wool merchant.' She pointed to a corner where the suit, minus arms, leaned crookedly against the walls. 'He probably found a use for the missing bits.'

April was studying a map of Europe. Blue-headed pins were dotted across several countries. 'My father's strategy,' explained Sebastian. 'That is the way he would have tackled the war. Thank God Sir Winston didn't take any notice.'

'Sir Winston?' gasped Yvonne.

'Oh, yes. He stayed here, apparently, and smoked many cigars while my father prattled on.' Sebastian looked closely at the map. 'We were never allowed to touch this. And now we daren't go near it because it is so frail.'

'What a character your father is,' remarked April, in a rare moment of understatement.

'Indeed.' Karam paused for thought. 'When we were children, we thought he was just Papa and that everyone else was similarly blessed. Then we went to school. Parents would not allow their children to visit us. That was because of the explosions, of course. Even after the war, Papa was employed by the Ministry of Defence.'

April chuckled mischievously. 'Guy Fawkes the Second.'

'Don't joke about it,' said Sebastian. 'Most of

354

the dining room went missing at one point. It can be very disturbing to a child, lying there at night and wondering whether the house will still be there in the morning.'

April was given a downstairs room with its own tiny bathroom. Karam and Yvonne were to share a large front bedroom where twin divans nestled among collected rubbish. Sebastian went up to his attic studio, a self-contained living area in which he also kept sound and video equipment.

On that first evening, Karam gave Yvonne and April a guided tour as thorough as the latter's limitations would allow. The visitors' heads finished up filled with memories of tumbledown rooms, faded tapestries, threadbare rugs, furniture stored in a jumble of legs and cushions.

They sat in the kitchen drinking Dolly's thick Yorkshire tea, which, according to a muted message from Karam, doubled up on its day off as an excellent paint-stripper. Dolly, whose mood had softened since the earlier encounter, was murdering a batch of batter in an earthenware bowl. She punished the mixture, then poured it into a tin. 'Yorkshire pud,' explained Karam. 'It's statutory on your first day.' The smell of roasting beef coloured the air deliciously.

'She's still got a fag in her mouth,' whispered Yvonne.

'Oh, absolutely,' replied the young mistress of the house. 'She can't work without that.'

'Doesn't it go in the food?' asked April.

'Better not to ask.' Karam drained her cup.

Yvonne was fascinated by the kitchen. It was sparkling clean and filled with appliances as old as

Noah. A Hoover washing-machine *circa* 1958 stood against one wall, its mechanism much improved by Stefan, who had 'done things to it', as Karam said darkly. A gigantic home-made electric mixer had pride of place on a side table, a sausage machine by its side. The cooker, a blue-mottled item with bowed legs, looked as if it had stepped from the advertisements in an early copy of *Mrs Beeton's Household Management.*

Dolly joined them at the table. She slammed down her mug, lit another cigarette and eyed each of the three women. 'The secret is', she announced, apropos of nothing, 'to keep watch all the time. He went off with some teenagers the other week and found magic mushrooms. The bloody old fool's bad enough without all that. I don't know what I'm supposed to do some days. He's ninety and I'm forty-eight—'

'Plus ten years,' muttered Karam.

'And I can't keep up with him. I've told him he'll end up in a straitjacket, but he won't listen. And don't let him kid you that he's deaf, because he can hear well enough when he wants, the owld bugger.'

The owld bugger wandered in, dressed this time in a pill-box hat with matching smoking jacket, both items in a dark-red satin material trimmed with gold braid. Over one eye, a ridiculous tassel dangled from the hat, swinging back and forth as he moved.

'He's trying to be suave,' said Karam.

Stefan sat next to Yvonne and blessed her with a brilliant smile. 'Tomorrow, I shall show you Huddersfield,' he threatened. 'It's not exactly Paris or Vienna, but it has its charms.'

356

Sebastian drifted in. He arrived at the table and placed two video-tapes in front of his father. 'Don't use my equipment for your videos, please,' he said.

'Bloody prude,' cursed the master of Horsefield Hall. 'Those are artistic films.' He addressed the whole room. 'This son of mine is not normal. He brings home no girl, no boy, no anything. And now he speaks to me as if I am a child. There is nothing wrong with my video-tapes.'

'Pornography,' Karam guessed aloud. 'Papa, when will you grow up? It's no wonder you're treated as a baby.'

Dolly snorted, causing her Embassy Regal to quiver more violently than usual. 'He'll sit up in his coffin begging for jelly-beans and chocolate. And no.' She addressed her employer directly. 'You are going nowhere near Huddersfield.' She swept an eye over the whole congregation. 'I won't bother telling you what he did, because he likes the attention. But there's three shops we don't go near any more.'

Stefan searched the realms of recent memory. 'I was only saying that those supermarkets should not have been built, that we should keep the old buildings and hold on to history.'

'I daren't shop in Sainsbury's, these days,' said Dolly angrily. 'I've never been so shown up in all my life.'

April burst out laughing. 'Bring him to Crosby and Blundellsands,' she hooted. 'I'd love to let him loose in one or two of our stores.'

Lord Laczynski of Horsefield was not amused. He glared fiercely at Dolly Isherwood. 'You, madam, are fired,' he announced.

Dolly raised fat shoulders. 'Not again. You fired me yesterday, last Thursday, the Friday before.' She stood up, her mountainous breasts hanging perilously near to full disclosure as she leant over the table. 'You'll be fired long before me,' she told her boss. 'In the bloody crematorium. I might not bother telling them to take your pacemaker out, because you'll go with a right good crack when the place blows up.' She drew herself to full height. 'In death, as in life, you'll explode. And take that hat off; it makes you look even dafter than you really are.'

April glanced at Karam, who was containing her laughter, just about. Sebastian, whose mask had begun to slip, made a fast getaway through the back door. Yvonne's face was buried in a table napkin.

Stefan addressed April. 'Multi,' he said sadly, 'I am ninety-one. When my children were born, I was already the age to be a grandfather. And here you witness all the respect I am to be given.' He stood up and walked to the door. 'The work I did for this, my adopted country, with my name attached to the Official Secrets Act, is no longer significant in the eyes of Sebastian and Karam.' He shook his head sadly. 'Do you have children, Multi?'

'No,' managed April, who was having one of her choking fits.

'Wise girl,' he pronounced.

When he had left and the muted laughter had died, Karam took hold of Yvonne's hand. 'See?' she said. 'I told you he was different. Please, please, don't let Papa see you laughing like that.

358

You'll never be rid of him.' She sighed, shook her head. 'What a family I have. Mad father, weird brother, crumbling homestead.'

Dolly swung round at the sink, fag ash dripping on the floor. 'Sebastian isn't weird,' she declared crossly. 'He's got morals, that's all.'

April regained her breath and sucked hungrily on an inhaler. There was no more to be said. As Sebastian had warned earlier, they had all entered the twilight zone.

It was a cool day, with a breeze scurrying round the corner from Deansgate, the resulting movement causing Honoria's skirt to dance slightly. Once more, she was outside the Bolton central police station, but this time her eyes were fastened on the closed doors of Paderborn House, which was just across the way. It was five minutes past three, and no one had entered or left the building for the past ten minutes.

She crossed the road and wandered on to Deansgate, her gaze skating over the contents of Whittaker's windows. This was a very select shop, but Honoria found it difficult to concentrate on Crown Derby and Waterford crystal. She was all dressed up, had bought a present, was waiting for her sister to emerge from Paderborn House register office with the man of her dreams. Something must have gone wrong. Perhaps the fire had caused the couple to alter the original plan.

Outside the police station once more, she fixed her eyes on the register office, flinching slightly when the town-hall clock reminded her that it was now three fifteen. She had not come with mischief in mind; she had merely intended to make her presence felt, had wanted to hand over the small gift.

A woman dawdled past, looked the well-dressed Honoria up and down. 'You all right, love?'

Honoria shook her head. 'I've come a long way to surprise a relative – she's getting married today.'

'Where?' asked the woman.

'At the register office, of course.'

The passer-by followed Honoria's gaze. 'It's not there no more,' she explained. 'They've shifted it up School Hill way, off Chorley Old Road. It were quite recent, I think. It's in Mere Hall Street.'

Honoria forced herself to keep smiling. The powers were conspiring against her yet again, it seemed. 'Oh, well.' She sighed. 'I suppose I must have missed it.'

Nevertheless, she drove home via Chorley Old Road, cutting through to the new register office on the way. The place was deserted. She inhaled deeply, hanging on to her temper and gripping the steering-wheel so tightly that her knuckles hurt.

A thought struck, a small moment during which Honoria realized that she was not quite as clever as she once had been. There she had stood, dressed to the nines, with a present in her hand. And why had she done that? How had she known the date of the wedding? Perhaps the fates had been with her after all, as some explaining would have been required. 'Am I losing my mind?' she asked herself aloud. 'I should have been forced to explain about the shop, about listening while they bought the wedding rings. Stupid, stupid.' Was this the beginning of senile dementia?

The suit had cost three hundred and fifty pounds, the hat, marked down in a sale, sixty, the shoes a small fortune. All designer labels, all bought to impress, all a waste of time and money now. She had only wanted to remind Hilda and the so-called Leo of her presence in the world, no more than that. Perhaps they were making for the airport. Would they actually go on honeymoon? she wondered.

After sitting for several minutes thinking about nothing in particular, she travelled out of the town, almost allowing the car to make its own decisions. The little Ford edged towards Moortop, grumbling slightly as it met the steeper gradients. Outside the house, Leo Stoneway's Rolls-Royce rested on its laurels. It had probably done a fine job of taking its master to his wedding.

Honoria found first gear and drove off. Her chance would come; she would make sure of that.

April was having the time of her life. She developed a curious liking for Dolly Isherwood and spent a great deal of time in the woman's company. The house went even further to pot while these two unlikely companions banded together over oceans of tea, and the rest of the household existed on a catch-as-catch-can basis, eating if there was food prepared, being chased from the kitchen each time they entered to make a snack.

Except for the lack of wrinkled stockings, Dolly was definitely a Nora Batty, a creature who harboured a set of ideals from a much earlier part of the century. Men were to be seen, but never heard. They were tolerated, encouraged to provide, nourished only if they brought home a wage. 'You can't be having them under your feet,' pronounced Dolly more than once. 'If you stick to your guns, they learn their place. Never let them have all their own road. If you do give them a bit of rope, make sure they're grateful for it.'

April began to believe in *Last of the Summer Wine*. She found herself almost waiting for Compo to put in an appearance, for Marina and Howard to pop up from behind a hedge, bicycles at the ready, grass in their hair, guilt printed in large letters over all they said and did.

'She's a caricature,' April told Karam later.

'No, she's a Yorkshire woman.'

'You're kidding.'

Karam shook her head. 'Dolly's a dying breed, I do admit, but she's not on her own. Men in these parts have not had easy lives. In fact, there was a marked need for men's liberation at one point. I suppose they would have burned jock-straps instead of bras.'

Yvonne entered the kitchen. Fresh from the bath, she glowed inside and out. Pregnancy was just beginning to suit her, as the sickness had disappeared and she was still slim enough to enjoy life to the full. Karam tried not to look at her. She had come dangerously close to declaring herself, but, being of a pragmatic and optimistic disposition, she was looking to her own future. After seeing Yvonne through this difficult time, Karam Laczynska intended to launch herself across the

362

Atlantic. A bit of her heart would remain in England, no doubt, yet she would go onward and upward. Nevertheless, she took care not to stare at her beautiful friend.

'Are we off, then?' Yvonne asked. She glanced at Karam. 'I see you've found a map or two.'

Karam snatched up maps and car keys, then led the others out. It was time to show off Yorkshire.

They progressed through the countryside, Yvonne's head trying to take in the names of villages they entered and left behind. All around them, green swatches of land dipped away into dales, rolling like waves, then rising up towards the mountains. April dabbed at her eyes, wondered how she could contain this spectacle without allowing emotion to spill. 'It's like my poor old Beethoven,' she said at last. 'Some days, he is too much for me to hear. This is too much for me to see.'

Yvonne agreed, but silently. She had seen Derbyshire, Dorset, Kent, Hampshire, Somerset, Devon – she had visited almost every county in England – but this was surely God's own place. There was peace, a special tranquillity that settled like a warm cloak about her shoulders. Yet the place was wild, too, with great monoliths dotted about, as if the Stone Age had decided to leave a few reminders for all who headed towards the Pennines.

Sheep ambled about, wandering off unfenced pasture, their respect for the internal combustion engine registering well below the zero mark. 'Sheep may safely graze,' Yvonne muttered quietly to herself.

They went through Fulstone and Butterley, paused to look at little terraces of stone houses, many churches, old pubs. Yvonne studied the map and read out names: Brockholes, Meltham, Helme, Slaithwaite, Golcar, Thongsbridge, Crimble Clough, Skelmanthorpe. Only in Yorkshire could such marvellous places exist.

They lunched in a pub nicknamed by Karam the Back of Beyond, though its real name was Nancy Dunn's. Poor old Nancy, a good Christian woman with a crooked eye, had been declared a witch and put to death several hundred years earlier, and the house had been named after her. A jolly female served them, asked where they were from and how did they like Yorkshire.

'I could live here for ever,' said Yvonne.

April gazed through a window at all the empty space between here and nowhere. 'I could run a sanctuary *par excellence* in these parts,' she said. 'Who comes to this pub? There aren't any houses for miles.'

'We're here for a start,' replied Yvonne. 'All the way from Liverpool, too.'

'And you'll soon see why,' smiled Karam.

Their hostess grinned knowingly. 'You'll not get food like mine over in Lancashire or whatever they call Liverpool now. Is it Merseyside? Aye, well, I reckon you won't be disappointed, girls.'

There was home-made bread, pea and ham soup, Yorkshire pudding so light that it threatened to float off the plate. 'I shall weigh this down with gravy before it makes a break for it,' announced Yvonne. She was eating for two, so she shifted three slices of beef and a pile of roast potatoes that tasted like heaven. 'What's your secret?' she asked the landlady. The woman tapped the side of her nose. 'Nancy Dunn,' she whispered conspiratorially. 'She came back and gave me the recipe.'

After treacle pudding and vanilla sauce made with cream, April could eat no more. She waltzed off in the direction of the ladies' room, finished up behind the bar. 'Bugger,' she said.

The landlady looked her up and down. 'What's up with you?'

'MS,' replied April.

'Get in the house,' she ordered, propelling April through a door marked PRIVATE.

When April returned to the living room, she found Karam and Yvonne waiting for her. Bloated and tired, the three women spread themselves all over the place, while Sally Houghton, licensee and cook *extraordinaire*, made coffee in the kitchen.

At first, it seemed like a touch of indigestion. Yvonne, trying hard not to seem critical of her hostess's culinary abilities, leant back in her chair and attempted to relax. But the pain persisted. She looked at Karam who had got up to examine some old prints on the chimney-breast, photographs of miners and people standing around in fields, scythes at the ready, smiles plastered across weather-worn faces.

April noticed. 'Are you all right, Yvonne?'

'No.'

Karam's head shot round to face her friend. 'What is it?'

'I don't know,' Yvonne lied. She was a nurse, and she did know. She was losing her baby.

Sally came in. 'My God, that's a fair sweat you're

in,' she told Yvonne. 'Has my dinner been a bit too much for you, love?'

'Get a doctor,' Yvonne gasped, before the pain hit again.

By the time the doctor arrived, Yvonne's baby was no more. She lay in Sally Houghton's bed, plastic bin liners protecting the sheets, her body racked with excruciating misery. 'Phone David,' she begged Karam. 'Tell him I couldn't help it. Tell him I tried my best.'

April sat next to the bed, her hands fastened tightly to Yvonne's arm. 'Don't fight it,' she whispered. 'Scream if you want to.'

Sally agreed. 'I've shut the pub and put a notice on the door. You yell your bloody head off if you feel like it, lass.'

The doctor, a brusque man of uncertain age, patted his patient's hand. 'We'll get you off to hospital, I think, just to make sure that you're out of the woods.'

Yvonne stared up at the ceiling. Until this moment, she had not realized how much she had wanted this clutch of cells to develop to full term. 'It was a person,' she mumbled. 'A child. I wanted it – didn't I, Karam?'

Karam could not speak. She was a strange mixture of sensitivity and practicality at the best of times, and this was the worst of times. She loved Yvonne with a quiet, hopeless passion she had never known before, and the child, Yvonne and David's, should have been a part of Yvonne's story. Now, a chapter was missing, because the little soul had decided not to stay among the living.

April wiped her eyes. The day had started out so

well, with four of them in the car, three women and an unborn baby. Yvonne would probably have been a good mother, too, while any young person living in the vicinity of Karam Laczynska could only have benefited from contact with such a gifted, lovely person. It wasn't fair, had never been fair. There again, nobody had ever promised that it would be.

The ambulance arrived eventually, picked up Karam and Yvonne and took them off in the direction of Huddersfield. April, faced with the prospect of driving an unfamiliar car along roads she didn't know, sat with Sally Houghton while the latter drew a map.

'Don't cry, love,' said Sally.

April wiped her face. 'I wish . . .' The words died.

'What do you wish?'

Although Yvonne and Karam could never be a couple, April had been looking forward to having them close by, just across the grove, the artist, the mother, the baby.

'What is it you were wishing for?' asked Sally again

'I don't know,' April answered, after a short pause. 'I truly don't know.'

Honoria packed her belongings into supermarket carrier-bags, picking up the timer plugs last of all and placing them in her handbag. It was all worked out. She smiled to herself, remembering how she had plucked Coca-Cola cans and cigarette packets out of a waste-bin in Blackburn Road, how she had scattered them outside the Chapel House before setting the fire. Whose fingerprints? she wondered idly. Certainly not hers, as she had worn gloves.

But this second scheme had become extraordinarily complicated. Being in two places at once was all very well, but when the two locations were over forty miles apart, wisdom was essential. She had given up the cottage, had bought the rented car, had sat a whole week making up the plan. It was honed as near to perfection as she could achieve.

She drove with extreme caution along the East Lancashire Road towards Liverpool, moving not too slowly, not too fast: this was one occasion on which the attention of police patrol cars might prove disastrous. At just after one in the morning, Honoria abandoned her car in a quiet Blundellsands street, locked its door, then walked on cushioned soles to Cavendish Mansions.

Inside, she switched on several lights and paced about for a few minutes, deliberately dropping a vase on the kitchen floor and slamming a couple of doors. She wanted to be heard, needed to be noticed. 'I'm back,' she mouthed at invisible neighbours, as she closed her bedroom curtains. When the timer plugs were fitted to the bedroom lamp, the radio and the television, Honoria sat and drank coffee, lingering for an hour or more before leaving the flat. With the light switching itself on and off all night, someone in the area might notice that she was in residence. At eight in the morning, the TV and the radio would come on for a few minutes, then the rest should prove as easy as pie.

It was almost four o'clock when Honoria parked her Ford on Moortop Lane. The soft-soled, sensible Clarks made no sound as she crept to the back door of Moortop. The dog, a dozy article who seemed to live on the landing, had made no fuss last time, so she did not fear him. She set the fire in the kitchen, making sure that it had taken hold before letting herself out and locking the back door with the spare key she had stolen before leaving for Liverpool all those years ago.

Her heart raced. If Hilda and Leo were on honeymoon, they would be safe. Except, of course, from their insurers, who would be bound to suspect that the happy pair had deliberately fired two houses within a few weeks. If they were in the house, they might die; if Hilda died, Honoria might well become a very rich lady.

Again, she crossed the border between Lancashire and Liverpool, her tired eyes drooping as she pulled into a country lane just off the Formby bypass. She picked a Baby Ben alarm clock out of her bag, set it for eight, wrapped herself in a tartan rug and dozed.

When the bell rang, Honoria jumped and gazed around herself. Where was she? Oh, yes, oh, yes. Her heart drummed in her ears when she thought about what she had done. Now the eleventh commandment must be the rule, as she must not be found out.

Everything was ready for her. There were pre-moistened face tissues, there was makeup, comb and brush. She slaked her thirst from a lemonade bottle, composed her thoughts, turned on the radio and drove to Sainsbury's in Crosby. When

369

the doors opened, she bought groceries, packed them in a carrier-bag and returned to the car. She was home and dry.

The garage belonging to Honoria West was positioned in a row behind the flats. When her car was put away, Honoria picked several Sainsbury's bags from the boot. One contained shopping, the others were packed with clothes. She had committed the perfect crime.

But, as she sat and watched Granada News, no report of a fire at Moortop Farm was given. Perhaps it hadn't been noticed yet. After all, Moortop was well off the beaten track.

Miss Honoria West made another pot of coffee, picked out some favourite biscuits and positioned herself at the corner window. With binoculars at the ready, she carried on where she had left off. A most peculiar-looking young man was walking about outside Philip Pointer's house. Surely he wasn't living there? He wore flowered trousers and his hair was extremely silly. Wouldn't Pointer's estate still be in the hands of lawyers?

She watched the creature, made up her mind that he had no right to be living here among executives and decent retired people like her good self. With a new project in mind, she forgot all about the previous night.

In his garden, Kevin shovelled leaves and felt the eyes boring into his back. She was there. The woman of letters had returned. He put down his spade and turned to face her, caught sight of the binoculars as she pulled them away from her face. He smiled, placed his right hand on his hip, then minced his way up the path, deliberately camp, deliberately provoking her.

Honoria smiled. She was all-powerful; the young man's days in Blundellsands were numbered.

Leo and Hilda sat at their vast kitchen table. Thanks to Mason, who was now basking in glory, they had been saved from a fiery death. Two cupboards were completely ruined, while the curtains no longer existed.

'It must have been her,' repeated Hilda.

'But how?'

'Where did my perfume go?' she asked. 'And I know she's been in this house. I feel it. She has been twice, Leo. Once just to have a look round, then last night to kill us. She probably burned your place, too.'

'No forced entry here,' he reminded his wife. 'And the fire at my house was started through a letterbox, so it was hardly the same thing.'

'Then she has a key.'

He knew that Hilda was right. The locks would have to be changed immediately. 'Shall I telephone the police?'

Hilda considered. 'No. My sister is a nightmare, a very clever one, too. She'll have an alibi. Even if she hasn't, she'll get bail. And if we rattle her, she'll strike again.'

Leo drummed his fingers on the table while he considered the problem. 'Right, I shall get a top-notch burglar alarm fitted today. They can put fire and smoke alarms everywhere, too.' He looked at his sad-faced wife. 'Hilda, don't let this make you ill. I shall put it out of my mind as quickly as possible – so must you.'

371

Hilda fiddled with a string of pearls. 'I wonder if she's still around here?'

'She left the Pack Horse weeks ago.'

'I know. And I can't telephone April, because she's in Yorkshire with her friends.'

'Phone the flat in Blundellsands, then.'

Hilda did not need to consider this suggestion before replying. 'Let the lioness sleep, wherever she is. We should be safe enough with alarms.'

Leo shivered as he flicked through the *Yellow Pages* in search of a joiner to mend the damage and a security company to install alarms and new locks. For over forty years, Miss Honoria West had affected his life. He was glad that he did not know her whereabouts as his fingers almost itched to strangle her. For Hilda's sake, he must keep his temper.

Kevin ascended the stairs and knocked on Honoria's door. He had applied some foundation, a nice, bright lipstick and two coats of mascara. This was unusual, as he was not a habitual wearer of cosmetics, but he wanted to give the old witch a heart-attack.

The chains were not on. Honoria had made herself more readily available than usual in order to make sure that people knew she was back, that she had returned the previous night. Kevin threw himself against the door and stepped inside.

'Who are—?' Honoria stopped when she noticed the bizarre decorations, the makeup, the bangles, a string of glass beads around his throat.

'Right,' began the unwelcome visitor. 'You're the sender of letters, I take it. The starer through windows, the employer of binoculars, the one who murdered Philip.'

She staggered back, a hand to her mouth.

'He hanged himself, you know. Everyone realizes that you're the poison pen, but people are vulnerable, as you have learnt only too well, and the letters gave away a little too much information for comfort. And you always stopped short of blackmail, didn't you? But you murdered my friend, Miss West.'

Honoria, thoroughly unused to direct confrontation, dropped into an armchair.

'So I thought I would introduce myself. My name is Kevin Brooks. Philip left me his house and made it possible for me to move in before probate is settled.'

Her heart was all over the place.

'I've looked for your letter, but he probably destroyed it. Many old queers are still frightened, frightened enough to do what Philip did.'

'I did nothing—'

'Don't start with me, you old bag,' he said evenly. 'Any more trouble from you and I'll fix you good and proper.' He sat down opposite her. 'You see, I'm HIV positive. Now, while I'm not a very big chap, I could quite easily overcome a dried-out old woman like you. I could get a hypodermic, draw off some of my filthy blood and stick it into you – no problem.' Inwardly, he shuddered. A gentle soul, he had never threatened anyone before. But this awful woman seemed to bring him down to her level, which inhabited a lower stratum than any earthworm.

She cried out, then clapped the hand against her mouth again.

373

'Another attitude taken by some out there is that you are ill and that your letters do no real harm. Well, the one you sent to Philip did damage. So we have collected together all your scribblings – except Philip's, of course. One more written syllable out of you and we get the police. If you so much as stir out of this flat, you will be watched.' He grinned. 'So now the hunter becomes the prey. We are all united against you, Miss West.'

She searched for an answer, found none.

'And I have people staying with me from time to time. They, too, have HIV – some of them have developed AIDS. Leave them alone. They don't want you staring and making trouble for them, so take care. There are many, many eyes on you.'

When the young man had left, Honoria grabbed a glass and poured herself a hefty measure of dry sherry. In all her life, no one had spoken to her in such an offensive manner. She gulped down the Harvey's, refilled the glass. No, no, she must keep her wits about her.

There was still no mention on TV of a fire at Moortop. Perhaps she hadn't lit it properly. Still, plans occasionally went awry, she told herself. But she couldn't settle, couldn't watch the television, didn't want to read. After several minutes of inactivity, during which time she tried not to worry about Kevin's threats, she walked to her famous corner window.

The sight before her would remain with her until her dying day. A solid mass of people stood below her flat, all silent, all motionless. She recognized many of the faces, realized that some of the men must have taken time off work to be here.

Before finding the presence of mind to close her curtains, Honoria saw David Benson, the Three Graces, Gill Collins. Her arms and legs shook, the latter almost refusing to support her. As far as Blundellsands was concerned, she was finished. Well, for the time being, at least.

Yvonne Benson felt empty, drained of all life and of most hope. Everyone was being very kind; if the medical people of Huddersfield were anything to go by, she was among gentle folk, men and women who truly cared about her. She had been given a single room in which to recuperate after her operation, yet she was never left alone for too long by the very busy staff.

David had been to visit. They had cried together, had clung to each other like two children left to drift on life's uncharted waters, only to part after an hour or so, both knowing that they must travel now in separate lifeboats.

Lord Laczynski, in the company of Dolly Isherwood, sat by Yvonne's bed, stroking the patient's hand and muttering words of consolation in a language he had scarcely used in years. Dolly, practical and sensible, brought Thermos flasks of home-made beef tea, a ring of scones, some parkin.

April struggled in, walked straight past Yvonne's bed, stopping only when the wall impeded her uncontrollable progress. She didn't say much, simply sitting and speaking if and when Yvonne wanted to talk. April Nugent was blessed in many ways, and one of her gifts was the ingrained knowledge that words were not always needed.

Karam, thinner and sadder, came every day. She always carried books, always left them on the hospital locker, hoping against hope itself that Yvonne would read eventually.

'You look worse than I do,' remarked Yvonne one afternoon.

'I care about you and you're hurt. I'm glad it shows, because you mustn't think you're on your own.' Karam bit her lip. Of late, there had been a subtle change in Yvonne, and Karam had wondered whether she had been about to throw in the towel and return to David.

At last, Yvonne's real tears started. 'What did I do wrong?' she wailed.

'Nothing.' Karam swallowed a huge ball of grief that had settled in her throat. 'I know this will sound trite, but many women lose their first.'

Yvonne slowed her sobs. 'And where do I get my second?'

Karam lowered her head as her own eyes spilled. 'Don't think about that just yet. Just rest and get well.'

'I don't conceive easily.'

'You've done it once; it can happen again.'

Karam closed her eyes and bit her tongue. David had visited her, too, had wept copiously in her arms. 'She just walked in and slammed the bill on my desk,' he had said.

Deirdre Mellor, on the brink of reconciliation with her husband, had aborted David's child. 'I didn't want the baby,' he had sobbed, 'so that's a cause for guilt, but two on one day, Karam? While Yvonne suffered all that pain, madam lay back in a five-star clinic, three hundred pounds' worth of sympathy and Earl Grey. A few hours later, she handed me the bill. What a bloody stupid game this life is.'

Karam laid her head on Yvonne's hard, narrow bed, and both women cried until exhaustion dried their tears. They were found asleep by a young nurse who left them in peace, her own eyes pricking as she left the scene.

On the third day, Sebastian arrived. He entered the room with enough flowers to decorate a small graveyard, muttered some words of consolation, then sat in a plastic chair as far away as possible from Yvonne's bed. For a couple of minutes, they both stared at the massive bouquet, then Sebastian got up and looked through the window. Having assessed the view, he sat down again, only to stand immediately and pick up a magazine from a table next to an easy chair that was far from relaxed, all high back, hard seat and tense wooden arms. This was his sister's lover. His head ached.

Yvonne sighed, wished that he would go, since he was a man who should not be allowed into company too often. How he managed to deliver sensible programmes on the arts she could not imagine. With strangers, he was inordinately uncomfortable; with the woman he assumed to be his sister's partner, he was almost silent. 'Why did you come?' she asked eventually.

A few beats of time passed while he organized his reply. 'To see you. To bring you the flowers.'

'Why?' she persisted. 'I'll be out of here tomorrow.' Endometriosis had been diagnosed. Getting pregnant again might prove difficult, though not impossible.

He walked to the door, opened it. 'I thought I heard someone,' he muttered lamely.

'You probably did. There are many someones around, since this is a hospital.' Recent events had made her acutely sensitive. Raw from the loss of a child, shocked by a diagnosis that promised a rather uncomfortable future, she was in no humour to tolerate this disconcerting visitor. 'Thank you for the flowers.' She sounded like a child delivering a compulsory and rehearsed message. 'Why don't you go now?'

He turned, looked her full in the face, his own features moulded carefully to show no expression. 'I am so, so sorry,' he managed.

She knew he was telling the truth.

'Are you feeling better?' he asked.

'Yes, thank you.' Physically, she was improving, though the psychological wound would take longer to heal. Why was he staring at her like that?

'I suppose I'd better . . .' He waved a hand in the direction of the corridor. 'Papa has asked me to record him. He wants to leave a message for the world.' Sebastian looked up at the ceiling. 'It will require careful editing, no doubt.'

Conversation. He had actually made a remark, had expressed an opinion. 'Your father's a good man. I expect you already know that.'

'Yes. Eccentricity becomes easier to deal with as the years go by. He did a lot for Great Britain, I suppose.'

It was hard work, hard for her as well as for him. There was a barrier of some kind. If Yvonne had erected it, she had never been aware of the fact. His assumptions had led him to this impasse, she concluded. Perhaps now, while he recognized her weakness, she should ask him about . . . About what? About an invisible wall, a moat, an insurmountable obstacle?

To the relief of both of them, Sally Houghton poked her head into the room. Yvonne introduced the two visitors, sighing the tension out of her body as Sebastian left.

'Nice-looking bloke,' said Sally. 'I wouldn't mind going a few rounds with him myself. He reminds me of somebody on the telly.'

'You've come a long way.' Yvonne was in no mood to talk about Sebastian. She accepted a huge basket of fruit. 'Who's running the pub?'

Sally Houghton raised her shoulders. 'Nobody, love. I've shut it. It's all right, don't worry. Weekends is when I make my brass. They come for miles just to get a whiff of my gravy.'

It was nice to have a visitor who was almost a stranger, someone who took a kindly interest in events without being too closely involved. They chatted about mundane topics – cooking, the weather, TV programmes.

Out in the corridor, Sebastian Laczynski wiped his brow. He sat for a few moments on another plastic chair, elbows on knees, head held between his hands. God, he hadn't asked to love her. She was the last woman in the world he would have chosen. Almost from their first encounter, he had been troubled, uneasy. Now he felt as if his mind didn't really belong to him, because it was occupied by visions, imaginings, hypothesis, lust, longing . . . She was Karam's. 'She is Karam's,' he mumbled softly.

A nurse passed. 'Are you all right, sir?'

'Yes, thank you.' Far from all right, he got up and walked towards the exit. And yet she wasn't Karam's. Yvonne Benson cared for Karam Laczynska; about that fact there could be no doubt. But she didn't truly belong with or to Karam. They would possibly stay together, as both were women of integrity. Also, the two were a perfect match, up to a point. Yet Yvonne, who had left a husband in order to be with Karam, gave off . . . something. Not quite a scent, not quite anything that responded to or reacted with the five identifiable senses of man. She was not a natural lesbian. She was a female who was drawn to another female whose brother was a damned fool. No. She had to be a lesbian – he must stop this wishful thinking.

He jumped into his car and sat for a while in the car-park. 'I have to fight this,' he told himself. 'I can't hurt Karam.' He adored his sister, admired her brilliant mind, her talent as a painter, her dry, wry humour. Above all, he loved her simply because she had always been there, had helped and encouraged him, had proved to be the best sister on earth.

'What must I do?' he asked the dashboard. How many beautiful women had he met over the years, several of them only too willing to jump into bed with a man of supposed influence? Sebastian was not a bed-hopper. Many chose to believe he was gay, since that excuse provided an acceptable explanation for his rejection of them. But he was not gay: he had simply waited for the right one, and the right one was the wrong one. 'I'm old-fashioned,' he explained to the speedometer. 'A relic from a bygone age.' He wanted a true relationship, a love story that would defy time and the corrosive laxity of today's society.

'She's been married, too.' It had been his intention to ally himself to a woman who had not travelled through other men's lives, never to fasten himself to a female who had jumped off the bus when the journey got rough. Divorce was the easy way out, the coward's route. 'It's driving me round the bend.' He turned the ignition key and drove homeward. Filming would start soon. He was to interview his own sister, April Nugent and the sister of Hyacinth West. The latter had contacted his employers and had been deemed interesting. From what he had heard, she was definitely that.

He reached Horsefield Hall and went up into his eyrie. Picking up a remote control, he fast-forwarded through several yards of video-tape until he found the footage he wanted. She was dancing about in Karam's back garden, the long hair flowing in her wake, Bertrand Russell chasing her, pretending to nip at pretty ankles. On bare feet, Yvonne Benson skipped and skidded, laughing when she fell into the pond, almost splitting her sides when one of Karam's frogs leapt out in protest because his home had been invaded.

'I'm going back to London,' he told the screen. 'I'm leaving you because I can't bear to look at you.' Her pain, the loss of her child, her very presence in Yorkshire was too much for him to tolerate. He went downstairs to root about in the fridge.

Karam was brewing tea. She looked up. 'How was she?'

'Slightly better, I'd say.'

She poured two cups while Sebastian found biscuits. He was not himself. 'What's the matter, little brother?'

'Nothing.'

'You can't fool me.' She stirred her tea, grabbed a digestive. 'Dolly, Papa and April have gone to Huddersfield,' she explained.

'I thought he'd been banned from most shops there?'

Karam raised a shoulder. 'At least we don't have to father-sit, so don't complain.'

She picked up a newspaper and started the crossword. 'You aren't happy – I hate to see you so miserable.'

For answer, he simply picked up his drink and walked to the window, turning his back on the sister he adored. There was nothing he could say.

Karam gripped the pen so hard it stung her fingers. She knew what he was going through, yet was unable to soothe him. It should have been easy: 'Sebastian, I love Yvonne to bits, I've loved her for months. She does not love me.'

She raised her head, took in the slope of his shoulders, the bone weariness, the despair. The urge to dash across the kitchen was strong, almost overpowering. Closing her eyes, she pictured Yvonne in the supermarket, remembered instant coffee, instant infatuation.

She never loved me. Oh, Sebastian, how I wish I could tell you the truth, tell you that she needs a husband, a child, a future. But I cannot open my mouth, because I promised that I would not explain her to anyone. She must tell you herself.

The pen did not work. She tossed it away and it clattered off the table's edge. He turned for a second, allowing his sister a brief glimpse of sad eyes, downturned mouth.

Yvonne said I hadn't to tell you. And now, with the baby lost, she will be more vulnerable than before. If I told you now, today, you might lose your head and declare yourself. This is the wrong time. She is too hurt, too bewildered, and she must not be imposed upon.

I've watched both of you for ages. How transparent you are. You give each other a berth wide enough to launch an ocean-going liner. She asks why you growl at her: you are forever pointing your video-camera at the garden when she happens to be there. The ritual has begun, but I can't enlighten you. The girl you love is not a lesbian, but I am forbidden to tell you.

Sebastian stared blindly ahead, not seeing the garden, not hearing the birds. He had wondered of late whether everything had been a nightmare. He was falling in love with his sister's lover. Often, he had come close to approaching Yvonne in spite of all that. Stupid. He could never offer himself to a lesbian, surely? Yet how tempted he had been . . .

And he could take nothing from Karam. She had always given him the bigger apple, the better toy. More than that, she had wrapped him in unconditional love.

Wordless, he turned and left the room, teacup still clutched in his hand. Locked in a bathroom, Sebastian Laczynski, a man who excelled in the concealment of emotion, found himself near to tears. Poor Yvonne, poor lost baby.

And Karam. Mother had died just before Karam's fourteenth birthday, had breathed her last in the room currently shared by Yvonne and Karam. How this beloved sister must have missed the guiding hand of Clare Casey, the gentlewoman who had married a Polish immigrant almost thirty years her senior. What a bloody mess this continued to be.

Downstairs, Karam made her decision. She would leave for Liverpool, allow her brother and Yvonne to find their own level without any interference.

She went up to pack her bags. She did not weep: she had drawn enough from that well in recent days. No. She was going on, going back, going home. 'Turn to him, Yvonne,' she told the photograph in her purse. 'You, too, must go home.'

Twenty

After five days during which the hospital staff monitored Yvonne's mental state as well as her physical condition, she was allowed home. Home, for the time being, was Horsefield Hall. April drove Yvonne from Huddersfield to Horsefield, her mind heavily occupied with Karam's recent disclosure. Before leaving for Liverpool, Karam had spoken in confidence to her, had told her about Sebastian's growing affection for Yvonne, about the latter's grudging admiration for him. 'She hasn't quite fallen for him, but, when she does, she'll need no safety-net, because my brother adores her,' Karam had said. 'And she won't allow anyone to tell anyone that she isn't a dyke.'

'Karam will be back at work, I suppose,' said Yvonne now.

'Yes.'

'And how is Lord Laczynski?'

April made a choking sound. 'Don't ask.'

'I have asked.'

'Last seen with a scythe in the jungle, the bit to

the right of the house. Muttering something about cultivation, potatoes, carrots and so forth.'

'He'll never clear that lot, not on his own.'

'Dolly's words exactly. She was behind him with a yard brush and a stream of curses. I don't know what that man's on, but I wish he'd give me some of it – he moves like the London express out of Lime Street. He's almost fifty years older than me, but he makes me feel as if I'm a hundred and he's sixteen.'

Yvonne wondered how she was going to cope without Karam's stoic support. 'Is Sebastian still around?'

'Yes.' April followed instructions to the letter. She was forbidden to discuss Sebastian with Yvonne, Yvonne with Sebastian. She was to travel back to Liverpool without Yvonne, who must be abandoned to the tender mercies of Dolly Isherwood, Stefan and Sebastian. 'Leave her only if she's not upset,' Karam had ordered. 'If she insists, bring her with you. But try to persuade her to stay.' Karam was turning into a real match-maker, it seemed.

Sebastian was waiting at the door. He helped Yvonne out of the car, flinched slightly when she drew away from him.

'I can walk,' she told him, rather tersely. 'I lost a baby, not my legs.' Immediately, she felt sorry about the harsh words, but she had not the energy for apologies.

April locked the car door and followed the two of them into the house. This was not going to be an easy few days.

Dolly had prepared a small feast of sandwiches

and cakes. April sat down with Yvonne while Sebastian made tea.

'Where's Dolly?' he asked.

'Still chasing your father,' answered April. 'He's trying to turn himself into a gardener.'

The three of them sat, no one eating, no one speaking. Sebastian took a sudden interest in the pattern on a sugar bowl. Yvonne stared down into her cup as if reading fortunes, while April, who sensed the tension acutely, simply sat and realized how right Karam had been. These two souls, concentrating on avoiding collision, were performing an age-old dance, a ritual that might last for hours, for months, even for years. Though neither fully recognized or acknowledged it, the orchestra was playing and courtship had already begun. At present, Yvonne would not be aware of much, yet her body language remained eloquent even now, after the miscarriage and the treatment necessitated by that unhappy event.

Stefan took the edge off the situation. He ran through the kitchen doorway, no sign of breathlessness or tiredness, then secreted himself in the broom cupboard. The small audience of witnesses did not react: it was as if the company was used to folk dashing about and hiding in cupboards.

Dolly came in, her face bright red and running with sweat. 'Hello, sweetheart,' she breathed at Yvonne. 'Where is that owld bastard?'

Nobody moved.

'He's in here somewhere. I saw him with my own eyes.'

'Who else's eyes would she use?' asked Sebastian quietly.

April snorted, changed the snort to a cough and rooted in the depths of her bag for a handkerchief.

Yvonne was having one of those other-worldly moments, those terrible times when a person feels that he or she is not really there. Empty, lonely, yet not alone, she was not making full contact with her surroundings.

'I'll bloody swing for him.' Dolly actually removed the cigarette from her mouth. She studied it for a few seconds, as if she didn't recognize it, then stuck it back where it belonged. On noisy, angry feet, Dolly marched across the flagged floor and threw open the broom cupboard.

Stefan stepped out. 'Good afternoon,' he said, with the air of a man greeting an unwelcome door-to-door salesperson.

Dolly grabbed him by the cardigan. 'What the hell do you think you're playing at? An hour and a flaming half I've been looking for you.'

'I was not lost,' he explained patiently. 'I was with myself. A person who is with himself is never lost or alone.'

Yvonne heard that, just about. Perhaps she should separate herself from others for a while; perhaps she should sit very still somewhere and find herself. There was a lot of talk these days about people finding themselves, understanding 'where they were coming from', delineating 'personal space' and getting 'in touch with their inner core'. She stood up and wandered out of the room.

Stefan approached the table. 'Multi,' he said, 'how is that poor girl? Is she very depressed?'

'Anybody'd be depressed looking at you,' said Dolly caustically.

Stefan ignored her. He was, for once, decently dressed in old moleskins and a green cardigan. 'Go up to her, Multi,' he suggested.

'She needs to be alone,' replied April.

He pondered, nodded sagely. 'Yes, that is probably so. I, of course, am not allowed the luxury of solitude. This female pursues me wherever I go. It has been my biggest burden in life, being followed hither and thither by women.'

Sebastian fiddled with a teaspoon. 'Are you going to take Yvonne back with you?' he asked April. 'To Blundellsands? You need to collect your stuff for the recording – the team will be up here in a few days. She might be better back in Liverpool – familiar faces and so forth. And she must need Karam.'

April, acutely aware of her brief, picked up the cue. 'Karam feels that Yvonne might be better here with you, your father and Dolly.' She watched hope in his eyes, saw it die straight away, knew that he had murdered it deliberately.

'She won't want to be here, April.' Sebastian threw down his spoon.

'And why not?' asked Stefan. 'This is a good place to be, plenty of fresh air, places where she can walk and regain her strength.'

'And she's pretty,' added Dolly, without malice.

'Let her do as she wishes,' said April. 'What she's been through takes some time to mend.'

Upstairs, Yvonne lay flat on the bed, hands folded on a belly that had so recently been the home of a very tiny person. She didn't want to be here, didn't want to go home, didn't care where she was, didn't care whether she was. She had never been suicidal, yet she suddenly wasn't interested in remaining alive.

The room still bore marks of Karam – a painting on a wall, some dried flowers in a vase, walking boots under the dressing-table. Yvonne turned away from these sights, closed her eyes and shut out the whole world. Karam, the one person in whom she might confide, was busy elsewhere. She woke in the middle of the night in a panic, yet although she reached back into her mind she failed to remember the dream. It had been bad – she knew that much.

On the landing, she regained her night vision slowly, then crept downstairs. Horsefield Hall was eerie in the moonlight. The famous armless armour seemed like a deformed person, while Lord Laczynski's aircraft engine was something from another planet, a mutated, hideous creature.

Would the baby have been deformed or diminished in some way? Had Mother Nature taken the child deliberately? 'I would have wanted you, no matter what,' Yvonne sobbed quietly. 'Had you been blind or deaf, or anything at all, you would have been loved.' She had worked during training with many children, some paralysed, some with poor sight or hearing, several with Down's syndrome, all special, all lovable, most capable of achieving a degree of pleasure from life. 'Why did you leave me?' she asked. 'Was I going to be such a bad mother?'

At the top of the stairs, Sebastian Laczynski

listened. Her whispers crept up the walls and into his ears. Tears pricked behind his eyelids, but he held them back. What right had he to cry when this poor young woman had lost so much? Like a thief in the night, he simply watched, listened and waited for the coast to clear.

Yvonne opened the front door and stepped out into a chilly world. She wanted clean air, space to move through, the timelessness of darkness. At first, she picked her way carefully through trees, past neglected urns, dried-up fountains and age-scarred statues. The waning moon silvered everything it touched, performing its magic so that the wild gardens were iced with a false prettiness.

After a few minutes, she began to run, not feeling briars as they tore at her clothes, unaware of thorns touching her face and neck. Inside, she was as senseless, as derelict as the hall's wild vegetation. There was no way forward, no way back. Her compass bore few points of reference; she heeded no sound, no sight, no sensation.

Behind her, he followed as closely as he could, realizing that this was possibly a part of Yvonne's cure. She had refused counselling, had torn up a prescription for tranquillizers. The running, the stumbling, the near-falls – these were her own treatments, her own medication.

At last, she stopped.

Sebastian hid in a clump of bushes, tried to quieten his breathing.

'Why?' she screamed at the stars. 'Why me? Why my baby? Is this to be my punishment because I stopped loving David? What sort of a God are you anyway? It's not fair, it's not, it's not!' Like a child, she stamped her feet as she cried out.

Sebastian parted the branches and looked at her, listened to the tantrum. She was kneeling now in a small clearing, her lovely face raised, her arms reaching up, fists balled as if ready to punch holes in the sky. He was glad that she had slept in her clothes, because the air was cutting right through his T-shirt and shorts.

Yvonne crumpled, lay down on the wild grasses, knees coming up to meet her chest, arms folded, hands gripping her shoulders. She had to go back now, had to wait for tomorrow so that she could pretend to be alive again. It was important to go on, to force herself to appear as part of whatever happened around her. The urge to carry on was so strong, even now, when the soul was weak and the mind remained depressed. Aching and lonely, she got up.

She passed so close that he could hear her breathing. Sighing with uncontainable relief, he prepared to follow her to the house.

'Who's there?' she asked.

He froze.

'Who is it?' she insisted. She turned, saw Karam's face peering over a low branch. Karam had cut her hair, had . . . 'Oh, it's you,' she said. 'Have you been following me?'

'Yes.' He stepped out.

'You're not even dressed.'

He didn't bother to tell her that he had slept on the landing, that he had watched and waited between short sessions of half-sleep.

'You'll get cold,' she remarked, her tone back to normal.

'I'm already cold,' he informed her.

They returned to the house without another word. Inside, they looked at one another for a couple of seconds. 'Hot chocolate?' asked Sebastian.

'Please.' While he went off to prepare the drink, Yvonne found a coat and carried it to the kitchen. 'Put this on,' she ordered.

He complied, then returned to the business of spooning powder into cups. Supposedly intelligent and sensitive, he did not know what to say, how to help this one particular person. He stirred the chocolate angrily, causing it to slop on to the surface next to the kettle.

'I feel dreadful,' Yvonne volunteered eventually.

Sebastian relaxed slightly. If she was going to talk, he could answer, at least. 'I'm sure you do,' he replied. 'A man must sound so glib saying that, but I've tried to imagine your pain and grief. It must be horrible.'

'It is.'

He brought the two drinks to the table. 'Here. Swallow some of that – it will warm you up.'

'You're the cold one.'

'Not as cold as you think, Yvonne.'

The *double entendre* was not wasted. 'I know that. You've been extremely kind. Thank you.'

He sat. 'We're all concerned about you. My father wants you to stay here to recuperate.'

Yvonne almost smiled.

He reached across the table and gripped her hand. 'Yvonne, most people find me an odd sort

393

of chap, a bit withdrawn and so forth, but—'

'Karam calls you weird.'

'I know. She says nothing behind my back that she wouldn't say to my face. But I am here, Yvonne. If you want to talk, or to sit by me and stay quiet, just use me. Come up into the attic and help me to practise my interview questions. Whatever – I'm here.'

'I'm grateful.'

He released her hand. He didn't want her gratitude. All he wanted was for her to be well, to find some hope, a future. 'I am to interview the terrible Honoria,' he said. 'It seems that her poetry is about to be published.'

'Oh.' She sipped the hot, sweet liquid.

'April, too.'

Yvonne nodded absently.

'And Karam.'

The penny finally dropped. 'Honoria? The last time she saw April, she threw water in her face.'

'Should be interesting, then.' Encouraged, he decided to elaborate. 'Hyacinth West had a book published shortly before she died. It was a slim volume, just a hundred or so pages and a small print-run, mainly for the people of Bolton.'

'And Honoria will not be outdone.'

'So it would seem.'

Yvonne nodded thoughtfully. 'Things promise to become lively if you intend to have Honoria and April under the same roof.' She paused. 'Tell April that Honoria is coming, but don't tell Honoria that April will be here.'

'Why?'

'Well, that will give April the edge. It's complicated.'

'That's what Karam said.'

Yvonne drained her cup. 'Will Karam come at the weekend?'

'I expect so.'

There was no more to be said. Yvonne wished her dear friend's brother good night, then went up to her room. She stripped off the dirty clothes and lay in a hot bath for twenty minutes. Karam should not have deserted her; surely the university could have managed without her for a few more days? Selfish, selfish, she chided herself. Karam loved her work; Karam had taken enough time off and could not endanger her position.

Warmer and clean, she curled up in the lonely room, feeling that even Karam could not have taken away this dreadful isolation. She was completely alone, and there seemed no cure for that. Sebastian had been so kind, so considerate. As she drifted towards sleep, his face appeared in her mind's eye. Yes, he was a good man after all. And he looked so much like his sister, so much like her . . .

In the dream, Yvonne saw Karam, not Sebastian. Karam was professing her love, was trying to persuade Yvonne to love her in return. She couldn't. Try as she might, the sleeping Yvonne was unable to change herself.

When Yvonne woke in the morning, the dream was clear. Oh, surely not? Karam had never indicated that she was in love with Yvonne. And yet . . . No, best not to think of that. It was all rooted in upset hormones, Yvonne concluded. The dream, the nightmare, had arisen from emptiness, lack of hope, fluctuating levels of oestrogen.

She suddenly realized that Sebastian was in her room. He lay near the door, a mattress underneath him, his body cocooned in a sleeping-bag. He had been instructed to look after her, no doubt, and was taking the job seriously. 'You look like a large blue caterpillar,' she informed him.

He opened one eye. 'I have waited all my life to hear those very words. Shall I go and make tea?'

'Please.' He had a first-class honours degree from Oxford in tea-making. He had followed her last night and had decided to keep close watch on her. Strangely, she did not mind.

'You cried in your sleep,' he advised her, as he struggled out of his navy blue prison.

'It will pass,' she answered. 'Yes, this, too, shall pass.'

He finally managed to stand. 'Damned sleeping-bag's a death trap,' he complained.

'Why are you in here?' she asked.

He felt a blush staining his cheeks. 'In case you took off again. We can't have you wandering into town at three in the morning.'

She was tired and could think of no clever reply. Neutral ground was the safest territory, mundane questions, aimless dialogue. 'Where do you live when you're in London?' she surprised them both by asking. Was that a suitable question? Was it too intimate, too interested? And did it matter?

He rolled up his bedding. 'On a friend's boat. This zip is going to break. Chelsea Reach. He's gone off filming in Africa, so I get to use *Jupiter*. I must buy a new sleeping-bag – there's a camping shop in Huddersfield. *Jupiter* is the name of the boat.'

'I gathered that.' He was so, so funny, like something out of a Marx Brothers film. The sleeping-bag was winning the battle. She got out of bed and yanked it away from him. 'For goodness' sake, Sebastian, go and make the tea.'

'Are you any good with zips?'

'No.'

He sighed. 'One can't get the staff, these days.' His hair stuck up around his head like the battered leaves of a palm tree after a hurricane. He tried to flatten it, failed miserably.

She stared at him for what felt like an eternity, remembered the unapproachable, silent creature who had arrived in Blundellsands, the TV star whose sister had designated him to the 'weird' category. The man was not weird: he was merely shy, slightly awkward. How hard he must have worked to overcome his true nature in order to pursue his goal. 'Give the thing to me,' she ordered, a mixture of unrecognizable emotions thickening her tone. She managed to re-set the zip so that it ran, though with several hiccups as it chattered over deformed teeth.

Sebastian returned with tea and toast, left her to her breakfast and went off to begin his day's work in the attic. Perhaps she would go up later on and watch the great man at work.

Dolly came in. 'Are you all right, lass?'

She was, but she didn't know why.

'Anything you want, Yvonne. Just ask.'

'I shall.' Yvonne lay back on her pillows. Life was difficult, but she was among decent people. Like many before her who had miscarried, she would survive.

Twenty-one

There had not been one single syllable spoken on radio or TV, not one word printed in the press about the fire at Moortop Farm.

Honoria took it on the chin, mostly because there was no other option, partly because she was about to be published. Not only would her poetry get an airing in print; it was also to be the subject of Sebastian Laczynski's Sunday *Arts Forum*. It seemed that the young man was about to dedicate several programmes to artists from the North West, and that Honoria, Karam Laczynska and April Nugent were to be subjects.

The Laczynska woman's involvement was as plain a piece of nepotism as Honoria had ever seen. That lesbian, that freak, was to have a whole programme to herself, while Honoria would be forced to share her forty minutes with Hyacinth West. Hyacinth, though dead, was still refusing to lie down.

Still, at least Honoria would get the chance to meet Lord Laczynski. She had heard that the old gentleman had a reputation for eccentricity, but he was, at the end of the day, a peer of the realm. To Honoria's knowledge, neither Hyacinth nor Hilda had ever enjoyed such illustrious company. Honoria was to be filmed at Horsefield Hall. She had bought clothes, silks for the filming, more tweeds and brogues to fit in with the country gentleman's environment. She pictured herself going on strolls with Lord Laczynski, imagined him leaning on her arm, hoped that he would recognize that she, too, was a person of good stock and excellent manners.

Honoria's long-term local hobby had been taken away from her. After that first day following her return, when residents of both avenues had stood beneath her corner window, people had been polite, yet distant. They had become very Blundellsands, she supposed, decorous, correct, slightly aloof. It didn't matter. Honoria, almost completely freed from the bondage of agoraphobia, was getting out and about in her little car. All she had to do was to start the engine, point herself in the right direction, then take off into Southport, Liverpool, Warrington – even Manchester. She joined a bridge club in Formby, went to the cinema once a week, often had lunch at the George on Crosby's Moor Lane.

People-watching remained an interest, though Honoria's involvement, at first, was kept very much on the surface. She would sit on a bench in Lord Street in Southport, her eyes raking over men, women and children as they passed by. She would probably never see them again, so she made up lives for them, colouring in the word sketches when she got home.

It was through this leisure activity that Honoria accidentally discovered her true ability as a writer. There had been no need for her to base her soon-to-be-published book on Hyacinth's leftovers, because Honoria had a marked talent whose existence she had never before suspected.

'Mary Wesley didn't produce a thing till she was seventy,' she told herself aloud one evening. Excitement bubbled in her chest: she could not sleep, could scarcely eat, because her whole being was moving in one direction only.

After poring over the *Writers' and Artists' Yearbook*, she picked out a female agent from Regent Street in London, then set about the business of compiling three chapters and a synopsis. No more would she deal with little back-street publishers: she wanted a proper book, a proper agent, a big publishing house.

As she scribbled, her feelings vacillated between blind confidence and total despair, yet the work took on a life of its own and pushed her along its own inexorable path. Each day, Honoria grew stronger, often walking for miles along the beach while characters formed in her head, stopping from time to time to speak into a tiny voice-activated tape-recorder, joy flooding her veins when an idea took hold. At last, she had found her true power.

When the work grew into a sizeable pile of handwritten pages, Honoria sent for help. The cavalry arrived in the form of a bespectacled young man with excellent manners, a computer and a laser-printer. He made it all look so easy, though Honoria had to summon him several times before the vagaries of Windows 95 became part and parcel of her everyday life.

Graham Mansell read some of Honoria's work as he helped her to print. 'This is good,' he told her seriously. He was always serious, but this time he was emphatic. 'You'll pay for this lot of equipment in no time,' he told her. 'You've got a way with words, Miss West.' The tale was gory, mysterious and disturbing. The outwardly sweet Miss Honoria pulled few punches when it came to sex, murder and revenge.

Miss West rewarded him with sweet coffee and two of Mr Kipling's exceedingly good Chocolate Fancies.

Graham became a regular visitor, calling in on Honoria whenever he happened to pass the Mansions. A well-read lad, he felt he recognized an author in the making. 'Why did you not write years ago?' he asked.

'I was never encouraged.' No, Hyacinth had been the gifted one. But even she had been published only by a local entrepreneur who paid peanut wages and achieved a limited circulation. 'I should pull out of that,' she said absently.

'I beg your pardon?'

Honoria smiled at him. 'Just thinking aloud.'

'I suppose you do that a lot. It's a lonely job, isn't it?'

Honoria hadn't considered that. 'Yes, I spend a great deal of time alone. It's essential. Writers cannot afford to waste time on being sociable.'

He looked uncomfortable. 'Would you rather I stopped coming?'

Graham was Honoria's first fan. 'Of course

402

you must visit me,' she told him.

When he had left, Honoria thought about her Bolton publisher. She was slightly uneasy, suddenly worried about the pieces she had submitted to that tiny, one-man firm. They weren't hers, not really. What if she got found out? But she had signed a contract, and any fuss might draw unwanted attention. Also, if she withdrew, the chance of appearing on television might be removed. No, she would take her chances.

The doorbell sounded. Honoria saved her work, backed it on to disk and went to identify the visitor. 'Oh,' she said, when the door was open, 'it's you.'

'May I come in?'

Honoria nodded stiffly.

April staggered forward, her limbs made sillier because she felt slightly nervous. After all, she had supposedly deprived Honoria West of her inheritance, had caused the woman to lose her temper at the reading of the will. 'I thought we should grow up and clear the air,' she said.

Honoria sat, folded her hands in her lap.

April placed herself in the other armchair, leant her stick against the wall. 'I understand that you have a book of poetry in the pipeline.'

Honoria nodded. 'Just a small one.' Her eyes wandered across the room, inviting April's gaze to follow suit. 'It was practice, really. I've started a novel.'

'Really?'

'Yes, really. Poetry and short stories were not enough for me. I needed to produce something more substantial.'

April tried not to be impressed by Honoria's

state-of-the-art computer with its CD Rom and very slick laser-printer. This was a serious purchase. The buyer had to be talented or deluded. It was easier to think of Honoria as deluded. 'You wrote to Sebastian Laczynski, I hear.'

The hostess bridled. 'My publisher wrote. He said that Hyacinth and I ought to be given an airing.'

April bit back a remark about other letters, one of which had probably curtailed the life of Philip Pointer. 'So we are all to be filmed at Horsefield Hall,' she said. 'I was staying there until yesterday. Perhaps we might travel over together.'

Honoria sniffed. 'I have my own car now,' she replied, with little grace and much self-congratulation. 'I bought it while I was on holiday. It helped so much with my recovery.'

The visitor forced her expression to remain unaffected. 'I spoke to Hilda on the phone several weeks ago. She said you were intending to visit her.'

'I never got round to it.'

'Pity.'

'Yes.'

The conversation was running drier than the Sahara, as was April's throat. She noted that she had been offered no refreshment, which slight carried a lot of meaning, particularly in northern counties. Even in the heady atmosphere of Blundellsands, kettles were activated almost before doorbells sounded. 'I suppose I'd better go.'

Honoria actually smiled. 'I'm sorry,' she said.

When had Honoria last apologized?

'I was somewhere else altogether.' She studied her visitor for a moment. 'Do you find that? When writing a play, do you become absent-minded?'

April tutted. 'Me? I don't need to be writing anything – I'm already absent-minded. But, yes, the characters can become more real than reality itself. A bit of advice – if you have no objection.'

'Not at all.' Hanging on every word, Honoria leant forward.

'Don't let the work run away with you. Take your time, don't wear yourself out.'

Honoria nodded wisely. 'I'll bear that in mind while I make a pot of tea.'

April relaxed. Now that this first post-baptismal meeting was over, things should improve. 'I'd better behave,' she told herself softly. 'Getting christened with cold water was one thing, but I don't fancy boiling hot tea.'

'Biscuits?' asked Honoria from the kitchen.

'No, thank you.'

Honoria returned with a tray and set about the business of filling cups

'How is the agoraphobia?' asked April.

Honoria handed over the cup of tea. 'Well, it varies. I can be going along very well, shopping and so forth, then it hits me. I feel as if I'm dying sometimes. The diazepam helps, though I have to be careful if I'm driving. The alternative, however, is even more terrifying – the idea of burying myself in the flat for the rest of my life.'

'I'm glad you made a break for it,' replied April. She knew she was lying. For the first time in her forty-five years, April Nugent felt hatred. This woman was a murderer. This woman had killed her own father, a child, a schoolmaster, some animals. Hyacinth had given the full story to April just months before her own death. Honoria may have killed Hyacinth, too.

The telephone rang. Honoria, slimmer, fitter, rose almost gracefully from her chair and picked up the receiver. 'Hello? Honoria West here.'

April watched with interest as her companion's mouth framed a couple of yesses. After these monosyllables had been uttered, the woman seemed to crumble, reaching out to support herself against the wall. 'I understand,' she said, before replacing the receiver.

'Are you all right?' asked April.

Honoria recovered some of her dignity. 'Yes. It was ... a researcher. Unfortunately, the information I require is difficult to track down.'

She was lying through her well-capped incisors, but April chose to change the subject. 'Have you titled your book yet?'

Honoria almost shook herself back into the here and now. '*Serendipity*, I think. The main character is called Serendipity. Serena for short.'

'Oh.' April waited, noted that Honoria's cup shook as it travelled to her lips. Whatever had happened on the phone had been momentous. Seeing Honoria in a state of fear was unusual, to say the least of it. 'I'd better go,' said April. 'Mark's on his own and we've a little bitch about to give birth. She was starved, so she'll need us with her. I'll probably have to get the vet, too.' Accusing herself of prattling and lying through her own teeth, April shut her mouth abruptly.

'Yes. Very well, dear,' answered Honoria vaguely.

'See yourself out. I shall telephone you tomorrow.'

Alone at last, Honoria closed her eyes and inhaled deeply. Leo Stoneway, as he called himself these days, had owned the voice on the phone. Lawrence Beresford, who had ruined poor Hyacinth's life, who had assaulted Honoria, who had married Hilda. 'We know you burnt down the Chapel House. No proof, but we are sure. We know you tried to set fire to Moortop. Hilda and I have lodged letters with our solicitors. If we die suddenly and in suspicious or unusual circumstances, you will be in trouble . . .' And so forth.

Confusion threatened. It started in her chest, moved up into her brain and made her head throb. 'Breathe into it,' she told herself. 'It's just panic, only panic.' She would defeat them all – Hyacinth, Hilda, Lawrence/Leo, April, Karam Laczynski, the rest of the neighbours. These anxiety attacks were a part of her persona, her brilliance.

It subsided. No coronary, no stroke, no lasting effects. And no diazepam, she thought, as she settled in front of the computer. She switched on the dream, switched off reality. Picking up her scribblings, she began the task of editing chapter two of *Serendipity*. This was the answer. This was the cure.

There was no bitch about to whelp, no real reason for April's sudden exit from Honoria's flat. April forgave herself for the untruth as she swung the Micra into her own driveway. She got out and walked across to Karam's house. The back door was unlocked, so April let herself in and found

Karam in transcendental mode on the kitchen rug. How the girl got herself into and out of such contortions was one of the wonders of the modern world.

Knowing better than to attempt conversation with the absent-in-all-but-body artist, April set the kettle to boil. She hadn't taken more than a couple of sips from Honoria's Crown Derby; the phone call had shortened her visit somewhat. She sat at Karam's table and downed two cups of tea.

'Hello.' Karam unwound her legs, stood up, touched her toes with all the ease of an Olympic athlete. 'How long have you been here?'

April grinned. 'You could get burgled and raped. Mind, I suppose you wouldn't notice. How do you get into these trances? More to the point, how does anyone with bones manage to tie so many knots in her body?'

'It's a knack.' Karam helped herself to tea. 'To enter deep meditation, I centre myself on my core. My core is pale orange.'

'Is it?'

'Yes. The rest is easy, just arms and legs.'

April sighed deeply. In her estimation, the world was going mad. 'Will you be seeing Yvonne at the weekend?'

'No.' Karam's tone was matter-of-fact. 'I'll come over for the shoots – can't wait to see you and Miss West locking horns again.'

April would not be diverted. 'Yvonne needs you.'

'She thinks she needs me. There is a difference.' The words were coated with a thick application of patience.

408

April grabbed a digestive. 'Karam, there's no need for you to be clever with me. I know you miss her.'

'I began missing her the day we met,' was the reply.

'So you knew all along that nothing would happen, that your affection would be sadly unrequited?'

'Most things are unrequited, April, and nothing ever lasts,' answered Karam.

'Clever again. There you sit with your heart broken, and you're trying to pass Yvonne to your brother like a birthday present. I wonder you didn't tie pink ribbons in her hair.'

'She's where she belongs, April. He will make her a damned good partner. She never knew how I felt about her. She'll be looked after and adored—'

'If she ever lets him near her.'

Karam peeled an orange. 'She's just lost a baby; she's not ready for commitment. When she is ready, she could end up with a lot worse than my weird baby brother.'

April groaned. 'And he thinks she's a lesbian. You should have told him.'

Karam, who felt like a wet rag, wished with all her heart that April would go home. 'Yvonne won't allow herself to be discussed. I promised.' She missed Yvonne so acutely that everything hurt; even her teeth were beginning to ache. Today had been particularly difficult. Today Karam had packed away as much pain as she could find – Yvonne's clothes, her perfume, some shoes, a birthday card, a pair of disgraceful wellington boots.

'What will you do if she does finish up with

Sebastian?' April asked, for the umpteenth time. 'Happy families at Christmas? Your father asking questions about who belongs to whom? The poor old fellow really believed that you and Yvonne were together.'

Karam closed her eyes. 'April, when you see two people who are so right for each other – never mind who they are, who their relations are – it's common sense to throw them together.'

'Love has nothing to do with common sense,' replied April, rather sharply. 'If it did, I'd never have finished up with Mark Nugent. And when did you appoint yourself matchmaker?'

'Oh, do shut up, dear,' replied Karam, her eyes still closed. 'Yes, I am hurting. No, I didn't want to lose her, though I could hardly lose what I'd never had. Yvonne has to move on – so must I. Things to do, places to go. I abandoned hope long before we went to Horsefield. The relationship between Yvonne and Sebastian began the moment they met in this house, the second they started not looking at each other. Even I could hear their orchestra tuning up. Destiny, April.'

April did not believe in destiny. She was a nuts-and-bolts sort, a down-to-earth woman whose feyness showed only in her plays and in her unfortunate choice of husband. In April Nugent's opinion, people made life happen, made choices, used free will for good or for evil. Evil reminded her of someone. 'Honoria is writing a book called *Serendipity*,' she said. 'I went to see her and was a witness to . . . Well, I wasn't an eye witness, wasn't even an ear witness, but I'd say she received a threatening phone call.'

Karam's eyes were suddenly wide open. 'Did she throw water on you again?'

'No. She gave me a cup of tea.'

Karam peered closely at her friend. 'How do you feel? Any stomach pain, any numbness?'

'No more than usual. No, I haven't been poisoned, but—'

The back door burst inward. Mark Nugent, looking as if he had just gone eight rounds with Mike Tyson, panted as he entered the room. His cardigan hung in tatters, strings of unravelled wool trailing towards the floor. There was a wildness in his eyes, while his mouth opened and closed without giving birth to any sound.

'Are you ill?' asked April.

Apparently struck dumb for several further seconds, he pointed over his shoulder. 'It's happened,' he managed at last. 'The animal from hell has arrived.'

April cheered up immediately. There was no dog she could not tame, no cat she could not mesmerize into reluctant submission. 'Canine or feline?' she asked.

'Neither,' he declared emphatically.

'Equine?'

'A flaming camel,' he murmured. 'Some very confused farmer has turned up with a bloody camel, buggered off and left it with us.'

April was thrilled but puzzled. 'How on earth did a farmer come to have a camel?' she asked.

Mark fell into a chair. 'He didn't have a camel. The camel very nearly had him – vicious, it is. I wouldn't worry, it's been sedated by a vet. God help us when the injection wears off. It spits and

411

eats clothes.' He waved his rags for all to see. 'The thing was running about all over the Formby bypass, then it got in with the cows.'

Karam looked at April; April looked at Karam, picked up the sugar bowl. 'One hump or two?' asked April eventually.

'One,' replied Mark. 'And it's one of those small camels, not a real camel. It's a wotsername.'

'Llama?' offered April.

'That's the one,' Mark said. 'We got it into a stable. It took three of us. It ate my cardie and the vet's glove. The farmer drove off like the clappers. He's put his name down for a nervous breakdown in a nice little rest home. And I reckon he'll have to take his Friesians with him.'

April clapped her hands. 'I've always wanted a llama,' she announced.

'So have I,' answered Mark drily. 'Could hardly wait.'

'So you were there when Honoria got a threatening phone call?' asked Karam.

'She went as white as a sheet and nearly collapsed. I think somebody's finally got her measure.' Yes, concluded April, everything always came back to Honoria. Come angry llamas, earthquakes, famines, Honoria would always loom large.

This pair was as crazy as a bag of nuts, Mark decided. Here he sat, having just survived an encounter with one of Satan's sidekicks, and these two were going on about . . . about what?

'It would take a lot to frighten Honoria,' Karam said.

'Try a llama,' mumbled Mark to himself.

412

'I wonder how they get on with sheep?' April asked.

'They're ruminants,' pondered Karam aloud. 'But so are cows.'

'Goats,' pronounced April. 'That farmer behind Stef's place has goats. One ate the best tablecloth – remember? Dolly tried to chase him off and he butted her.'

'So we need to ask the farmer behind Horsefield Hall if he'll accept a llama. Then, if he gives permission, we hire a horsebox. You don't think Kevin's threatening her, do you? I mean, you said he got nasty when she first came back, promised to hypodermic her with some of his blood.'

'He wouldn't hurt a fly,' said April. 'All wind and water, bless him. The poor lad was in bed for two days after confronting Honoria. Too sensitive by far. No, it can't be him.'

Mark got up and walked outside. He had had no experience of psychiatric facilities, yet he chose to cross the road towards the valley of the damned rather than to listen to a conversation between two intelligent, crazy women. Taken all round, the llama made more sense.

Twenty-two

The llama was not a thing of beauty. It looked as if it had been cobbled together from waste left behind by the cotton industry, just lumps and clumps of matted mess dangling and dragging around him whenever he moved. He moved quite frequently, very quickly and usually in the direction of the two-legged creatures who tried to dominate him. When he failed to attack the human of his choice, he spat with devastating accuracy, often catching the fleeing coward on the back of the head, or, as in April's case, right in the middle of her face.

April was amused by him. She understood his attitude, even approved of it. Some soft clowns had brought these normally docile, yet arrogant and superior creatures to be stared at in zoos or to roam aimlessly around safari parks, never considering how a llama would feel about his change of circumstances. 'I shall call you Dalai Harold,' she told the irate animal. She lowered her open umbrella just in time to cover her face. Moisture dripped down the fabric and landed at April's feet. 'I am not afraid of you, Harold.'

Mark stood at the opposite side of the yard, his back against rabbit and ferret cages. He was out of reach, just about, though the creature certainly put some power behind the spits.

Karam wandered across from her house. 'What time's the vet coming?' she asked Mark.

'Soon, I hope. He's fetching a posse with him – two off-duty firemen and a dentist.'

Karam wondered about the dentist.

'The dentist just happened to be there at the time, having his chow inoculated. Anyway, he's six foot four and eighteen stone, so he'll be handy.'

April lowered her guard and marched forward, veering off to the left slightly, then homing in on her target. She eyed him. He was chewing morosely, grinding his teeth and staring at her with utter malevolence in his eyes. She felt so sorry for him. He should not have been here. 'Where do llamas come from?' she shouted.

'The llama shop,' replied Mark caustically. 'Next door to Oxfam.'

April turned and gave her ex-husband a look that was no stranger to Harold's expression. 'Shut up, Mark,' she advised coldly.

Once again, she swivelled uncertainly and gave her full attention to Dalai Harold. He reminded her of someone, someone who behaved nastily most of the time. He forgot his naughtiness as soon as it was finished, simply standing and waiting for the next well-meant approach. Like all animals, he was amoral: he had not been blessed or cursed with humanity's wide set of choices. Honoria. He was Honoria on four legs. She, too,

had the ability to forget her misdeeds, the deliberate amnesia that enabled her to expect her victims
to give her a clean sheet. So there was something
missing in Honoria, a sliver of genetic program-
ming that might have made her humane, or at
least decent.

Harold chewed rhythmically. After several hours
of playing dodgems with cars and irate cows, he
felt slightly anxious and out of sorts. But this
woman was not impressed. She just stood there
like a tree, though the wind blew through her
from time to time, causing her to stagger a bit. He
was running out of energy. He was reaching that
stage where even a close relative to the camel concluded that what must be must be.

Karam crept closer to April and the beast. 'You
mustn't worry about him,' she told April. 'His
ancestors were domesticated by the Inca. Llamas
actually like people. Harold's state of mind has
been altered by traffic and those frightened cows.
You know, I read that if you put one with the
sheep, predators stay away.'

'But he needs a Mrs Harold,' said April.

Karam approached the animal, reached out and
patted the coarse fleece. 'A Gillette razor for
Christmas,' she promised. 'And a mate, if the
Yorkshire farmer allows it.'

Harold looked from Karam to April, then made
a sound like an improbable cross between whoop-
ing cough and Concorde.

'Tell him he's going to Yorkshire,' Karam
advised. 'Open spaces, sheep and goats to keep in
order.'

'Will he understand?' laughed April.

'Oh, yes. I have communicated with his inner core. He also has a beautiful aura.'

April wished that Karam would stop being so whimsical. There was nothing transcendental about Harold. He was a mess, a challenge, a nuisance. Inner core? Beautiful aura? Yet April still pitied him.

Inner core or no inner core, Harold went into a flat spin when the horsebox arrived. He lay down on the floor of the stable, spat, kicked and made as much noise as the contents of an infant school playground. He was going nowhere. After a great deal of trouble and pain, the firemen trapped the flailing legs, the dentist managed to wrap a sack around Harold's head, while the vet, panting and red in the face, stuck the needle in.

This time, the sedation worked. Mollified and weak in the legs, poor Harold was led into the horsebox and left alone.

In April's kitchen, firemen, vet, dentist, Mark and the two women drank coffee. One fireman said he would rather deal with burning buildings than grapple with a llama, while the dentist announced that he would prefer to drill and fill a mouthful of teeth any day. Everyone refused payment, saying that this would be their contribution to April's sanctuary.

Honoria had decided to make her own way to Horsefield. Travelling in a hired Land Rover with a llama fastened to the rear end was not Honoria West's idea of style. Glad that they were to be without Miss Honoria and her *Serendipity*, April and Karam threw their bags into the vehicle, checked on Harold, who had fallen asleep, then set off towards the cooler, drier climes of their Yorkshire neighbours.

A large section of the motorway was akin to a parking lot. The powers had decided to place acres of cones along the route, though no work was in progress. Karam expressed once again her long-held belief that traffic cones bred in the night, doubling their numbers hourly. 'They cull seals,' she muttered resignedly, 'beautiful little seals, then they leave these things to multiply.'

Harold, up and as much about as horsebox and tranquillizer would allow, was peering over the tailgate and making rude faces at other vehicles. Still doped, he had not yet reached the spitting stage, though he was working his way up to that. Then, as if by magic, the cones suddenly disappeared, allowing traffic to spurt forward like a series of corks emerging from the necks of several very agitated champagne bottles.

The Ford Transit van behind Karam, April and Harold shot ahead a little too quickly. Whether the driver had lost control because of Harold's antics ceased to be significant within a few minutes of the collision. He bounced off the horsebox and into the central reservation, dying almost immediately when the steering column impaled him to the seat.

The horsebox tried to follow the path of the van, was dragged back by the Land Rover, then, after a half-hearted attempt at jack-knife, rolled over on to the hard shoulder and into a ditch. The Land Rover, too, turned over, its wheels spinning aimlessly in the air like an upended turtle treading air in a futile attempt to right itself.

April, upside down in the passenger seat, thanked God for her seat belt, though her relief lasted for just a split second. Karam was covered in blood and her breathing rasped like a file against iron. Cars crashed all around the Land Rover, many moving too quickly after crawling for miles past cones whose placement had seemed so unnecessary. Road rage, pondered April stupidly, was often encouraged by the silliness of people who sat in offices setting up imaginary roadworks.

She found herself thinking all sorts of crazy things while metal made contact with metal, while cars and lorries smashed themselves to pieces all around her. What about Sebastian's programmes? Would Honoria be involved in this messy accident? Would Karam die? How was Yvonne going to cope? Had the llama perished? She passed out and worried no more.

After what seemed like hours, during which April revived from time to time, police and ambulances arrived. The doors of the Land Rover were ripped away, Karam was neck-braced, injected and stretchered into a helicopter in a nearby field, then April was placed in an ambulance. She was reassured by paramedics that the RSPCA would collect Harold, who seemed to be perfectly well, though asleep.

In a green-curtained cubicle that reminded April of BBC 1's *Casualty*, she was pummelled, prodded and questioned. What was her name, her address, her date of birth? What day was it, who was president of the USA, was she on medication?

She eyed her tormentors, advised them to wander off and help those whose need was greater

419

than hers. 'What is this – *Fifteen to One?*' she asked. 'I don't matter,' she continued, tears trickling down her face. 'I'm already ill, but she wasn't. Karam. Karam Laczynska, daughter of Lord Laczynski of Horsefield, she's the important one. She assesses for the Tate and the National, for God's sake! Save her, not me. She can't die.'

They diagnosed severe shock and, after X-rays and further questions about presidents and prime ministers, the doctors decided that this was, indeed, April Nugent, playwright and pest. She was shoved into a bed next to a toothless woman who snored, and was given sleeping tablets which she pretended to swallow. Minutes later, April set about the business of finding Karam.

With a borrowed Zimmer, she stumbled down corridors, peering at notices that were suddenly blurred. 'Damned MS,' she muttered repeatedly. If her eyes went, she would be scuppered.

The hospital casualty department was still in uproar. April was pleased to hear that only one person had died, and that most were being treated for shock and minor injuries. She sat on a chair in a long row and chatted to the woman next to her. 'So you're all right, then?'

'Yes, it's my husband. Just a broken arm – a nice clean break, the doctor called it. And you?'

'Shock,' replied April. 'I've got MS,' she added, to explain the walking frame. 'And they told me to stay the night, but I want to find out about my friend.'

'Was she in a Land Rover?'

April nodded eagerly.

'Intensive Care,' said the woman. 'She was the

420

one brought in by helicopter, wasn't she? Intensive Care's down there – just follow the red line.'

When she achieved her destination, April barged through the doors and past a clutch of nurses. Karam was all tubes and bleeps. Her head was wrapped, and her face, apart from bruising, was whiter than newly fallen snow.

'You can't stay in here unless you're a relative,' whispered a nurse. 'This is ICU.'

'I'm not a relative, but I'm all she has just at present. So you may have to throw me out.' Like Harold, April fell to the floor, though she managed, just about, not to spit at the staff. 'Pick me up and shift me,' she challenged. 'I've told you, I'm all she's got at the moment.' Too upset to hide her fears, April pleaded, 'Someone has to be here.' If the worst should happen, at least Karam would not die alone.

The sister recognized April, remembered reading in the *Sunday Express* supplement that April Nugent was an MS victim. 'I'll get you a chair,' she said. 'Please try to keep quiet. There are some really ill people in here. All right?'

Two men brought in a fairly comfortable seat. April, prepared to watch over Karam for as long as necessary, got up off the floor with the help of the chair-fetchers, then went into what she always termed an MS zonk, a deep sleep that missed out the usual courtship ritual.

When she came to, it was morning. At the other side of the bed, Stefan Laczynski prayed softly in Polish. 'Stef?'

He lifted his weary, tear-stained face. 'Hello, Multi. Are you hurt?'

She ached all over, but she often did. 'I'm OK. Where's Sebastian?'

'Dealing with Yvonne,' was his reply. 'She is very distraught, as is my son, because he thinks this is his fault.'

They both studied Karam for a few seconds. 'His fault?' asked April.

Stefan nodded. 'He arranged to film at Horsefield Hall.'

'He didn't do this. It was me, since I was the one fetching Harold. That's the llama we told you about on the phone. The box pulled us over when we got hit.' She concentrated on Karam's poor face. 'What did the doctors say?'

He wiped the five-fingered hand across his brow. 'My Karam is lucky, or so I am told. No bones broken, fortunate to be alive. She had inhaled some blood from her nose, her face is cut and bruised.' He shook his head. 'Lucky? This is lucky? She has bad concussion and is in a coma. She may wake tomorrow or she may be like this . . . for ever. Until I turn her off, that is. Oh, yes, my beautiful daughter is lucky, Multi.' He wept silently, mopping his tears with a large handkerchief. 'Dolly is in shock. Our doctor gave her something to knock her out.'

April didn't know what to say.

'I phoned Sebastian a few minutes ago. He told me that a terrible woman arrived. She pretends to be sad, but she isn't. Sebastian is sending her away. She was quite put out. I think she expected him to carry on and film her, as she is not in a coma or in shock, as you are, my good friend.' He blew his nose. 'Thank you for being with my little girl. You

422

were asleep when I arrived, so I did not disturb you.'

April had a sudden urge to stand up and scream, but she was among people whose lives hung by a thread. Instead of screaming, she sobbed for Karam and for her father, who also continued to cry.

They were taken into a small room and given a breakfast that was actually edible. April, strangely hungry, polished off an egg and four slices of toast before swallowing her little clutch of pills. 'They have even phoned my doctor about the medicines,' she said vaguely. 'This is a very kind hospital, Stef.'

'It should have been me,' he said. 'I was the age of a grandfather when my children were born. How can this happen to such a lovely young woman?'

'She will get better,' said April firmly.

He looked at her, his eyes suddenly cloudy and ancient. 'Can you give me a written guarantee, Multi?'

'God, I wish I could.'

'So do I, my dear. So do I.'

They finally got rid of Honoria. She left in an angry shower of wheel-churned gravel and in a mood that could only be guessed at by Sebastian. He had been uncomfortable in the woman's presence, as if evil had suddenly entered his childhood home and polluted its atmosphere.

He concentrated on Yvonne, who seemed to be nearing a state of catatonia. When she made no attempt to eat, he pulled a chair up to hers, sat with one arm round her stiff body, spooning corn-flakes and milk into her mouth with the other hand. When the food dribbled out, he scraped it from her chin and pushed it back between her lips. Like a baby, she simply allowed life to happen to her.

'Yvonne? Yvonne? Look at me.'

She obeyed, though there was no light in her eyes.

'You must try. Please try.'

Her mouth moved to frame words. 'I don't know what I did wrong,' she said finally. 'And if I did make a mess of things, why should Karam suffer? God took my baby, now . . .' Her eyes glazed over again. 'David's a good man. I should have forced myself to stay.' In her eyes, confusion reigned, was emphasized by the wild, tangled mass of hair that framed her head. What if Karam had truly loved her? Had she encouraged that love? 'Have I done this to your sister? Am I some kind of Jonah?'

'Yvonne?'

She sank back in the chair and would not be drawn into further conversation.

He was flummoxed. He wanted to get to the hospital to visit Karam, yet he could not leave Yvonne with Dolly, as the latter was still in a state of drug-assisted unconsciousness. With few choices to hand, he went up to his attic, bringing with him a compliant Yvonne, who sat where she was put and stared into the middle distance, her lips moving from time to time, though no words were delivered.

Sebastian phoned the hospital and was told that

his sister's condition remained unchanged. Unchanged meant that the sweetest girl and the finest art historian in Britain were both comatose.

'Sebastian?'

Ah, at last, Yvonne had spoken again.

'Sebastian?'

'Yes?'

'It's all gone wrong.'

'Yes, sweetheart, it has.'

Honoria turned into the lane outside Horsefield Hall, parked in a little lay-by near a farm gate. She was not in a good humour, had not been best pleased since receiving the phone call from Leo Stoneway. The man had almost accused her of attempted murder, but what could she do about that? Nothing. And now the lesbian had got herself mangled in a car crash, so there had to be a postponement of the filming at Horsefield Hall. Horsefield Hall. How terribly grand that sounded, yet the house had been a dump. As for the village of Horsefield – well, that had turned out to be about ten houses, a pub and a crestfallen church.

The flowers she had bought as a present for Lord Laczynski's household were pretty enough, she supposed, an adequate decoration for Karam's bedside cabinet. She should go along and visit the woman in hospital, she pondered, though she would probably be turned away. After all, the patient was in Intensive Care. Honoria all but grinned when she thought about the comatose freak. 'Some people get what they deserve. This might teach her to leave other women alone.' Though some people never learnt, Honoria concluded. Not for one instant did she consider her own inability to learn from past mistakes and sins. As ever, Honoria remained completely convinced of her own rectitude.

After deciding to have a doze before her return journey to Liverpool, Honoria closed her eyes and leant back against the headrest. She pictured the expression on Sebastian Laczynski's face, wondered why he had seemed so reluctant to talk to her. He had been indoctrinated, deduced Honoria. Behind him, Yvonne Benson had lingered, dirty shirt hanging from her shoulders, hair like a disordered haystack, face as white as lint. To hell with all of them.

Honoria woke with a start and glanced at her watch, discovering that she had been asleep for the best part of an hour. Someone was rapping on the window. She wound it down and stared into the face of April Nugent. The woman might be a cripple, but she certainly managed to get about. There was no avoiding her, it seemed. 'Oh,' she mumbled sleepily, 'it's you.'

'Yes. It's me, Honoria.' April, raw from fighting to get herself discharged, could scarcely manage to look into the murderer's eyes. 'I'm going to change places with Sebastian so that he can visit his sister.'

'Sad business.' Honoria tried to stretch the sleep out of her legs, but was impeded by clutch, brake and accelerator. She opened the door and stepped out of her car. 'Yvonne Benson didn't look too well, either.'

'The loss of a baby affects most women.'

'Oh. I see.' Honoria looked across the lane, saw

a taxi waiting to take April the rest of the way to the house. 'His meter will be ticking,' she remarked.

'All our meters are ticking, Honoria.'

'What? Oh, yes, quite.'

The two women faced one another. April was no longer interested in civility. Seeing Honoria West so near to the vulnerable Karam made April's blood boil. 'Are you intending to visit the hospital?'

'I thought I might.'

April moved until her nose almost touched the other woman's. 'I know everything,' she whispered. This murderer had never had much time for poor Karam.

'I beg your pardon?'

'Hyacinth told me the full story.'

Honoria swallowed audibly.

'Keep away from Karam.'

Honoria bristled. 'My sister was confused towards the end of her life. She was so ill.'

'Yes, I saw her almost every day. There were no symptoms of confusion.' April paused. 'She wrote a great deal of poetry during those last weeks. I typed it up on my computer after she recorded it on tape because Hyacinth's hands were not good.' She waited again, saw Honoria's expression change slightly. Was that trepidation in her eyes? 'If any of Hyacinth's work were to turn up in a publication bearing a different name, I should recognize it immediately.'

Honoria shuffled slightly, moved away towards her car.

'Plagiarism is not tolerated in my sphere of

work.' Honoria's complexion was becoming a rather dirty white. 'Even if a writer is dead, the work is protected for many, many years,' continued April.

'Why are you telling me this?'

April raised her shoulders. 'Because if I see anything at all of Hyacinth's work published under your name, I shall reduce your circumstances by making a couple of phone calls. Who will believe then that *Serendipity* is your own?'

'But it is.'

'Of course it is. But who will give you credence? Use a *nom de plume* if you wish, but that will not protect you. A writer's actual identity is always discovered.'

'But—'

'But nothing. Remember that I know a great deal about you, Miss Honoria West. Suffice it to mention one rabbit, one child, one horse, one teacher, one father. And, perhaps, a little extra insulin?'

Honoria staggered against the Ford's bonnet, her hands spreading wide as she sought to support herself.

'Life is cruel,' said April softly. 'To Hyacinth, it was particularly vicious. You made it so.'

Honoria sidled along, opened the door and sat in the driver's seat.

April smiled grimly. 'And now your future rests with me. Do not cross me, because I have not Hyacinth's sweetness of temper.'

'You don't know everything,' hissed the seated woman. 'Even Hyacinth didn't know the biggest of all my family's secrets.'

428

'I see. So you hid behind another sofa, did you? Or did you read letters, follow someone?'

'Shut up,' replied the well-mannered Miss West. 'Just shut your mouth, you stupid—' A jogger passed by, causing Honoria's words to dry up at source.

'Go home,' advised April. 'There is nothing you can do to me, nothing at all. I am stronger than I used to be. I am not afraid of you or of your bullying tactics.'

Honoria laughed, though there was no merriment in the sound. 'If I want to publish, I shall.'

'And be damned.'

'You wouldn't dare.'

'If necessary, I shall go public. I can tell from your reaction that you have used your sister's work. The answer is in your hands, Honoria. Either I make a few discreet phone calls, or I denounce you publicly. It makes no difference to me.' April walked as steadily as possible towards the taxi.

Honoria slumped in the chair. Again, she was about to be cheated, ignored, beaten at the winning-post. *Serendipity* was her own work, born of her own long-neglected talent. Just because of a few poems, her real work would never see the light of day.

April stopped in the middle of the lane, turned and shouted, 'Forget Sebastian's film. Your assistance is no longer required.'

429

Twenty-three

As Christmas approached, Dolly and Sebastian made some attempt to decorate the house. Dolly, who had lived with Stefan's piles of books for more years than she cared to think of, finally managed to clear the hall table. She was delighted to find beneath the yellowing tomes a piece of furniture so ancient that axe and file marks showed on its forgotten surface. With an air of martyrdom that fooled no one, Dolly Isherwood caressed the wood with beeswax, almost making love to planks of long-neglected elm. The table repaid her after four days with a dazzling smile in which were reflected a small Christmas tree and vases of holly rich with ruby berries.

April, whose mother had died in the middle of November, absented herself for much of the time, popping over the mountains occasionally to visit Yvonne, Karam and the rest of the Laczynski family. Although she continued to worry about her 'Yorkshire folk', she had other concerns that required her attention, including, of course, the burial of her mother and the subsequent legal niceties required by the law of the land.

Karam had not regained consciousness in the seven weeks since the accident. Successive bulletins declared her to be stable, but her father, her brother, Yvonne and Dolly became increasingly concerned about her condition. Sebastian, whose career had been put on hold, spent much of his time visiting his sister, caring for Yvonne and watching over Stefan, whose health had taken a sudden downturn after Karam's accident.

'I feel like an undermanned nursing home,' Sebastian told Dolly as they plucked the Christmas goose. 'And I'm not complaining about you, Dolly, because you have been a brick.'

Dolly brushed goosedown off the end of her nose. 'It's Yvonne that worries me,' she replied. 'Mooning about reading poetry and listening to dead music.' For Dolly, all classical music was moribund to a point miles beyond rigor mortis. It wasn't cheerful. All the folk who had composed it had long doffed their powdered wigs and returned to the soil. Dolly preferred Meatloaf, the Manic Street Preachers and, at a pinch, she could tolerate the Beatles and a bit of Abba.

'She feels guilty,' answered Sebastian. 'She thinks she should have been with Karam, that she ought to be the one in a coma.'

'Well, she shouldn't.'

'I know that, you know that, Papa knows that. Wherever poor Karam's mind is, she agrees with the rest of us.' He ceased plucking for a moment. 'If she does come out of the coma, will she be Karam?' He had realized for a while that he would have chosen death for his

431

sister rather than a wheelchair and brain damage.

Dolly carried on working. She had made mince-pies and Christmas puddings. She had scrubbed and cleaned and washed and ironed until she could scarcely walk. And none of it counted because nobody wanted Christmas. 'Sebastian?'

'Yes?'

'You can't do anything about Karam – right?'

He nodded.

'But you can keep your dad going and you can look after Karam's friend.' She shoved a pile of feathers into a bin bag. 'I know you love Yvonne. It shines out of your eyes every time she walks into the room.'

'And I'm Karam's brother.'

'Sod that,' muttered Dolly, with customary directness. 'Yvonne's no more a ladies' woman than I am. Go to it. Put some love back into her life, then she'll stop listening to that bloody lager.'

'Handel's Largo, Dolly.'

'I don't care who brewed the flaming ale or wrote the rotten theme tune, she wants a bit of cheering up. I've offered to lend her my Simply Red, but she said no.'

Sebastian smiled. Simply Red was as close as Dolly Isherwood came to pretty music. 'Yvonne will come round. She's already asked about Bertrand Russell – that's her dog. He's been taken care of for weeks by the animal-sanctuary people. And I told her that Dalai Harold is quite content on the farm.' If only he could quieten Yvonne's worries about Karam. 'Yvonne will come round,' he repeated determinedly.

'Aye, she will if you drag her round. Stop

pussy-footing about, lad. Take her somewhere – I'll look after your dad. Christmas shopping in Huddersfield might do the trick.'

'Is Yvonne ready for Huddersfield, Dolly?'

Dolly, Huddersfield born and bred, waved a fist at her companion. 'Don't take the you-know-what out of me. Remember, I do your washing.'

Sebastian laughed. The sound was rusty and dry. He realized that he had not laughed properly for weeks. How on earth could he laugh now, while Karam lay in a sleep so profound that her eyelids didn't flicker? How could he chuckle while Yvonne wandered about like a pale ghost who spoke sense, yet not complete sense?

'Get this bloody goose plucked,' ordered Dolly, 'or there'll be no dinner on Christmas Day.'

Sebastian plucked.

Dolly glanced at him from time to time, wondering what had happened to the Sebastian of six months earlier. On screen, he had always been excellent, a listener, a drawer-out of folk, a man who knew the right questions, which buttons to press to irritate or encourage an interviewee. At home, he had been contained, kind, but distant. Now, his heart was on his sleeve. Worried beyond measure about an adored sister, about his father and about Yvonne, he was wide open and hurtable.

'Why are you staring at me?' he asked.

'Look after yourself as well, son,' she advised him.

He grinned. 'I've no intention of becoming another patient, Dolly. Haven't I enough on my plate already?'

'You know what I mean.'

He knew. And he carried on plucking.

Honoria sipped dry sherry. April Nugent should die. April Nugent should never have been born. She was behind all Honoria's new problems, was a threat, a nuisance, a blot on the landscape. How? Too difficult, too dangerous. What a pity. The removal of April would have brought so much satisfaction . . .

Yvonne dozed. She was back in Karam's kitchen at Jasmine Cottage, peeling vegetables at the table. Karam came into the room, stood behind Yvonne, embraced her. It felt wrong. In the dream, Yvonne turned and found that Karam was crying. 'I can't love you. I'm so sorry,' Yvonne told her good friend. Then, in the dream, Karam became Sebastian and all problems seemed resolved. No, no, everything was more complicated and . . .

'God be praised!'

Yvonne's eyes shot open, propelling her swiftly into the present tense and back into the hospital. In a chair at the opposite side of Karam's bed, Stefan Laczynski was crying and smiling simultaneously.

Karam, whose head ached beyond measure after her too-long and too-deep sleep, looked from one to the other. 'Yvonne,' she breathed before falling asleep again.

'What a Christmas gift,' cried the old man. 'Such a blessing, such a wonderful blessing. Get the nurse, Yvonne.'

Yvonne remained where she was. Karam had spoken her name. Karam loved her, and Yvonne

434

should have realized months earlier, should have stayed away from—

'Nurse!' screamed Stefan. When she arrived, he grabbed her arm. 'She spoke,' he wept. 'She said Yvonne.'

'There, there,' smiled the nurse. 'Didn't we tell you to hope for the best? I've seen them come round after months. Oh, let me get the doctor.' She bustled away.

Yvonne studied Karam's face closely. She looked different, as if her sleep had become normal. 'Thank God,' she whispered.

Stefan dried his eyes. 'When she started to speak just then, I thought all my Christmases had come on the one day.'

'We must tell Sebastian and Dolly.'

Stefan noticed colour in Yvonne's cheeks, heard a lighter voice, saw that her eyes were suddenly clearer. 'We can tell them when we go home,' he said.

Yvonne insisted. 'No, no. I promised Seb I'd tell him immediately – he made the same promise to me.' She ran off towards the phone in a nearby corridor

Alone with his daughter, Stefan took her hand and held it. What would happen now? he wondered. When would Karam wake again?

In Horsefield Hall, Dolly Isherwood and Sebastian Laczynski danced up and down the stairs, John Travolta's 'You're The One That I Want' blaring all over the house. It was Christmas Day. The goose was done to a turn, but the vegetables had begun to fall and spoil due to overcooking. The two of them did not care. Dolly wiggled ample hips, while Sebastian leant over her, his shoulders moving with the rhythm. Karam was the one that they wanted. Olivia Newton Isherwood pouted, while Sebastian Travolta tried to look macho and stern. It was over. Life could begin again.

Drunk on sherry, Honoria had little control over her thoughts. Could she kill April Nugent? Could she? Should she? A fire would not do. There had been two fires already, one successful, the other a failure. Another way? Even in her cups, Honoria still sensed danger. She might have to allow the wretched woman to remain alive.

Christmas lunch had become Christmas supper. Stefan, almost back on form, pinched Dolly's bottom as she passed his chair, got clipped round the ear with a linen napkin. 'Keep your bloody hands to yourself,' Dolly pretended to snap.

Stefan grinned, picked up Yvonne's hand and kissed it. His chest infection had cleared up miraculously after his daughter's little sign of life. 'Happy Christmas and God bless us every one,' he said.

Yvonne blushed. Sebastian, as silent as ever, simply stared at her. The attempted camaraderie of recent weeks seemed to have burst like a soap bubble landing on a candle flame. He had not taken up growling again, but he looked as if he might be thinking in snarls.

Dolly had cooked a second lot of vegetables – since the first had disintegrated and were now ear-marked for next door's pigs. Perhaps Harold would get some of them, Yvonne thought obliquely. Harold, who lived among goats and sheep, was as happy as a sandboy. Karam had opened her eyes. April was spending Christmas with her ex-husband. Sebastian was not eating. Yvonne's head was fuzzy, confused, as if she had suffered a bump. No. Poor Karam was the one in a hospital bed. Yvonne should have recognized the signals, should have felt Karam's love, her need, should have stayed away from Jasmine Cottage.

When supper was finished, Stefan declared that everyone was on strike. The dishes could sit until tomorrow, he said. The party dispersed, each person repairing to his or her room until ten o'clock, at which time party games would be compulsory.

Yvonne was not surprised when her door opened. She watched Sebastian as he strode into the room, stopped, walked this way, that way, passing a hand through unruly hair, looking at her, looking away from her, opening his mouth, closing it. Did he still think of her as a lesbian? wondered Yvonne. Or were his instincts honed to a point where he did not need to ask?

She sat on the edge of her bed, hands folded in her lap.

Sebastian threw himself into a wicker chair, leant forward, leant back, stood up again. By this time, his eyes were riveted to her face.

Yvonne twiddled her thumbs, wished that he would go away. She needed to think and to rest, wanted to plan the future, to settle, look for a job, make sure that Karam was safe and fully recovered.

'I've tried my level best,' he said finally, 'and I can't go on mooning about like an anorak at

Stringfellow's.' He saw her bewilderment. 'String-fellow's in London. An anorak would be—'

'Slightly out of place?'

'Yes.'

She waited. Lines of communication seemed to be opening up at last.

He wiped moisture from his upper lip, was clearly uncomfortable. 'Since I saw you that first day . . . I really didn't want this to happen . . .'

Would he ever finish a sentence? Up to now, he had achieved a handful of clauses, had concluded no statement. He was struggling. A part of Yvonne knew what was coming, though she allowed no space for it in her clouded thoughts.

'And I don't know whether you are well enough to bear what I'm saying to you.'

Yvonne studied a painting above his head. It was one of Karam's, a parody of *Venus Rising*. This Venus was dressed in military uniform and the shell from which she emerged was weaponry. The sea beneath Venus Victoria was frothed with the wasted blood of humankind, while the sky was brightened by explosions. 'That's subtitled *Whatever Happened to Motherhood?*,' said Yvonne. It was as if she had switched to automatic pilot, because the sentence had formed itself without referring to her brain.

Sebastian turned, glanced at the work. 'Yes, she was young and angry when she painted that. About fourteen, I think.'

Yvonne waited.

'I have, unfortunately, grown fond of you,' he said quietly.

'Yes.'

He blinked. 'Yes'? What on earth did 'yes' mean?

Yvonne awarded him a smile of painful sweetness. 'You washed my hands and face, didn't you? On the worst days, you looked after me. I am so grateful.'

Sebastian did not want gratitude. He decided that he had spoken too soon, that he ought to have waited. Had he declared himself today because Karam had shown signs of improvement? Was he trying to make sure of Yvonne before Karam could reclaim her? After all, the accident might have wiped sections of his sister's memory. Hating himself, he walked to the door.

'Sebastian?'

He froze.

'Don't go. Just hold me, please. I need someone to hold me.' She did, too. The relief she felt concerning Karam's improvement seemed to have exhausted her. He was a wholesome, decent man who respected her. 'And don't growl, snarl or bark,' she ordered.

'I won't.'

They lay on the bed, each wrapped hungrily around the other. She wept, he wept. There were no kisses, no words, just the holding, the clinging on to life, to warmth, to the sense of another's blood coursing nearby, to the comfort of heartbeats keeping time.

'Sebastian?'

'What?'

'Remember Deirdre?'

'Yes.'

'She killed David's other baby. He lost two on

the same day. That one cost him several hundred pounds – mine was free, at least.' Yvonne moved her head and looked into a face of startling beauty. 'Pity is akin to love, you know. Had David not found someone else, I might have gone back to him.'

He smiled encouragingly, hoped that she would continue to talk.

'I don't know myself yet,' she added, 'so allow me to understand myself first. The baby, Karam – so much has happened. I'm changing. You are a part of the change, but I don't know which part. Wait a while.'

'Of course.'

'Thank you.'

Like young animals hiding from a harsh world, they curled together and slept peacefully.

Dolly found them, stood and allowed her tears to fall. This was just a job, she told herself. Right from the start, Dolly had kept on muttering that this was only a job. But the Laczynskis had become her family, while Sebastian was her particular favourite. He and Yvonne looked a lovely couple, wrapped in innocence, clinging together even while asleep. 'I can see me wanting a new hat,' she mouthed, as she dashed wetness from her cheeks. 'A nice blue, I think. And I'd best go on a diet before your wedding.'

She closed the door behind her and went downstairs.

'Where are they?' Stefan was setting up the Monopoly board.

'Asleep.'

'Together?' There was hope in his eyes.

440

'Aye, they're together.'

'Karam will understand.'

'Yes. Yes, she will.'

Poison was messy and could be inaccurate. Knives were such obvious evidence. Tampering with brakes required specialist knowledge. How? How best to kill April Nugent? Even as she planned, Honoria knew that her killing days were over. Still, this was a happy dream. Oh, if only she dared . . .

Karam was discharged from hospital at the end of January. She was tired and quiet, though she insisted on speaking to everyone on her first day home. 'I want to see people in bits,' she told her father. 'One at a time. I've been alone for so long that a crowd of four might well overwhelm me.'

Her brother came in first. Had Yvonne told him that she had never been Karam's other half? He remained a picture of misery. 'You looked after Yvonne so well,' she said, after a few moments of safe, mundane conversation.

'She and I are like brother and sister,' he replied.

She heard the irony. 'Oh.' Brother and sister? Even now, after all this time? 'She'll still be upset about the miscarriage.'

'I expect so.' He tried to wear a grin, failed. 'You gave us one hell of a fright, too, sis. Glad you made it. We were all scared stiff.'

'Attention-seeking,' she quipped weakly. 'At least you got a bit of peace while I was out of it.'

He sat in the wicker chair under Karam's

441

bloodstained Venus. 'Whatever, it's great to have you home.'

'Is it?'

He frowned deeply. 'Of course it is.'

'You've ... er ... spent a lot of time with Yvonne, I suppose?'

He nodded mutely.

'And you haven't snarled or growled?'

'Not at all.'

She watched his hands. They were clasped so tightly together that knuckles showed white through healthy tanned skin.

'Has she mentioned me?' asked Karam carefully.

'Of course.'

She gritted her teeth and looked at the ceiling. It was like trying to tap blood from concrete. He adored Yvonne – that was very clear. As for Yvonne, she probably wasn't ready just yet. Unready – but, for all that, head over heels. What an impasse.

Sebastian muttered a few words, then kissed the top of his sister's head before leaving the room.

Yvonne came in. 'It's like queuing for a job interview,' she mumbled nervously.

Karam studied her. Yvonne was holding back, keeping her distance. 'I'm sorry,' whispered Karam.

'For what?'

Another blood-and-concrete situation, then. 'You know the answer. If you don't, I suggest a white stick and a golden retriever.'

Yvonne frowned, shook her head.

Exasperated, Karam almost ground her teeth

before speaking again. 'You've realized that I was in love with you. I admit freely that I sheltered you under false pretences. I was so happy while you lived with me. Did you never guess?' The threat of a headache came as no surprise to Karam. Concussion and coma seemed small-fry compared to this impossible task.

Yvonne swallowed. 'Not at the time.'

'And now?'

'It dawned on me finally.'

A few seconds crawled by in silence.

'My brother still believes that you and I were lovers. Obeying your instructions, I have not dared to enlighten him.'

Yvonne paced about, said nothing.

'Don't you think you ought to put the poor chap out of his misery one way or the other?'

'I don't know.' She leant her forehead against the cool glass of the overmantel mirror. 'I need time. I know he's holding back because he believes I've been in a relationship with you.'

'And?'

'And that keeps me safe.'

'From what.'

Yvonne swivelled and faced the bed. 'From decision-making. I loved David – remember? It all changed, died. I'm afraid of mistakes.'

'Safety in solitude, eh?'

'Something like that.'

Karam heaved herself up on to a mound of pillows. She had to move in for the kill, had to try to clear a path, clear her own mind, Yvonne's, Sebastian's. 'If he went away tomorrow, how would you feel? He might, you know. He has a lot of catching up to do.' She saw panic flash across Yvonne's face.

'Is he going away?'

'Possibly. And although you've been through a lot and feel uneasy about decisions, I know you'd miss him.'

Yvonne blinked rapidly.

Karam continued. 'He can take just so much pain and no more, like the rest of us. He's suffered too. When you were in hospital, he was demented with worry. Then he thought he'd lost me, then Papa got ill. I think he'll just clear out of here if . . . well . . . if there's nothing to keep him.'

Yvonne took a few steps and sat on the end of the bed. Cocoa, midnight talks, strong arms dragging her out of the cold. Tender fingers straightening her hair, mopping tears from her face, buttering the morning toast. 'I . . . have to be sure.'

'So tell him the truth.'

No reply was offered.

'I have to make some decisions myself soon,' continued Karam. 'I've been invited back to Florence, then to New York. The first's a part of the endless clean-up. The second's slightly longer term, a mobile post in acquisitions for various institutions across the States.'

'Oh.'

'So I'll sell the house.'

'No!' The response was quick, automatic. 'Let me buy or rent it from you.'

Relief flooded Karam's veins. Yvonne was thinking rationally, just as she always had before the miscarriage. Karam lowered her tone. 'I really did

444

love you, Yvonne, but I knew you weren't for me.'

Yvonne held back a rising sob. 'Yes, and I've always cared for you. You taught me how to find happiness – more than that, freedom. It's just . . . Sebastian . . .' The words died.

'I do understand.'

Yvonne took a very deep breath. 'I thought I hated your brother. He was always growling at me, staring at me as if I had a smudge on my nose or lipstick on my teeth. In my book he was criticizing me, assessing my worth.'

'He *was* assessing your worth, Yvonne.'

'I still don't know what I feel for him.' But he must not go. She would miss him. Oh, God.

'He won't expect you to jump into bed with him ten minutes after you tell him you're not a lesbian.'

An impish smile paid a brief visit to Yvonne's lips. 'We've already slept together.'

'What?' Karam's jaw hung.

'Slept,' repeated Yvonne. 'Just holding one another, nothing more.'

Karam's mouth changed shape and gave birth to a whistle. 'Hecky thump,' she added.

Yvonne stopped smiling. Eight Items or Less, the sign had said. Dark slate-grey eyes, shining hair, marked-down scones, Heinz beans. Poor Karam had fallen in love, while Yvonne had looked for no more than companionship. 'I'm scared,' she managed.

'Of what?' Karam asked yet again.

'Of being a serial monogamist.'

'You just need the right person.'

Yvonne dabbed at her eyes. 'I suppose so.'

'Everyone has to move on, you know.'

It was so difficult to explain, yet Yvonne had to try. She concentrated for a while, marshalling her thoughts into some kind of discipline, seeking the right words, the best phrases. 'I think I really like him.' She stopped, began again. 'He visited me in hospital and I wanted to scream at him, "I'm not a lesbian," because there was all this . . . this stuff in the air, like electricity. I'd just lost the baby, so I was strange, but there was an atmosphere, real feelings, and I didn't know whether I hated him, loved him, or simply resented everyone.' She stopped, drew a hand across her face. 'He's kind, isn't he?'

'The best,' answered Karam.

Yvonne cleared her throat. 'He followed me outside one night, here, at the hall. I was running, just running and screaming at God about the baby. Sebastian came for me. The way he looks at me as if I'm special. I'm not. What I am is frightened to death of doing it all wrong again. So.' She dragged in a long, shuddering breath, placed a hand on her stomach when she exhaled. 'I have to hide behind you for just a little while longer. If he insists on believing I'm gay, he'll hold his horses while I sort my head out. Does that make sense?'

Twin tears ran down Karam's cheeks. 'Yes. Yes, it does make sense.'

'He loves me. He's tried to tell me that. I sort of half listen when he says things. Then, when he starts to walk away, I get him to hold me.' She smiled ruefully. 'Near him, I want to curl up and borrow his warmth. When he leaves me I'm cold.'

'Sounds like love,' ventured Karam.

Yvonne looked at her friend. 'I used you.'

'No.' The answer was firm. 'We helped each other.'

'And Sebastian?'

Karam almost giggled. 'Don't worry about him. He always gets his own way.'

'Really?'

'Really. Get measured for the frock, girl, he'll brook no refusal.'

Twenty-four

The binoculars had taken early retirement in a kitchen cupboard. Occasionally, Honoria felt drawn to them in much the same way as an alcoholic drifts in the direction of a tantalus, but she resisted. Now it was her turn to be looked at, and she revelled in the limelight she imagined to be pointing in her direction.

At least twice a week she made up one of a bridge four, the other players culled from the club in Formby. She left the curtains open so that anyone passing by or living within the scope of two avenues could watch and envy her. She and her partner, a widow from Freshfield, had worked out a system that made them very successful. Honoria's abilities of calculation and communication, together with her terrible need to win, made her a force much admired and feared within the world of bridge.

When she wasn't playing cards, Honoria slaved over her novel. April Nugent, who was out to ruin her, had been put on a slow-burner for the time being. Honoria was beginning to realize that elimination was not always the answer, that retribution often presented too many difficulties. She could not remove April, so she had to win in a different way: by becoming a brilliant novelist. The greatest pity was that the television programme was now out of the question. If Honoria advertised her wares, April would denounce them as stolen from Hyacinth. The publisher was not playing fair. Half a dozen telephone conversations had proved his stubborn nature. Honoria would have to deal with him in person.

She saved the work, backed it on to disk and switched off her computer. *Serendipity* was taking so much time and energy, yet the book would never be published if April Nugent had her way. Should Honoria fail to withdraw from publication the work supposedly stolen from Hyacinth, April would denounce Honoria as a plagiarist. The man in Bolton must be forced to co-operate. *Serendipity* had to be published.

Honoria tapped her teeth with a ballpoint, arranged her thoughts. *Serendipity* was a brilliant novel. It pulled no punches, was raunchy, hard hitting, written from experience, from knowledge of life. Honoria grinned. What was that expression much used by Gill Collins? 'That'll wipe their eyes'? Yes, that was the one. Who in Blundellsands would believe that a spinster in her seventies could write so freely about sex and murder, about a woman who, like the counterpart to Jack the Ripper, categorized and culled men, acting as judge, jury and executioner? 'An unusual work,' she mused. 'And so well done.' Not for an instant did Honoria question her own certainty. April

Nugent continued as the fly in the ointment, though.

April knew something of the West family's history, closely guarded secrets divulged by Hyacinth. What a traitor Honoria's older sister had been. Yet Honoria still held an ace, kept it hidden until such time as it might be employed. Had that time arrived? No, not just yet. She grinned, imagined the expression on certain faces when facts finally came to light . . .

So the local playwright, the brave sufferer from multiple sclerosis, that much-loved celebrity, was blackmailing a fellow writer. Even if all that stuff about rabbit, horse, boy and man got aired, who would want to investigate so-called crimes that were as old as God? Honoria was not a criminal: she had simply sought equality and recognition in an unfair world. But she dared take no chances, not where her talent was concerned.

She stared at her reflection in the overmantel mirror, saw a slimmed-down version of her former self, a woman who creamed and polished herself morning and night, a woman in a designer suit, who enjoyed aromatherapy, massage, manicure and hairdo every week. She was all new, and refused to be threatened by the woman who produced silly little plays and facile comedies for television.

And as for Hilda – what did a few cakes and puddings matter? she asked herself. Compared to a work of literature, baking scarcely signified. She smiled at the image in the mirror. The London agent had taken her on, had submitted the three chapters to a publisher, and an editor was interested in seeing the finished product. Soon, soon.

Well, it was time to prepare for the next move. Honoria switched out the lights and repaired to her bedroom. She cleaned and moisturized her face, applied Gayle Hayman Youth Lift, lay down for five minutes with slices of iced cucumber on her eyes. Dumpy, frumpy Hilda could keep her sticky toffee puddings and her ancient husband. It was Honoria's turn at last.

Paul Greenhalgh leant back in his seat. 'No can do, lady,' he drawled.

In Honoria's opinion, this one had watched too many James Cagney movies. His accent hovered somewhere between Brooklyn and Manchester, as if he had melted himself down and reconstituted all the DNA factors, rearranging each molecule to suit his imagined position in society. A publisher? If this was a publisher, Honoria was Queen of the May. 'Why not?' she asked. She would brook no further nonsense. On the phone, he had been impossible for weeks, going on about contracts, lawsuits, loss of income. He had to be dealt with.

He rooted in a drawer and brought out a folder. 'Contract, Miss West. The typescript is already at the print shop. Nothing can stop production now.'

'I can stop it,' she replied mildly. 'With a stroke of the pen.' She drew a pigskin case from her handbag, opened it to reveal a cheque book. 'There is nothing on earth that cannot be purchased, Mr Greenhalgh. Why do you think God created the *Financial Times* Index?'

Clever bugger, admitted Greenhalgh inwardly.

'You do not need to know my reasons, but I want to buy the whole print-run, then the contract must be destroyed. Name your price.'

Her eyes were . . . unusual, he thought. 'I stand to lose around six thousand,' he said. In actuality, his losses promised to kiss the hem of four figures, no more than that. Publishers of local work tended to make little money, as did the authors. 'With repeat runs,' he went on, 'I might have made a lot more.' He could not look at her: something in her expression made his skin mobile, as if it tried to lift away and crawl off the bone.

She wrote the cheque. 'A receipt,' she snapped. 'And sign this declaration of intent not to publish the work at some later date. All rights in the matter now revert to me.' She paused. 'Well? Sign it, Mr Greenhalgh.'

He complied, wondering what the hell she was up to. This was not a woman to be gainsaid. This was not a woman who recognized the normal barriers in life, the legal or moral restrictions that had been instituted by God, or fought for by generations of human beings. This was not a woman, not really. What was she, then?

'The copies will be delivered to me,' she said.

'It was certainly worth publishing,' he commented, as he read the cheque.

'But much more valuable not published, wouldn't you say?'

'Well . . .'

'I am not fooled by you, Mr Greenhalgh. You are here to make a living and you must be compensated for my withdrawal from our arrangements. However, disabuse yourself of the concept that you have fooled me. Were I to remove a nought from the sum on my cheque, that would be nearer the mark. But we understand one another, you and I.' She stood up. 'I bid you goodbye, then, Mr Greenhalgh.'

Paul Greenhalgh of Yesteryear Ltd sat very still for a couple of minutes. He was not of a fanciful turn, seldom indulging in any mental activity that involved imagination. In fact, his wife had been called upon to invent a name for his company, so limited were the man's capabilities. His wife read submissions at home, chose what would be published, what would be rejected. All he did was sit here and take the money.

He shivered. Someone was performing a rapid tap dance on his grave. Miss Honoria West probably had a birthmark somewhere about her person, an arrangement of three sixes dictated by her real father. The number of the beast? He'd watched a few too many Films on Four, he decided grimly. All the same, he wanted to get Honoria West's cheque out of his office and into the bank. After which, he intended to treat his lovely wife to a little car, a new dress and a slap-up meal. The money must be disposed of as quickly as possible.

He stood up, walked to the window, rubbed a small, clear circle into years of nicotine and grime. Miss West was crossing the road. When she reached the other side, she turned and stared right at him. Like a child caught eavesdropping, Paul Greenhalgh stumbled away and sat down. Shortly, he would go out for a double brandy – for medicinal purposes, of course. She was gone, thank God. He hoped that she would never return.

After coffee and a fruit salad, Honoria decided to visit her sister and brother-in-law. The telephone call from Leo had been nasty, of course, but blood was thicker than the watery lump who had once been Lawrence Beresford. The fire at Moortop had never taken hold, so no harm had been done there. As for the Chapel House – was there any proof? And she wanted them to see her as she was now, the revived product of Estée Lauder, healthy exercise and a diet that was usually sensible.

In a suit that had cost over five hundred pounds, she was ready for anyone and anything. She was an author, a writer in whom a large publishing house had expressed an interest. She was a dab hand at bridge and she had almost overcome agoraphobia. She wanted them to know that she feared no man and was not even remotely alarmed by letters lodged with a solicitor.

Hilda opened the door.

'Hello,' said Honoria, the tone coated in honey.

The lady of the house staggered back a pace. 'Honoria?'

'Of course.'

'But you're . . . so thin.'

Elegant would have been more apt, thought the visitor, as she entered her childhood home.

'Leo's out,' stammered Hilda. 'But my dailies are somewhere about.'

Honoria smiled inwardly. Mother's little baby seemed keen to impart the information that she was still protected, still swaddled within the bosom of the farmhouse. 'I understand that you are married.' She kept the tone light. 'And that you are something of a business success, too. Cakes, isn't it?'

Hilda heard the sarcasm. 'We do some savouries, too.'

'Really?' Honoria sat in what had once been Father's chair in the smaller drawing room. 'I shan't stay,' she explained. 'I've just been firing my publisher. Why drink water while there's champagne in the cooler?'

'Did you want a drink?'

'No.' It was like talking to a child. 'I am to be published nationally, not locally. If I'm fortunate, I might even sell abroad. But, then, I was always the creative one, while you were practical and—'

'Hyacinth was creative,' said Hilda rather smartly.

'Shallow, though.'

Hilda knew that her trembling was visible. 'Hyacinth was very, very clever. She was kind, too. Nobody ever told me the truth about what happened all those years ago, but—'

'I beg your pardon?'

Flustered, the lady of the house dried damp hands on her apron. Trust Honoria to call during a baking session. Trust poor Leo to choose this time to go to the bakery with the wages. 'You did things when you were little. Mother said you were a . . . difficult child.' She heard the Hoover upstairs, plucked up courage. 'My husband never touched you in that barn, Honoria. You just wanted to steal him away from Hyacinth.'

Honoria laughed. 'I didn't want him.'

'No, but you made sure Hyacinth couldn't have him, either.'

The unwelcome guest remained unmoved and,

apparently, immovable. 'I came to visit you, Hilda, dear. Let the past rest, please. I only wanted to—'

'Do you have a key to this house? It would have to be the back door, as the front locks have been changed several times.'

'I have no keys but my own.' The big iron key to the rear door was hers. This was her home, her heritage, her place of birth.

'New locks everywhere now,' said Hilda. 'Front and back. Bolts, chains and a burglar alarm connected to the police station.' She paused. 'We've got fire alarms, too.'

'Really?'

'Yes, really.' Hilda perched on the edge of Mother's chair. 'We know you burned down Leo's house. There's no proof, but we're sure.'

A couple of seconds ticked by. 'Nonsense, my dear. You have always tended towards hysteria. I blame Mother for over-indulging you.' She allowed her gaze to travel round the room where Father had lain in his coffin, where Mother had wept, where Honoria had hidden to listen as her own parents had plotted against her. 'Not many changes here,' she remarked.

'There's no point in mending what isn't broken.'

Marriage seemed to have strengthened Hilda. Honoria noticed the quick recovery as Hilda settled herself more comfortably, while the voice gained power with every word. 'You are looking well,' said Honoria. 'Perhaps a little pale, a few more wrinkles, but quite happy, I'm sure.'

Hilda had always been even-tempered, yet she bubbled now beneath the surface, memories

456

churning, half-truths colliding and mixing in a cauldron where her stomach had recently resided. 'I want you to leave my house,' she said.

'Oh, I shall. In fact, I shall probably leave the north behind altogether quite soon. So drab and dreary, so sad and angry. I intend to live in the south.'

'Good.' Hilda rose. 'Now, if you don't mind, I have a lot to do.' She faltered, then continued. 'Our lawyer has letters in case anything—'

'I know. It's all nonsense, of course, and—'

'So has April Nugent's solicitor. If and when she dies, a whole can of worms will crawl across that silly grin of yours. She knows you mean her harm.' Unused to being nasty, Hilda blinked away a tear. 'You must keep away from all of us.'

Honoria stood up, a smile pinned across her features. 'The biggest truth is known to no one but myself. I keep it in reserve for a rainy day. Perhaps when I have finished my novel I shall tell you and your dear husband. There again, I may not bother.' She grinned broadly. 'Try Youth Lift, dear. I'm afraid your face is quite the worse for wear.' With this sweet message, she left her sister and slammed the front door in her wake.

Hilda shook with rage. If Leo had been here, Honoria would never have got past the front door. She needed to talk to someone now, this instant. With uncertain feet, she walked into the hall, picked up the cordless phone and brought it into the smaller drawing room. 'April?'

'Oh, is that you, Hilda?'

'Yes.' April's voice seemed to have lost its bounce. 'Is Karam all right?' Of late, Hilda had kept in touch with April on a more-or-less fort-nightly basis.

'She's fine.'

'And you?'

'Mum's death laid me low, I'm afraid. And the legal stuff was so complicated. What's the matter, Hilda?'

'Guess who turned up here today.'

Seconds ticked. 'She didn't.'

'Bold as brass in a suit that must have cost a bomb. She said she'd just fired her publisher.'

After a short pause, April laughed. 'That'll be my fault. I'm afraid I deprived her of her few minutes on the box. She was to be interviewed by Karam's brother. Karam is due to be filmed next week over in Yorkshire. So am I, but I need written permission from my left foot if I'm to get any-where at all.'

'Oh dear. Is it dropping again?'

'I wish it would drop off, Hilda. It's a perishing nuisance. Anyway, I warned Honoria that I would deal with her if she published anything of Hyacinth's. She'll have paid the man off, I dare say.'

'I bet she did steal Hyacinth's work. Honoria has to win, no matter what the cost. Well, she's still writing, this time a novel.'

'I know.'

'And she set fire to my kitchen and burned down Leo's beautiful house.'

'Yes.'

'April?'

'Yes?'

'Did Hyacinth . . . did she ever tell you about

458

things? You know, about Honoria when she was young?'

'Leave well alone, Hilda,' replied April promptly. 'You, Leo and I are going to be very pleasant to your sister. In a few months, *Monday's Child* will go ahead. I want you and Leo to come on the last night. Honoria will be there – I shall flatter her and invite all her bridge friends along, free tickets if necessary. You know how easily she forgets trouble. I have faced up to her several times, but she takes little advice and respects no one, seems to wipe the more unpleasant scenes from her mind. So have you put her in her place, too?'

'I told her to leave my house. And she knows that we all have letters lodged in case of accident or sudden death.'

'No matter,' answered April. 'In a couple of weeks, she will act as if nothing untoward has happened. That's the nature of the beast, as you already know, I'm sure.'

'What are you planning?' asked Hilda.

April paused. She had so much to say, but she had to think first, had to work things out for herself. It was almost like writing yet another play, she mused. The final scene of *Monday's Child*. So far, it's had at least five endings, but I'll get there eventually. And I'll keep in touch – in fact, I'll visit you when this blasted foot decides to behave. Don't worry. The last act is almost ready.'

'You're being so secretive,' said Hilda.

'Don't worry, my friend. It will be worth the wait, believe me.'

* * *

459

The problem was solved. In a wardrobe in the spare bedroom, twelve hundred copies of Honoria's slim book lay beneath an old blanket. They would never see the light of day – not during Honoria's lifetime, at least.

She worked for at least six hours a day. When she wasn't working, she thought about working, finding herself almost incapable of concentrating on TV, radio or reading. Honoria did not realize that this was a situation common to all compulsive writers. The fact that she scarcely ate or slept did not signify. *Serendipity* had taken over, and Honoria allowed the clever woman in the story to have her way.

She stopped answering the door, unplugged the phone and objected to the smallest sound from outside. Forgetting April Nugent's insistence that creative writing had to be controlled, she carried on regardless, her mind racing, her heart maintaining its steady, even pace. 'Don't let it get the better of you, don't let the characters lead you astray,' April had told her.

Honoria knew better, as did Graham Mansell, the computer boffin who was her only daytime visitor. He had no living relatives, and seemed to have adopted Honoria as a grandmother, bringing her flowers, listening with bated breath while she read chapters to him. She was happier than she had ever been in her whole life. Nothing could touch her now. She was home and dry.

People would wonder, no doubt, about the source of Honoria's knowledge on sexual behaviour. To the world around her, she was a spinster, a woman who would die intact, unversed.

But, like Serendipity, Miss Honoria West had experienced life to the full, had needed to take charge. The paper heroine had been neglected and abused as a child; Honoria, though unmolested in her infancy, had suffered by being the middle child, the least important, the black sheep.

Attention! she had screamed silently into the blackness of night while Hyacinth had sat with Father, while Hilda had been comforted by Mother. As a young woman, she had dealt with Lawrence Beresford, causing him to run away and change his identity. In her thirties, she had deliberately ruined marriages, with the result that two high-ranking tax officers had been forced to relocate, wifeless, childless and hopeless. Oh, yes, she knew all about life, about men and their little vagaries.

She poured a second sherry and remembered the most spectacular of her conquests. A frumpy woman in twinset and pearls had arrived at the office, had slapped Honoria's cheek, had called her a harlot. Honoria had kept her temper, had washed her face, returned to her desk, carried on working. Sex had been a hobby until her forties, when she had grown tired of it.

She laughed aloud. Let them all read and wonder: she would not be here, would go to London where no one raised an eyebrow while flicking through a Jackie Collins.

What had the names been? she wondered sleepily. Nine or ten men, she had known in the biblical sense. God alone knew where they all were now. They had been experiments, creatures of no particular significance. But, oh, how much she owed them now. They had wakened Serendipity in

461

Honoria, had allowed the author to walk through the part before starting to plot the story. After all, a writer did best when expressing what she knew.

A noise summoned her to the window. Cars pulled up outside Philip Pointer's house, now the home of the peculiar chap who wore those strange clothes. He didn't like her. Many people didn't like her. No matter. Soon, she would be leaving them all behind.

In the end, it came down to three biscuit tins, each with a decorated lid. The first portrayed a crinolined lady, the second a drummer boy, the third, which had originally contained Keiller's butterscotch, bore a Christmas theme. On the lid sat a partridge in a pear tree, while the sides were covered in faded holly, berries paling towards pink, leaves eroding to allow silvery metal to show through.

It was all in here, the whole of April's life: birth certificate, photographs, mementoes of her wedding, newspaper cuttings with reviews of her earliest works. Until almost ten years ago, Enid Charnock had kept a faithful record of her daughter's progress, the neat, almost shy handwriting accounting for each item in the boxes. How proud of April this sweet, sensible woman had been. April remembered a happy household, good parents, a settled and comfortable childhood, teenage, young adulthood. Then, like a bolt from the blue, Mother's confusion had arrived.

April closed her eyes and leant back against the cushions of her sofa. 'Mother,' she whispered. Dad had died quite young, had simply keeled over in the garden, short-handled planting fork in one hand, geranium in the other. 'He knew nothing about it,' the family doctor had said. Mother had planted all those geraniums, consulting her daughter about their positioning, then feeding and watering the flowers, taking cuttings, perpetuating Dad's favourite blooms.

Enid's descent into dementia had been rapid. At the end, April Nugent had visited a shell, a wispy-haired crone much older than her true age, which was a mere sixty-five. And now, with the funeral long over, probate settled, the family home in Chester due to go on the market, April sat with the three tins and a headful of memories, some sweet, some painful.

'Cup of coffee?' Mark Nugent's head was poking its way into the room. He was back, probably for good.

'Please,' she answered. She stared at a photograph of Dad at *Aramis*'s wheel, a silly captain's hat cocked over one eye, the dead pipe clenched between his teeth. *Aramis*, their little boat, had carried them along the Dee on many sunny Sundays. There was another snap of Mother with her skirts spread out as she lay on the riverbank, ankles crossed, feet clad in strappy white sandals. And here was April, about eight years old, cartwheeling, limbs slightly blurred as she tumbled and turned about.

Mark came in with the coffee. 'Don't brood,' he said.

April shrugged. 'I'm not brooding, just remembering.'

He went out to nurture dogs and horses.

So here it was, a bundle of papers, a few folders of photographs, some pressed flowers, love letters tied with narrow ribbons, April's baby curls sealed in a silver locket. And, right at the bottom of the Keiller's tin, the most important message of all.

She shoved everything back into place and snapped all three lids shut. Mother had been in no condition to explain. Mother's brain had predeceased its owner, leaving her with few memories and no pleasures. 'I'll do the thinking for both of us,' said April now. She looked at her cats, glanced at the parrot, smiled to herself. 'The time of reckoning is nigh,' she explained to Velcro.

Unimpressed, the cat rolled over and fell asleep.

April sighed, closed her eyes and followed suit. She was going to need all her strength. Times of reckoning were invariably arduous.

Twenty-five

Although the weather was wet and cold, April Nugent threw herself against the wind and continued her walk. She looked across the water, enjoyed a clear view of New Brighton, then Wales. Behind her, Mark sat in the animal-shelter van; she could feel his eyes on her. The strangest thing was that the man truly loved her at last. He needed to be needed, it seemed. Mark asked nothing for himself, worked hard with the animals, took just a small wage, accounting for every penny he spent on food for dogs, cats and other members of April's ever-expanding menagerie. People could change, she supposed. Well, most people, that was. Honoria West was the probable exception.

April had wanted to walk alone this morning. Mark had developed the disconcerting habit of clicking into her thoughts as effectively as a computer mouse, entering her program, punctuating the script, reading right through to the bottom of the page. And, yes, she loved him, too.

She felt a hand on her shoulder. 'I told you to stay in the van—' April turned her head. 'Oh, hello, Graham. Sorry – I thought you were Mark. Funny, I was thinking about computers a moment ago, and here you are, the Blundellsands trouble-shooter. How's business?'

Graham Mansell smiled. After a session in Cavendish Mansions, he was experiencing a sudden need for fresh, mobile air. 'Good – going well. I've just left Miss West,' he explained. 'She's still struggling a bit with the word-processor.' Miss West hated Mrs Nugent. He could not understand why anyone should dislike this sweet lady. Here she was, buffeted by the wind, still insisting on making her own way along the promenade. 'Do you want to be alone?' he asked.

'Come a little way with me. This breeze is turning rather boisterous.'

They continued for a dozen of his paces, twenty of hers. 'Honoria's writing a novel,' remarked April casually.

He stopped walking and placed a hand on April's arm. 'She's always reading bits aloud. It's very . . . Well, it doesn't pull many punches.'

'Sexy?' April ground to a halt, one hand on her walking-stick, the other arm supported by her companion.

Graham reddened. 'Strange,' he replied eventually. 'Very strange.'

'In what way?'

The boy swallowed, Adam's apple rasping up and down the thin throat. 'Well, it's called *Serendipity*. That's the name of the main character, too.'

'I knew that.' April kept her tone light.

'She keeps killing people. Serendipity, I mean. Men. She kills men.'

466

'Ah.' April waited.

'She does it during – while she's in bed with them.'

'Really?'

He jerked his head quickly several times. 'Miss West says it's like the behaviour of a black widow spider.'

'Yes.'

'Very well written,' he continued. 'Good English, interesting in a peculiar way. I read a lot, you see,' he said, by way of explanation. 'And Miss West seems extremely clever, clever enough to write any sort of book really. So I've become more and more . . .' The words tailed away.

'Shocked?' suggested April.

'Surprised,' he amended. Miss West almost glowed while mouthing the most salacious passages. The old lady seemed to have no shame, no pity for her characters. 'She likes describing the deaths, I think. Loads of blood and gore, stabbings, that sort of carry-on. It's a bit like one of those snuff movies – the ones where the actors really get murdered. Viewers want to look away but they can't, or so I've heard. Miss West's agent's talking about *Serendipity* being entered for some big thriller prize.' He nodded again. 'It's certainly a thriller, not the kind of book you'd want to read at midnight during a thunderstorm.'

April patted his hand, turned round. She had walked far enough for one day. Graham led her in the direction of her van, said goodbye, then set off towards his home on the Serpentine.

Leaning on the rail that divided car-park from shore, April gazed down upon dirty sand, tangles

467

of seaweed, dead jellyfish, a few drinks cans. So Honoria was writing her autobiography – well, almost. She had reinvented herself, probably as a devastatingly beautiful woman with enormous sex appeal, large breasts, small waist, eyes big enough to drown in. Honoria West was celebrating herself, revelling in a past murkier than today's grey, choppy waters.

'You have to do it,' April told herself softly. 'Only you have the wherewithal to see her off completely.' Honoria had announced her intention to leave the north, but would she? April's skin crawled. The murderess was writing about murder, about the pleasure she had derived from killing. Had there been an extra dose of insulin for Hyacinth? How long was Honoria's real list of victims?

'April?' called Mark.

She walked to the van. It had to be done. Honoria had to disappear for ever.

The idyll stretched through winter and into spring, a time upon which Yvonne would always reflect with joy coloured by a feeling of otherwordliness, as if the two of them had been folded in a warm cloud of magic where they dwelt in total isolation. Soon, she would tell him that she had never loved any woman. Each day, her confidence grew.

Sebastian surprised and excelled himself. He had never considered himself romantic, though Karam had often advised him that he was incurably so. 'Weird', he began to suppose, meant old-fashioned, hesitant, cautious. Certainly, he had not stepped easily into love. The internal quarrelling had gone on for ages, reason battling with emotion, the latter beating the former into submission after many rounds.

Yvonne had been married, which made her rather more exotic than he might have wanted. Love didn't follow any leader – it eliminated the psyche, ignored personality and character, would not negotiate, refused to do business with rational thought. I love you. Three tiny monosyllabic words spoken so fearlessly, so often, so carelessly. But they had stuck in Sebastian's throat until the white flag of truce had put a stop to all his inner doubts. He wanted Yvonne, could not imagine continuing without her. Whatever she was, whatever she might have been, he wanted and needed her.

For her part, Yvonne remembered the growler, the man whose wordless criticisms had plagued her, the seeker of fault, that sulky creature who came to life only on Sundays and from within a television tube. He was so different now, so amiable and approachable. A flower on her pillow, a silver locket for her birthday, this gift secreted in her individual pack of Coco Pops, for which she had maintained a fondness since childhood. And it wasn't only gifts: there were poems marked for her in an anthology, quiet moments when he would brush her hair, massage her shoulders, hold her hand, share her uncontainable delight while she revelled in Nora Batty and company's synchronized tea-drinking in *Last of the Summer Wine*.

The silences still existed, but she no longer felt excluded. He would look up at her, smile, even drop a comment or two before returning to his studies. She admired and respected Sebastian Laczynski; she also adored him.

Stefan, worried at first about his daughter, was eventually delighted. Once Karam left Horsefield, the old man had the rare privilege of watching love developing between two wonderful young people. His son was normal after all, as was Yvonne. He thought none the less of her for her temporary lapse into lesbianism, saying quite openly that she had been 'going through adolescence rather later than normal', and that she would make an excellent mother for his grandchildren.

Yvonne was almost happy at last. There was little she could do about Karam, nothing she needed to do about David. At least he was no longer on her conscience. The divorce was under way, David had met his policewoman and they would move to Manchester within the foreseeable future. Deirdre's house had been sold; she and her husband had sought pastures new in Kent, where Paul Mellor would sell expensive houses to weary commuters and time-shares in Spain to retired businessmen. Karam had gone back to Liverpool, was preparing to cross the Atlantic after serving out her notice period at the university. Yvonne, who had stayed in Yorkshire, spent some time worrying about Karam. Nothing Sebastian or Stefan said could comfort her. But, apart from her concern for her friend, Yvonne was a contented woman.

In the end, Sebastian phoned April, who was coming over to put some finishing touches to her interview, the airing of which had been scheduled for the end of May. 'Bring Karam,' he said.

'She may not want to come. What do I do if she refuses?' enquired April, who was not in the best frame of mind after receiving a litter of kittens rescued from the brink of a watery death in some poor old chap's fishpond. 'She's very busy, preparing for America and so forth. And she spends a lot of time at Kevin's house. They're all decorating, trying to cover poor old Philip's years of nicotine with some ghastly green paint.'

'Persuade her,' pleaded Sebastian. 'Yvonne needs to tie up loose ends.'

'And what about Karam's needs?' Like the kittens, Karam was displaced at the moment, insecure but terribly brave.

'I know my sister. Trust me.'

An unexpectedly warm day in early May found Yvonne and Sebastian preparing a picnic. Some of Horsefield Hall's jungle had been tamed by an odd-job man, a very odd man with an Irish accent as thick as Dolly's stews, two teeth and a big dog called – everyone thought – Charlie Brown. Man and dog had taken a shine to Dolly, who thought Mr McWhatever might have been all right with teeth and a going-over with the power hose. The dog stank, so Dolly bathed him, only to stand by helplessly while the creature returned to the mud from which he had probably crawled at the dawn of creation.

The chap leant on his spade and watched Yvonne struggling with a tablecloth. After a few seconds, he picked up some stones and helped her to weight the thing down, all the while muttering under his breath in a language that bore some distant relationship to English. Yvonne managed to pick out 'eejit' and 'woman', though the rest of the diatribe would remain a perpetual mystery.

Sebastian wandered across the lawn, an area of flattened and unevenly mown weed, carrying on a tray some tepid dips in white bowls. The fridge, a remnant from the early seventies, had given up the ghost yet again. 'Father's doing heart massage on it,' he said. 'He'd have a better chance of raising the *Titanic*.' Sebastian dumped his burdens and kissed Yvonne's nose. 'Karam's coming.'

She noticed the contrived insouciance of his tone.

'You may want to spend a little time with her,' he continued. 'Tie up loose ends about the house and so forth.'

Yvonne was not fooled. She looked back on the whole Karam episode as if reading a chapter in someone else's story. The queue in Sainsbury's, the man with his coupon, Karam's friendly, gentle eyes, three Domestos for the price of two, a special offer on frozen chicken drumsticks. 'I shall never know what to say to her.' You should have realized, insisted the inner voice of conscience. You ought to have noticed that Karam was looking for more than companionship.

'Darling, Karam takes life as it comes. She loves you, I know.' He paused. 'Have I told you the good news about her?'

'America?'

'No. It's inexplicable, but her style changed after the accident. My big sister is now extremely saleable. Her more recent daubs are all over

London. And no, it's not graffiti, dearest. Galleries, exhibitions.'

'Oh.' Words weren't easy, not where Karam was concerned.

'So she will launch herself into the next stage of her life, and I know she'll meet someone – she always does. One day, Karam will find her life partner.'

'Yes.' Yvonne stared straight ahead. 'Sebastian?'

'What?'

She swallowed. 'There was no relationship.'

'What?' he repeated. He sat down abruptly, dragging at Yvonne's hand until she, too, was seated on the grass.

'I have not been your sister's lover. I am not a lesbian and I never was.'

His mouth gaped for a split second. 'Then why didn't you say – why did you let everyone think—?'

'Loyalty,' replied Yvonne swiftly. 'And I made Karam promise to keep quiet, too. What's the big deal? I was angry at the idea of her being judged, while I, Mrs Yvonne Benson, could get away scot-free with my behaviour. She was hurting no one. I, on the other hand, was running away from a decent man just because I was bored with him.' Her chin jutted out defiantly. 'It wasn't fair.'

'So you never—'

'No, I never. Even if I had, you would have messed it up. Right from the start, I knew you'd be trouble,' said Yvonne.

There followed a silence that stretched through five long minutes. Sebastian, relieved and confused, wondered yet again about the peculiarities

473

of the female mind. It was almost as if women saw events differently, their vision impaired by thin fog, or by some kind of fluid. Yes, water could cause refraction, was capable of bending light so that objects appeared to have shuffled off towards the side. Amazing.

Yvonne gave him time to think. In her experience, even the most able of men took a while to classify and file new information.

'I'd be trouble?' he asked suddenly. 'What do you mean by that?'

She refused to laugh. 'You got into my head. I thought it was hormones, but it was you. You were a challenge, an argument that was about to happen at any minute. I couldn't let you win with crosswords. I started reading all kinds of stuff so that I could toss quotations into the pool during your more cerebral conversations with Karam.' She turned her head and stared hard at him. 'I could scarcely bear to look at you then in case . . . Oh, I don't know. You were in my head, Sebastian.'

'Ah.' He discovered himself to be nearly dumb-struck.

'Then you moved.'

'Moved?'

'You touched my arm.'

'So I was then in your arm?'

'Don't mock me. I may be a weak and feeble woman, but I have the fist of Mike Tyson. I began to find you attractive.' In spite of herself, she grinned. 'You're really enjoying this, aren't you?'

He laughed. 'My story is just as silly. I loved you from the moment I saw you murdering that first tomato for spaghetti sauce. You are a very lovable woman.'

'I know.'

'So?' he asked. 'When did you realize you loved me?'

'When I knew how much I hated you.' She pondered. 'No, that's not quite true. You weren't actually around when the light began to dawn. Chasing a sculptor or an actor – I can't remember which. It was your clothes.'

Finding no sensible comment or question, Sebastian remained mute. His clothes?

'They looked so lonely and empty hanging there in the porch. There was that disgraceful green jacket – Karam calls it your poacher's coat. And your wellies were parked the wrong way round, as if a child might be preparing to put them on crossed over.' She sighed. 'And I realized that I was empty and crossed over, too. So I hated you all the more.' She pretended not to notice as he dashed a drop of moisture from his cheek.

'That is almost unbearably sweet,' he announced after a short pause. 'Fairytaleish.'

'Sickening,' she agreed. 'And very confusing for both of us. I was in love with a green jacket, while you fell for a tomato-killer.'

He pulled her close and kissed her forehead, her nose, her mouth. She was good for him, right for him. As soon as her divorce was through, they could marry, travel through Europe, settle in London, keep the house in Liverpool . . . The kiss became urgent, clouded his thoughts.

Yvonne eased herself away from him. The unmistakable voice of Stefan Laczynski warned of his imminent arrival. The old chap was striding with remarkable vigour across the newly flattened area of yellowish green. He wore the cricket cap at a rakish angle, a faded blue shirt, some khaki shorts. 'He cometh,' said Yvonne.

Sebastian laughed. 'We must try to prise him into a suit one of these days.'

Stefan marched towards them, a screwdriver in his hand and a look of devilment in his eyes. 'I give up,' he said. 'Today, after the picnic, Dolly and I go for a new refrigerator.'

Yvonne smiled. This was a good example of progress, surely?

Serendipity, a mistress of disguise, continued to work her way across the world as an astute businesswoman and serial killer. Honoria, who took time out now only for bridge, food and sleep, kept very much to herself for most of the time. Even Graham Mansell, computer genius and *Serendipity* fan, had forsaken her. Like everyone else, he had turned out to be shallow and useless, had discussed the plot of Honoria's *magnum opus* all over Crosby. Being accosted in Farm Foods by Kevin Brooks had been embarrassing, to say the least of it. The mincing, stupid little man had not attempted to lower his voice. 'Mass murder now, Miss West?' he had called. 'Progress, I suppose; better than poisonous letters.'

Honoria backed up her work and walked to the corner window. The cans of spray paint had been deposited in the dead of night, in Kevin Brooks's dustbin and, of course, she had worn gloves. Kevin and his diseased friends were scrubbing away, trying to eradicate the filthy words that decorated the front of the house. 'Never threaten me again,' Honoria mouthed to herself. 'Hypodermic, indeed. You couldn't swat a fly, you sad little man.'

She sat down near the fireplace and closed her eyes. *Serendipity* was in complete charge these days. Had Honoria been possessed of any true vision, she might have realized that her relationship with reality had become rather casual. The flat, which was tidied only when bridge players were expected, had assumed an air of neglect, a mustiness in the air, a lack of polish in its overall presentation. Often, there was little fresh food, and Honoria took to eating from cans, shopping just once each week, rushing home to get back to the keyboard. Clothes were tightening once more. She watched little television, even ignoring *Morse* and *The Bill*, while *EastEnders*, which she had followed avidly from its inception, was a mere memory shaded in the depressing browns and sepias that seemed to have dominated most scenes.

Determined to try again, she switched on the set. A man called Jerry Springer was trying to interview two transvestites and their families. The result of his efforts was displayed in a blur of tangled limbs and bleeped-out language. Wigs and curses flew in all directions; security men tried to separate lipsticked males from each other and from a crowd of fat, ill-dressed relatives.

'Serendipity's world is not so strange, then,' Honoria mumbled to herself.

The doorbell sounded. Honoria switched off the TV and waited.

'We know it was you!' called a voice from the landing.

She wandered into the kitchen and set the kettle to boil.

'You did it,' shouted Kevin Brooks. 'And you killed PP.'

Honoria found a clean mug. She had given up saucers long ago. Yesterday's dishes were balanced uncertainly in a corner, greasy pans and plates, glasses whose lustre was a distant memory. She would fill the dishwasher later. Would Serendipity ever be caught? Could she leave the poor heroine to languish in prison? Instant coffee would do. Cheese on toast later, she decided. And there were some chocolate digestives in the barrel. To kill her heroine would be a grievous sin indeed. Suicide? Tomorrow the diet must begin again. She would shop in the morning, buy ready-made salads and . . .

Perhaps Serendipity's final act should be to remove herself, thereby going to her grave clean and free. After all, what had she done that was so wrong, so punishable? Jack the Ripper had got away with murder, so why should a woman not remove from society those men who fornicated their way through life?

'You'll go too far again one of these days,' yelled a voice from the wings. Who was that? Ah, yes, it was PP's little buddy from across the way. No matter. She used the milk frother to jazz up her Gold Blend, sprinkling a little powdered chocolate on top. Kevin Brooks. He was the one with . . . What was it? HIV. He needed shifting, but Honoria was tired. Her hair was dirty. Her hands had not been creamed for over a week, and she would soon require a manicure.

She carried her cup to the window, raised it when she saw Kevin standing in the street. 'Cheers,' she mouthed.

Kevin re-entered his home. 'I feel like murdering someone,' he announced loudly.

Karam Laczynska, head bound up in an ancient scarf, glanced down from her position on a ladder. 'Shut up and paint.' She pointed towards Kevin's discarded roller and tray. 'I shall be in New York by the time you finish that wall. Then there's all your stencils.'

He slumped in a chair. 'You'd never believe an old woman capable of language like that. She sprayed it all over the stucco.'

'The outside needs repainting anyway. Now, get on with this awful green.'

Kevin continued furious. He drew up his legs and sat like a miniature Buddha, his slight frame curled tightly in Philip Pointer's enormous leather chair. 'She has to be dealt with,' he muttered darkly.

Karam wiped a bit of moss-coloured emulsion from the picture rail. 'She will be dealt with. April is up to something. She keeps walking round in circles and talking to herself. There is to be a meeting soon.'

'A meeting?'

Karam nodded. 'It's all top secret. We shall probably have to sign our names to some document.'

'Really?'

479

'Really. Couldn't you have chosen a pleasanter colour, Kevin? This is so depressing.' She, too, had been infuriated by the sight of Honoria's latest handiwork, but the days were spinning by, the decorating needed finishing, there was packing to do, her own house to sort out, the visit to Horsefield and—

'Honoria can't be stopped,' said Kevin.

'April believes that she can put Honoria in her place.'

'Six feet under?'

Karam loaded her brush. 'Hardly. April has trouble swatting wasps. But she feels she knows enough to call Honoria's bluff. There will be many witnesses at the dénouement, I expect, sufficient to scare even Honoria out of the district. Where's Peter? He's let this gloss run, you know.' She scraped at a blob of brilliant white. 'Can't get the staff these days,' she grumbled amiably.

'Everyone's gone out,' replied Kevin. 'It seems all three of my guests are required just to carry home a few gallons of exterior paint.' He paused. 'I bet she'll spray it again when we've gone over her naughty words.'

'Security camera,' said Karam. 'We've got one at home.' She rested for a moment. 'Unless Papa's been at it with his screwdrivers. Still, even a dummy camera should suffice. Take heart.'

He took heart, stood up and resumed painting. 'Karam?'

'What?'

'What does April know? Is she going to say something—?' He laid down his roller. 'Is she going to denounce the old bag after the play? In the church hall? In front of a whole audience?'

Karam considered the question. 'Well,' she began, thoughts consolidating before she carried on, 'I know that the play's been altered since Hyacinth's death. Alice survives, outlives Amelia. Now, if Alice is supposed to be Hyacinth, then if Amelia is Honoria, and if—'

'If I'm a monkey's uncle,' interrupted Kevin. 'Remember, I'm taking over your job as set manager, not Philip's as director. Say it plainly, Karam. Pretend I know nothing.' Which was, he thought, precisely the case.

'There are some digs in the play, some bits which might just get on Honoria's nerves.'

'If she has any.'

'Quite. But this meeting is a separate issue, I think. I get the distinct impression that Honoria's past has been rather murky. My guess is that Hyacinth told April some nasty stuff and that April has got past the point of no return in the patience department. Beans will be spilt. So get on with your painting and forget it all for now.'

Kevin painted. He wanted to dash across the road and batter Honoria's door down. He felt like kicking her, kicking her again, then strangling her. The word QUEER was spread right across his front door. QUEER? She was the queer one, the one who spread gloom and fear wherever she went, the one who—

'Kevin?'

'Yes?'

'Did you want a green sofa? The dust sheet has slipped.'

He slowed down. 'The furniture's leather,' he

replied. 'The paint will come off when it's dry.'

'Good. Stop thinking about her. Just do the job.'

'Right.' He wasn't sure about the colour any more, wasn't sure about much. But he hoped with all his heart that April Nugent was about to play a strong hand. Moss green would do for now. And Honoria West had to go.

Twenty-six

Sebastian grabbed Karam's arm and pushed her without ceremony into the coal shed. 'Sit,' he ordered. 'Where have you been?'

'Painting walls a particularly nasty green,' she answered, tossing her crash helmet on to a beer crate. Sebastian was in an odd frame of mind, she decided. In fact, he looked slightly unhinged, all tousled hair and raised eyebrows. For a man supposedly immersed in the glories of art in its various forms, he seemed suddenly earthbound and harassed. 'I know I'm a bit late, and I'm sorry,' she concluded lamely.

Perching on the edge of an old garden bench, Karam stared up at her sibling's outline. Framed in the doorway, with the light behind him, he loomed even larger than he actually was. 'Where's Yvonne?' she asked.

He drew a hand through locks that already needed a good combing. 'I've camera and sound people waiting for a picnic lunch to begin,' he said hurriedly. 'They and I have a job to do, once April gets here. There's no time for all your clever gibes, Miss Perfect. So. Come on, out with it.'

Karam shrugged. 'If you'll tell me what to say, I'll say it. Give me a clue. Pretend we're on *Arts Forum* and deliver one of your leading questions.'

He looked up at the ceiling, cursed under his breath, then awarded his full attention to the leather-clad vision on the bench. She had travelled alone on the dreaded motorbike. He wondered obliquely whether she would go the whole hog and get tattooed. 'Yvonne is preparing the picnic,' he answered belatedly. 'Papa is having a nervous breakdown near the fridge, Dolly is chain-smoking in the kitchen, that new Mr McWhatever is wielding a scythe, and—'

'And you have kidnapped your sister.'

Sebastian inhaled deeply. He felt like hugging her, slapping her, shouting at her. But he kept his tone under strict control. 'Why didn't you tell me?'

Karam leaned back and studied a mound of coal. 'To what are you referring, sir?'

'To Yvonne, of course.'

'Ah.' There was enough coal stored in this shed to fire the *Flying Scotsman* from here to eternity. 'Yvonne.'

He waited, grew impatient. 'I can understand her,' he said. 'She was acting out of some kind of loyalty to you. But I'm your brother, your kin – and you must have noticed—'

'I noticed,' she replied, her tone quiet but firm. 'Yvonne imagined that you resented her, but I knew the real truth of the matter, Seb.' She paused. 'You resented me. You saw me as the obstacle in your path. But what does it matter

484

now? Why start pulling the scabs off? Leave well alone.'

His jaw hung for a split second. 'You allowed me to think that she was a lesbian, that I had no chance with her. That was so, so cruel.'

Karam stood up. 'Was it? Was what I did – or didn't do – really bad? Think about it. You've been up to your armpits in attractive women since before you started to shave. Girls hung around you like a cloud of flies near a midden. Never once have you fallen in love. We were beginning to have visions of you going through life as the eternal bachelor, all Pot Noodles and instant mash. Then, out of the blue, it happened. I saw it, I was there.'

'Yes, yes, you were.' His temper simmered.

'Don't glower at me, Sebastian Laczynski. Remember, I'm the one who bathed your cut knees and took the rap every time you messed about with Papa's stuff. You played with dynamite quite literally in the old days.' She took a step nearer to him. 'After our mother died, we had just each other. The result is that I understand you better than anyone else in this world ever could. Believe me, I knew what I was about.'

'That is so reassuring.'

'Sarcasm doesn't suit you.' She placed a hand on each of his shoulders. 'The imagined barrier was huge, Seb. You thought she was my lover, yet your instincts drew you towards her. I knew you really loved her when you hung on in there.'

'I see. Some sort of test, was it?' His fury ebbed away on a sigh. There had been no malice, then. How could he have imagined that his sister was capable of causing such distress?

Karam continued, 'At first I wondered if Yvonne was the apple you couldn't quite reach, suspected that the attraction might have been seated in the idea that she was unattainable. Were you still keeping yourself safe? If you weren't playing safe, how many Herculean labours were you willing to perform in order to secure her? Well, you proved yourself.'

'Did I? And were you sure of her response?'

She grinned at him. 'Absolutely. She couldn't even look at you. Every time you came into the room, she blushed and started dropping things. Had I not been infatuated with her at the time, I'd have been giggling. It was so sweet, so juvenile. I'm happy for you, and I mean that. Yvonne was not for me.'

He drew her close. 'Oh, Karam, it was like a sledgehammer. And, as you've told me so often, it hit me when I was least expecting it. Then I worried about your feelings because I realized that you were very much in love. But nothing could have stopped me. I was like a bus without brakes—'

'On a winding road in a very hot country, sheer drops all round you, no safety-net.'

He breathed in the scent of his beloved sister's hair. 'You've been there.'

'Oh, yes. My passport's been stamped many times.' She pulled herself away. 'Yvonne has loved you for ages. Of course, losing the baby, ending her marriage – those things clouded her thinking. But when you two were together in my kitchen the air was electric. You could have run Blackpool illuminations on the atmosphere.' She smoothed tumbling curls from his forehead. 'You will marry, her, I suppose.'

'If she'll have me.'

'Of course she will. She'd be a damned fool to refuse you.' Karam walked towards the door. 'Just one point on the subject of weddings, Seb.'

'Yes?'

'If she wants bridesmaids, I refuse to walk up the aisle looking like a pink meringue.'

'OK,' he replied. 'What will you wear?'

She looked down at her leather jacket and trousers. 'A compromise,' she said eventually. 'Life is full of those, isn't it?'

He swallowed. 'I don't half love you, sis. Nobody could have had a better sister. If I've hurt you, I'm very sorry.'

'As I've already told you, she wasn't for me. Don't worry, I always get by.'

Sebastian lingered in the doorway while his sister walked away, crash helmet swinging from a hand, steps firm but light. She was such a positive person, such an ambitious woman, too. Karam Laczynska would get where she was going. Although she was not particularly hard, there was a spine of pure steel under the soft exterior. With or without passengers, she would make her way. For a moment, he wished he owned her confidence. But, no, he begrudged her nothing.

He closed the decaying door of the coal shed and wandered off to look for the rest of the party. This was going to be a great day, the first of many.

Twenty-seven

London had proved disappointing. It retained its vibrance, continued to embrace many influential people, was the most suitable place in Britain for a writer to live. Honoria had been spoilt by her publishing house. She had breakfasted with her publicity girl, had lunched with her editor, had enjoyed a champagne reception at a very up-market hotel. She had also spent weeks investigating the housing market and was not pleased by her discoveries. The capital was so expensive that a flea would have needed a mortgage to secure a foothold in a matchbox.

She was perplexed. If she sold most stocks, decimated her bank accounts and disposed of her flat, she might have afforded a claustrophobic, two-bedroomed 'bijou' residence on the fringes of Chelsea and Kensington. Such drastic fiscal transactions would have left her a moderate nest egg, but she had no idea how she would fare as a writer. Poverty was a terrifying concept. Miss Honoria West had no intention of starving in a garret for the sake of her art. If writing would not keep her . . . The prospect was awesome.

She sat at her dining-table and doodled on a pad. 'I am supposed to be writing,' she announced to the teapot. One book was no good: if she was going to make it, she had to carry on with a second novel. Where, though? Here? No, no, she had to get away. Perhaps she should try the Home Counties . . .

Oh, what a nuisance. She wanted London, wanted her own home there, at the centre of everything, just a stride from her agent's place, a few miles from her publisher's offices. There was so much going on, and she wanted to miss none of it. But Honoria was unwilling to rent. Renting was for those who voted Labour and depended on handouts. Rent was dead money.

She had searched and searched. Even Islington had come up in the world, was populated by TV stars and suchlike, a select group whose members pretended not to be select, choosing instead to wear old jumpers and jeans instead of dressing to suit their status. These tiresome young folk stuck rigidly to instant coffee and Sainsbury's hock. Even had she been able to afford it, Honoria would not have chosen to live amongst such arrant inverted snobbery. For a multiplicity of reasons, London seemed unreachable.

She chomped on a stick of celery and wondered about her next piece of work. There was nothing in her head. Serendipity had committed suicide very gracefully, and the thought of dredging up another worthy woman was rather frightening. Was she going to be a one-book wonder, a here-today-gone-tomorrow author? She needed a move, needed to get away from the *nouveau-riche* mentality with which she considered herself surrounded. Perhaps she would never fit in anywhere. Until now, fitting in had never been important. She suddenly wanted to live among her own kind, people who made their way by using brains and imagination.

Walking to the window, she glanced out at the dreary prospect. That silly man across the road was tiptoeing through his tulips. This time, his clothing was relatively quiet, burgundy sweater, faded jeans, black trainers, hair tied back in a silly, girlish pony-tail. He had taken over as stage manager for the STADS, had replaced the famous Karam Laczynska. In just under a year, Karam had become a global name, both as a painter and as an expert in art acquisitions for all those vulgar Americans who wanted to hang some culture on a living-room wall.

The doctor had gone to Manchester. Once divorced, he had married someone from the police force and had moved to pastures new. His ex-wife was now Mrs Sebastian Laczynski. Yvonne Benson had landed on her feet, all right. She was enjoying the good life without having to work for it. As for April Nugent – three radio plays in one year, a television series due to start filming in the autumn. Sometimes Honoria's palms itched when she thought about April, as if her hands had decided to wipe the woman out, as if a weapon was just a fraction of a centimetre out of reach.

Kevin Brooks was looking remarkably well for someone with an immunity problem. As for his lodgers – what a motley crew, long hair on one of them, another with a shaved head and earrings in nose, eyebrow, lip, tongue. They all wanted shooting. 'Why can't people take pride in themselves?' she mumbled. 'Society is crumbling, no standards any more.'

She sat down. The next book would be called *Purity*. Now, that was a good name for a central character, especially one as impure as Honoria intended to invent. Yes. She would go to Southport again, might sit on one of the Lord Street benches until Purity walked by. Camera, car keys, purse. It was time to begin again.

April was having a lazy morning. The year had whizzed by, punctuated by Karam's departure, Yvonne and Sebastian's register-office wedding, continuing rewrites of *Monday's Child*, another spate of letters from Honoria West. Now published and hovering on the brink of fame, Honoria was campaigning to be rid of Kevin and his household. She no longer stooped to aerosol sprays, preferring instead to complain to the council about noise pollution, untidy gardens and anything else she could hang her hat on. And she showed few signs of moving away from the area.

April's day had dawned with birdsong, a bright blue sky and a left leg that was almost her own. It was the anniversary of her birth, and a full year had passed since Mark Nugent's re-entry into her schedule. 'You'll have to change that new aftershave,' came her sharp greeting as he opened the bedroom door. They had occupied the same room for several months now. He was older, wiser, gentler, happier. And she had almost forgotten the original game, could scarcely remember the words they had used long ago, when they had been young in hope and in love. Everything improved with practice, she reassured herself inwardly. As long as he changed his aftershave.

With a single red rose grasped between his teeth, Mark found himself at a slight disadvantage in the speech department. His heart was all but bursting with love and gratitude. The tousled, auburn-haired and rather unsteady moppet in the bed was his once more. But he would have to behave himself this time: fewer nights out with the lads, no spending sprees, no taking unfair advantage.

'Good morning,' she said belatedly.

He spat the rose on to the bed. 'Happy birthday, shut up about aftershaves and eat your breakfast.'

April studied the feast of incinerated toast, spilt milk and watery marmalade. 'My cup runneth over,' she remarked drily.

'Well, it's playtime, isn't it? Celebration time.' He dumped the tray on a table. 'So be cheerful. Think about tonight, your final moment of triumph.'

'*Monday's Child* will be over,' she mused. 'Thank God.' She turned over a slice of milk-drenched toast. This was to be the last night, the final curtain and the true, long-awaited telling of the tale.

'The daft beggars across the road are having a bit of bother,' said Mark. He was referring to the visitors at Jasmine Cottage, now the home of Sebastian and Yvonne. Yorkshire folk had arrived on the previous evening. Mark continued, 'That old chap with fingers missing is mending their lawnmower. Yvonne says good morning, happy birthday, and can you do something about her father-in-law? He's ruined a lot of stuff, apparently. Tried to make the dishwasher more efficient, so it doesn't work at all now.'

April nodded, poured milk into her cup and swallowed the day's first lot of tablets. Stefan was in residence across the way. Was Blundellsands ready for the old devil's particular brand of eccentricity? She rattled her prescribed medication. 'Did you know that most of these medicines are prescribed to fight each other? Stomach pills to deal with the anti-inflammatories, diuretics to drain away the water retained by the red ones, which, in turn, disguise the effects of the purple torpedoes? Mind, it all makes for a colourful life. It's not everybody gets a chance to swallow a rainbow three times a day.'

He smiled. If she threw him out again, he wouldn't go. 'I never stopped loving you,' he said, before a sob threatened to undermine him completely.

'Really? Then what was Mrs Blimp? An interval? An attack of hiccups? A pause for thought?'

'A mistake.'

'Oh, that's all right, then.' She munched thoughtfully for a few seconds. 'Have I put everyone in the picture, Mark?'

He sat on the edge of the bed. 'Everyone who needed forewarning was at the meeting last June. Leo, Hilda, the Laczynskis, Philip's little buddy . . . and the rest.'

'Am I doing the right thing, Mark?'

'Of course you are. It's all set.'

'I feel . . . cruel.'

Mark sniffed. 'Huh. You feel cruel? You? What about poor Philip Pointer? All those letters, Leo's chapel, Hyacinth, their father. Look, think about the horse that had to be shot. You love horses.'

April gave him a withering glance. 'Are you saying that I put animals before people?'

'No, but I—'

'I know. I'm the only one who can chase her out of here.' She sighed. 'Three acts to get through first, too. And I've already done two nights. It's exhausting. And while I'm doing it, I'm thinking, Who wrote this flaming rubbish? As Alice, I have to sit through the lot, watch my own life and do the commentary.' She decided to stop moaning. 'Never mind, soon be over, eh?' She ate another mouthful of soggy toast. 'Sorry. Sometimes I get sick and tired of being sick and tired.'

'I know, love.' Mark walked to the window and gazed out at his wife's animal sanctuary. Often, he wondered what the hell he'd been thinking of when he'd left April for someone as interesting as a pile of wet washing. He had never treated April well, had perhaps been envious of her abilities. And he had spent her earnings without thought or shame. 'I don't want anything from you,' he muttered now.

'Just as well, because you'll get nothing.'

'Except love. I'd like some of that,' he said wistfully.

A spoon clattered. 'There'll be no more of anything until you change your aftershave. What is it?'

He shrugged. 'Something in a green bottle.'

'Then hang it up with the other nine and let them all accidentally fall.' She drank tea and

494

studied the back of his head. He was good with animals – well, except llamas. 'I do love you,' she informed him. 'But I am keeping my distance in the cerebral department.' She glanced at the clock. 'My getter-upper will be here shortly.' April was now the proud employer of a woman who showered and dressed her each day.

'Love isn't cerebral,' he stated.

He was right, of course. 'Bugger off, Mark.'

He buggered off, paused in the doorway. 'For your birthday, I've enrolled you in line-dancing classes.'

April roared with laughter. 'Well done.' His sense of humour was returning, she thought happily. She had married him because of his wit.

Mark closed the door, opened it again. 'Aromatherapy, actually.' A pillow flew through the air, so he shut the door firmly and wandered off to feed dogs. She was so alive, he thought, as he walked downstairs to be greeted by cats and parrot. Multiple sclerosis might have depleted April's body, yet her mind remained razor sharp, her silliness intact.

April closed her eyes and leant back against the headboard. A longer than long, busy day stretched out before her. Yvonne and Sebastian were to have their civil marriage blessed at lunchtime. After several months abroad, Karam had returned for the ceremony and for the long-awaited play. Karam Laczynska, toast of the international well-to-do, the glorious and the famous, had dragged across the Atlantic a tall blonde with a rose tattoo just above the right ankle, a silver sleeper through an eyebrow and a penchant for black nail varnish.

This extraordinarily beautiful import sported a crew-cut that managed to look damp at all times, and a smile as bright as this lovely spring morning.

'I suppose I've taken long enough,' mumbled April to herself. 'It has to be done before Honoria goes completely insane.' She looked up at the ceiling. 'Well, PP, the play might be a year or two late, but here goes nothing.' She frowned. 'I won't be sticking strictly to the script tonight, Philip. Forgive me.' She cleared her throat. 'And then, of course, there's the bit afterwards.' Could she really do it? Could she stand there and tear Honoria West limb from limb in front of all those at the last-night party? 'Hatred is a sin,' she murmured, 'but I've been driven to it.'

The getter-upper came in. 'Nice day for it,' she said vaguely.

'Give it time,' answered April. Tonight promised to be extremely interesting . . .

Sebastian lingered at the bedroom window, his eyes fixed on his father. Stefan sat on a plastic chair, pieces of lawnmower strewn about his feet. 'Another consumer durable ruined,' Sebastian remarked to himself. Dolly Isherwood tottered into the garden, her hair completely obscured by plastic curlers in orange, pink and blue. In her wake walked Sally Houghton, landlady of the inn where Yvonne had lost her baby. The management of Lord Laczynski took two people now, it seemed.

'Hiya, bro.'

Sebastian swung round. 'Karam. Are you alone?' He found his sister's new girlfriend rather awesome. 'Where is she?'

Karam raised a shoulder. 'She'll be messing about with car engines somewhere.' She laughed. 'No. Seriously, Melinda's an expert beautician, hairdresser and makeup lady, much in demand in Hollywood and on Broadway. She's doing your wife's hair as we speak.'

Sebastian gasped. 'Really? Are we talking about the same woman – your new Melinda? The Yank with the shorn head and more piercings than our kitchen colander? What would she know about hairdressing and so forth?'

Karam shrugged. 'She's experienced in hair. She used to have some herself.'

'But—'

Karam punched him. 'Listen, you, she's done Julia Roberts, Jodie Foster, Whoopi Goldberg, that woman with the big doo-dahs – country singer, very large hair—'

'Done them? *Done* them?'

'Their hair and makeup.'

'Ah.' He relaxed until a thought hit home. 'Have you seen Whoopi Goldberg's hair?'

Karam jumped up. 'Yes. Try not to worry, dear. Yvonne will look delicious with dreadlocks.'

Alone again, he smiled to himself. Karam, his dearly loved sister, was happy. Above all things, Sebastian needed Karam to be content. He had married Yvonne as soon as her divorce had been finalized. Neither of them had wanted to wait. His grin broadened. He had never imagined such joy, such fun. Yvonne, down-to-earth, pragmatic, sensible, was capable of great daftness. He loved her so much that words could not encompass his feelings. Yvonne had managed, though. 'It hurts,' she had said more than once. 'It's wonderful, but exquisitely painful.' That summed up true love, he decided.

So, because the ceremony had been performed during Karam's absence, a church blessing was scheduled for today. Karam had demanded it. Such a generous, open-minded, big-hearted woman had to be a one-off. 'Let me see you both dressed up,' she had begged long-distance. 'And please allow God in on it. One of us ought to be properly done in church. That can never happen to me.'

He blinked. There were lesbian 'marriages', but he knew what Karam meant. And what a wonderful mother she would have made. Still, she could be a wonderful aunt instead.

He looked at the grey pin-stripe suit on its hanger, at a pristine white shirt folded on the bed next to a silk tie, grey socks, gold tie-pin and cufflinks. He had to be presentable today. As a putative expert and commentator on art in its several guises, Sebastian was newsworthy. There would be photographers, columnists, fans with Polaroids and autograph books, Granada TV, BBC Manchester, the inevitable clutch of hopefuls carrying examples of their work. Tonight, the happy band of reporters would be joined by critics, since April's rewrite of *Monday's Child* looked set to be a rip-roaring success. The whole business seemed to have come together under April's magic charm, because this was her day, her defining moment.

What a play *Monday's Child* had become, though. April – ignoring, as usual, what was smart, fashionable, or even acceptable – had gone completely OTT with the project. The level of audience participation went way beyond pantomime, since the gatherings in St Thomas's church hall were required to sing hymns and psalms during brides' progressions up the centre parting to the altar/stage, then while a coffin travelled to its bier behind a vestmented 'priest'. Such courage, April had, such disdain for correctness and criticism. To turn audience into congregation was no mean feat. And she had won, because the play would be in the West End within months.

He closed his eyes, leant back in the chair. Tomorrow, at nine in the morning, he and his wife would fly out of Manchester and into the welcoming arms of the Seychelles. Tonight, Yvonne was to make her final appearance in the play. After the last curtain, April would . . . April would do whatever she had planned.

'I don't want curls!' This muffled cry struggled through ancient plaster and tumbled into Sebastian's ears. He laughed. His wife didn't like curls, Big Macs, Mahler, garlic, Chris Evans, modern jazz, Woody Allen films. She loved mushy peas, Thora Hird, freesias, LeAnne Rimes, Mozart, old gravestones, windy days. 'And me,' he said firmly. 'She loves me.'

Outside, Dolly Isherwood was in a mood. 'Leave the bloody mower alone,' she spat at her employer. 'You're supposed to be getting ready.' She clouted Stefan's shoulder. 'In the house, get showered, shaved and dressed immediately. Your son's marriage is being blessed in ninety minutes. You are not turning up at that church with a

499

screwdriver and a can of WD 40. Don't bother arguing, else I'll cut your privileges off.' She stormed towards the house, curlers and pins bouncing from their moorings and landing on the grass.

Sebastian closed his eyes and called to mind his fragrant, lovely, frail mother. He could not remember her clearly, but he recalled the photographs of an English rose, blonde, happy-eyed, laughing, who had married a man more than twice her age. The old bugger had worn her out, had worn her down, yet she had loved him. Eastern Europeans were not without charisma, it seemed.

Papa was picking up mower parts when Sebastian opened his eyes. The old man looked up, grinning at his son.

Sebastian blinked away a tear. This second wedding was getting to him, he supposed, as it was a marker, a semi-colon on the pages of his own life. Father would not last for ever. Time, the unseen and often unheeded enemy, ticked on relentlessly. Even Lord Laczynski's brilliance could not disarm that particular bomb. As the pair stared at one another through the thin barrier of aged window glass, clocks seemed to stop for a breath or two. Frozen on the lower rungs of life's ladder, the younger man looked at his father, who, though positioned at ground level, had reached the higher steps, the dizzying zenith of weary age.

'Get dressed, boy,' shouted the peer. 'Had you forgotten that today is your blessing? And, oh, what a prize is Yvonne. You are lucky, so lucky.'

Sebastian realized that he had not been inhaling during those precious, timeless moments.

He knew that he would always envisage Stefan as he was today, dirty moleskins, open-necked shirt with its sleeves rolled, eyes crinkling against the morning light. This was Papa. Wedding photos would be taken, yet Sebastian's father would be remembered as he was now, oil-streaked, thin, henpecked and so delighted with life.

Oh, well. It was time to dress, time to turn the leaf and begin the next chapter.

After the second post had been delivered, Honoria West was walking on air. Her armada had docked at last, bringing with it the promise of exquisite recognition.

She smoothed the single page, read it yet again. Miss West was informed that she had been short-listed for the Carrington prize, a prestigious title awarded once a year to the best new thriller writer. *Serendipity* had paid off. 'Fifteen thousand for the winner, too,' she chortled. How much she would have to tell tonight. 'I never needed Hyacinth's help,' she reminded herself yet again. 'She wasn't a writer; she was a mere dabbler with little conviction and, therefore, no courage.'

It was one o'clock. In an hour, Sebastian Laczynski's marriage to Yvonne Benson was to be blessed. Yvonne Benson, a recycled lesbian, was about to be joined anew to the brother of her erstwhile lover. Compared to the ongoings hereabouts, *Serendipity*'s tale was almost tame.

Few had been invited to the actual ceremony, but there was to be a huge celebration following the last performance of April Nugent's play. An exciting thought struck, causing Honoria to sink into an armchair. There would be press. She could steal a small corner of limelight intended for April Nugent and Sebastian Laczynski, would be able to show this precious letter to critics, to photographers. And six members of the bridge club would be present, so Honoria would have her own audience within the larger gathering.

Standing at the mirror, Honoria smoothed firming cream across a slackening jawline. She smiled in a half-hearted effort to improve the reflected face. It was time to give everyone the benefit of the doubt, to be gracious in triumph. All the nasty business of the past was forgotten, surely? People talked to her these days, greeted her in the street. Even the stupid, diseased powder-puffs across the way had stopped goading her recently. There could not possibly be any ulterior motive in the sudden switch to polite acceptance. People forgot; time healed.

But time itself was working its way across Honoria's skin, leaving thin but noticeable tracks. Her vacillations between strict dieting and self-indulgence were doing little to improve her appearance. At present, she was in control of her eating, but small pockets of cellulite alternated with furrows that deepened each time she lost weight. 'Keep a grip,' she ordered her reflection. 'The world is at your feet. Where it belongs.'

April was pretty in apple green. The silk suit, which had cost an arm and both legs – one of which had begun to wander off on its own again – consisted of a long, flowing skirt and a loose jacket over a blouse in muted shades of green and rust.

She had chosen a broad-brimmed hat, rust-coloured shoes and bag. 'If I sit still, I look normal,' she told Karam. 'How's the bride?'

'Not half as pretty as you,' replied Karam.

'She's gorgeous.'

'Yes.'

April cleared her throat. 'Are you coping with this?'

'Yes, yes, yes, yes,' cried Karam. 'She's gone and I'm getting on with my life.'

'And Melinda?'

Karam tapped the side of her nose. 'No more questions.'

April reached for her stick and stood up. 'I thought Yvonne was the love of your life. I've been worried about you.'

'Watch my lips, April. Yvonne is doing the right thing and I'm over it, I'm recovered, I'm enjoying myself.' She paused. 'Mind, Yvonne's being very brave, taking my brother on. Sebastian is—'

'Weird,' interrupted April resignedly. 'Leave him alone. He has his own way of doing things.'

'Or of not doing them.' Karam studied her old friend. April seemed tired, distracted. 'You're still following your plan this evening, then?'

April nodded.

'Well, stop mithering about me, dear heart. You have quite enough on your plate without worrying over an old dyke. And I'm ecstatic, I promise. America is so wonderful, so big and crazy – I should have emigrated years ago. They're generous and they love success and there's a McDonald's on every street.'

'Good.'

Karam reached out her long, elegant arms and drew April close. 'I can't even imagine what you must have gone through, love. Especially after your mother died. Finding out all that and— Oh, it scarcely bears thinking about.'

April sighed. 'It was hard. She never deserved senile dementia. I suppose no one deserves to be locked inside himself or herself for a dozen years. She scarcely recognized me for the last five, you know. When I look back, she was never right after my dad's death. It was as if she gave up trying. And now, with hindsight, I wonder whether God might have handed out one of His teaspoonfuls of kindness, because Mother was saved some pain.' The pain had been contained in those tins, had been packed away with photographs and mementoes.

'A complicated business,' muttered Karam. 'And that's as great an example of understatement as I have ever produced.'

They separated and sat in a pair of armchairs.

'Are you up to it?' Karam asked.

'No, but it has to be done.' April adjusted her hat. 'This is a happy day, my dear, good friend. It's my birthday and it's the celebration of two splendid young people coming together in the sight of God.'

'And Honoria West's day of reckoning.'

April shrugged. 'Perhaps. But she does have a habit of rising from the ashes like some evil phoenix.'

'Not this time,' promised Karam. 'This time she will be well and truly finished.'

April blinked and fixed her gaze on the middle distance. 'It's all so unlike me,' she whispered. 'I have never hated anyone.'

'And now?'

The playwright lifted her head. 'She deserves what's coming to her.'

'At last you're talking sense. And remember, you're doing this for everyone, for a whole community.'

'And for the dead.' April breathed deeply. 'Come on, let's collect the populace together. It's time for Yvonne to make an honest man of your brother.' She paused for thought. 'I hope Stef behaves himself.'

'He will,' vowed Karam. 'I've programmed Dolly in killer mode. One false move and he's a dead peer.'

Twenty-eight

The last night of *Monday's Child* was over. In the new version of the play, Alice, Amelia and Annie had all been married. Alice/Hyacinth had survived, while Amelia, the Honoria-type character, had been punished for doing her worst. April Nugent, arms stuffed with flowers, led the cast out for another bow. She wondered whether Honoria had received the tiny messages contained within the script. Probably not. Rumour had it that Honoria was over the moon after being nominated for the Carrington. Ah, well, let the woman have her moment.

The last-night audience was always special, but this one had risen to its many feet so noisily that April had begun to fear for the stability of the church hall's roof. The stage, too, was packed. With three Alices, three Amelias, three Annies and sundry other characters, curtain calls were quite a crush.

More and more flowers arrived, some tossed singly, some in beribboned bunches, every fragrant offering accompanied by applause and whistling. After a full five minutes, the curtains closed, leaving the playwright alone on the apron, wheelchair ready and parked nearby in case she needed to rest. She was strangely calm. With the grey wig and painted, aged face, she looked every inch the eighty-year-old Alice, the *Monday's Child* whose sell-by date was long past. Yet April stood firm and solid, no symptom of her disease on show, no tremor, no twitch.

Smiling, she thanked the gathering before paying particular attention to the press, members of which august body were gathered at the back, pens poised, cameras ready. The press had usually been kind to her; now she intended to repay their generosity, though many would be disappointed, she thought, as a press release was never as exciting as an exclusive. 'You wanted my life story,' she told them. 'It will be available tomorrow. I can assure you that it will curl your hair, which should save on the price of perms for the foreseeable future. First, though, I must thank you all once again for your support over the years. I wish you good night and a safe journey home.'

She stepped back through the curtains and into the waiting arms of Yvonne. 'Whoa,' she muttered, as the familiar problems struck without warning. Her legs ached, while every organ in her body ticked and trembled. 'Ants in the stomach again,' she said. The headache she did not mention. The pain in her temples was beginning to spill down her face, producing the neuralgic agony so often visited on sufferers of multiple sclerosis. She had no time for MS just now. She was the one. Only April had the power to chase Honoria away from

Kevin, from Yvonne and Sebastian, from herself.

'Are you well enough to face the monster?' Yvonne asked.

'Yes, of course I am. You were wonderful, incidentally. You should go to drama school.'

Yvonne laughed. 'Oh, yes? Isn't life hard enough, April? Sebastian comes and goes enough for both of us. Anyway, I like being here for him.'

'You're happy.' This was not a question.

'Blissful. Terrifyingly so. When life is so perfect, you just don't trust it, do you? I have to keep pinching myself and saying, "Yes, he will come home and, no, he won't become a grouch." Am I silly?'

'No, you're deliriously, annoyingly joyful. Come on, we have to beard the lioness. Did you notice her nipping off towards the press folk? She's over the moon about her nomination.'

Yvonne led April towards the dressing rooms. 'Remember how angry you were when you first found the truth. Hang on to that.'

April nodded. 'I'm still angry,' she said softly. 'I never stopped being angry. It's just so hard – it leaves me drained.'

Karam, waiting in the dressing-room doorway, heard and understood. It had become plain over the years that stress contributed to April's discomfort, often acting as trigger to an attack. 'Four hundred miles,' she said to herself.

'What?'

'The nervous system of the average human is four hundred miles long.'

April grimaced. 'And mine's mostly roadworks, pneumatic drills, steamrollers, a few JCBs doing their excavations.' She straightened. 'Let me get this rubbish off my face, then we'll go back and eat Dolly's buffet.' She smiled at Yvonne. 'Our houses have been wall-to-wall sausage rolls since yesterday, haven't they? So much to celebrate, girls, what with the play over, Yvonne properly married, Stefan behaving himself for eight hours.' On this optimistic note, she went to clear her face of makeup.

In the mirror, Alice slowly disappeared, all remnants of the old lady resting in balls of cotton wool on the table. April looked at herself, skin pink from exertion, eyes tired, the lids darkening slightly, pain sparking in the irises. 'Honoria will never give up,' she reminded her reflection. 'We both know that. Remember Hyacinth trying to dig up reasons, excuses for Honoria's behaviour? She'd been a middle child, her mother had been terribly ill, she'd been ignored? Even Hyacinth found all that hard to swallow. Honoria enjoys her wickedness a little too well for anyone's good. So it's up to thee and me.'

The 'thee' smiled at the 'me', and vice versa. April undressed and pulled on a rather smart kaftan in blue and green shot silk from Singapore, a gift from Karam, who had travelled rather a lot of late. She combed her hair, applied a little foundation, a touch of mascara, some lipstick. Before getting up to leave, she winked at her other half. 'Break a leg,' they mouthed at each other.

Mark came in. 'Ready for off?'

Ah, here came the other other half. 'Yes.'

He stood beside her, obviously summing up what he saw. The neuralgia was back. It showed in her eyes, in a slightly turned-down lower lip, in her voice. 'Listen, if it's going to be too much for you, I'll do it.'

'Really?'

'Of course I will. What are husbands for?' He held out an arm for support. 'You're not blubbering, are you?'

'No,' she lied, determined not to cry.

'Right, I'm doing the reading of the Riot Act. You've had enough, love, writing the play, starring in it, doing your radio stuff and now this TV contract. Leave Honoria to me.'

April almost fell against him. He really, truly cared about her. 'Thank you,' she replied, pulling herself up physically and mentally. 'Just be there, Mark. Though only I can do what must be done – you know that. But if I stumble—'

'You can fall on me, our kid. I'll always be here.'

Yes, he would always be there. Knowing that, she could be strong. Knowing that, she could face the demon.

The party had spilled into both houses. April, resolved to remain sober, polished off two glasses of champagne, then stuck rigidly to orange juice. Mark stuck rigidly to her, though he did indulge his partiality for lager and the odd shot of Irish whiskey whenever he passed the drinks table. While most of the younger folk had skipped across to Jasmine Cottage, the older ones remained in April's house, clutches of middle-aged people talking seriously about the Arts Council's level of investment in Liverpool theatre, about golf, the weather, politics.

As the evening wore on, conversations became louder, slightly muddled, the level of sense diminishing in accordance with disappearing stocks of alcohol. April spotted Honoria talking to a nice-looking widower from Thornton. Soon, the smile would be wiped from the woman's over-powdered face.

Across the road, in the attic that had once served as Karam's studio, the main cast of tonight's second drama was gathering. Leo, Hilda, Kevin Brooks, David Benson and his new wife were already *in situ*, while Sebastian had gone to April's house to fetch Honoria. As the presenter of an arts programme, he was by far the best bait. Karam's Melinda was to hold the fort at the bottom of the attic stairway, her brief being to keep all outsiders away from the studio.

Karam and Yvonne entered together. 'Why is David's Paula here?' whispered Karam.

'She's family and she's police,' replied Yvonne. She and David got along so much better these days. As brother and sister, they were perfect. She waved at him, smiled at Paula. 'Paula is one of our aces. However old the crimes, they can still merit investigation.'

'Old crimes? What are Honoria's——?'

'Shush. Wait and see.' Yvonne wandered off to talk to her ex-husband and his second wife, a very pretty, tall, elegant lady with dark hair and deep-set violet eyes.

Karam sat down, closed her eyes and breathed deeply, using yoga methods she had practised for years to settle her racing imagination. Old crimes? April had hinted at the Wests' dark past, had occasionally let fall a crumb from the table she had shared with Hyacinth. Now the tablecloth was to be shaken here, in this very room.

Yvonne, having greeted David, his wife, Kevin and the rest, perched on the edge of a wicker seat, hands gripping each other to prevent her from biting her nails. The waiting was awful, terrifying. Then she thought about Sebastian and smiled. As long as he was within calling distance, nothing could frighten her. The only alarming thing about Sebastian was how close she had come to not knowing him at all. The idea of a life without him was unthinkable.

Karam emerged from her reverie and placed herself next to Yvonne. 'How much is there?' she whispered. 'How much is there to tell?'

'Enough,' Yvonne replied. 'April will say insufficient for slander action, I'm sure. But the old witch won't dare sue, no matter what. She has far too much to lose. Remember, we have a police presence.'

Kevin Brooks, the new stage manager, tottered across the room. 'We didn't like the green,' he told Karam. He longed to talk about ordinary things, things unconnected to—

'What?'

'The paint,' he said patiently. 'We went over it with Wedgwood blue and a nice border.' He hesitated. 'I'm dreading this. Yet I can't wait for it to happen.'

They understood him. Tolerating Miss Honoria West had probably been a huge pain in Kevin's neck, but here came the pay-off. He removed his shoes and settled himself on the boards at Karam's feet. 'I hope April goes for the jugular,' he mumbled. Honoria had virtually murdered Kevin's buddy, and Kevin needed above all things to be a witness to the retribution.

Honoria entered, Sebastian on her heels. The moment she arrived, all mouths seemed to snap closed, while the temperature in the room appeared to plummet by several degrees. She turned as if intending to leave, but Sebastian loomed large against the closed door. 'Do find a seat,' he invited politely.

She walked tentatively towards the window, then placed herself in an old carver, handbag clutched on her knee like a shield. She saw her sister, that silly Leo chap, Dr Benson, someone who was probably his second wife, Yvonne, Karam, the dreadful Kevin. Sebastian Laczynski opened the door again. April, depending heavily on the support of Mark Nugent, entered the room. After staring at Honoria for what seemed like minutes, she sat on an easy chair. Mark joined Sebastian; they looked like a pair of sentries guarding the entrance to a monarch's castle.

Mark Nugent made eye-contact with his wife, smiled encouragingly, then offered a double thumbs-up sign. In his newly cleaned suit with one of April's birthday roses in a lapel, he felt very much the gentleman. He was proud of her, prouder of the verbal striptease to come than he was of *Monday's Child*. This was April's day, her privilege, the dénouement of her personal plot. For her own sake, and out of love for Hyacinth, April was about to lay her soul bare.

Seconds crept by. Cold fingers of anticipation

danced up and down Honoria's spinal column. Although she could not imagine what was about to happen, her senses were on raw alert. Why had she been brought here? There was no one she wished to talk to, no one with whom she would have chosen to spend time. Perhaps they were about to congratulate her on the shortlisting . . .

April took a deep breath. 'Most of us know why we're here,' she began, her eyes fixed on Honoria. 'Life has been rather less than pleasant of late. Some of us – most of us – have received nasty, unsigned letters. A few such items were sent to the authorities, too. In our midst, we have the person who penned those terrible things. Philip Pointer hanged himself after receiving one of them.' She paused. 'I have always believed that a sender of anonymous letters is a coward.' Her eyes hardened. 'Why, Honoria?'

Honoria gulped into the heavy silence. 'I don't know what you mean.' The voice was high-pitched and uncertain.

'What about the graffiti on Kevin Brooks's house?' asked April.

'Nothing to do with me.'

April nodded slowly. 'Arson? A chapel, a farmhouse?'

After a weighty pause, the speaker took a sheet of paper from her pocket. She made much of unfolding and flattening it before placing it on her lap. 'Hyacinth told me so much about you, Honoria. The attempted rape was a fine piece of work. Do you recall that occasion, I wonder? You could not allow Hyacinth to be happy, so you trampled all over her, blackened her young man's reputation and separated her from him. Leo?'

Leo cleared his throat. 'I went abroad, made my fortune, came home, married Hilda.' He smiled at his wife. 'My house was burnt down last year, then a fire was set at the farmhouse where Hilda and I now live.'

'The West family's home,' explained April. 'The scene of many crimes.'

Honoria leapt to her feet.

'Stay where you are,' boomed Leo. 'Stay and listen.'

Almost mesmerized by the man's glare, Honoria sank back into the chair.

'When you were a child, you killed a child.' April's voice was very soft.

The whole room gasped, drawing in so much oxygen that the air seemed to become unnaturally thick. Karam stood up and opened a window, her body curving sideways as she passed Honoria's chair.

'After practising on animals first, of course,' continued April. 'That is quite common in cases such as this. You are a serial predator, Honoria. Dr Benson has looked you up in some of his medical books. Quite a phenomenon, as few such creatures are female. Yet you are not insane. We must conclude, then, that you are simply evil.'

'Preposterous,' gabbled Honoria.

'I agree.' April leant forward. 'Hyacinth found the plank of wood, you know, the weapon you used to kill your father. Afraid and hysterical, she tossed it into the well. She knew that your mother would never have coped with the facts. You murdered your own father.'

515

This was a tissue of lies, naturally. Honoria knew that all these people were out to get her. There had been some difficulties in the past, but her actions had always been perfectly justifiable. Misunderstood all her life, Miss Honoria West continued to be treated unfairly. She would not listen. She would shut down and concentrate on *Serendipity*, the prize she might win, the next book—

'You also tried to kill your mother by causing her to fall downstairs,' said April.

Honoria smiled. Yes, Purity would be the name of her second heroine.

'But arson was your favourite trick. Your father told Hyacinth everything, eventually. All about Brian Cullen, the headmaster, who perished in a fire. Your clothes stank of paraffin, Honoria. And your recent behaviour is enough to warrant arrest.' April turned her head. 'Isn't that right, Detective Constable Benson?'

Paula Benson nodded.

'And perhaps the well can be excavated?' April asked. 'Forensic science has come along in strides of late.'

'It's amazing what can be found – even after many years,' answered Paula. 'Of course, hand-writing is easily analysed. Then there's the fingerprint.'

The new voice brought Honoria's attention back to the here and now. Fingerprints? She had always worn gloves. 'Try proving all that rubbish,' she muttered. 'Nonsense.'

Paula Benson shivered. In her capacity as a CID officer, she had met some hard cases, but this one was a brilliant piece of nastiness. 'I am a member of the Manchester police force,' she said quietly.

Honoria stared levelly at this latest challenge.

Paula continued. 'At the back of the chapel, cans and cigarette packets were found. From a Cola can, the print of a boy was lifted. He was known to the Bolton police, but he did not fire that chapel, Miss West.'

Honoria shrugged. 'The can must have been planted, then.'

'Yes, it must have been,' replied Paula. 'Because when that fire was started, the lad was under arrest for mugging an old lady in Atherton. Atherton is several miles away from the arson.'

Feeling like a prisoner in the dock, Honoria was on the point of blurting out that the boy must have been there at some stage, since the can had been taken from a nearby bin. She must be careful, must tread softly. 'Are there not ways of delaying the start of a fire?' she asked, her tone cold and disinterested.

Paula nodded thoughtfully. 'It seems plain to me that you know a lot about fire-starting, Miss West. And, no, there was no evidence of any device. The arsonist simply lit up and ran.'

'Nothing to do with me,' answered Honoria.

'You were away from home at that time. You had been staying in Bolton.' Again, the well-trained officer felt a shudder in her bones. Like many members of the police force, Paula had developed a strange inner knowledge, a sixth sense that homed in on the guilty quite of its own accord. This creature was as black-hearted as original sin.

April took the reins again. 'You have no future,'

she told Honoria. 'Hyacinth signed a statement before she died. She begged me to use it only if and when your behaviour deteriorated. Hyacinth was worried for the rest of us. Your crimes are listed here in black and white, so numerous, too many to be ignored. No smoke without fire? How very appropriate that saying has become. We all need to be saved from your ruthlessness.'

'Especially you,' said Honoria clearly. 'Especially Hyacinth's very dear friend.' There was a muted note of triumph in the words.

'Yes.' April smiled grimly. 'Especially me.'

Honoria squirmed slightly. What did this dreadful April woman know? Not everything. Oh, no, she didn't know the best, the juiciest bit.

'Why do you keep hurting people?' April asked now.

A curtain fluttered in Honoria's brain, allowing her a glimpse of actions taken so long ago that they had lain dormant, forgotten almost. The child on the bridge, falling, drowning. Mother and Father plotting, saying things – nasty things. The well. Pushing, heaving, waiting for something to land at the bottom, in the mud.

'Hiding behind furniture was a favourite trick of yours. Hyacinth saw you once, warned your father, but it was too late for him, too late for a lot of people.'

Honoria jabbed the air with a finger. 'Be careful,' she warned. 'Don't go too far, April.'

'Too far? Too far? How much further is there to go? Patricide, infanticide, attempted matricide. There is hardly a crime left. You know it all, don't you, Honoria?' April waved the document. 'That

518

last big truth, the final secret you mentioned so often to your sisters. Well, I discovered the facts for myself a few months ago.'

Honoria swallowed painfully. She was hemmed in, could not possibly make her escape.

April carried on, this time addressing the whole company. 'After Honoria managed to separate Hyacinth from Leo, poor Hyacinth had a complete mental breakdown. She was sent away.'

Honoria half smiled.

'Honoria kept her ear to the ground, of course, was probably continuing to open letters, listen at doors and so on.' April swallowed. 'While she was ill, Hyacinth had a Caesarian section. She didn't even know that she was pregnant. It was explained away afterwards as an appendectomy.'

Honoria almost laughed.

April closed her eyes. For approximately sixty seconds, she remained silent. 'I was adopted by Enid and Bob Charnock,' she said eventually. 'It was a private arrangement, all very discreet, of course. Illegitimacy was quite a crime in those days.'

Honoria's grin had been replaced by a snarl.

'My mother told me early on that I was a special, chosen child. She offered several times to explain about my true beginnings, but I never needed to know. I was so happy. My parents were wonderful people, you see.' April's eyes were suddenly wide open. 'My father died quite young. Mum deteriorated over the last decade of her life. She was in a home and, although I visited her often, her mind was damaged by senile dementia, so my day-to-day life meant nothing to her. I used to talk to her about Hyacinth. But she seemed not to hear. Had she been in possession of her faculties, she might have enlightened me with regard to my dear friend.'

Honoria's breathing was suddenly rapid and audible.

'A biscuit tin held all I needed to know. Hyacinth West was my birth mother, so Honoria, who had kept in touch with my adopted mother, was my aunt.' April glared at Honoria. 'You told Mum that Hyacinth was crackers and that you would be my sole sensible relation in the event of Mum's death.' Another pause followed. 'If you were my sole relation, I'd be very poor indeed.'

Honoria stumbled to her feet. 'She promised me that she would never tell you. She promised to leave it to me, to—'

'To deny Hyacinth?' April leapt out of her chair. 'I sat in that room in your flat with my birth mother's corpse. You knew. You knew that my mother had just died.'

'Yes. I did know that.'

'You watched us together for years.'

'Indeed I did.'

'I lost two mothers.' April drew herself to full height. 'But remember this, Honoria. Hyacinth and I came together naturally, were drawn to one another. Really, you deprived us of nothing, because we were such close friends. I loved her and she loved me. It was an extraordinary relationship. In spite of you, we found more common ground than you could ever imagine.'

The two women stared into one another's eyes like contenders in a boxing ring. 'She never learnt who you really were,' snarled the older.

'She knows now.' April sighed. 'Where both my mothers are, everything is understood. You are the loser, not I. Tomorrow, this story will be in several newspapers. Eventually, you will be questioned. "What was your reason for withholding such information, Miss West?" You may win a prize, but you'll lose public sympathy.'

Honoria leapt forward, fingers curled like claws, but Yvonne and Karam dragged her back.

'You killed my grandfather,' said April. 'You may even have killed Hyacinth. I don't know what you said to Mum, whether you threatened to claim me, whether you frightened her. But, Honoria, look what I have gained.' She smiled. 'Leo is my father. I have a father and a lovely stepmother who is also my aunt Hilda.'

Honoria struggled to break free of restraining arms, but Sebastian came to the aid of his wife and his sister. He pushed the suddenly much older woman back into her chair. 'Stay,' he snapped, as if talking to a difficult dog.

Breathing was becoming difficult. To make a move towards freedom, Honoria would have been forced to squeeze past several angry people. The room was closing in on her. Panic rose, swelled up, engulfed her like a hot, wet blanket. Sweat poured down her face, her neck, her back.

'It's all about power, isn't it?' asked April. 'Absolute, corrupt power.'

Honoria's back was wet through, while her palms were so slick that she wiped them on the skirt of a Jaeger suit. This was a nightmare, surely? This was not supposed to happen, because she had

521

been shortlisted for— Anger joined despair and panic until all three emotions melded together into a curdled scream. She didn't know what to say, so she simply howled her distress. Hyacinth had been so damned stupid. Only a complete idiot could have mistaken a Caesarian section for a ruptured appendix. But Honoria could not explain, was unable to justify herself in the face of so much animosity. There were too many witnesses to April's testimony. And the other business – fires and so forth – there was a policewoman here and—

'Your sister was the best of women,' said April now, 'while you are the very worst.' She looked her adversary up and down. 'That's all,' she said. 'You may go now.'

Honoria picked up her handbag and staggered to the door.

Sebastian opened it. 'Watch your step,' he advised. 'Those stairs are dreadfully steep.'

'You did it,' Yvonne called to April, when the door was closed.

'Are you all right?' asked Karam.

Kevin fluttered across, tears lingering on disgracefully abundant lashes.

April managed a weak grin. 'Of course I'm all right. Except I'm starving and I'd kill for a glass of wine.' She stood up and embraced her friends, lifting her head and shouting upwards, 'See, Mothers? No wheelchair. God bless you both. Now I shall get stinking drunk and unmanageably relieved.' With these immortal words, April Nugent followed her left foot towards the stairs.

Before disappearing altogether, she looked over

her shoulder at Leo and Hilda. 'Come on, Dad,' she said, her tone steady. 'And Mum number three. Let's go and enjoy ourselves.'

Leo, his eyes moist, knew now that he had found the missing piece of his own jigsaw. He had a daughter, a wonderful, proud and talented daughter.

Twenty-nine

Honoria failed to notice that dawn was lightening the sky, pale colours extending from the east, graded blues, muted purples, a tinge of pink here and there. Nor did she hear the heralds chirruping and squawking in trees along the avenues, blackbirds, starlings, a few ringed doves surfacing to purr at the new day. Her sense of smell was affected, too, causing her not to react to acrid fumes that rose from vomit spilled down the front of her clothing.

At six in the morning, Honoria West was seated at the corner window, no binoculars, no *Woman's Own* to hand. Unaware of the ice in her stiffening limbs, she remained motionless, scarcely breathing, seldom blinking. Vaguely, she remembered a party, snatches of conversation, a handsome man, a terrible scene at the top of a house. Nothing was clear.

But, in another place inside her head, the senses worked on and she saw, heard and felt everything.

The lavatory stank. Whitewash in her hair. Ding dong bell, who's in the well? Not Pussy, that was certain. Who put the man in the well? Hyacinth's laugh, a light, tinkling sound, another little ding dong bell.

Looking after . . . children. Someone in hospital, bright faces around a farmhouse kitchen table . . . Father's in the well. Scones for tea, honey thick and yellow, sweet jam made at home, butter patted, scraped into curls to make it pretty. Who put him in the well?

Not me, no, no, never me.

Lawrence Beresford – Leo who? Chasing the wrong girl through cowslips and daisies. Buttercups golden, sky patchy blue, thin traces of cloud scudding, breeze fanning the watcher's cheek.

Stay low, stay low.

Behind the sofa, stay low.

Isobel West, conspirator, traitor. Thomas James West, another just the same. The accused. They cannot put me away. Hyacinth was the one who went, a child in her belly, brain on strike, no words, no more tinkling ding dong bell.

Another child, skinny and afraid, dripping nose, thin arms, a wild child. Hyacinth did poetry, made it rhyme. Was he a Kershaw? The scent of fear.

With that I shared human milk? Thickset woman, huge breasts, pillows on which I laid my head then, when I knew nothing, when my world had already been taken from me . . . On the bridge he hung, slimy boy, tight knuckles, bang, bang, you're dead.

Never tell, never say.

Thomas did not love me. He went into the well. She mourned and could not be happy again.

Isobel. Iso-bell. Another bell. Hyacinth fragrant, Hilda pretty. A coffin in the small drawing room, his wife so white, so drawn.

Running, running, praising the sky, reaching for paradise, finding it in his arms. They made a baby. She lay down with him; I was not invited.

Isobel crying softly, secretly into the telephone. A little girl. She will live in Chester, all done tidily, quietly, no fuss, letters to open, seal them up, seal my lips, never say, never tell.

How loved. Standing across the road I watched, a park close by, a church, shops and school down the lane in a precious, walled city, a Roman place. April. Skipping along between a mother and a father, all to herself, no one to share, no one to take away the love. Hyacinth's daughter, straight and strong, golden hair that would darken over years, limbs that would fail.

Don't tell.

Laughter again. Oh, smell the new bread carried in by April. It is still warm, so crusty, wholemeal, seeds and grains pressed into its skin. A piece for me. But I am left to break my bread alone. I am not welcome in their company, am banished from their society. They write, paint pictures. I am trapped here. Why? Why do I fear the outside? Do I tremble because of what I might do?

I never did anything.

Hide away behind a chair, hide away behind the front door of a shared flat. Is she watching me? Is that why she is here? Am I locked in by her? If I went out, she would tell, would say that I did all those things, things that simply happened beyond my reach. It was always beyond my reach.

This is her daughter, new bread, legs that hardly work, Flora instead of butter, Hyacinth's cholesterol. I could have told them, mother and daughter, but I did not say. They have so much time for each other, none for me, so I will not speak.

Hide away in the stable where his horse used to stay. A burning school – no, a burning chapel made into a mansion. Torn clothing, a scream – look what he did to me.

Yes, yes, he did.

I brought Lawrence Beresford home, selected him, allowed him into my party in my garden, but the other two Hs were there, as ever. Hyacinth and Hilda. I am the silent H, the one who isn't really here. Honoria. In my name, the H is never used. Like me, it is unwanted, unimportant, *de trop*.

The man chose Hyacinth. Like Father, he picked her. Hilda was unplucked, but she needed nothing, nobody. Even so, she got him. She has April's father, Hyacinth's lover, my choice. He was mine and they stole him.

I never had anything or anyone all to myself.

Isobel fell downstairs. The child fell into the river. Thomas fell down the well. Fires happen. Life happens. She is still alive, that child of love.

Oh, how I hate her.

Oh, I can hurt the man now; I can hurt Hilda.

They have April, the child of his love, the daughter of Hyacinth. I can take away your stepdaughter/niece, Hilda. She is frail, unsteady on her feet. I am Serendipity.

This is my destiny. There is just one thing left for me to do and no one must stand in my way. She will die; she will go to her birth mother and her adoptive mother. Let them fight over her.

Beloved daughter.

I was not beloved by anyone.

Good heavens, walking is not easy. I must have sat in this chair all night. A job to do now. What was it? Ah, yes, I remember. A shower, a change of clothes, the carving-knife.

She did this to me. April tore me down, left me to stand alone, for ever alone. So I shall cleanse my life and start again in another place. It is April. This is her month. In April, she was ripped from the belly of a thief. My sisters are both thieves. This is the end and the beginning, both the same. I will not be diverted.

Honoria West sat in her car and stared straight ahead. She had showered, made up her face, had put on a sensible suit, some flat shoes, a warm jacket.

Thinking about nothing, feeling little, she was calm and sure. Driving came naturally. The traffic of the day had scarcely touched the roads, leaving Honoria a free hand as she sped along the Formby bypass, through Ince Blundell, back to the main carriageway, just driving, just moving.

In a layby, she parked for a while, attention given now to an item on the passenger seat. Hyacinth's turquoise scarf, silk, shot through with a colour that was supposed to match her name. A gift from April. Inside, wrapped loosely, the kitchen knife nestled, its bright surface concealed beneath a caress of soft material.

'I must make my will,' she said absently. Having

destroyed the original, Honoria was now intestate. 'It would go to Hilda,' she continued. 'And Hilda would give it all to April. Hilda does not want my money, but April isn't getting it.'

As sudden as bolts of summer lightning, events of the previous evening played across her mind, quickly at first, then slowing, staggering like old film across sticky reels.

This was no nightmare, no plague of demons. The boy with girlish hair, beads dangling from little plaits, his stupid shoes, a grin threatening to render him even uglier. Hilda with her Leo, Yvonne Benson, both her lovers in tow, husband sitting wordless while his second wife spoke of crime. Fingerprints. Forensic. Arson. April Nugent – patricide, infanticide, big words to mark a big occasion . . . Everyone listening, everyone ready to go out and spread the gossip.

A shuddering sigh rattled through Honoria's chest. Like the very first breath of life, it brought a special kind of pain, a shock that caused her body to tremble from head to feet. She had power, the angry strength that came with rebirth. She was all new.

As she drove towards Crosby and Blundellsands, Honoria travelled fast, eyes fixed on her goal, mind concentrating on one thing only. April's day had come; April's last hour on the planet was now.

The Fiesta swung round the bend at the bottom of the bypass, curving at speed past large houses, until the parade of shops and a petrol station hove into view. She had to hurry before the day woke completely.

April should not have said those things.

Honoria was Serendipity. Serendipity was a kind of fate, an element that stretched beyond the reach of human management.

She had forgotten the traffic-lights.

The truck caught her on the passenger side, shunting her effortlessly across the road. This was not meant to happen, not to Honoria, not to Serendipity. On the forecourt of Tom England's garage, the car turned over with the weight of the lorry behind it.

There was little discomfort. She knew that her spine was broken and that there was a lot of blood. As the life seeped out of her, one final thought crept through the mists. April would get everything. Hilda had no need . . . Those animals would benefit . . . The one Honoria had meant to eradicate would inherit the flat, the money . . . Thoughts stuck, stopped developing properly. This was the end of Serendipity's road. It was so unfair.

The recovery of Honoria West's body took time, since cutting gear could not operate within such easy reach of stored petrol. A crowd gathered, like vultures hovering over remains, people whose curiosity overcame their sense of propriety. For safety's sake, police were drafted in to clear away the living.

The lorry driver, white and trembling with shock, was taken off in an ambulance, scarcely a mark on him. The wreck of Honoria's Fiesta was crane-lifted away from the filling station, no hurry, no yelling of orders, since the vehicle's sole occupant was so clearly dead.

By two in the afternoon, the only reminders of the accident were a shattered window, a BUSINESS AS USUAL sign on the door and a few policemen looking for witnesses. Cars and vans stopped, filled up, moved on, obeyed the traffic-lights.

It was almost as if Miss Honoria West had never existed.

April heard the news and went out to visit her dogs. She had spoken on the phone to Hilda and Leo, the father she had known for just a few months. Honoria was dead.

A litter of pups tumbled about, youthful enthusiasm making them loud and clumsy. The bitch lapped at water, one eye fixed on the nearby tangle of stupidity that was her family. A pair of failed greyhounds played with a ball, tossing it across the play run, chasing after it on stick-thin limbs much stronger than they looked. Soon, all these dogs would have new homes.

April felt numb. She had heard the relief in Leo's tone. Even Hilda had not wept. It was so sad to know that a human being had been so bad, so unloved. Still, it was no one's fault, she supposed. The woman was dead, and many could now breathe again.

Mark came out. 'Are you all right, girl?'

Girl. She was in her mid-forties, yet she was still his girl. 'Just thinking.'

'Well, don't. If you think too much, the government'll slap tax on it.' He went into the cattery with a tray of fish pieces.

April steaded herself before walking towards the house. Today, she had a red-hot-needle feeling in her right eye.

Mark emerged empty tray in his hand. 'April?'
'Yes?'

'According to the garage manager, Honoria had a kitchen knife in her car. One of the firemen handed it to the copper in charge.'

'I'm not surprised.'

'Where had she been?' asked Mark. 'Coming down from Formby, she was.'

April smiled sadly. 'Where was she going is the real question.' After a pause, she added, 'And what does that matter now?'

They stared hard at one another. Although no further words were spoken, they each understood the situation. The knife had been for April.

Mark reached out and helped his wife into the house, noticing how heavily she depended on his physical support. Ah, well, never mind. Honoria had done her worst, had done her last.

April placed the flowers on her parents' grave. On the attached card, in neat print, the message read,

For Hyacinth, who gave me life, love and friendship.
For Enid, who nurtured, loved and guided me.
For Bob, my guardian, my dad for twenty-one
   wonderful years.

With difficulty, April stood up. She had wanted to do this alone, had needed a few minutes to think about her two dead mothers, about her father. Memories poured into her mind, pictures of days that could never come again, magical times, cotton-candy afternoons by the sea, skipping ropes in a park, evenings spent reading and laughing with Hyacinth.

He came up behind her and patted her shoulder. Yes, there was still some magic left, because the touch was familiar, comfortable.

'Good people,' said Leo, the words gruff with emotion.

'Yes.' She took his hand. They had a lot of catching up to do, this parent and offspring who had come to visit the cemetery. 'Come on, Dad,' she said, her tone determined. 'Let's go home.'

They walked towards the Rolls.

'Look,' cried April, a hand extended towards the sky.

He looked. A perfect rainbow stretched across the clouds, its colours radiant after a recent heavy shower. 'The blue is particularly bright.'

'Yes,' she answered. 'A lovely colour. I think it's called Hyacinth.'

Afterthoughts – Meeting April

A couple of years ago, Avril Cain's left foot took a turn and propelled its owner sideways into my life. Using her walking stick as a maypole, she explained to me, as she circled, that it had all been another dreadful mistake. She had *definitely not* been shoplifting when she had picked up two minted lamb chops from the display outside Frank Smith's butcher shop. Her left foot had suffered a digression in the direction of Maud Smith's (matching surnames coincidental), where she had tried to pay for the meat at a greeting cards counter.

Behind such tales of hilarity (and there are many of them), there is a wonderful, vibrant and gifted woman who suffers from multiple sclerosis. In spite of depleted motor control and severe pain, she paints exquisite watercolours, crochets and has even decorated her own bathroom (plus two of her cats who happened to come between brush and wall). She also writes brilliant poetry.

In my almost sixty years, I have been privileged to know three victims of MS. The first, Auntie

Jessie, made cakes on the floor. We accepted this unquestioningly. Most folk mixed cakes on tables; Auntie Jessie used the floor. The second was Audrey Moss of Rainford, whose sympathy and humour carried me through the early death of my mother and helped me to 'hang on in there' during two dreadful pregnancies and one mildly annoying divorce.

I am indebted to those people, as they taught me so much about the true value of life and the curative properties of laughter. Because of our aunt, we never developed the 'Does he take sugar?' mentality, since we learned while young to converse not just with the navigator, but also with the occupant of the wheelchair.

My friend Avril cannot always speak to me. Sometimes, she opens her mouth and talks in a language we call 'broken biscuits'. Frustrated and often in agony, she communicates with me by our now infamous fill-in-the-missing-word method. This reduces us both to hysterical wrecks and renders innocent visitors immobile, as they don't yet know how to play.

I feel honoured because Avril has chosen to fit me into her very full and deliberately active life. We talk (or mumble) on the phone every day. Recently, my own health problems laid me low for some weeks, and Avril visited me frequently. She made coffee – 'See, I haven't spilled all of it; your cup's still half full' – and cheered me with stories about playschool (Bootle Day Centre) and painting class. Tales of the latter are particularly funny, as a lot of damage can be done by involuntary muscle spasm and a brush overloaded with blue paint.

Avril's secret is, I think, that the cup is half full, not half empty. She makes me ashamed, as my own attitude tends to gravitate towards the half-empty theory.

All three – Auntie Jessie, Audrey and Avril – have been so positive, lively, enthusiastic, talented. This may be a series of coincidences, yet I have wondered, over the years, whether only the best people are tormented by this incurable, wearisome and unpredictable disease.

I wish we could take away some of the symptoms. If Avril could have a few days when she could see, talk and walk without suffering. She treats her illness with near-contempt, blaming herself when a severe attack knocks her out for days on end. I have learned to hear pain in her voice; she can no longer fool me. Avril's bravery is truly extraordinary.

I pay tribute, too, to all those who care for victims of the disease. MS puts careers and/or education on hold, forcing family members to stay at home to nurse the afflicted, their incomes replaced by allowances so paltry as to be almost laughable. Well, God bless them, every one. And God speed a cure for MS.

Ruth Hamilton

MS . . . Most Stupid?

neither miss nor mrs, just MS.
Million Stars. Mindless Stare.
Mute Swan. Much Sympathy.
a Midweek Scoop. a Missing Share.

wild Manic Secrets. Mystic Symbols.
Music Score. Movie Screen.
Minute Steak. Mushroom Stalks.
crying over a Moving Scene.

Mini Skirts. Mesh Stockings. Muscle Strain.
Maiden Spinsters at home.
Mud Slips. pale Mauve Sunsets.
Mixed Singles spending time alone.

Myeline Sheath. Major Symptoms.
Misting Sight. closing door.
Multiple Sclerosis.
Me Staggering across the floor.

                                        Avril Cain

THE CORNER HOUSE
by Ruth Hamilton

When, one dark night in 1939, young Theresa Nolan was brutally raped by three young men, it was the beginning of a series of tragic and dramatic events. For the young men were not criminals or vagrants, but the sons of wealthy and privileged business men. Pregnant, thrown out of her home by her bigoted father, Theresa vowed a lifetime of vengeance on the men who had wrecked her future. Physically frail, but filled with a burning anger that fuelled her weak body, she determined that nothing and no one was going to deflect her from her path of retribution, not even the gentle man who cared for her during her sickness and whom she eventually came to love.

But there were others caught into the web of violence and deceit, Bernard Walsh and his brother Danny, Eva, the midwife who had befriended Theresa and had seen her through her pregnancy. Above all there were two children, bonded together from birth, whose lives were to play their part in the drama of Theresa Nolan.

With all the rich characters and traditions of Liverpool and the north-west, Ruth Hamilton has created another magnificent story of passion and conflict.

0 552 14567 X

THE DREAM SELLERS
by Ruth Hamilton

The Shawcross family was a strange and unhappy one. Edward Shawcross absented himself as much as possible and kept a red-haired mistress in Tintern Avenue. Alice, his wife, sought solace in chocolate and continually carped at Connie, her beautiful daughter. And Connie and Gilbert, their children, formed an uneasy alliance in the face of their parents' antipathy.

Twenty years before, Edward Shawcross had been an impoverished millhand, born in a slum to feckless parents. Overnight his fortunes had changed. To everyone's surprise he had married the plain and awkward daughter of the wealthy Fishwick family. Almost at once the Fishwicks, owners of a lucrative mill and a grand house, went to live abroad leaving Edward in charge of all their business interests. No one could understand why Edward had suddenly made this leap of fortune.

But as the new generation began to grow up, so the truth behind old scandals began to emerge. Then, after many years, the Fishwicks returned and violence swiftly followed. Before Connie and Gilbert could throw off the legacies of the past and build their own lives, there were to be many shocking revelations.

'Gritty, down-to-earth writing and strong female characters have become the trademarks of her writing'
Bookworld

0 552 14566 1

THE BELLS OF SCOTLAND ROAD
by Ruth Hamilton

To the Liverpool of the 1930s came Bridget O'Brien, a young widow with two children, about to be forced into marriage with a man she had never met. Her destination was the infamous Scotland Road, with its noise, its colour, its poverty and humour, where the people lived lives of deprivation and courage backed by rich tradition and a folklore they had themselves evolved.

For Bridget, straight from Ireland, fleeing from a brutal and bigoted father, Scotland Road was, at first, noisome and terrifying. Her sense of isolation was made worse when she met her bridegroom, Sam Bell, a middle-aged pawnbroker whose twin sons were older than she was. Grimly, thankful that at last she and her daughters had a roof over their heads, she settled to make the best of it she could.

It was the rough and vibrant Costigan family who first made her welcome. Diddy, a huge warm-hearted Liverpudlian and Billy, her docker husband, did their best to ease the young widow into her new life. Anthony, one of her so-called stepsons, also held out the strong hand of friendship, but Liam, the favourite of his father, had the power to terrify her. Liam was cold, compelling, mysterious and antagonistic. He was also a priest.

Against the backdrop of a unique culture, through the depression of the 30s and the savagery of the Second World War, the story of Bridie, her daughters, and the two men who were to shape her destiny was played out.

0 552 14385 5

PARADISE LANE
by Ruth Hamilton

There were only four houses in Paradise Lane, and young Sally Crumpsall lived at No.1. If it hadn't been for the kindly inhabitants of the Lane she would have been even more neglected than she was, for with a father too ill to care for her, and a mother who was to abandon her, she led a ragged and lonely existence. When – finally – both mother and father had gone, then the Lane moved in and, with the help of Ivy, Sally's old and stubbornly aggressive grandmother, they decided to raise Sally as best they could.

But Paradise Lane was built in the shadow of Paradise Mill – and Andrew Worthington, owner of the mill, loomed menacingly over the lives of everyone about him. A corrupt, evil and greedy man, he had totally destroyed his own family, and soon his venom was directed towards Ivy, her friends in Paradise Lane, and finally threatened the very existence of young Sally.

As events moved towards a violent and terrible climax, only the combined efforts of all who loved the young girl were able to save her.

0 552 14141 0

A CROOKED MILE
by Ruth Hamilton

In the shadow of the Althorpe mills, the Myrtle Street residents endure cramped and often verminous conditions.

Joe Duffy, a Bolton tradesman, strives to lift his family out of the 'garden' streets. But as more children are born, Joe's wife Tess sinks deeper into the obsession that will be her undoing. When Tess screams her belief that the area is cursed, few people heed her ravings. She is ignored, even as the Myrtle Street tragedies become more frequent and begin to feature in local gossip.

It is left to Megan, the third Duffy child – the one who felt she was unworthy and unloved because she had been born a girl – to end the curse. When she becomes embroiled in a web of deceit, Megan needs all her strength, talents, and wit in order to survive. But it is her capacity to give love that ensures her family's stability, the future of the Althorpe cotton mills, and the safekeeping of the Hall i' the Vale.

0 552 14140 2

THE SEPTEMBER STARLINGS
by Ruth Hamilton

Laura Starling, now wealthy and succesful, has survived a bitter past. She fled from a tyrannical mother into the clutches of a sadistic man. She endured poverty, fear and pain. Then along came Ben Starling, older, wiser, who smoothed her path and gave her love and security.

But now Ben has become a stranger who has slipped beyond her reach. As her stability threatens to disintegrate once more, a thin, waif-like girl from Liverpool thrusts her way into Laura's life – a girl who is to prove a link with the past. But no one can help Laura make the decisions that will alter the course of her existence. As the September starlings gather, Laura realises she must take courage and forge her own future.

0 552 14139 9

A SELECTED LIST OF FINE NOVELS
AVAILABLE FROM CORGI BOOKS

14060 0	MERSEY BLUES	*Lyn Andrews*	£5.99
14537 8	APPLE BLOSSOM TIME	*Kathryn Haig*	£5.99
14538 6	A TIME TO DANCE	*Kathryn Haig*	£5.99
13897 5	BILLY LONDON'S GIRLS	*Ruth Hamilton*	£5.99
13755 3	NEST OF SORROWS	*Ruth Hamilton*	£5.99
13384 1	A WHISPER TO THE LIVING	*Ruth Hamilton*	£5.99
13616 6	WITH LOVE FROM MA MAGUIRE	*Ruth Hamilton*	£5.99
13977 7	SPINNING JENNY	*Ruth Hamilton*	£5.99
14139 9	THE SEPTEMBER STARLINGS	*Ruth Hamilton*	£5.99
14140 2	A CROOKED MILE	*Ruth Hamilton*	£5.99
14141 0	PARADISE LANE	*Ruth Hamilton*	£5.99
14385 5	THE BELLS OF SCOTLAND ROAD	*Ruth Hamilton*	£5.99
14566 1	THE DREAM SELLERS	*Ruth Hamilton*	£5.99
14567 X	THE CORNER HOUSE	*Ruth Hamilton*	£5.99
14686 2	CITY OF GEMS	*Caroline Harvey*	£5.99
14692 7	THE PARADISE GARDEN	*Joan Hessayon*	£5.99
14603 X	THE SHADOW CHILD	*Judith Lennox*	£5.99
14492 4	THE CREW	*Margaret Mayhew*	£5.99
14693 5	THE LITTLE SHIP	*Margaret Mayhew*	£5.99
14658 7	THE MEN IN HER LIFE	*Imogen Parker*	£5.99
14752 4	WITHOUT CHARITY	*Michelle Paver*	£5.99
10375 6	CSARDAS	*Diane Pearson*	£5.99
14577 7	PORTRAIT OF CHLOE	*Elvi Rhodes*	£5.99
14655 2	SPRING MUSIC	*Elvi Rhodes*	£5.99
14636 6	COME RAIN OR SHINE	*Susan Sallis*	£5.99
14671 4	THE KEYS TO THE GARDEN	*Susan Sallis*	£5.99
14657 9	CHURCHILL'S PEOPLE	*Mary Jane Staples*	£5.99
14708 7	BRIGHT DAY, DARK NIGHT	*Mary Jane Staples*	£5.99
14740 0	EMILY	*Valerie Wood*	£5.99
14640 4	THE ROMANY GIRL	*Valerie Wood*	£5.99